THE FALL OF ATLANTIS

**Baen Books
by Marion Zimmer Bradley**
✣ ✣ ✣

The Fall of Atlantis

Glenraven (with Holly Lisle)

In the Rift: Glenraven II (with Holly Lisle)

THE FALL OF ATLANTIS

MARION ZIMMER BRADLEY

BAEN

THE FALL OF ATLANTIS

This is a work of fiction. All the characters and events portrayed in this book
are fictional, and any resemblance to real people or incidents is purely coincidental.

A Baen Book

Baen Publishing Enterprises
P.O. Box 1403
Riverdale, NY 10471
www.baen.com

ISBN: 978-1-4767-3629-7

Cover art by Sam Kennedy

First Baen trade paperback printing, March 2014

Distributed by Simon & Schuster
1230 Avenue of the Americas
New York, NY 10020

Library of Congress Cataloging-in-Publication Data

Bradley, Marion Zimmer.
  The fall of Atlantis / Marion Zimmer Bradley.
    pages cm
  ISBN 978-1-4767-3629-7 (pbk.)
  I. Title.
  PS3552.R228F33 2014
  813'.54--dc23
                                2013049452

Printed in the United States of America

10 9 8 7 6 5 4 3 2 1

✠ ACKNOWLEDGEMENT ✠

First, to my dear friend and mentor Dorothy G. Quinn, who, more years ago than I like to think about, explored the past with me, and wrote, with me, a thin sheaf of handwritten scenes exploring the characters of Domaris and Micon. The book has been through four rewritings since, and Dorothy would probably not recognize her brainchild; but it was in her company that I first trod this path, and the debt is inestimable.

Second, to David R. Bradley, my son, who prepared the final draft of this manuscript for publication and who provided, from various sources, including the unpublished writings of his late father, Robert A. Bradley, the philosophical excerpts which appear at the head of each section.

—*Marion Zimmer Bradley*

✠ CONTENTS ✠

BOOK ONE
✠ MICON ✠

"All events are but the consummation of preceding causes, clearly seen but not distinctly apprehended. When the strain is sounded, the most untutored listener can tell that it must end with the keynote, although he cannot see why each successive bar must lead at last to the concluding chord. The law of Karma is the force which leads all chords to the keynote, which spreads the ripples from the tiny stone dropped into a pool, until the tidal waves drown a continent, long after the stone has sunk from sight and been forgotten.

"This is the story of one such stone, dropped into the pool of a world which was drowned long before the Pharaohs of Egypt piled one stone upon another."
— *The Teachings of Rajasta the Mage*

CHAPTER ONE
✠ EMISSARIES ✠

I

At the sound of sandaled feet upon stone, the Priest Rajasta raised his face from the scroll he held open on his knee. The library of the Temple was usually deserted at this hour, and he had come to regard it as his peculiar privilege to study here each day undisturbed. His forehead ridged a little, not with anger, for he was not given to anger, but with residual annoyance, for he had been deep in thought.

However, the two men who had entered the library had aroused his interest, and he straightened and watched them; without, however, laying aside the scroll, or rising.

The elder of the two was known to him: Talkannon, Arch-Administrator of the Temple of Light, was a burly, cheerful-faced man, whose apparent good nature was a shrewd dissemblance for an analytical temperament which could turn cold and stern and even ruthless. The other was a stranger, a man whose graceful dancer's body moved slowly and with effort; his dark smile was slightly wry, as if lips shut tight on pain could grimace more easily. A tall man, this stranger, deeply tanned and handsome, clad in white robes of an unfamiliar pattern, which glimmered with faint luminescence in the sunlit shadows of the room.

"Rajasta," the Arch-Administrator said, "our brother desires further knowledge. He is free to study as he will. Be he your guest." Talkannon bowed slightly to the still-seated Rajasta, and, turning back to the stranger, stated, "Micon of Ahtarrath, I leave you with our greatest student. The Temple, and the City of the Temple, are yours, my brother; feel free to call upon me at any time." Again Talkannon bowed, then turned and left the two men to further their acquaintance.

As the door scraped slowly shut behind the Arch-Administrator's powerful form, Rajasta frowned again; he was used to Talkannon's abrupt manners, but he feared that this stranger would think them all lacking in civility. Laying down his scroll, he arose and approached the guest with his hands outstretched in courteous welcome. On his feet, Rajasta was a very tall man, long past middle age; his step and manner disciplined and punctilious.

Micon stood quite still where Talkannon had left him, smiling still that grave, one-sided smile. His eyes were deeply blue as storm-skies; the small creases around them spoke of humor, and a vast tolerance.

This man is one of us, surely, thought the Priest of Light, as he made a ceremonious bow, and waited. Still the stranger stood and smiled, unheedful. Rajasta's frown returned, faintly. "Micon of Ahtarrath—"

"I am so called," said the stranger formally. "I have come here to ask that I may pursue my studies among you." His voice was low and resonant, but held an overlay of effort, as if kept always in careful control.

"You are welcome to share in what knowledge is mine," Rajasta said with grave courtesy, "and you are yourself welcome—" He hesitated, then added, on a sudden impulse, "Son of the Sun." With his hand he made a certain Sign.

"A fosterling, only, I fear," said Micon with a brief, wry smile, "and overly proud of the relationship." Nevertheless, in answer to the ritual identifying phrase, he raised his hand and returned the archaic gesture.

Rajasta stepped forward to embrace his guest; they were bound, not only by the bonds of shared wisdom and search, but by the power behind the innermost magic of the Priesthood of Light: like Rajasta, Micon was one of their highest initiates. Rajasta wondered at this— Micon seemed so young! Then, as they stepped apart, Rajasta saw what he had not noticed before. His face shadowed with sorrow and pity, and he took Micon's emaciated hands in his and led him to a seat, saying, "Micon, my brother!"

"A fosterling, as I said," Micon nodded. "How did you know? I was—told—that there is no outward scarring, nor—"

"No," Rajasta said. "I guessed. Your stillness—something in your gestures. But how did this come upon you, my brother?"

"May I speak of that at another time? What is—" Micon hesitated again, and said, his resonant voice strained, "—cannot be remedied. Let it suffice that I—returned the Sign."

Rajasta said, his voice trembling with emotion, "You are most truly a Son of Light, although you walk in darkness. Perhaps—perhaps the only Son of that Light who can face His splendor."

"Only because I may never behold it," Micon murmured, and the blank eyes seemed to gaze intently on the face they would never see. Silence, while that twisted and painful smile came and went upon Micon's face.

At last Rajasta ventured, "But—you returned the Sign—and I thought surely I was mistaken—that surely you saw—"

"I think—I can read thoughts, a little," Micon said. "Only a little; and only since there was need. I do not know, yet, how much to trust to it. But with you—" Again the smile lent brilliance to the dark, strained face. "I felt no hesitation."

Again the silence, as of emotions stretched too tightly for speech; then, from the passageway, a woman's young voice called, "Lord Rajasta!"

Rajasta's tense face relaxed. "I am here, Domaris," he called, and explained to Micon, "My disciple, a young woman—Talkannon's daughter. She is unawakened as yet, but when she learns, and is—complete, she holds the seeds of greatness."

"The Light of the Heavens grant knowledge and wisdom to her," said Micon with polite disinterest.

Domaris came into the room; a tall girl, and proudly erect, with hair the color of hammered copper that made a brightness in the dark spaces and shadows. Like a light bird she came, but paused at a little distance from the men, too shy to speak in the presence of a stranger.

"My child," Rajasta said kindly, "this is Micon of Ahtarrath, my brother in the Light, to be treated as myself in every respect."

Domaris turned to the stranger, in civil courtesy—then her eyes widened, a look of awe drew over her features, and with a gesture that seemed forced, as if she made it against her will, she laid her right hand over her breast and raised it slowly to forehead level, in the salute given only to the highest initiates of the Priesthood of Light. Rajasta smiled: it was a right instinct and he was pleased; but he let his voice break the spell, for Micon had gone grey with a deep pallor.

"Micon is my guest, Domaris, and will be lodged with me—if that is your will, my brother?" At Micon's nod of assent, he continued, "Go now, daughter, to the Scribe-Mother, and ask her to hold a scribe always in readiness for my brother."

She started and shivered a little; sent a worshipful glance at Micon; then inclined her head in reverence to her teacher and went on her errand.

"Micon!" Rajasta spoke with terse directness. "You are come here from the Dark Shrine!"

Micon nodded. "From their dungeons," he qualified immediately.

"I—I feared that—"

"I am no apostate," Micon reassured firmly. "I served not there. My service is not subject to compulsion!"

"Compulsion?"

Micon did not move, but the lift of his brows and the curl of his lip gave the effect of a shrug. "They would have compelled me." He held out his mutilated hands. "You can see that they were—eloquent in persuasion." Before Rajasta's gasp of horror, Micon drew back his hands and concealed their betrayal within the sleeves of his robe. "But my task is undone. And until it is completed, I hold death from me with these hands—though he companion me most closely."

Micon might have been speaking of last night's rain; and Rajasta bowed his head before the impassive face. "There are those we call Black-robes," he said bitterly. "They hide themselves among the members of the Magician's Sect, those who guard the shrine of the Unrevealed God—whom we call Grey-robes here. I have heard that these . . . Black-robes—torture! But they are secret in their doings. Well for them! Be they accursed!"

Micon stirred. "Curse not, my brother!" he said harshly. "You, of all men, should know the danger of that."

Rajasta said tonelessly, "We have no way of acting against them. As I say, we suspect members of the Grey-robe sect. Yet, all are—gray!"

"I know. I saw too clearly, so—I see nothing. Enough," Micon pleaded. "I carry my release within me, my brother, but I may not yet accept it. We will not speak of this, Rajasta." He arose, with slow carefulness, and paced deliberately to the window, to stand with his face uplifted to the warm sunlight.

With a sigh, Rajasta accepted the prohibition. True, the Black-robes always concealed themselves so well that no victim could ever identify his tormentors. But why this? Micon was a stranger and could hardly have incurred their enmity; and never before had they dared meddle with so highly-placed a personage. The knowledge of what had befallen Micon initiated a new round in a warfare as old as the Temple of Light.

And the prospect dismayed him.

II

In the School of Scribes, Mother Lydara was in the process of disciplining one of her youngest pupils. The Scribes were the sons and daughters of the Priest's Caste who showed, in their twelfth or thirteenth year, a talent for reading or writing: and thirty-odd intelligent boys and girls are not easy to keep in order.

Mother Lydara felt that no child in all her memory had ever been such a problem to her as the sullen little girl who faced her just now: a thin angular girl, about thirteen, with stormy eyes and hair that hung dishevelled in black, tumbled curls. She held herself very stiff and erect, her nervous little hands stubbornly clenched, taut defiance in her white face.

"Deoris, little daughter," the Scribe-Mother admonished, standing rock-like and patient, "you must learn to control both tongue and temper if you ever hope to serve in the Higher Ways. The daughter of Talkannon should be an example and a pattern to the others. Now, you will apologize to me, and to your playmate Ista, and then you will make accounting to your father." The old Priestess waited, arms crossed on her ample breast, for an apology which never came.

Instead the girl burst out tearfully, "I won't! I have done nothing wrong, Mother, and I won't apologize for anything!" Her voice was plangent, vibrating with a thrilling sweetness which had marked her, among the children of the Temple, as a future Spell-singer; she seemed all athrob with passion like a struck harp.

The Scribe-Mother looked at her with a baffled, weary patience. "That is not the way to speak to an elder, my child. Obey me, Deoris."

"I will not!"

The old woman put out a hand, herself uncertain whether to placate the girl or slap her, when a rap came at the door. "Who is it?" the Priestess called impatiently.

The door swung back and Domaris put her head around the corner. "Are you at leisure, Mother?"

Mother Lydara's troubled face relaxed, for Domaris had been a favorite for many years. "Come in, my child, I have always time for you."

Domaris halted on the threshold, staring at the stormy face of the little girl in the scribe's frock.

"Domaris, I *didn't!*" Deoris wailed, and, a forlorn little cyclone, she flung herself on Domaris and wrapped her arms around her sister's neck. "I didn't do anything," she hiccoughed on a hysterical sob.

"Deoris—little sister!" chided Domaris. Firmly she disengaged the clinging arms. "Forgive her, Mother Lydara—has she been in trouble again? No, be still, Deoris; I did not ask *you.*"

"She is impertinent, impudent, impatient of correction and altogether unmanageable," said Mother Lydara. "She sets a bad example in the school, and runs wild in the dormitories. I dislike to punish her, but—"

"Punishment only makes Deoris worse," said Domaris levelly. "You should never be severe with her." She pulled Deoris close, smoothing the tumbled curls. She herself knew so well how to rule Deoris through love that she resented Mother Lydara's harshness.

"While Deoris is in the Scribe-School," said the Scribe-Mother with calm finality, "she will be treated as the others are treated, and punished as they are punished. And unless she makes some effort to behave as they behave she will not be long in the School."

Domaris raised her level brows. "I see . . . I have come from Lord Rajasta. He has need of a scribe to serve a guest, and Deoris is competent; she is not happy in the school, nor do you want her here. Let her serve this man." She glanced at the drooping head, now snuggled into her shoulder; Deoris looked up with wondering adoration. Domaris always made everything right again!

Mother Lydara frowned, but was secretly relieved: Deoris was a problem quite beyond her limited capabilities, and the fact that this spoilt child was Talkannon's daughter complicated the situation. Theoretically, Deoris was there on an equal footing with the others, but the daughter of the Arch-Administrator could not be chastised or ruled over like the child of an ordinary priest.

"Have it as you will, Daughter of Light," said the Scribe-Mother gruffly, "but she must continue her own studies, see you to that!"

"Rest assured, I shall not neglect her schooling," said Domaris coldly. As they left the squat building, she studied Deoris, frowning. She had seen little of her sister in these last months; when Domaris had been chosen as Rajasta's Acolyte, the child had been sent to the Scribe-School—but before that they had been inseparable, though the eight years difference in their ages made the relationship less that of sisters than of mother and daughter. Now Domaris sensed a change in her young sister that dismayed her. Always before, Deoris had been merry and docile; what had they done to her, to change her into this sullen little rebel? She decided, with a flare of anger, that she would seek Talkannon's permission to take Deoris again under her own care.

"Can I really stay with you?"

"I cannot possibly promise it, but we shall see." Domaris smiled. "You wish it?"

"Oh yes!" said Deoris passionately, and flung her arms about her sister again, with such intensity that Domaris's brow furrowed into lines of deep trouble. What had they *done* to Deoris?

Freeing herself from the clinging arms, Domaris admonished, "Gently, gently, little sister," and they turned their steps toward the House of the Twelve.

III

Domaris was one of the Twelve Acolytes: six young men and six young women, chosen every third year from the children of the Priest's Caste, for physical perfection, beauty, and some especial talent which made them archetypal of the Priest's Caste of the Ancient Land. When they reached maturity, they dwelt for three years in the House of the Twelve, studying all the ancient wisdom of the Priest's Caste, and preparing themselves for service to the Gods and to their people. It was said that if some calamity should destroy all of the Priest's Caste save only the Twelve, all the wisdom of the Temples could be reconstructed from these Twelve Acolytes alone. At the end of this three-year term, each married his or her allotted mate, and so carefully were these six young couples chosen that the children of Acolytes rarely failed to climb high in the Priesthood of their caste.

The House of the Twelve was a spacious building, crowning a high green hill apart from the clustered buildings of the precinct; surrounded by wide lawns and green enclosed gardens, and cool fountains. As the sisters sauntered along the path which climbed, between banks of flowering shrubs, toward the white walls of the retreat, a young woman, barely out of childhood, hurried across the lawns toward them.

"Domaris! Come here, I want you—oh, Deoris! Have you been freed from the Scribe's prison?"

"I hope so," said Deoris shyly, and the girls hugged one another. The newcomer was between Domaris and Deoris in age; she might almost have been another sister, for the three were very much alike in form and feature, all three very tall and slender, finely-boned, with delicate hands and arms and the molded, incised features of the Priest's Caste. Only in coloring did they differ: Domaris, the tallest, her fiery hair long and rippling, her eyes cool, shadowed grey. Deoris was slighter and smaller, with heavy black ringlets and eyes like crushed violets; and Elis's curls were the glossy red-brown of polished wood, her eyes merry and clear blue. Of all those in the House of the Twelve, or in all the Temple, the daughters of Talkannon loved their cousin Elis the most.

"There are envoys here from Atlantis," Elis told them eagerly.

"From the Sea Kingdom? Truly?"

"Yes, from the Temple at Ahtarrath. The young Prince of Ahtarrath was sent here with his younger brother, but they never arrived. They were kidnapped, or shipwrecked, or murdered, and now they're searching the whole seacoast for them or their bodies."

Domaris stared, startled. Ahtarrath was a formidable name. The Mother-Temple, here in the Ancient Land, had little contact with the Sea Kingdoms, of which Ahtarrath was the most powerful; now, twice in one day, had she heard of it.

Elis went on excitedly, "There's some evidence that he landed, and they're talking of Black-robes! Has Rajasta spoken of this, Domaris?"

Domaris frowned. She and Elis were of the Inner Circle of the Priest's Caste, but they had no right to discuss their elders, and the presence of Deoris should restrain such gossip in any case. "Rajasta does not confide in me; nor should an Acolyte listen to the gossip of the Gates!"

Elis turned pink, and Domaris relented a little. "There is no swarm that does not start with a single bee," she said pleasantly. "Rajasta has a guest from Ahtarrath. His name is Micon."

"Micon!" Elis exclaimed. "That is like saying that a slave's name is Lia! There are more Micons in the Sea Kingdoms than leaves on a songtree—" Elis broke off as a tiny girl, barely able to stand alone, clutched at her skirt. Elis looked down, impatient, then bent to take up the child; but the dimpled baby laughed, scampered toward Deoris, then tumbled down and lay squalling. Deoris snatched her up, and Elis glanced with annoyance at the little brown-skinned woman who scuttled after her refractory charge. "Simila," she rebuked, "cannot you keep Lissi from under our feet—or teach her *how* to fall?"

The nurse came to take the child, but Deoris clung to her. "Oh, Elis, let me hold her, I haven't seen her in so long, why she couldn't even creep, and now she's walking! Is she weaned yet? No? How do you endure it? There, Lissi love, you *do* remember me, don't you?" The baby girl shrieked with delight, plunging both hands into Deoris's thick ringlets. "Oh, you fat little darling!" Deoris gurgled, covering the chubby cheeks with kisses.

"Fat little nuisance." Elis looked at her daughter with a bitter laugh; Domaris gave Elis an understanding little pat. Because the women of the Acolytes were given in marriage without any regard for their own wishes, they were free until the very day of their marriage; and Elis, taking advantage of this freedom, had chosen a lover and borne him a child. This was perfectly allowable under the laws of the Temple, but, what was *not* allowable, her lover had failed to come forward and acknowledge paternity. Terrible penalties were visited on an unacknowledged child; to give her child caste, Elis had been forced to throw herself on the mercy of her allotted husband, an Acolyte like herself, called Chedan. Chedan had shown generosity, and acknowledged Lissi, but everyone knew he was not the father; not even

Domaris knew who had fathered little Lissi. The real father would have suffered a severe penalty for his cowardice, had Elis denounced him; this she steadfastly refused to do.

Domaris said, gently, before Elis's bitter eyes, "Why don't you send the child away, Elis, since Chedan dislikes her so much? She cannot be important enough to disturb the peace of the Acolytes this way, and you will have other children—"

Elis's mouth twisted briefly, cynically. "Wait until you know what you are talking about before you advise me," she said, reaching out to reclaim her child from Deoris. "Give me the little pest, I must go back."

"We're coming, too," Domaris said, but Elis tucked Lissi under her arm, beckoned to the nurse and hurried away.

Domaris looked after her, troubled. Until this moment her life had moved in orderly, patterned channels, laid out as predictably as the course of the river. Now it seemed the world had changed: talk of Black-robes, the stranger from Ahtarrath who had so greatly impressed her—her quiet life seemed suddenly filled with strangeness and dangers. She could not imagine why Micon should have made such a deep impression on her.

Deoris was looking at her, her violet eyes disturbed, doubtful; Domaris returned, with relief, to the world of familiar duties, as she arranged for her sister's stay in the House of the Twelve.

Later in the day, a courteously worded request came from Micon, that she might bring the scribe to him that evening.

IV

In the library, Micon sat alone by a casement, shadowed; but the white robes he wore were faintly luminescent in the dimness. Except for his silent form, the library was deserted, with no light except that slight luminescence.

Domaris sang a low-toned note, and a flickering, golden light sprang up around them; another note, more softly pitched, deeped the light to a steady radiance with no apparent source.

The Atlantean turned at the sound of her voice. "Who is there? Is it you, Talkannon's daughter?"

Domaris came forward, Deoris's little hand nestled shyly in hers. "Lord Micon, I bring you the scribe-student Deoris. She has been assigned for your convenience at all times and will attend you." Encouraged by Micon's warm smile, she added, "Deoris is my sister."

"Deoris." Micon repeated the name with a soft, slurred accent. "I thank you. And how are you called, Acolyte to Rajasta? Domaris," he recalled, his softly vibrant voice lingering on the syllables. "And the little scribe, then, is your sister? Come here, Deoris."

Domaris withdrew as Deoris went timidly to kneel before Micon. The Atlantean said, disturbed, "You must not kneel to me, child!"

"It is customary, Lord."

"Doubtless, a Priest's daughter is well schooled." Micon smiled. "Yet if I forbid it?"

Deoris rose obediently and stood before him.

"Are you familiar with the contents of the library, little Deoris? You seem very young, and I shall have to depend on you wholly, for writing as well as reading."

"Why?" Deoris blurted out uncontrollably. "You speak our language as one born to it! Can you not read it as well?"

Just for a moment a tormented look flitted across the dark, drawn face. Then it vanished. "I thought that your sister had told you," he said quietly. "I am blind."

Deoris stood for a moment in dumb surprise. A glance at Domaris, who stood off to one side, showed her that her sister had gone chalky white; she had not known, either.

There was a moment of awkward silence; then Micon picked up a scroll which lay near him. "Rajasta left this for me. I should like to hear you read." He handed it to Deoris with a courteous gesture, and the child, wrenching her eyes from Domaris, unfastened it, seating herself upon the scribe's stool which was placed at the foot of Micon's chair. She began to read, in the steady and poised voice which never failed a trained scribe, whatever her emotions.

Left to herself, Domaris recovered her composure: she retired to a niche in the wall and murmured the soft note which lighted it brilliantly. She tried to become absorbed in a page of text, but, try as she might to fix her attention on her own tasks, her eyes kept returning, as with separate will of their own, to the man who sat motionless, listening to the soft monotonous murmur of the child's reading. She had not even guessed! So normal his movements, so beautiful the deep eyes—why should it affect her so? Had *he*, then, been the prisoner of the Black-robes? She had seen his hands, the gaunt twisted travesties of flesh and bone that had once, perhaps, been strong and skillful. Who and what was this man?

In the strange confusion of her emotions, there was not a shred of pity. Why could she not pity him, as she pitied others who were blinded or tortured or lamed? For a moment she felt sharp resentment—how dared he be impervious to her pity?

But I envy Deoris, she thought irrationally. *Why should I?*

CHAPTER TWO
✠ OF DISTANT ✠ STORMS

I

There was no thunder, but the insistent flicker of summer lightning came and went through the opened shutters. Inside it was damply hot. The two girls lay on narrow pallets placed side by side on the cool brick floor, both nearly naked beneath a thin linen sheet. The thinnest of net canopies hung unstirring above them. The heat clung like thick robes.

Domaris, who had been pretending to sleep, suddenly rolled over and freed one long plait of her loosened hair from Deoris's outflung arm. She sat up. "You needn't be so quiet, child. I'm not asleep either."

Deoris sat up, hugging her lanky knees. The thick curls clung heavily to her temples: she tossed them impatiently back. "We're not the only ones awake, either," she said with conviction. "I've been hearing things. Voices, and steps, and, somewhere, singing. No—not singing, chanting. Scary chanting, a long way off, a very long way off."

Domaris looked very young as she sat there in her filmy sleeping garment, limned in sharp patches of black and white by the restless lightning; nor, on this night, did she feel much older than her little sister. "I think I heard it, too."

"Like this." Deoris hummed a thread of melody, in a whisper.

Domaris shuddered. "Don't! Deoris—where did you hear that chanting?"

"I don't know." Deoris frowned in concentration. "Far away. As if it came from under the earth—or in the sky—no, I'm not even sure whether I heard it or dreamed it." She picked up one of her sister's plaits and began listlessly to unravel it. "There's so much lightning, but no thunder. And when I hear the chanting, the lightning seems to brighten—"

"Deoris, *no!* That is impossible!"

"Why?" asked Deoris fearlessly. "Singing a note in certain rooms will bring light there; why should it not kindle a different light?"

"Because it is blasphemous, evil, to tamper with nature like that!" A coldness, almost fear, seemed to have clamped about her mind. "There is power in the voice. When you grow older in the Priesthood you will learn of this. But you must not speak of those evil forces!"

Deoris's quick thoughts had flitted elsewhere. "Arvath is jealous, that I may be near you when he may not! Domaris!" Her eyes held merry laughter that bubbled over into sound. "Is *that* why you wanted me to sleep in your apartments?"

"Perhaps." A faint stain of color etched the older sister's delicate face with crimson.

"Domaris, are you in love with Arvath?"

Domaris turned her eyes from the searching glances of her sister. "I am betrothed to Arvath," she said gravely. "Love will come when we are ready. It is not well to be too eager for life's gifts." She felt sententious, hypocritical, as she mouthed these sentiments; but her tone sobered Deoris. The thought of parting from her sister, even for marriage, filled her with jealousy which was partly jealousy for the children she knew Domaris would have. . . . All her life *she* had been Domaris's baby and pet.

As if to avoid that loss, Deoris said imploringly, "Don't ever make me go away from you again!"

Domaris slipped an arm around the meager shoulders. "Never, unless you wish it, little sister," she promised; but she felt troubled by the adoration in the child's voice. "Deoris," she said, squirming her hand beneath the small chin and turning Deoris's face up to hers, "you mustn't idolize me this way, I don't like it."

Deoris did not answer, and Domaris sighed. Deoris was an odd child: mostly reserved and reticent, a few she loved so wildly that it scared Domaris; she seemed to have no moderation in her loves and hates. Domaris wondered: *Did I do that? Did I let her idolize me so irrationally when she was a baby?*

Their mother had died when Deoris was born. The eight-year-old Domaris had resolved, on that night, that her newborn sister would never miss a mother's care. Deoris's nurse had tried to enforce some moderation in this, but when Deoris was weaned, her influence was ended: the two were inseparable. For Domaris, her baby sister replaced the dolls Domaris had that day discarded. Even when Domaris grew older, and had lessons, and later duties in the world of the Temple, Deoris tagged continually at her heels. They had never been parted for a single day until Domaris had entered the House of the Twelve.

Domaris had been only thirteen when she had been betrothed to Arvath of Alkonath. He also was an Acolyte: the one of the Twelve whose Sign of the Heavens was opposite to and congenial to her own. She had always accepted the fact that one day she would marry Arvath, just as she accepted the rising and setting of the sun—and it affected her just about as much. Domaris really had not the slightest idea that she was a beautiful woman. The Priests among whom she had been fostered all treated her with the same, casual, intimate affection; only Arvath had ever sought a closer bond. To this, Domaris reacted with mixed emotions. Arvath's own youth and love of life appealed to her; but real love, or even conscious desire, there was none. Too honest to pretend an acquiescence she did not feel, she was too kind to repulse him utterly, and too innocent to seek another lover. Arvath was a problem which, at times, occupied her attention, but without gravely troubling it.

She sat, silent, beside Deoris, vaguely disturbed. Lightning flickered and glimmered raggedly like the phrases of a broken chant, and a coldness whispered through the air.

A long shiver ripped through Domaris then, and she clung to her sister, shuddering in the sudden, icy grip of fear. "Domaris, what is it, what is it?" Deoris wailed. Domaris's breath was coming in gasps, and her fingers bit sharply into the child's shoulder.

"I don't . . . I wish I knew," she breathed in terror. Suddenly, with deliberate effort, she recovered herself. Rajasta's teaching was in her mind, and she tried to apply it.

"Deoris, no force of evil can harm us unless we permit it. Lie down—" She set the example, then reached in the darkness for her sister's hands. "Now, we'll say the prayer we used to say when we were little children, and go to sleep." Despite her calm voice and reassuring words, Domaris clasped the little cold fingers in her own firm ones a little too tightly. This was the Night of Nadir, when all the forces of the earth were loosed, good and evil alike, in balance, for all men to take as they would.

"Maker of all things mortal," she began in her low voice, now made husky with strict self-control. Shakily, Deoris joined in, and the sanctity of the old prayer enfolded them both. The night, which had been abnormally quiet until then, seemed somehow less forbidding, and the heat did not cling to them so oppressively. Domaris felt her strained muscles unlock, taut nerves relax.

Not so Deoris, who whimpered, cuddling closer like a scared kitten. "Domaris, talk to me. I'm so frightened, and those voices are still—"

Domaris cut her off, chiding, "Nothing can harm you here, even if they chant evil music from the Dark Shrine itself!" Realizing she had spoken more harshly than was wise in the circumstances, she quickly went on, "Well, then, tell me about Lord Micon."

Deoris brightened at once, speaking almost with reverence. "Oh, he is so kind, and good—but not *inhuman,* Domaris, like so many of the Initiates; like Father, or Cadamiri!" She went on, in a hushed voice, "And he suffers so! He seems always in pain, Domaris, though he never speaks of it. But his eyes, and his mouth, and his hands tell me. And sometimes—sometimes I pretend to be tired, so that he will send me away and go to his own rest."

Deoris's little face was transparent with pity and adoration, but for once Domaris did not blame her. She felt something of the same emotion, and with far less cause. Though Domaris had seen Micon often, in the intervening weeks, they had not exchanged a dozen words beyond the barest greetings. Always there was the strange sense of something half-perceived, felt rather than known. She was content to let it ripen slowly.

Deoris went on, worshipfully, "He is good to everyone, but he treats me like—almost like a little sister. Often when I am reading, he will stop me simply to explain something I have read, as if I were his pupil, his chela. . . ."

"That is kind," Domaris agreed. Like most children, she had served as a reader in her childhood, and knew how unusual this was: to treat a little scribe as anything more than an impersonal convenience, like a lamp or a footstool. But one might expect the unexpected of Micon.

As Rajasta's chosen Acolyte, Domaris had heard much of the Temple talk. The lost Prince of Ahtarrath had not been found, and the envoys were planning to return home, their mission a failure. By devious paths, Domaris had discovered that Micon had kept himself from their knowledge, that he had not even let them guess his presence within the Temple of Light. She could not fathom his motives—but no one could attribute any motive, other than the highest, in connection with Micon. Although she had no proof of it, Domaris felt sure that Micon was one whom they sought; perhaps the young brother of the Prince. . . .

Deoris's thoughts had drifted to still another tangent. "Micon speaks often of you, Domaris. Know what he calls you?"

"What?" breathed Domaris, her voice hushed.

"Woman-clothed-with-the-sun."

The grateful darkness hid the glimmer of the woman's tears.

II

Lightning flickered and went dark over the form of a young man who stood outlined in the doorway. "Domaris?" questioned a bass voice. "Is all well with you? I was uneasy—on such a night."

Domaris focussed her eyes to pierce the gloom. "Arvath! Come in if you like, we are not sleeping."

The young man advanced, lifting the thin netting, and dropped cross-legged on the edge of the nearer pallet, beside Domaris. Arvath of Alkonath—an Atlantean, son of a woman of the Priest's Caste who had gone forth to wed a man of the Sea Kingdoms—was the oldest of the chosen Twelve, nearly two years older than Domaris. The lightning that flared and darkened showed chastened, tolerant features that were open and grave and still loved life with a firm and convinced love. The lines about his mouth were only partly from self-discipline; the remainder were the footprints of laughter.

Domaris said, with scrupulous honesty, "Earlier, we heard

chanting, and felt a—a wrongness, somehow. But I will not permit that sort of thing to frighten or annoy me."

"Nor should you," Arvath agreed vigorously. "But there may be more disturbance in the air. There are odd forces stirring; this is the Night of Nadir. No one sleeps in the House; Chedan and I were bathing in the fountain. The Lord Rajasta is walking about the grounds, clad in Guardian-regalia, and he—well, I should not like to cross his path!" He paused a moment. "There are rumors—"

"Rumors, rumors! Every breeze is loaded with scandal! Elis is full of them! I cannot turn around without hearing another!" Domaris twitched her shoulders. "And has even Arvath of Alkonath nothing better to do than listen to the clatter of the market-place?"

"It is not all clatter," Arvath assured her, and glanced at Deoris, who had burrowed down until only the tip of one dark curl was visible above the bedclothing. "Is she asleep?"

Again Domaris shrugged.

"No sails stir without wind," Arvath went on, shifting his weight a little, leaning toward Domaris. "You have heard of the Black-robes?"

"Who has not? For days, in fact, I seem to have heard of little else!"

Arvath peered at her, silently, before saying, "Know you, then, they are said to be concealed among the Grey-robes?"

"I know almost nothing of the Grey-robes, Arvath; save that they guard the Unrevealed God. We of the Priest's Caste are not admitted into the Magicians."

"Yet many of you join with their Adepts to learn the Healing Arts," Arvath observed. "In Atlantis, the Grey-robes are held in great honor. . . . Well, it is said, down there beneath the Grey Temple, where the Avatar sits, the Man with Crossed Hands, there is a story told of a ritual not performed for centuries, of a rite long outlawed—a Black Ritual—and an apostate in the Chela's Ring. . . ." His voice trailed into an ominous whisper.

Domaris, her fears stirred by the unfamiliar phrases with their hints of unknown horrors, cried out, "Where did you hear such things?"

Arvath chuckled. "Gossip only. But if it comes to Rajasta's ears—"

"Then there will be trouble," Domaris assured him primly, "for the Grey-robes, if the tale is true; for the gossips, if it be false."

"You are right, it concerns us not." Arvath pressed her hand and smiled, accepting the rebuke. He stretched himself on the pallet beside her, but without touching the girl—he had learned that long ago. Deoris slept soundly beside them, but her presence enabled Domaris to steer the conversation into the impersonal channels she wished; to avoid speaking of their personal affairs, or of Temple matters. And when Arvath slipped away to his own chambers, very late, Domaris lay wakeful, and her thoughts were so insistent that her head throbbed.

For the first time in the twenty-two summers of her young life, Domaris questioned her own wisdom in electing to continue as Priestess and student under Rajasta's guidance. She would have done better, perhaps, to have withdrawn from the Priesthood; to become simply another woman, content with dwelling as a Priest's wife in the Temple where she had been born, one of the many women in the world of the Temple; wives and daughters and Priests, who swarmed in the city without the faintest knowledge of the inner life of the great cradle of wisdom where they dwelled, content with their homes and their babies and the outward show of Priestly doings. . . . *What is the matter with me?* Domaris wondered restlessly. *Why can't I be as they are? I will marry Arvath, as I must, and then—*

And then what?

Children, certainly. Years of growth and change. She could not make her thoughts go so far. She was still vainly trying to imagine it when she fell asleep.

CHAPTER THREE
✦ THE LOOM OF FATE ✦

I

The Temple of Light, set upon the shores of the Ancient Land, was near the sea; it was set high above the City of the Circling Snake, which ringed it like a crescent moon. The Temple, lying between the spread horns of the crescent, at the focus of certain natural forces which the walls were built to intercept and conduct, was like a woman in the encircling glow of a lover's arm.

It was afternoon; summer and sun lay like smooth butter on the city, and like topaz on the gilded sea, with the dream of a breeze and the faint, salt-sweet rankness of tidewaters.

Three tall ships lay lifting to the swell of sails and sea, in the harbor. A few yards from the wharves, merchants had already set up their stalls and were crying their wares. The coming of the ships was an event alike to city-folk and farmer, peasant and aristocrat. In the crowded streets, Priests in luminous robes rubbed elbows uncaring with stolid traders and ragged mendicants; and a push or chance blow from some unwary lout, that would have meant a flogging on another day, now cost the careless one only a sharp look; tatterdemalion boys ran in and out of the crowd without picking the scrip of a single fat merchant.

One little group, however, met with no jostling, no familiarities: awed smiles followed Micon as he moved through the streets, one hand resting lightly on Deoris's arm. His luminous robes, fashioned of a peculiarly stainless white, cut and girdled in an unusual style, marked him no ordinary Priest come to bless their children or energize their farmlands; and, of course, the daughters of the powerful Talkannon were known to all. Many a young girl in the crowd smiled as Arvath passed; but the young Priest's dark eyes were jealously intent on Domaris. He resented Micon's effect on his betrothed. Arvath had almost forced himself on them, today.

They paused atop a sandy ridge of dunes, looking out over the sea. "Oh!" Deoris cried out in childish delight, "the ships!"

From habit, Micon turned to her. "What ships are they? Tell me, little sister," he asked, with affectionate interest. Vividly and eagerly, Deoris described to him the tall ships: high and swaying above the waves, their serpent banners brilliantly crimson at the prow. Micon's face was remote and dreamy as he listened.

"Ships from my homeland," he murmured wistfully. "There are no ships in all the Sea Kingdoms like the ships of Ahtarrath. My cousin flies the serpent in crimson—"

Arvath said bluntly, "I too am of the Golden Isles, Lord Micon."

"Your lineage?" queried Micon with interest. "I am homesick for a familiar name. Have you been in Ahtarrath?"

"I spent much of my youth beneath the Star-mountain," the younger man said. "Mani-toret, my father, was Priest of the Outer Gates in the New Temple; and I am son by adoption to Rathor in Ahtarrath."

Micon's face lighted, and he stretched his gaunt hands joyfully to the young man. "You are my brother indeed, then, young Arvath! For Rathor was my first teacher in the Priesthood, and guided me first to Initiation!"

Arvath's eyes widened. "But—are you *that* Micon?" he breathed. "All my life have I been told of your—"

Micon frowned. "Let be," he warned. "Speak not of that."

In uneasy awe, the young man said, "You *do* read minds!"

"That took not much reading, younger brother," Micon said wryly. "Do you know these ships?"

Arvath looked at him steadily. "I know them. And if you wish to conceal yourself, you should not have come here. You have changed, indeed, for I did not recognize you; but there are those who might."

Mystified and intrigued, the two girls had drawn together, alternately gazing at the two men and exchanging glances with one another.

"You do not—" Micon paused. "Recognize me? Had we met?"

Arvath laughed ringingly. "I would not expect you to know me again! Listen, Domaris, Deoris, and I will tell you about this Micon! When I was a little boy, not seven years old, I was sent to the home of Rathor, the old hermit of the Star-mountain. He is such a man as the ancients call saint; his wisdom is so famed that even here they do reverence to his name. But at that time, I knew only that many sober and serious young men came to him to study; and many of them brought me sweets and toys and petted me. While Rathor taught them, I played about on the hills with a pet cat. One day, I fell on a slide of rocks, and rolled down, and twisted my arm under me—"

Micon smiled, exclaiming, "Are you *that* child? Now I remember!"

Arvath continued, in a reminiscent tone, "I fainted with the pain, Domaris, and knew no more until I opened my eyes to see a young Priest standing beside me, one of those who came to Rathor. He lifted me up and set me on his knee, and wiped the blood from my face. There seemed to be healing in his hands—"

With a spasmodic movement, Micon turned away. "Enough of this," he said, stifled.

"Nay, I shall tell, elder brother! When he cleaned away the blood and dirt, I felt no pain, even though the bones had pierced through the flesh. He said, 'I have not the skill to tend this myself,' and he carried me in his arms to Rathor's house, because I was too bruised to walk. And then, because I was afraid of the Healer Priest who came to set the broken bone, he held me on his knees while the bone was set and bandaged; and all that night, because I was feverish and could not sleep, he sat by me, and fed me bread and milk and honey, and sang and told me stories until I forgot the pain. Is that so terrible a tale?" he asked softly. "Are you afraid these maidens might think you womanish, to be kind to a sick child?"

"Enough, I say," Micon pleaded again.

Arvath turned to him with a disbelieving stare; but what he saw in the dark blind face made his own expression alter into a gentler pattern. "So be it," he said, "but I have not forgotten, my brother, and I shall not forget." He pulled back the sleeve of his Priestly robe, showing Domaris a long livid streak against the tanned flesh. "See, here the bone pierced the flesh—"

"And the young Priest was Micon?" Deoris asked.

"Yes. And he brought me sweets and playthings while I was abed; but since that summer I had not seen him again."

"How strange, that you should meet so far from home!"

"Not so strange, little sister," said Micon, in his rich and gentle voice. "Our fates spin their web, and our actions bear the fruits they have sown. Those who have met and loved cannot be parted; if they meet not in this life, they meet in another."

Deoris accepted the words without comment, but Arvath asked aggressively, "Do you believe, then, that you and I are bound to one another in such manner?"

The trace of a wry smile touched Micon's lips. "Who can tell? Perhaps, when I picked you up from the rocks that day, I merely redeemed an old service done me by you before these hills were raised." He gestured, with a look of amusement, toward the Temple behind them. "I am no seer. Ask of your own wisdom, my brother. Perhaps the service remains to be met. The Gods grant we both meet it like men."

"Amen to that," Arvath said soberly. Then, because he had been deeply moved, his quick emotions swung in another direction. "Domaris came to the city to make some purchases; shall we return to the bazaar?"

Domaris came alive out of deep preoccupation. "Men have no love for bright cloth and ribbons," she said gaily. "Why do you not remain here upon the docks?"

"I dare not let you from my sight in the city, Domaris," Arvath informed her, and Domaris, piqued, flung her proud head high.

"Think not that you can direct my steps! If you come with me— you *follow*!" She took the hand of Deoris, and the two walked ahead, turning toward the marketplace.

II

The sleepy bazaar, wakened into life by the ships from the Sea

Kingdoms, hummed with the bustle of much buying and selling. A woman was selling singing birds in cages of woven rushes; Deoris stopped, enchanted, to look and listen, and with an indulgent laugh Domaris directed that one should be sent to the House of the Twelve. They walked slowly on, Deoris bubbling over with delight.

A drowsy old man watched sacks of grain and glistening clay jugs of oil; a naked urchin sat cross-legged between casks of wine, ready to wake his master if a buyer came. Domaris paused again at a somewhat larger stall, where lengths of brilliantly patterned cloth were displayed; Micon and Arvath, following slowly, listened for a moment to the absorbed girlish voices, then grinned spontaneously at one another and strolled on together past the flower-sellers, past the old country-woman. Chickens squawked in coops, vying with the cries of the vendors of dried fish and fresh fish, or plump fruits from cakes and sweetmeats and cheap sour beer, the stalls of bright rugs and shining ornaments, and the more modest stalls of pottery and kettles.

A little withered Islandman was selling perfumes under a striped tent, and as Micon and Arvath passed, his shrivelled face contracted with keen interest. He sat upright, dipping a miniature brush into a flask and waving it in air already honey-sweet with mingled fragrances. "Perfumes from Kei-lin, Lords," he cried out in a rumbling, wheezy bass, "spices of the West! Finest of flowers, sweetest of spice-trees. . . ."

Micon halted; then, with his usual deliberate step, went carefully toward the striped tent. The scent-seller, recognizing Temple nobility, was awed and voluble. "Fine perfumes and essences, Lords, sweet spices and unguents from Kei-lin, scents and oils for the bath, all the fine fragrances of the wide world for your sweetheart—" The garrulous little man stopped and amended quickly, "For your wife or sister, Lord Priest—"

Micon's twisted grin came reassuringly. "Neither wife nor sweetheart have I, Old One," he commented dryly, "nor will I trouble you for unguents or lotions. Yet you may serve us. There is a perfume made in Ahtarrath and only there, from the crimson lily that flowers beneath the Star-mountain."

The scent-seller looked curiously at the Initiate before he reached back into his tent and searched for a long time, fumbling about like a mouse in a heap of straw. "Not many ask for it," he muttered in apology; but, finally, he found what was wanted, and wasted no time in extolling its virtues, but merely waved a scented droplet in the air.

Domaris and Deoris, rejoining them, paused to breathe in the spicy fragrance, and Domaris's eyes widened.

"Exquisite!"

The fragrance lingered hauntingly in the air as Micon laid down some coins and picked up the small flask, examining it closely with his hands, drawing his attenuated fingers delicately across the filigree carving. "The fretwork of Ahtarrath—I can identify it even now." He smiled at Arvath. "Nowhere else is such work done, such patterns formed . . ." Still smiling, he handed the phial to the girls, who bent to exclaim over the dainty carven traceries.

"What scent is this?" Domaris asked, lifting the flask to her face.

"An Ahtarrath flower, a common weed," said Arvath sharply.

Micon's face seemed to share a secret with Domaris, and he asked, "You think it lovely, as I do?"

"Exquisite," Domaris repeated dreamily. "But strange. Very strange and lovely."

"It is a flower of Ahtarrath, yes," Micon murmured, "a crimson lily which flowers beneath the Star-mountain; a wild flower which workmen root up because it is everywhere. The air is heavy with its scent. But I think it lovelier than any flower that grows in a tended garden, and more beautiful. Crimson—a crimson so brilliant it hurts to look on it when the sun is shining, a joyous, riotous color—a flower of the sun." His voice sounded suddenly tired, and he reached for Domaris's hand and put the flask into it with finality, gently closing the fingers around it with his own. "No, it is for you, Domaris," he said with a little smile. "You too are crowned with sunlight."

The words were casual, but Domaris swallowed back unbidden tears. She tried to speak her thanks, but her hands were trembling and no words came. Micon did not seem to expect them, for he said, in a low voice meant for her ears alone, "Light-crowned, I wish I might see your face . . . flower of brightness. . . ."

Arvath stood squarely, frowning ferociously, and it was he who broke the silence with a truculent, "Shall we go on? We'll be caught by night here!" But Deoris went swiftly to the young man and clasped his arm in a proprietary grip, leaving Domaris to walk ahead with Micon—a privilege which Deoris usually claimed jealously for herself.

"I will fill her arms with those lilies, one day," Arvath muttered, staring ahead at the tall girl who walked at Micon's side, her flaming hair seeming to swim in sunlight. But when Deoris asked what he had said, he would not repeat it.

CHAPTER FOUR
✠ THE HEALER'S ✠ HANDS

I

Rajasta, glancing from the scroll that had occupied his attention, saw that the great library was deserted. Only moments ago, it seemed, he had been virtually surrounded by the rustle of paper, the soft murmurings of scribes. Now the niches were dark, and the only other person he could see was a librarian, androgynously robed, gathering various scrolls from the tables where they had been left.

Shaking his head, Rajasta returned the scroll he had been poring over to its protective sheath and laid it aside. Although he had no appointments to keep that day, he found it faintly annoying that he had spent so long reading and re-reading a single scroll—one which, moreover, he could have recited phrase for phrase. A little exasperated, he rose to his feet and began to leave—only then discovering that the library was not so empty as he had thought.

Micon sat at a gloomy table not far away, his habitual wry smile almost lost in the shadows felling across his face. Rajasta stopped beside him and stood for a moment, looking down at Micon's hands, and what they betrayed: strange hands, with an attenuated look about them, as if the fingers had been forcibly elongated; they lay on the table, limp but also somehow tense and twisted. With a deft gentleness, Rajasta gathered up the strengthless fingers into his own, cradling them lightly in his strong grasp. Questioningly, Micon raised his head.

"They seemed—such a living pain," the Priest of Light heard himself say.

"They would be, if I let them." Micon's face was schooled to impassivity, but the limp fingers quivered a little. "I can, within certain limits, hold myself aloof from pain. I feel it—" Micon smiled tiredly. "But the essential *me* can hold it away—until I tire. I hold away my death, in the same manner."

Rajasta shuddered at the Atlantean's calm. The hands in his stirred, carefully and deliberately, to free themselves. "Let be," Rajasta pleaded. "I can give you some ease. Why do you refuse my strength?"

"I can manage." The lines around Micon's mouth tightened, then relaxed. "Forgive me, brother. But I am of Ahtarrath. My duty is undone. I have, as yet, no right to die—being sonless. I must leave a son," he went on, almost as if this were but the spoken part of an argument he had often had with himself. "Else others with no right will seize the powers I carry."

"So be it," said Rajasta, and his voice was gentle, for he, too, lived by that law. "And the mother?"

For a moment Micon kept silent, his face a cautious blank; but this hesitancy was brief. "Domaris," he answered.

"Domaris?"

"Yes." Micon sighed. "That does not surprise you, surely?"

"Not altogether," said Rajasta at last. "It is a wise choice. Yet, she is pledged to your countryman, young Arvath. . . ." Rajasta frowned, thoughtful. "Still, it is hers to choose. She has the right to bear another's child, if she wishes. You—love her?"

Micon's tense features brightened, relaxing, and Rajasta found himself wondering what those sightless eyes beheld. "Yes," Micon said softly. "As I never dreamed I could love—" The Atlantean broke off with a groan as Rajasta's clasp tightened.

Chastened, the Priest of Light released Micon's abused hands. There was a long and faintly uneasy silence between them, as Micon conquered the pain once again, patiently, and Rajasta stood watching, helpless so long as Micon refused his aid.

"You have attained greatly," said Rajasta suddenly. "And I am not, as yet, truly touched by the Light. For the time allotted you—will you accept me as disciple?"

Micon lifted his face, and his smile was a transcendent thing.

"What power of Light I can give, will surely shine in you despite me," he promised. "But I accept you." Then, in a lower, more sober tone, Micon continued, "I think—I hope I can give you a year. It should suffice. And if not, you will be able to complete the Last Seal alone. That I vow to you."

Slowly, as he did everything, Micon rose up and stood facing Rajasta. Tall and thin, almost translucent in the shadowy sunlight that shone upon them through the library windows, the Atlantean laid his twisted hands lightly on the Priest's shoulders and drew him close. With one hand he traced a sign upon Rajasta's forehead and breast; then, with a feather-touch, ran his expressive fingers over the older man's face.

Rajasta's eyes were wet. This was an incredible thing to him: he had called a stranger to that most meaningful of relationships; he, Rajasta, Priest of Light, son of an ancient line of Priests, had asked to be a disciple to an alien from a Temple referred to, contemptuously, among the Priest's Caste, as *"that upstart backwoods chantry in the middle of the ocean!"*

Yet Rajasta felt no regret—only, for the first time in his life, true humility. *Perhaps my caste has become too proud,* the Priest thought, *and so the Gods show themselves through this blind and tortured foreigner, to remind us that the Light touches not only those ordained by heredity. . . . This man's simplicity, his courage, will be as talismans to me.*

Then Rajasta's lips tightened, stern and grim. "Who tortured you?" he demanded, as Micon released him. "Warrior of Light—*who?*"

"I do not know." Micon's voice was wholly steady. "All were masked, and in black. Yet, for a moment, I saw too clearly. And so, I see no more. Let it be. The deed will carry its own vengeance."

"No, that may be so, but vengeance delayed only gives time for further deeds. Why did you beg me to let you remain concealed while the envoys from Ahtarrath were among us?" Rajasta pressed.

"They would have slain many, tortured more, to avenge me—thus setting a worse evil in motion."

Rajasta started to make reply, but hesitated, again wondering at the strength of this man. "I will not question your wisdom, but—is it right to let your parents grieve needlessly?"

Micon, once more sitting down, laughed lightly. "Do not let that disturb you, my brother. My parents died before I was out of childhood. And I have written that I live, and how, and for how long, and sealed it with—with that my grandsire cannot mistake. My message travels on the same ship with the news of my death. They will understand."

Rajasta nodded approvingly, and then, remembering that although the Atlantean seemed to gaze into the Priest's very soul, Micon could not see him, said aloud, "That is as it should be, then. But what was done to you? And for what reason? Nay," he went on, more loudly, overriding Micon's protest, "it is my right—even more, my *duty*, to know! I am Guardian here."

Unknown to Rajasta, and all but forgotten by Micon, Deoris perched on the edge of her scribe's stool not far away from them. Silent as a little white statue, she had listened to all that they had said in mute absorption. She understood almost nothing of it, but Domaris had been mentioned, and Deoris was anxious to hear more. The fact that this conversation was not intended for her ears bothered her not at all; what concerned Domaris, she felt, was her affair as well. Fervently, Deoris hoped that Micon would continue, forgetful of her presence. Domaris must know of this! Deoris's hands clenched into small fists at the thought of her sister as the mother of a baby. . . . A smothered and childish jealousy, of which Deoris was never to be wholly aware, turned her dismay into hurt. Why should Micon have chosen *Domaris?* Deoris knew that her sister was betrothed to Arvath—but that marriage was some time in the future. This was now! How could Micon and Rajasta dare to talk of her sister this way? How could Micon dare to love Domaris? If only they did not notice her!

They did not. Micon's eyes had grown dark, their queer luminosity veiled with suppressed emotion. "The rack, and rope," he said, "and fire, to blind, because I ripped away one mask before they could bind me." His voice was low and hoarse with exhaustion, as if he and Rajasta were not robed Priests in an ancient and sacred place, but wrestlers struggling on a mat. "The reason?" Micon went on. "We of Ahtarrath have an inborn ability to use—certain forces of nature: rain, and thunder, lightning, even the terrible power of the earthquake and volcano. It is—our heritage, and our truth, without which life in the Sea Kingdoms would be impossible, perhaps. There are legends . . ." Micon shook his head suddenly, and smiling, said lightly, "These things you must know, or have guessed. We use these powers for the benefit of all, even those who style themselves our enemies. But the ability to control this power can be—stolen, and bastardized into the filthiest kind of sorcery! But from me they gained nothing. I am not apostate—and I had the strength to defeat their ends, although not to save myself . . . I am not certain what befell my half-brother, and so I must force myself to live, in this body, until I am certain it is safe to die."

"Oh, my brother," said Rajasta in a hushed voice, and found himself drawing nearer Micon again.

The Atlantean bent his head. "I fear Reio-ta was won over by the Black-robes. . . . My grandsire is old, and in his dotage. The power passes to my brother, at my death, if I die without issue. And I will not leave that power in the hands of sorcerers and apostates! You know the law! *That is* important; not this fragile body, nor that which dwells in it and suffers. I—the essential I—remain untouched, and because nothing can touch that unless I allow!"

"Let me lend you strength," Rajasta pleaded, again. "With what I know—"

"Under necessity, I may do so," Micon returned, calm again, "but now I need only rest. The need may come without warning. In that event, I shall take you at your word. . . ." And then the timbre of Micon's rich voice returned, and his face lighted with his rare, wonderful smile. "And I do thank you!"

Deoris fixed her eyes studiously upon her scroll, to appear absorbed, but now she felt Rajasta's stern gaze upon the top of her head.

"Deoris," said the Priest severely. "What are you doing here?"

Micon laughed. "She is my scribe, Rajasta, and I forgot to dismiss her." Rising, he moved toward Deoris and put a hand upon her curly head. "It is enough for today. Run away, my child, and play."

II

Dismissed with Micon's one-sided smile, Deoris fled in search of Domaris, her young mind filled with entangled words: Black-robes, life, death, apostasy—whatever that was—torture, Domaris to bear a son. . . . Kaleidoscopic images twisted and glimmered in her dismayed young mind, and she burst breathlessly into their apartments.

Domaris was supervising the slave women as they folded and sorted clean garments. The room was filled with afternoon sunlight and the fragrance of fresh, smooth linens. The women—little dark women, with braided hair and the piquant features of the pygmy race of the Temple slaves—chattered in birdlike trills as their diminutive brown bodies moved and pattered restlessly around the tall girl who stood in their midst, gently directing them and listening to their shrill little voices.

Domaris's loose hair moved smoothly upon her shoulders as she turned, questioning, toward the door. "Deoris! At this hour! Is Micon—?" She broke off, and turned to an older woman; not a slave, but one of the townspeople who was her personal attendant. "Continue with this, Elara," Domaris requested gently, then beckoned Deoris to her. She caught her breath at sight of the child's face. "You're crying, Deoris! What is the matter?"

"No!" Deoris denied, raising a flushed but tearless face. "I just— have to tell you something—"

"Wait, not here. Come—" She drew Deoris into the inner room where they slept, and looked again at the girl's flushed cheeks with dismay. "What are you doing here at this hour? Is Micon ill? Or—" She stopped, unable to voice the thought that tortured her, unable even to define it clearly in her own mind.

Deoris shook her head. Now, facing Domaris herself, she hardly knew how to begin. Shakily, she said, "Micon and Rajasta were talking about you . . . they said—"

"Deoris! Hush!" Shocked, Domaris put out a hand to cover the too-eager lips. "You must never tell me what you hear among the Priests!"

Deoris twisted free, stinging under the implied rebuke. "But they talked right in front of me, they both knew I was there! And they were talking about you, Domaris. Micon said that you—"

"*Deoris!*"

Before her sister's blazing eyes, the child knew this was one of those rare occasions when she dared not disobey. She looked sulkily down at the floor.

Domaris, distressed, looked at the bent head of her little sister. "Deoris, you know that a scribe must never repeat anything that is said among the Priests. That is the first rule you should have learned!"

"Oh, leave me alone!" Deoris blurted out wrathfully, and ran from the room, her throat tight with angry sobs, driven by a fear she could neither control nor conceal. What right had Micon—what right had Rajasta—it wasn't right, none of it was right, and if Domaris wouldn't even listen, what could she do?

III

Deoris had no sooner left the library than Rajasta turned to Micon. "This matter must be brought to Riveda's attention."

Micon sighed wearily. "Why? Who is Riveda?"

"The First Adept of the Grey-robes. This touches him."

Micon moved his head negatively. "I would rather not disturb him with—"

"It must be so, Micon. Those who prostitute legitimate magic into foul sorcery must reckon with the Guardians of what they defile, else they will wreak havoc on us all, and more than we can undo, perhaps. It is easy to say, as you say, 'Let them reap what they sow'—and a bitter harvest it will be, I have no doubt! But what of those they have injured? Would you leave them free to torture others?"

Micon looked away, silenced, and his blind eyes moved randomly. Rajasta did not like the idea of what visions were in the Atlantean's mind then.

At last, Micon forced a smile, and a kind of laugh. "I thought I was to be the teacher, and you the pupil! But you are right," he murmured. Still, there was a very human protest in his voice as he added, "I dread it, though. The questioning. And all the rest. . . ."

"I would spare you, if I could."

Micon signed. "I know. Let it be as you will. I—I only hope Deoris did not hear all we said! I had forgotten the child was there."

"And I never saw her. The scribes are pledged to silence about what they hear, of course—but Deoris is young, and it is hard for mere babies to keep their tongues in silence. Deoris! That child!"

The weary exasperation in Rajasta's voice prompted Micon to ask, in some puzzlement, "You dislike her?"

"No, no," Rajasta hastened to reassure him. "I love her, much as I love Domaris. In fact I often think Deoris the more brilliant of the two; but it is only cleverness. She will never be so—so *complete* as Domaris. She lacks—patience. Steadfastness is not Deoris's virtue!"

"Come now," Micon dissented, "I have been much with her, and found her to be very patient, and helpful. Also kind and tactful as well. And I would say that she is more brilliant than Domaris. But she is only a child, and Domaris is—" His voice trailed off abruptly, and he smiled. Then, recalling himself, "Must I meet this—Riveda?"

"It would be best, I think," Rajasta replied. About to say more, the Priest stopped and bent to peer closely at Micon's face. The deepening lines he saw etched there made the Priest turn and summon a servant from the hall. "I go to Riveda now," Rajasta said as the servant approached. "Guide Lord Micon to his apartments."

Micon yielded gracefully enough—but as Rajasta watched him go, the muscles in his face were tight with worry and doubt. He had heard that the Atlanteans held the Grey-robes in a kind of reverence that bordered on worship—and this was understandable, in a way, when one considered the illnesses and disease that constantly troubled the Sea Kingdoms. The Grey-robes had done wonders there in controlling plague and pestilence. . . . Rajasta had not expected Micon to react in quite this way, however.

Rajasta dismissed his faint misgivings swiftly. It could only be for the best. Riveda was the greatest of their Healers, and might be able to help Micon where Rajasta could not; that, perhaps, was why the Atlantean was disturbed. *After all,* Rajasta thought, *Micon is of a noble lineage; despite his humility, he has pride. And if a Grey-robe tells him to rest more, he will have to listen!*

Turning, Rajasta strode from the room, his white robes making sibilant whispers about his feet. Even before this, Rajasta had heard the rumors of forbidden rituals among the Grey-robes, of Black-clad sorcerers who worked in secret with the old and evil forces at the heart of nature, forces that took no heed of humanity and made their users less human by degrees.

The Priest paused in the hall and shook his head, wonderingly. Could it be Micon believed those rumors, and feared Riveda would open the way for the Black-robes to recapture him? Well, once they had met, any such doubts would surely melt away. Yes, surely Riveda, First Adept among the Grey-robes, was best fitted to handle this problem. Rajasta did not doubt, either, that justice would be done. He knew Riveda.

His mind made up, Rajasta strode down the hallway, through a covered passageway and into another building, where he paused before a certain door. He knuckled the wood in three firm and evenly-spaced knocks.

IV

The Magician Riveda was a big man, taller even than the tall Rajasta; firmly-knit and muscular, his broad shoulders looked, and were, strong enough to throw down a bull. In his cowled robe of rough gray frieze, Riveda was a little larger than life as he turned from contemplation of the darkling sky.

"Lord Guardian," he greeted, courteously, "what urgency brings you to me?"

Rajasta said nothing, but continued to study the other man quietly for a moment. The cowl, flung loose on Riveda's shoulders, revealed a big head, set well on a thick neck and topped with masses of close-clipped fair hair—silver-gilt hair, a strange color above a stranger face. Riveda was not of the true Priest's Caste, but a Northman from the kingdom of Zaiadan; his rough-hewn features were an atavism from a ruder age, standing out strangely in contrast to the more delicate, chiselled lineaments of the Priest's Caste.

Under Rajasta's silent, intense scrutiny, Riveda flung back his head and laughed. "The need must be great indeed!"

Rajasta curbed his irritation—Riveda had always had the power to exasperate him—and answered, in a level voice that sobered the Adept, "Ahtarrath has sent a son to our Temple; the Prince Micon. He was apprehended by Black-robes, tortured, and blinded—to the end that he serve their Illusion. I am come to tell you: look to your Order."

The frigid blue of Riveda's eyes was darkened with troubled

shadows. "I knew nothing of this," he said. "I have been deep in study . . . I do not doubt your word, Rajasta, but what could the Hidden Ones hope to achieve?"

Rajasta hesitated. "What do you know of the powers of Ahtarrath?"

Riveda's brows lifted. "Almost nothing," he said frankly, "and even that little is no more than rumor. They say that certain of that lineage can bring rain from reluctant clouds and loose the lightning—that they ride the storm-wrack, and that sort of thing." He smiled, sardonic. "No one has told me how they do it, or why, and so I have reserved judgment, so far."

"The powers of Ahtarrath are very real," said Rajasta. "The Black-robes sought to divert that power to—a spiritual whoredom. Their object, his apostasy and—service to their demons."

Riveda's eyes narrowed. "And?"

"They failed," Rajasta said tersely. "Micon will die—but only when he chooses." Rajasta's face was impassive, but Riveda, skilled in detecting involuntary betrayals, could see the signs of emotion. "Blinded and broken as he is—the Releaser of Man will not conquer until Micon wills it. He is a—a Cup of Light!"

Riveda nodded, a trifle impatiently. "So your friend would not serve the Dark Shrine, and they sought to force apostasy upon him? Hmm . . . it *is* possible . . . I could admire this prince of Ahtarrath," Riveda murmured, "if all you say is true. He must be, indeed, a man." The Grey-robe's stern face relaxed for a moment in a smile; then the lips were harshly curled again. "I will find the truth of this business, Rajasta; believe me."

"That I knew," said Rajasta simply, and the eyes of the two men met and locked, with mutual respect.

"I will need to question Micon."

"Come to me then, at the fourth hour from now," Rajasta said, and turned to go.

Riveda detained him with a gesture. "You forget. The ritual of my Order requires me to make certain lengthy preparations. Only when—"

"I have not forgotten," said Rajasta coolly, "but this matter is urgent; and you have some leeway in such cases." With this, Rajasta hurried away.

Riveda stood looking at the closed door, troubled, but not by Rajasta's arrogance; one expected such things of the Guardians, and circumstances generally justified them.

There were always—would always be, Riveda suspected—a few Magicians who could not be restrained from dabbling in the black and forbidden arts of the past; and Riveda knew all too well that his Order was automatically suspected in any Temple disturbance. It had been foolish to submerge himself in study, leaving the lesser Adepts to govern the Grey-robes; now even the innocent might suffer for the folly and cruelty of a few.

Fools, worse than fools, Riveda thought, *that they did not confine their hell's play to persons of no importance! Or, having dared so high, fools not to make certain their victims did not escape alive to carry tales!*

Riveda's austere face was grim and ruthless as he swiftly gathered up and stored away the genteel clutter of the studies which had so long preoccupied him.

It was, indeed, time to see to his Order.

V

In a corner of the room set aside for Rajasta's administrative work, the Arch-Priest Talkannon sat quietly, for the moment apparently altogether detached from humanity and its concerns. Beside him Domaris stood, motionless, and with sidelong glances watched Micon.

The Atlantean had refused a seat, and stood leaning against a table. Micon's stillness was uncanny—a schooled thing that made Rajasta uneasy. He knew what it concealed. With a thoughtful frown, Rajasta turned his gaze away and saw, beyond the window, the grey-robed figure of Riveda, easily identifiable even at a distance, striding along the pathway toward them.

Without moving, Micon said, "Who comes?"

Rajasta started. The Atlantean's perceptivity was a continuing source of wonder to him; although blind, Micon had discerned what neither Talkannon nor Domaris had noticed.

"It is Riveda, is it not?" Micon said, before Rajasta could reply.

Talkannon raised his head, but he did not speak. Riveda entered, saluting the Priests carelessly but with enough courtesy. Domaris, of course, was ignored completely. She had never seen Riveda before, and now drew back in something like wonder. Her eyes met the Adept's for a moment; then she quickly lowered her head, fighting unreasoning fear and immediate dislike. In an instant she knew that she could hate this man who had never harmed her—and also that she must never betray the least sign of that hatred.

Micon, touching Riveda's fingers lightly with his own, thought, *This man could go far.* . . . Yet the Atlantean was also uneasy, without knowing why.

"Welcome, Lord of Ahtarrath," Riveda was saying, with an easy deference devoid of ceremony. "I deeply regret that I did not know, before—" He stopped, and his thoughts, running in deep channels, surfaced suddenly. This man was signed to Death; signed and sealed. It spoke in everything about Micon: the fitfully-fanned, forced strength; the slow, careful movements; the banked fires of his will; the deliberate husbanding of energy—all this, and the almost-translucence of Micon's thin body, proclaimed that this man had no strength to spare. And yet, equally clearly, the Atlantean was an Adept—as the high Mysteries made Adepts.

Riveda, with his thirst for knowledge and the power that was knowledge, felt a strange mixture of envy and regret. *What terrible waste!* he thought. *This man would better serve himself—and his ideals—by turning to Light's darker aspects!* Light and Dark, after all, were but balanced manifestations of the Whole. There was a kind of strength to be wrested from the struggle with Death that the Light could never show or grant. . . .

Micon's greetings were meaningless sounds, forms of polite speech, and Riveda attended them with half an ear; then, amazed and disbelieving, the Grey-robe realized just what Micon was saying.

"I was incautious." The Atlantean's resonant voice rang loud in the closed room. "What happened to me is of no importance. But there was, and is, one who must return to the Way of Light. Find my half-brother if you can. As for the rest—I could not, now, point out the guilty to you. Nor would I." Micon made a slight gesture of finality. "There shall be no vengeance taken! The deed carries its own penalty."

Riveda shook his head. "My Order must be cleansed."

"That is for you to decide. I can give you no help." Micon smiled, and for the first time Riveda felt the outpouring warmth of the man. Micon turned his head slightly toward Domaris. "What say you, light-crowned?" he asked, while Riveda and Talkannon stood scandalized at this appeal to a mere Acolyte—and a woman at that!

"You are right," Domaris said slowly, "but Riveda is right, too. Many students come here in search of knowledge. If sorcery and torture go unpunished, then evil-doers thrive."

"And what say you, my brother?" Micon demanded of Rajasta. Riveda felt a surge of envious resentment; he too was Adept, Initiate, yet Micon claimed no spiritual kinship with him!

"Domaris is wise, Micon." Rajasta's hand closed very gently on the Atlantean's thin arm. "Sorcery and torture defile our Temple. Duty demands that others must not face the peril you have tasted."

Micon sighed, and with a helpless gesture said, "You are the judges, then. But I have, now, no way of knowing those involved. . . . They took us at the seawall, treating us with courtesy, and lodged us among Grey-robes. At nightfall we were led to a crypt, and certain things demanded of us under threat of torture and death. We refused. . . ." A peculiar smile crossed the lean, dark features. Micon extended his emaciated hands. "You can see their threats were no idle ones. And my half-brother—" He broke off again, and there was a brief, sorrowful silence before Micon said, almost in extenuation, "He is little more than a boy. And him they could use, although not fully. I broke free from them for a moment, before they bound me, and ripped the mask from one face. And so—" a brief pause, "I saw nothing more. After that—later, much later I think—I was freed; and men of kindliness, who knew me not, brought me to Talkannon's house, where I was reunited with my servants. I know not what tale was told to account for me." He paused, then added quietly, "Talkannon has told me that I was ill for a long time. Certainly there is a period which is wholly blank to me."

Talkannon's iron grip forced quiet on his daughter.

Riveda stood, with clasped hands, looking at Micon in thoughtful silence; then asked, "How long ago was this?"

Micon shrugged, almost embarrassed. "I have no idea. My wounds were healed—what healing was possible—when I awakened in Talkannon's house."

Talkannon, who had said almost nothing so far, now broke his silence and said heavily, "He was brought to me, by commoners—fishermen, who said they found him lying on the shore, insensible and almost naked. They knew him for a Priest by the ornaments he still wore about his throat. I questioned them. They knew nothing more."

"*You* questioned!" Riveda's scorn was withering. "How do you know they told truth?"

Talkannon's voice lashed, whiplike and stern: "I could not, after all, question them under torture!"

"Enough of this," Rajasta pleaded, for Micon was trembling.

Riveda bit off his remarks unvoiced and turned to Micon. "Tell me more of your brother, at least."

"He is only my half-brother," Micon replied, a bit hesitant. Gone now was the uncanny stillness; his twisted, strengthless fingers twitched faintly at his sides, and he leaned more heavily against the table. "Reio-ta is his name. He is many years younger than I, but in looks we are not—were not—very dissimilar." Micon's words trailed away, and he wavered where he stood.

"I will do what I can," said Riveda, with a sudden and surprising gentleness. "If I had been told before—I cannot say how much I regret—" The Grey-robe bowed his head, maddened by the futility of his words. "After so long, I can promise nothing—"

"And I ask nothing, Lord Riveda. I know you will do what you must. But I beg you—do not ask for my aid in your—investigations." Micon's voice was an apology beyond words, "I have not the strength; nor could I be of much use, having now no way to—"

Riveda straightened, scowling: the intent look of a practical man. "You told me you saw one face. Describe him!"

Everyone in the room bent slightly toward Micon, waiting. The Atlantean drew himself erect and said clearly, "That is a secret which shall die with me. I have said, *there will be no vengeance taken!*"

Talkannon settled back in his seat with a sigh, and Domaris's face betrayed her conflicting emotions. Rajasta did not question Micon even in his mind; of them all he knew the Atlantean best and had come to accept Micon's attitude, although he did not really agree.

Riveda scowled fiercely. "I beg you to reconsider, Lord Micon! I know your vows forbid you to take vengeance for your personal hurt, but—" He clenched his fists. "Are you not also under oath to protect others from evil?"

Micon, however, was inflexible. "I have said that I will not speak or testify."

"So be it!" Riveda's voice was bitter. "I cannot force you to speak against your will. For the honor of my Order, I must investigate—but be sure I shall not trouble you again!"

The anger in Riveda's voice penetrated deep; Micon slumped, leaning heavily on Rajasta, who instantly forgot all else and helped the Atlantean into the seat he had previously refused.

Swift pity dawned in the stern features of the Adept of the Grey-robes. Riveda could be gracious when it suited him, and his urge now was to conciliate. "If I have offended, Lord Micon," he said earnestly, "let this excuse me: this thing that has befallen you touches the honor of my Order, which I must guard as carefully as you guard your vows. I would root out this nest of evil birds—feather, wing, and egg! Not for you alone, but for all who will follow you to our Temple's doors."

"With those aims I can sympathize," Micon said, almost humbly, his blind eyes staring up at Riveda. "What means you employ are none of my affair." He sighed, and his drawn nerves seemed to relax a little. Perhaps no one there except the abnormally sensitive Domaris had known how much the Atlantean had dreaded this interview. Now, at least, he knew that Riveda himself had not been among his tormentors. Tensed to this possibility, and prepared to conceal it if it had been so, relief left him limp with weariness. "My thanks are worth nothing, Lord Riveda," he said, "but accept my friendship with them."

Riveda clasped the racked fingers in his own, very lightly, secretly examining them with a Healer's eye to see how long they had been healed. Riveda's hands were big and hard, roughened by manual work done in childhood, yet sensitive as Micon's own. The Atlantean felt that Riveda's hands held some strong force chained—a defiant strength harnessed and made powerful. The strengths of the two Initiates met; but even the briefest contact with so much vitality was too much for Micon, and swiftly he withdrew his hand, his face ashen-pale. Without another word, trembling with the effort to seem calm, Micon turned and went toward the door.

Rajasta took a step to follow, then stopped, obeying some inaudible command that said, plainly, *No.*

VI

As the door scraped shut, Rajasta turned to Riveda. "Well?"

Riveda stood, looking down at his hands, frowning. Uneasily, he said, "The man is a raw, open channel of power."

"What do you mean?" Talkannon demanded roughly.

"When our hands touched," Riveda said, almost muttering, "I could feel the vital strength leaving me; he seemed to draw it forth from me—"

Rajasta and Talkannon stared at the Grey-robe in dismay. What Riveda described was a secret of the Priest's Caste, invoked only rarely and with infinite caution. Rajasta felt unreasoningly infuriated: Micon had refused such aid from him, with a definiteness that left no room for argument. . . . Abruptly, Rajasta realized that Riveda had not the slightest understanding of what had happened.

The Grey-robe's harsh whisper sounded almost frightened. "I think he knew it too—he drew away from me, he would not touch me again."

Talkannon said hoarsely, "Say nothing of this, Riveda!"

"Fear not—" Uncharacteristically, Riveda covered his face with his hands and shuddered as he turned away from them. "I could not—could not—I was too strong, I could have killed him!"

Domaris was still leaning against her father, her face as white as Talkannon's robes; her free hand gripped the table so tautly that the knuckles were white knots.

Talkannon jerked up his head. "What ails you, girl!"

Rajasta, his stern self-control reasserted at once, turned to her in concern. "Domaris! Are you ill, child?"

"I—no," she faltered. "But Micon—" Her face suddenly streamed with tears. She broke away from her father and fled the room.

They watched her go, nonplussed; the room was oppressively silent. At last Riveda crossed the room and closed the door she had left open in her flight, remarking, with sarcastic asperity, "I note a certain lack of decorum among your Acolytes, Rajasta."

For once Rajasta was not offended by Riveda's acerbic manner. "She is but a girl," he said mildly. "This is harsh business."

"Yes," said Riveda heavily. "Let us begin it, then." Fixing his ice-blue eyes on Talkannon, the Adept proceeded to question the Arch-Administrator with terse insistence, demanding the names of the fishermen who had "discovered" Micon, the time when it all had happened, probing for the smallest revealing circumstance, the half-forgotten details that might prove significant. He had hoped to fuse overlooked bits of information into a cohesive basis for further investigation. He learned, however, little more than he had known already.

The Grey-robe's cross-examination of Rajasta was even less productive, and Riveda, whose temper was at the best of times uncertain, at last grew angry and almost shouted, "Can I work in the dark! You'd make me a blind man, too!"

Yet, even as his bafflement and irritation ignited, Riveda realized that he had truly plumbed the limits of their knowledge of the matter. The Adept flung back his head, as if to a challenge. "So, then! If Priests of Light cannot illuminate this mystery for me, I must learn to see black shapes moving in utter blackness!" He turned to go, saying over his shoulder, "I thank you for the chance to refine my perceptions!"

VII

In his secluded apartments, Micon lay stretched on his narrow bed, his face hidden in his arms, breathing slowly and with deliberation. Riveda's vitality, flooding in through Micon's momentary incaution, had disturbed the precarious control he held over his body, and the surging imbalance left the Atlantean dumbly, rigidly terrified. It was paradoxical that what, in a less critical situation, would have speeded Micon's recovery, in this instance threatened him with a total relapse, or worse. He was almost too weak to master this influx of strength!

Micon found himself thinking, with grim sureness, that his initial torture and what he suffered now were only the preliminaries of a long-drawn-out and bitter punishment—and for what? Resisting evil!

Priest though he was, Micon was young enough to be bitterly bewildered. *Integrity,* he thought, in a sudden fury, *is far too expensive a luxury!* But he arrested the questing feelers of this mood, knowing such thoughts for a sending of the Dark Ones, insinuating further sacrilege through the pinholes that their tortures had opened. Desperately, he fought to still the mental rebellion that would diminish the already-fading control he barely held, and must keep, over his body's torment.

A year. I thought I could bear this for a year!

Yet he had work to finish, come what might. He had made certain promises, and must keep them. He had accepted Rajasta as disciple. And there was Domaris. *Domaris . . .*

CHAPTER FIVE
✠ THE NIGHT OF ✠ THE ZENITH

I

The night sky was a silent vault of blues piled up on blues, purple heaped high on indigo, dusted with a sprinkle of just-blossoming stars. A tenuous luminescence, too dim for starlight, too wispy for any light belonging to earth, hovered faintly around the moonless path; by its glimmer Rajasta moved unerringly, and Micon, at his side, walked with a quiet deliberation that missed no step.

"But why go we to the Star Field tonight, Rajasta?"

"Tonight—I thought I had told you—is the night when Caratra, the Star of the Woman, touches the Zenith. The Twelve Acolytes will scan the heavens, and each will interpret the omens according to their capability. It should interest you." Rajasta smiled at his companion. "Domaris will be there, and, I expect, her sister. She asked me to bring you." Taking Micon's arm, he guided the Atlantean gently as the path began to ascend the rim of a hill.

"I shall enjoy it." Micon smiled, without the twist of pain that so frequently marred his features. Where Domaris was, was forgetfulness; he was not so constantly braced. She had somehow the ability to give him a strength that was not wholly physical, the overflowing of her own abundant vitality. He wondered if this were deliberate; that she was capable of just such outpouring generosity, he never doubted. Her gentleness and graciousness were like a gift of the Gods. He knew she was beautiful, with a faculty that went beyond seeing.

Rajasta's eyes were sad. He loved Domaris; how dearly, he had never realized until now, when he saw her peace threatened. This man, whom Rajasta also loved, walked ever more closely with death; the emotion he sensed between Micon and Domaris was a fragile and lovely thing to hold such seeds of grief. Rajasta, too, knew that Domaris would give so generously as to rob herself. He would not and could not forbid, but he was saddened by the inevitable end he foresaw with such clarity.

Micon said, with a restraint that gave point to his words, "I am not wholly selfish, my brother. I too can see something of the coming struggle. Yet you know, too, that my line must be carried on, lest the Divine Purpose strive against too great odds. That is not pride." He trembled, as if with cold, and Rajasta was quick to support him with an unobtrusive arm.

"I know," said the Priest of Light, "we have discussed this often. The cause is already in motion, and we must ensure that it does not turn against us. All this I understand. Try not to think of it, tonight. Come, it is not far now," he assured. Rajasta had seen Micon when he surrendered to his pain, and the memory was not a good one.

To eyes accustomed to the starshine, the Star Field was a place of ethereal beauty. The sky hovered like folded wings, brushed with the twinklings of numberless stars; the sweet fragrance of the breathing earth, the rumor of muted talk, and the deep velvet of black shadows, made dreamy fantasy around them, as if a harsh word would dissolve the whole scene and leave an emptiness.

Rajasta said in a low tone, "It is—beyond words—lovely."

"I know." Micon's dark unquiet face held momentary torment. "I feel it."

Domaris, her pale robes gleaming silver as if with frost, seemed to drift toward them. "Come and sit with us, Teachers of Wisdom," she invited, and drew Deoris closely against her.

"Gratefully," Rajasta answered, and led Micon after the tall and lovely shape.

Deoris abruptly freed herself from the arm that encircled her waist, and came to Micon, her slender immaturity blending into the fantastic imagery of the place and the hour.

"Little Deoris," the Atlantean said, with a kindly smile.

The child, with a shy audacity, tucked her hand into his arm. Her own smile was blissful and yet, somehow, protective; the dawning woman in Deoris frankly took notice of all that the wiser Domaris dared not admit that she saw.

They stopped beside a low, sweet-smelling shrub that flowered whitely against the night, and Domaris sat down, flinging her cloak of silver gossamer from her shoulders. Deoris pulled Micon carefully down between them, and Rajasta seated himself beside his Acolyte.

"You have watched the stars, Domaris; what see you there?"

"Lord Rajasta," the girl said formally, "Caratra takes a strange position tonight, a conjunction with the Harpist and the Scythe. If I were to interpret it . . ." She hesitated, and turned her face up to the sky once again. "She is opposed by the Serpent," Domaris murmured. "I would say—that a woman will open a door to evil, and a woman will bar it. The same woman; but it is another woman's influence that makes it possible to bar the door." Domaris was silent again for a moment, but before her companions could speak, she went on, "A child will be born; one that will sire a line to check this evil, forever."

With an unguarded movement, the first one anyone had seen him make, Micon caught clumsily at her shoulders; "The stars say that?" he demanded hoarsely.

Domaris met his unseeing eyes in an uneasy silence, almost glad for once of his blindness. "Yes," she said, her voice controlled but husky. "Caratra nears the Zenith, and her Lady, Aderes, attends her. The Seven Guardians ring her about—protecting her not only from the Serpent but the Black Warrior, El-cherkan, that threatens from the Scorpion's claws . . ."

Micon relaxed, and for a space of minutes leaned weakly against her. Domaris held him gently, letting him rest against her breast, and in a conscious impulse poured her own strength into him. It was done unobtrusively, graciously, in response to a need that was imperative, and in the instinctive act she placed herself in rapport with Micon. The vistas that opened to her from the Initiate's mind were something far and away beyond her experience or imaginings, Acolyte of the Mysteries though she was; the depth and surety of his perceptions, the profundity of his awareness, filled her with a reverence she was never to lose; and his enduring courage and force of purpose moved her to something like worship. The very limitations of the man proclaimed his innate humanity, his immense humility blending with a kind of pride which obliterated the usual meaning of the word. . . . She saw the schooled control inhibiting emotions which would have made another savage or rebellious—and suddenly she started. She was foremost in his thoughts! A hot blush, visible even in the starlight, spread over her face.

She pulled out of the rapport quickly, but with a gentleness that left no hurt around the sudden vacancy. The thought she had surprised was so delicately lovely that she felt hallowed, but it had been so much his own that she felt a delicious guilt at having glimpsed it.

With a comprehending regret, Micon drew himself away from her. He knew she was confused; Domaris was not given to speculation about her effect upon men.

Deoris, watching with mingled bewilderment and resentment, broke the filmy connection that still remained. "Lord Micon, you have tired yourself," she accused, and spread her woolly cloak on the grass for him.

Rajasta added, "Rest, my brother."

"It was but a moment's weakness," Micon murmured, but he let them have their way, content to lie back beside Domaris; and after a moment he felt her warm hand touch his, with a feather-soft clasp that brought no pain to his wrecked fingers.

Rajasta's face was a benediction, and seeing it, Deoris swallowed hard. *What's happening to Domaris?* Her sister was changing before her eyes, and Deoris, clinging to what had been the one secure thing in the fluid world of the Temple, was suddenly terrified. For a moment she almost hated Micon, and Rajasta's evident acceptance of the situation infuriated her. She raised her eyes, full of angry tears, and stared fiercely at the blurring stars.

II

A new voice spoke a word of casual greeting, and Deoris started and turned, shivering with a strange and unfamiliar excitement, half attraction and half fascinated fear. *Riveda!* Already keyed to a fever pitch of nervousness, Deoris shrank away as the dark shadow fell across them, blotting out the starlight. The man was uncanny; she could not look away.

Riveda's courtly, almost ritualistic salute included them all, and he dropped to a seat on the grass. "So, you watch the stars with your Acolytes, Rajasta? Domaris, what say the stars of me?" The Adept's voice, even muted in courteous inquiry, seemed to mock at custom and petty ritual alike.

Domaris, with a little frown, came back to her immediate surroundings with some effort. She spoke with a frigid politeness. "I am no reader of fortunes, Lord Riveda. Should they speak of you?"

"Of me as well as any other," retorted Riveda with a derisive laugh. "Or as ill . . . Come, Deoris, and sit by me."

The little girl looked longingly at Domaris, but no one spoke or looked at her forbiddingly, and so she rose, her short, close-girdled frock a shimmer of starry blue about her, and went to Riveda's side. The Adept smiled as she settled in the grass beside him.

"Tell us a tale, little scribe," he said, only half in earnest. Deoris shook her head bashfully, but Riveda persisted. "Sing for us, then. I have heard you—your voice is sweet."

The child's embarrassment became acute; she pulled her hand from Riveda's, shaking her dark curls over her eyes. Still no one came to the rescue of her confusion, and Micon said softly in the darkness, "Will you not sing, my little Deoris? Rajasta also has spoken of your sweet voice."

A request from Micon was so rare a thing, it could not be refused. Deoris said timidly, "I will sing of the Seven Watchers—if Lord Rajasta will chant the verse of the Falling."

Rajasta laughed aloud. "I, sing? My voice would startle the Watchers from the sky *again,* my child!"

"I will chant it," said Riveda with abrupt finality. "Sing, Deoris," he repeated, and this time there was that in his voice which compelled her.

The girl hugged her thin knees, tilted her face skyward, and began to sing, in a clear and quiet soprano that mounted, like a thread of smoky silver, toward the hushed stars:

On a night long ago, forgotten,
Seven were the Watchers
Watching from the Heavens,
Watching and fearful
On a black day when
Stars left their places,
Watching the Black Star of Doom.

Seven the Watchers,
Stealing a-tiptoe,
Seven stars stealing
Softly from their places,
Under the cover
Of the shielding sky.

The Black Star hovers
Silent in the shadows,
Stealing through the shadows,
Waiting for the fall of Night;
Over the mountain,
Hanging, hovering,
Darkly, a raven
In a crimson cloud.

Softly the Seven
Fall like shadows,
Star-shadows, blotted
In starless sunlight!
In a flaming shower,
Seven stars falling
Black on the Black Star of Doom!

Others who had gathered on the Star Field to observe the omens, attracted by the song, drew nearer, hushed and appreciative. Now Riveda's deep and resonant baritone took up a stern and rhythmic chant, spinning an undercurrent of weird harmonies beneath the silvery treble of Deoris.

The mountain trembles!
Thunder shakes the sunset,
Thunder at the summit!
As the Seven Watchers
Fall in showers,
Star-showers falling,
Flaming comets falling
On the Black Star!

The Ocean shakes in torment,
Mountains break and crumble!
Drowned lies the Dark Star
And Doomsday is dead!

In a muted, bell-like voice, Deoris chanted the lament:

Seven stars fallen,
Fallen from the heavens,
Fallen from the sky-crown,
Drowned where the Black Star fell!

Manoah the Merciful, Lord of Brightness,
Raised up the drowned ones,
The Black Star he banished
For endless ages,
Till he shall rise in light.
The Seven Good Watchers
He raised in brightness.

Crowning the mountain,
High above the Star-mountain,
Shine the Seven Watchers,
The Seven Guardians
Of the Earth and Sky.

The song died in the night; a little whispering wind murmured and was still. The folk that had gathered, some Acolytes and one or two

Priests, made sounds of approval, and drifted away again, speaking in soft voices.

Micon lay motionless, his hand still clasped in Domaris's fingers. Rajasta brooded thoughtfully, watching these two he loved so much, and it was for him as if the rest of the world did not exist.

Riveda inclined his head to Deoris, his harsh and atavistic features softened in the starlight and shadows. "Your voice is lovely; would we had such a singer in the Grey Temple! Perhaps one day you may sing there."

Deoris muttered formalities, but frowned. The men of the Grey-robe sect were highly honored in the Temple, but their women were something of a mystery. Under strange and secret vows, they were scorned and shunned, referred to contemptuously as saji—though the meaning of the word was not known to Deoris, it had a bleak and awful sound. Many of the Grey-robe women were recruited from the commoners, and some were the children of slaves; this in great part accounted for their being shunned by the wives and daughters of the Priest's Caste. The suggestion that Deoris, daughter of the Arch-Administrator Talkannon, might choose to join the condemned saji so angered the child that she cared little for Riveda's compliment to her singing.

The Adept only smiled, however. His charm flowed out to surround her again and he said, softly. "As your sister is too tired to advise me, Deoris, perhaps you would interpret the stars for me?"

Deoris flushed crimson, and gazed upward intently, mustering her few scraps of knowledge. "A powerful man—or something in masculine form—threatens—some feminine function, through the force of the Guardians. An old evil—either has been or will be revived—" She stopped, aware that the others were looking at her. Abashed at her own presumption, Deoris let her gaze fell downward once more; her hands twisted nervously in her lap. "But that can have little to do with you, Lord Riveda," she murmured, almost inaudibly.

Rajasta chuckled. "It is good enough, child. Use what knowledge you have. You will learn more, as you grow older."

For some reason, the indulgent tolerance in Rajasta's voice annoyed Riveda, who had felt some astonishment at the sensitivity with which this untaught child had interpreted a pattern ominous enough to challenge a trained seer. That she had doubtless heard the others discussing the omens that beset Caratra made little difference, and Riveda said sharply, "Perhaps, Rajasta, you can—"

But the Adept never finished his sentence. The stocky, heavy-set figure of the Acolyte Arvath had cast its shadow across them.

III

"The story goes," Arvath said lightly, "that the Prophet of the Star-mountain lectured in the Temple before the Guardians when he had not told his twelfth year; so you may well listen to the least among you." The young Acolyte sounded amused as he bowed formally to Rajasta and Micon. "Sons of the Sun, we are honored in your presence. And yours, Lord Riveda." He leaned to twitch one of Deoris's ringlets. "Do you now seek to be a Prophetess, puss?" He turned to the other girl, saying, "Was it you singing, Domaris?"

"It was Deoris," said Domaris curtly, ruffled. Was she never to be free of Arvath's continual surveillance?

Arvath frowned, seeing that Micon was still almost in Domaris's arms. Domaris was his! Micon was an intruder and had no right between a man and his betrothed! Arvath's jealousy kept him from thinking very clearly, and he clenched his fists, furious with suppressed desire and the sense of injustice. I'll teach this presumptuous stranger his manners!

Arvath sat down beside them, and with a decisive movement encircled Domaris's waist with his arm. At least he could show this intruder that he was treading on forbidden ground! In a tone that was perfectly audible, but sounded intimate and soft, he asked her, "Were you waiting long for me?"

Half-startled, half-indignant, Domaris stared at him. She was too well-bred to make a scene; her first impulse, to push him angrily away from her, died unborn. She remained motionless, silent: she was used to caresses from Arvath, but this had a jealous and demanding force that dismayed her.

Irked by her unresponsiveness, Arvath seized her hands and drew them away from Micon's. Domaris gasped, freeing herself quickly from both of them. Micon made a little startled sound of question as she rose to her feet.

As if he had not seen, Rajasta intervened. "What say the stars to you, young Arvath?"

The life-long habit of immediate deference to a superior prevailed. Arvath inclined his head respectfully and said, "I have not yet made any conclusions, Son of the Sun. The Lady of the Heavens will not reach absolute zenith before the sixth hour, and before then it is not possible to interpret correctly."

Rajasta nodded agreeably. "Caution is a virtue of great worth," he said, mildly, but with a pointedness that made Arvath drop his eyes.

Riveda, predictably, chuckled; and the tension slackened, its focus diffused. Domaris dropped to the grass again, this time beside Rajasta, and the old Priest put a fatherly arm about her shoulders. He knew she had been deeply disturbed—and did not blame her, even though he felt that she could have dealt more tactfully with both men. But Domaris is still young—too young, Rajasta thought, almost in despair, to become the center of such conflict!

Arvath, for his part, began to think more clearly, and relaxed. After all, he had really seen nothing to warrant his jealousy; and certainly Rajasta could not permit his Acolyte to act in opposition to the customs of the Twelve. Thus Arvath comforted himself, conveniently forgetting all customs but those he himself wished enforced.

Most powerful, perhaps, in alleviating Arvath's anger was the fact that he really liked Micon. They were, moreover, countrymen. Soon the two were engaged in casual, friendly conversation, although Micon, hypersensitive to Arvath's mood, answered at first with some reserve.

Domaris, no longer listening, hid herself from inner conflict in the earnest performance of her duty. Her eyes fixed on the stars, her mind intently stilled to meditation, she studied the portents of the night.

IV

Gradually, the Star Field quieted. One by one the little groups where the watchers clustered fell silent; only detached words rose now and then, curiously unearthly, from a particularly wakeful clique of young Priests in a far corner of the field. An idle breeze stirred the waving grasses, riffled cloaks and long hair, then dropped again; a cloud drifted across the face of the star that hovered near Caratra; somewhere a child wailed, and was hushed.

Far below them, a sullen flicker of red marked where fires had been built at the sea-wall, to warn ships from the rocks. Deoris had fallen asleep on the grass, her head on Riveda's knees and the Adept's long grey cloak tucked about her shoulders.

Arvath, like Domaris, sat studying the omens of the stars in a meditative trance; Micon, behind blind eyes, pursued his own silent thoughts. Rajasta, for some reason unknown even to himself, found his own gaze again and again turning to Riveda: still and motionless, his rough-cut head and sternly-straight back rising up in a blacker blackness against the starshine, Riveda sat in fixed reverie for hour after hour: the sight hypnotized Rajasta. The stars seemed to alternately fade and brighten behind the Adept. For an instant, past, present, and future, all slid together and were one to the Priest of Light. He saw Riveda's face, thinner and more haggard, the lips set in an attitude of grim determination. The stars had vanished utterly, but a reddish-yellow, as of thousands of filmy, wind-blown strips of gossamer, danced and twisted about the Adept.

Suddenly and brilliantly, a terrible halo of fire encircled Riveda's head. The dorje! Rajasta started, and with a shudder that was at once within him and without, his actual surroundings reasserted themselves. I must have slept, he told himself, shaken. That could have been no true vision! And yet, with every blink of the Priest of Light's eyes, the awful image persisted, until Rajasta, with a little groan, turned his face away.

A wind was blowing across the quiet Star Field, turning the perspiration on the Priest of Light's brow to icy droplets as Rajasta wavered between lingering, mindless horror, and intermittent waves of reasoning thought. The moments that passed before Rajasta calmed himself were, perhaps, the worst of his life, moments that seemed an unending prison of time.

The Priest of Light sat, hunched over, still unable to look in Riveda's direction for simple fear. It could only have been a nightmare, Rajasta told himself, without much conviction. But—if it was not?

Rajasta shuddered anew at this prospect, then sternly mastered himself, forcing his keen mind to examine the unthinkable.

I must speak with Riveda about this, Rajasta decided, unwillingly. I must! Surely, if it was not a dream, it is meant for a warning—of great danger to him. Rajasta did not know how far Riveda had gotten in his investigations, but perhaps—perhaps the Adept had gotten so close to the Black-robe sect that they sought to set their hellish mark on him, and so protect themselves against discovery.

It can only mean that, Rajasta reassured himself, and shivered uncontrollably. Gods and spirits, protect us all!

V

With tired and sleepless eyes, Domaris watched the sun rise, a gilt toy in a bath of pink clouds. Dawn reddened over the Star Field slowly; the pale and pitiless light shone with a betraying starkness on the faces of those who slept there.

Deoris lay still, her regular breathing not quite a snore; Riveda's cloak remained, snuggled around her, although Riveda himself had gone hours ago. Arvath sprawled wide-limbed in the grass as if sleep had stolen up upon him like a thief in the night. Domaris realized how much like a sturdy small boy he looked—his dark hair tumbled around his damp forehead, his smooth cheeks glowing with the heavy, healthy slumber of a very young man. Then her eyes returned to Micon, who also slept, his head resting across her knees, his hand in hers.

After Rajasta had gone away, hurrying after Riveda with a pale and shaken look, she had returned to Micon's side, careless of what Arvath might say or think. All night Domaris had felt the Atlantean's thin and ruined hands twitch, as if even in sleep there remained an irreducible residue of pain. Once or twice, so ashen and strengthless had Micon's face appeared in the grey and ghastly light before dawn that Domaris had bent to listen to his breathing to be sure he still lived; then, her own breathing hushed to silence, she would hear a faint sigh, and be at once relieved and terrified—waking could only bring more pain for this man she was beginning to adore.

At the uttermost ebb-tide of the night, Domaris had found herself half-wishing Micon might drift out silently into the peace he so desired . . . and this thought had frightened her so much that she had but barely restrained herself from the sudden longing to clasp him in her arms and by sheer force of love restore his full vitality. How can I be so full of life while Micon is so weak? Why, she wondered rebelliously, is he dying—and the devil who did this to him still walking around secure in his own worthless life?

As if her thoughts disturbed his sleep, Micon stirred, murmuring in a language Domaris did not understand. Then, with a long sigh, the blind eyes opened and the Atlantean drew himself slowly upright, reaching out with a curious gesture—and drawing his hand back in surprise as he touched her dress.

"It is I, Micon—Domaris," she said quickly, addressing him by name for the first time.

"Domaris—I remember now. I slept?"

"For hours. It is dawn."

He laughed, uneasily but with that peculiar inner mirth which never seemed to fail him. "A sorry sentry I should make nowadays! Is this how vigil is kept?"

Her instant laughter, soft and gentle, set him at ease. "Everyone sleeps after the middle hour of the night. You and I are likely the only ones awake. It is very early still."

When he spoke again, it was in a quieter tone, as if he feared he might wake the sleepers she had referred to so obliquely. "Is the sky red?"

She looked at him, bemused. "Yes. Bright red."

"I thought so," said Micon, nodding. "Ahtarrath's sons are all seamen; weather and storms are in our blood. At least I have not lost that."

"Storms?" Domaris repeated, dubiously glancing toward the distant, peaceful clouds.

Micon shrugged. "Perhaps we will be lucky, and it will not reach us," he said, "but it is in the air. I feel it."

Both were silent again, Domaris suddenly shy and self-conscious at the memory of the night's thoughts, and Micon thinking, *So I have slept at her side through the night.* . . . *In Ahtarrath, that would amount almost to a pledge.* He smiled. *Perhaps that explains Arvath's* temper, last night . . . yet in the end we were all at peace. She sheds peace, as a flower its perfume.

Domaris, meanwhile, had remembered Deoris, who still slept close by them, wrapped warm in Riveda's cloak. "My little sister has slept here in the grass all night," she said. "I must wake her and send her to bed."

Micon laughed lightly. "That seems a curiously pointless exercise," he remarked. "You have not slept at all."

It was not a question, and Domaris did not try to make any answer. Before his luminous face, she bent her head, forgetful that the morning light could not betray her to a blind man. Loosening her fingers gently from his, she said only, "I must wake Deoris."

VI

In her dream, Deoris wandered through an endless series of caverns, following the flickering flashes of light sparkling from the end of a strangely shaped wand held in the hand of a robed and cowled figure. Somehow, she was not afraid, nor cold, though she knew, in a way oddly detached from her senses, that the walls and the floor of these caverns were icy and damp. . . .

From somewhere quite nearby, a familiar but not immediately recognizable voice was calling her name. She came out of the dream slowly, nestling in folds of grey. "Don't," she murmured drowsily, putting her fingers over her face.

With tender laughter, Domaris shook the child's shoulder. "Wake up, little sleepyhead!"

The half-open eyes, still dream-dark, unclosed like bewildered violets; small fingers compressed a yawn. "Oh, Domaris, I meant to stay awake," Deoris murmured, and scrambled to her feet, instantly alert, the cloak felling from her. She bent to pick it up, holding it curiously at arm's length. "What's this? This isn't mine!"

Domaris took it from her hands. "It is Lord Riveda's. You went to sleep like a baby on his lap!"

Deoris frowned and looked sulky.

Domaris teased, "He left it, beyond doubt, so that he might see you again! Deoris! Have you found your first lover so young?"

Deoris stamped her foot, pouting. "Why are you so mean?"

"Why, I thought that would please you," said Domaris, and merrily flung the cloak about the child's bare shoulders.

Deoris cast it off again, angrily. "I think you're—horrid!" she wailed, and ran away down the hill to find the shelter of her own bed and cry herself back to sleep.

Domaris started after her, then stopped herself; she felt too ragged to deal with her sister's tantrums this morning. The Grey-robe's cloak, rough against her arm, added to her feeling of unease and apprehension. She had spoken lightly, to tease the little girl, but now she found herself wondering about what she had said. It was unthinkable that the Adept's interest in Deoris could be personal—the child was not fourteen years old! With a shudder of distaste, Domaris forced the thoughts away as unworthy of her, and turned back to Micon.

The others were waking, rising, gathering in little groups to watch what remained of the sunrise. Arvath came and put an arm about her waist; she suffered it absent-mindedly. Her calm grey eyes lingered dispassionately on the young Priest's face. Arvath felt hurt, bewildered. Domaris had become so different since—yes—since Micon had come into their lives! He sighed, wishing he could manage to hate Micon, and let his arm fall away from Domaris, knowing she was no more conscious of its removal than she had been of its presence.

Rajasta was coming up the pathway, a white figure faintly reddened in the morning light. Drawing near them, he stooped to pick up Micon's cloak of stainless white. It was a small service, but those who saw wondered at it, and at the caressing, familiar tone in Rajasta's normally stern voice. "Thou hast slept?" he asked.

Micon's smile was a blessing, almost beatific. "As I seldom sleep, my brother."

Rajasta's eyes moved briefly toward Domaris and Arvath, dismissing them. "Go, my children, and rest. . . . Micon, come with me."

Taking Domaris's arm, Arvath drew the girl along the path. Almost too weary to stand, she leaned heavily on his offered arm, then turned and laid her head for a moment against his chest.

"You are very tired, my sister," said Arvath, almost reproachfully—

and, protective now, he led her down the hill, holding her close against him, her bright head nearly upon his shoulder.

Rajasta watched them, sighing. Then, his hand just touching Micon's elbow, he guided the Initiate unobtrusively along the opposite path, which led to the seashore. Micon went unerringly, as if he had no need whatsoever for Rajasta's guidance; the Atlantean's expression was dreamy and lost.

They paced in silence for some minutes before Rajasta spoke, without interrupting the slow rhythm of their steps. "She is that rarest of women," he said, "one born to be not only mate but comrade. You will be blessed."

"But she—accursed!" said Micon, almost inaudibly. The strange, twisted smile came again to his lips. "I love her, Rajasta, I love her far too much to hurt her; and I can give her nothing! No vows, no hope of real happiness, only sorrow and pain and, perhaps, shame . . ."

"Don't be a fool," was Rajasta's curt reply. "You forget your own teachings. Love, whenever and wherever it is found, though it last but a few moments, can bring only joy—if it is not thwarted! This is something greater than either of you. Do not stand in its way—nor in your own!"

They had stopped on a little rocky outcropping that overlooked the shore. Below, the sea crashed into the land, relentless, insistent. Micon seemed to regard the Priest of Light with his sightless eyes, and Rajasta felt for a moment that he was looking at a stranger, so oddly changed did the Atlantean's face appear to him.

"I hope you are right," said Micon at last, still peering intently at the face he could not see.

BOOK TWO
✠ DORMARIS ✠

"If a scroll bears bad news, is it the fault of the scroll, or that which is described by the scroll? If the scroll is a bearer of good news, in what way does it differ from the scroll which bears the bad news?

"We begin life with a seemingly blank slate—and, though the writing that gradually appears on that slate is not our own, our judgment of the things written thereon determines what we are and what we will become. In much the same way, our work will be judged by the use to which other people put it. . . . Therefore, the question becomes, how can we control its use when it passes out of our control, into the hands of people over whom we have no control?

"The earliest teachings of the Priest's Caste have it that by performing our work with the wish and desire that it work for the betterment of man and the world, we endow it with our blessing which will reduce the user's desire to use it for destructive purposes. Doubtless this is not untrue—but reduction is not prevention."

—from the introduction to
The Codex of the Adept Riveda

CHAPTER ONE
✠ SACRAMENTS ✠

I

A heavy, soaking rain poured harshly down on the roofs and courts and enclosures of the Temple precinct; rain that sank roughly into the thirsty ground, rain that splashed with a musical tinkling into pools and fountains, flooding the flagged walks and lawns. Perhaps because of the rain, the library of the Temple was crowded. Every stool and table was occupied, each bench had its own bent head.

Domaris, pausing in the doorway, sought with her eyes for Micon, who was not in his usual recess. There were the white cowls of the Priests, the heavy grey hoods of Magicians, the banded filletings of Priestesses, bare heads of student-priests and scribes. At last, with a little joyous thrill, she saw Micon. He sat at a table in the farthest corner, deep in conversation with Riveda, whose smoky, deep-cowled robe and harsh, gaunt face made a curious contrast to the pallid and emaciated Initiate. Yet Domaris felt that here were two men who were really very much alike.

Pausing again, even as she directed her steps toward them, her intense, unreasoning dislike of Riveda surged back. She shuddered a little. *That man, like Micon?*

Riveda was leaning forward, listening intently; the Atlantean's blind, dark features were luminous with his smile. Any casual observer would have sworn that they felt no emotion but comradeship—but Domaris could not dispel the feeling that here were two forces, alike in strength but opposite in direction, pitted against each other.

It was the Grey-robe who first became aware of her approach; looking up with a pleasant smile, Riveda said, "Talkannon's daughter seeks you, Micon." Otherwise, of course, he did not move or pay the least attention to the girl. Domaris was only an Acolyte, and Riveda a highly-placed Adept.

Micon rose painfully to his feet and spoke with deference. "How may I serve the Lady Domaris?"

Domaris, embarrassed by this public breach of proper etiquette, stood with her eyes cast down. She was not really a shy girl, but disliked the attention Micon's action called upon her. She wondered if Riveda was secretly scornful of Micon's evident ignorance of Temple custom. Her voice was hardly more than a whisper as she said, "I came on your scribe's behalf, Lord Micon. Deoris is ill, and cannot come to you today."

"I am sorry to hear that." Micon's wry grin was compassionate now. "Flower-of-the-Sun, tell her not to come to me again until she is quite well."

"I trust her illness is nothing serious," Riveda put in, casually but with a piercing glance from beneath heavy-lidded eyes, "I have often thought that these night vigils in the damp air do no good to anyone."

Domaris felt suddenly annoyed. This was none of Riveda's business! Even Micon could sense the chill in her voice as she said, "It is nothing. Nothing at all. She will be recovered in a few hours." As a matter of fact, although Domaris had no intention of saying so, Deoris had cried herself into a violent headache. Domaris felt disturbed and guilty, for she herself had brought on her sister's distress with her teasing remarks about Riveda that very morning. More, she sensed that Deoris was furiously jealous of Micon. She had begged and begged Domaris not to leave her, not to go to Micon, to send some slave to tell him of her illness. It had been difficult for Domaris to make herself leave the miserable little girl, and she had finally forced herself to do it only by reminding herself that Deoris was not really ill; that she had brought on the headache by her own crying and fussing, and that if Deoris once and for all learned that her tantrums and hysterics would not get her what she wanted, she would stop having them—and then there would be no more of these headaches, either.

Riveda rose to his feet. "I shall call to inquire further," he said definitely. "Many serious ills have their beginnings in a mild ailment."

His words were far from uncourteous—they were indeed stamped with the impeccable manners of a Healer-Priest—but Riveda was secretly amused. He knew Domaris resented him. He felt no real malice toward Domaris; but Deoris interested him, and Domaris's attempts to keep him away from her sister impressed him as ridiculous maneuvers without meaning.

There was nothing Domaris could say. Riveda was a high Adept, and if he chose to interest himself in Deoris, it was not for an Acolyte to gainsay him. Sharply she reminded herself that Riveda was old enough to be their grandsire, a Healer-Priest of great skill, and of an austerity unusual even among the Grey-robes.

The two men exchanged cordial farewells, and as Riveda moved sedately away, she felt Micon's light groping touch against her wrist. "Sit beside me, Light-crowned. The rain has put me out of the mood for study, and I am lonely."

"You have had most interesting company," Domaris commented with a trace of asperity.

Micon's wry grin came and went. "True. Still, I would rather talk to you. But—perhaps it is not convenient just now? Or is it—improper?"

Domaris smiled faintly. "You and Riveda are both so highly-placed in the Temple that the Monitors have not reproved your ignorance of our restrictions," she murmured, glancing uneasily at the stern-faced scribes who warded the manuscripts, "but I, at least, may not speak aloud." She could not help adding, in a sharper whisper, "Riveda should have warned you!"

Micon, chagrined, chuckled. "Perhaps he is used to working in solitude," he hazarded, lowering his voice to match the girl's. "You know this Temple—where can we talk without restraint?"

II

Micon's height made Domaris seem almost tiny, and his rugged, wrenched features made a strange contrast to her smooth beauty. As they left the building, curious heads turned to gaze after them; Micon, unaware of this, was nevertheless affected by Domaris's shyness, and said no word as they went through a passageway.

Unobtrusively, graciously, Domaris slowed her light steps to match his, and Micon tightened his clasp on her arm. The girl drew back a curtain, and they found themselves in the anteroom to one of the inner courts. One entire wall was a great window, loosely shuttered with wooden blinds; the soft quiet fragrance of rain falling on glass and expectant flowers came faintly through the bars, and the dripping music of raindrops pouring into a pool.

Domaris—who had never before shared this favorite, usually-deserted nook even with Deoris—said to Micon, "I come here often to study. A crippled Priest who seldom leaves his rooms lives across the court, and this room is never used. I think I can promise you that we will be quite alone here." She found a seat on a bench near the window, and made room for him at her side.

There was a long silence. Outside, the rain fell and dripped; its cool, moist breath blowing lightly into their faces. Micon's hands lay relaxed on his knees, and the flicker of a grin, which never quite left his dark mouth, came and went like summer lightning. He was content just to be near Domaris, but the girl was restless.

"I find a place where we may talk—and we sit as dumb as the fish!"

Micon turned toward her. "And there is something to be said—Domaris!" He spoke her name with such an intensity of longing that the girl's breath caught in her throat. He repeated it again; on his lips it was a caress. "Domaris!"

"Lord Micon—Sir Prince—"

A sudden and quite unexpected anger gusted up in his voice. "Call me not so!" he ordered. "I have left all that behind me! You know my name!"

She whispered, like a woman in a dream, "Micon."

"Domaris, I—I am humbly your suitor." There was an oddly muted tone in his voice, as of self-deprecation. "I have—loved you, since you came into my life. I know I have little to give you, and that only for a short time. But—sweetest of women—" He paused, as if to gather strength, and went on, in hesitant words, "I would that we might have met in a happier hour, and our—our love flowered—perhaps, slowly, into perfection. . . ." Once again he paused, and his dark intent features betrayed an emotion so naked that Domaris could not face it, and she looked away, glad for once that he could not see her face.

"Little time remains to me," he said. "I know that by Temple law you are still free. It is your—right, to choose a man, and bear his child, if you wish. Your betrothal to Arvath is no formal bar. Would you— will you consider me as your lover?" Micon's resonant voice was now trembling with the power of his emotions. "It is my destiny, I suppose, that I who had all things, commanding armies and the tribute of great families, should now have so little to offer you—no vows, no hope of happiness, nothing but a very great need of you—"

Wonderingly, she repeated, slowly, "You love me?"

He stretched questing hands toward her; found her slim fingers and took them into his own. "I have not even the words to say how great my love is, Domaris. Only—that life is unendurable when I am not near you. My—my heart longs for—the sound of your voice, your step, your—touch. . . ."

"Micon!" she whispered, still dazed, unable to comprehend completely. "You do love me!" She raised her face to look intently into his.

"This would be easier to say if I could see your face," he whispered—and, with a movement that dismayed the girl, he knelt at her feet, capturing her hands again and pressing them to his face. He kissed the delicate fingers and said, half stifled, "I love you almost too much for life, almost too much. . . . you are great in gentleness, Domaris. I could beget my child upon no other woman—but Domaris, Domaris, can you even guess how much I must ask of you?"

With a swift movement, Domaris leaned forward and drew him to her, pressing his head against her young breasts. "I know only that I love you," she told him. "This is your place." And her long red hair covered them both as their mouths met, speaking the true name of love.

III

The rain had stopped, although the sky was still grey and thickly overcast. Deoris, lying on a divan in the room she shared with her sister, was having her hair brushed by her maid; overhead, the little red bird, Domaris's gift, twittered and chirped, with gay abandon; Deoris listened and hummed softly to herself, while the brush moved soothingly along her hair, and outside the breeze fluttered the hangings at the window, the fringed leaves of the trees in the court. Inside, the room was filled with dim light, reflecting the polished shine of dark woods and the glint of silken hangings and of ornaments of polished silver and turquoise and jade. Into this moderate luxury, allotted to Domaris as an Acolyte and the daughter of a Priest, Deoris nestled like a kitten, putting aside her slight feeling of self-consciousness and guilt; the scribes and neophytes were curtailed to a strictness and austerity in their surroundings, and Domaris, at her age, had been forbidden such comforts. Deoris enjoyed the luxury, and no one had forbidden it, but under her consciousness she felt secretly shamed.

She twisted away from the hands of the slave girl. "There, that's enough, you'll make my head ache again," she said pettishly. "Besides, I hear my sister coming." She jumped up and ran to the door, but at seeing Domaris, the eager greeting died on her lips.

But her sister's voice was perfectly natural when she spoke. "Your headache is better, then, Deoris? I had expected to find you still in bed."

Deoris peered at Domaris dubiously, thinking, _I must be imagining things._ Aloud, she said, "I slept most of the afternoon. When I woke, I felt better." She fell silent as her sister moved into the room, then went on, "The Lord Riveda—"

Domaris cut her off with an impatient gesture. "Yes, yes, he told me he would call to inquire about you. You can tell me another time, can't you?"

Deoris blinked. "Why? Are you in a hurry? Is it your night to serve in the Temple?"

Domaris shook her head, then stretched her hand to touch her sister's curls in a light caress. "I'm very glad you are better," she said, more kindly. "Call Elara for me, will you, darling?"

The little woman came and deftly divested Domaris of her outer robes. Domaris then flung herself full-length upon a pile of cushions, and Deoris came and knelt anxiously beside her.

"Sister, is something wrong?"

Domaris returned an absent-minded "No," and then, with a sudden, dreamy decision, "No, nothing is wrong—or will be." She rolled over to look up, smiling, into Deoris's eyes. Impulsively, she started, "Deoris—" Just as suddenly, she stopped.

"What *is* it, Domaris?" Deoris pressed, feeling again the inexplicable inner panic which had risen in her at her sister's return only moments ago.

"Deoris—little sister—I am going to the Gentle One." Abruptly she seized Deoris's hand, and went on, "Sister—come with me?"

Deoris only stared, open-mouthed. The Gentle One, the Goddess Caratra—her shrine was approached only for particular rituals, or in moments of acute mental crisis. "I don't understand," Deoris said slowly. "Why—why?" She suddenly put out her other hand to clasp Domaris's between both of her own. "Domaris, what is happening to you!"

Confused and exalted, Domaris could not bring herself to speak. She had never doubted what answer she would bring Micon—he had forbidden her to decide at once—yet something deep within her heart was disturbed, and demanded comfort, and for once she could not turn to Deoris, for, close as they were, Deoris was only a child.

Deoris, who had never known any mother but Domaris, felt the new distance between them keenly, and exclaimed, in a voice at once wailing and strangled, "*Domaris!*"

"Oh, Deoris," said Domaris, freeing her hand with some annoyance, "*please* don't ask me questions!" Then, not wanting the gap between them to widen any further, quickly added, gently, "Just—come with me? Please?"

"Of course I will," murmured Deoris, through the peculiar knot in her throat.

Domaris smiled and sat up; embracing Deoris, she gave her a quick little kiss and was about to pull away, but Deoris clutched her tight, as if, with the bitter intuition of the young, she sensed that Micon had not so long ago rested there and wished to drive his lingering spirit away. Domaris stroked the silky curls, feeling the impulse to confide again; but the words would not come.

IV

The Shrine of Caratra, the Gentle Mother, was far away; almost the entire length of the Temple grounds lay between it and the House of the Twelve, a long walk under damp, flowering trees. In the cooling twilight, the scent of roses and of verbena hung heavily on the moist and dusky air. The two sisters were silent: one intent on her mission, the other for once at a loss for words.

The Shrine shone whitely at the further end of an oval pool of clear water, shimmering, crystalline, and ethereally blue beneath the high arch of clearing sky. As they neared it, the sun emerged from behind an intervening building for a few moments as it sank in the west, lightening the Shrine's alabaster walls. A pungent trace of incense wafted to them across the water; twinkling lights beckoned from the Shrine.

Noticing that Deoris was dragging her feet just the least bit, Domaris suddenly sat down on the grass to the side of the path. Deoris joined her at once; hand in hand they rested a little while, watching the unrippling waters of the holy pool.

The beauty and mystery of life, of re-creation, was embodied here in the Goddess who was Spring and Mother and Woman, the symbol of the gentle strength that is earth. To approach the Shrine of Caratra, they would have to wade breast-high through the pool; this sacred, lustral rite was undertaken at least once by every woman of the precinct, although only those of the Priest's Caste and the Acolytes were taught the deeper significance of this ritual: every woman came this way to maturity, struggling through reluctant tides, deeper than water, heavier and harder to pass. In pride or maturity, in joy or in sorrow, in childish reluctance or in maturity, in ecstasy or rebellion, every woman came one day to this.

Domaris shivered as she looked across the pale waters, frightened by the symbolism. As one of the Acolytes, she had been initiated into this mystery, and understood; yet she hung back, afraid. She thought of Micon, and of her love, trying to summon courage to step into those waters; but a sort of prophetic dread was on her. She clung to Deoris for a moment, in a wordless plea for reassurance.

Deoris sensed this, yet she looked sulkily away from her sister. She felt as if her world had turned upside down. She would not let herself know what Domaris was facing; and here, before the oldest and holiest shrine of the Priest's Caste into which they had both been born, she too was afraid; as if those waters would sweep her away, too, into the current of life, like any woman. . . .

She said moodily, "It is cruel—as all life is cruel! I wish I had not been born a woman." And she told herself that this was selfish and wrong, to force herself on Domaris's attention, seeking reassurance for herself, when Domaris faced this testing and her own was still far in the future. Yet she said, "Why, Domaris? Why?"

Domaris had no answer, except to hold Deoris tightly in her arms for a moment. Then all her own confidence flooded back. She was a woman, deeply in love, and she rejoiced in her heart. "You won't always feel that way, Deoris," she promised. Letting her arms drop, she said slowly, "Now I shall go to the Shrine. Will you come the rest of the way with me, little sister?"

For a moment, Deoris felt no great reluctance; she had once entered the Shrine beyond the pool, in the sacred rite undertaken by every young girl in the Temple when, at the first commencement of puberty, she gave her first service in the House of the Great Mother. At that time she had felt nothing except nervousness at the ritual's solemnity. Now, however, as Domaris rose from the grass, panic fixed chilly knuckles at Deoris's throat. If she went with Domaris, of her own free will, she felt she would be caught and trapped, handing herself over blindly to the violence of nature. Scared rebellion quivered in her denial. "No—I don't want to!"

"Not even—if I ask it?" Domaris sounded hurt, and was; she had wanted Deoris to understand, to share with her this moment which divided her life.

Deoris shook her head again, hiding her face behind her hands. A perverse desire to inflict hurt was on her: Domaris had left her alone— now it was *her* turn!

To her own surprise, Domaris found herself making yet another appeal. "Deoris—little sister—please, I want you with me. Won't you come?"

Deoris did not uncover her face, and her words, when they came, were barely audible—and still negative.

Domaris let her hand fall abruptly from her sister's shoulder. "I'm sorry, Deoris. I had no right to ask."

Deoris would have given anything to retract her words now, but it was too late. Domaris took a few steps away, and Deoris lay still, pressing her feverish cheeks into the cold grass, crying silently and bitterly.

Domaris, without looking back, unfastened her outer garments, letting them fall about her feet, and loosened her hair until it covered her body in a smooth cascade. She ran her hands through the heavy tresses, and suddenly a thrill went through her young body, from fingertips to toes: *Micon loves me!* For the first and only time in her life, Domaris knew that she was beautiful, and gloried in the knowledge of her beauty—although there was a chill of sadness in the knowledge that Micon could never see it or know it.

Only a moment the strange intoxication lasted; then Domaris divided her long hair about her neck and stepped into the pool, wading out until she stood breast-high in the radiant water, which was warm and tingling, somehow oddly not like water at all, but an effervescent, living light. . . . Blue and softly violet, it glowed and shimmered and flowed in smooth patterns around the pillar of her body, and she thrilled again with a suffocating ecstasy as, for an instant, it closed over her head. Then she stood upright again, the water running in scented, bubbling droplets from her glowing head and shoulders. Wading onward, toward the beckoning Shrine, she felt that the water washed away, drop by drop, all of her past life, with its little irritations and selfishness. Filled and flooded with a sense of infinite strength, Domaris became—as she had not on any earlier visit to Caratra's Shrine—aware that, being human, she was divine.

She came out of the water almost regretfully, and paused a moment before entering the Temple; solemnly, with sober, intent concentration, the young Priestess robed herself in the sacramental garments kept within the anteroom, carefully not thinking of the *next* time she must bathe here. . . .

Entering the sanctuary, she stood a moment, reverent before the altar, and bound the bridal girdle about her body. Then, arms wide-flung, Domaris knelt, her head thrown back in passionate humility. She wanted to pray, but no words came.

"Mother, lovely goddess," she whispered at last, "let me—not fail. . . ."

A new warmth seemed to envelop Domaris; the compassionate eyes of the holy image seemed to smile upon her, the eyes of the mother Domaris could barely remember. She knelt there for a long time, in a sober, listening stillness, while strange, soft, and unfocussed visions moved in her mind, indefinite, even meaningless, yet filling her with a calm and a peace that she had never known, and was never entirely to lose.

V

The sun was gone, and the stars had altered their positions considerably before Deoris, stirring at last, realized that it was very late. Domaris would have returned hours ago if she had intended to return at all.

Resentment gradually took the place of alarm: Domaris had forgotten her again! Unhappy and petulant, Deoris returned alone to the House of the Twelve, where she discovered that Elara knew no more than she—or, at least, the woman refused to discuss her mistress with Deoris. This did not sweeten her temper, and her snappish response, her fretful demands, soon reduced the usually patient Elara to silent, exasperated tears.

The servants, and several of the neighbors, had been made as miserable as Deoris was herself when Elis came in search of Domaris, and innocently made things even worse by asking her cousin's whereabouts.

"How would I know!" Deoris exploded. "Domaris never tells *me* anything any more!"

Elis tried to placate the angry girl, but Deoris would not even listen, and at last Elis, who had a temper of her own, made herself clear. "Well, I don't see why Domaris *should* tell you anything—what concerns her is none of your business—and in any case, you've been spoilt until you are absolutely unbearable; I wish Domaris would come to her senses and put you in your place!"

Deoris did not even cry, but crumpled up, stricken.

Elis, already at the door, turned and came back swiftly, bending over her. "Deoris," she said, contritely, "I'm sorry, really, I didn't mean it quite like that. . . ." In a rather rare gesture of affection, for Elis was undemonstrative to a fault, she took Deoris's hand in hers, saying, "I know you are lonely. You have no one but Domaris. But that's your own fault, really you could have many friends." Gently, she added,

"Anyway, you shouldn't stay here alone and mope. Lissa misses you. Come and play with her."

Deoris's returning smile wavered. "Tomorrow," she said. "I'd— rather be by myself now."

Elis had intuitions that were almost clairvoyant at times, and now a sudden random impression almost as clear as sight made her drop her cousin's hand. "I won't try to persuade you," she said; then added, quietly and without emphasis, "Just remember this. If Domaris belongs to no one but herself—then you, too, are a person in your own right. Good night, puss."

After Elis had gone, Deoris sat staring at the closed door. The words, at first simple-seeming, had turned strangely cryptic, and Deoris could not puzzle out their meaning. At last she decided that it was just Elis being Elis again, and tried to put it out of her mind.

CHAPTER TWO
✤ THE FOOL ✤

I

Unmarried Priests, above a certain rank, were housed in two dormitories. Rajasta and Micon, with several others of their high station, dwelt in the smaller and more comfortable of these. Riveda might have lived there as well—but, of his own free will, from humility or some inversion of pride, the Adept had chosen to remain among the Priests of lesser accomplishment.

Rajasta found him writing, in a room which doubled as sleeping-room and study, opening on a small, enclosed courtyard. The main room was sparsely furnished, with no hint of luxury; the court was laid simply with brick, without pools or flowers or fountain. A pair of smaller rooms to one side housed the Grey-robe's attendants.

The day was warm; throughout the dormitory most of the doors were wide open, to allow some circulation of the deadening air. So it was that Rajasta stood, unnoticed, gazing at the preoccupied Adept, for several moments.

The Priest of Light had never had any cause to distrust Riveda—and although the vision of the *dorje* sign still troubled Rajasta, courtesy demanded that he speak not again of the warning he had delivered to the Adept on the night of Zenith; to do so would have been an insulting lack of confidence.

Yet Rajasta was Guardian of the Temple of Light, and his responsibility no slight one. Should Riveda somehow fail to set his

Order to rights, Rajasta would share the guilt in full, for by the strict interpretation of his duty, the Guardian should have persuaded, even forced Micon to give testimony about his ordeal at the hands of the Black-robes. The matter properly should have been laid before the High Council.

Now, thinking all these things over yet again, Rajasta sighed deeply. *Thus it is that even the best of motives ensnare us in karmic webs,* he thought tiredly. *I can spare Micon, but only at my own expense—so adding to his burdens, and binding us both more closely to this man. . . .*

Riveda, very straight at his writing-table—he said often that he had no liking for having some silly brat of a scribe running about after him—incised a few more characters in the heavy, pointed strokes which told so much about him, then abruptly flung the brush aside.

"Well, Rajasta?" The Adept chuckled at the Priest of Light's momentary discomfiture. "A friendly visit? Or more of your necessities?"

"Let us say, both," Rajasta answered after a moment.

The smile faded from Riveda's features, and he rose to his feet. "Well, come to the point—and then perhaps I shall have something to say, too. The people of my Order are restless. They say the Guardians intrude. Of course—" He glanced at Rajasta sharply. "Intrusion is the business of the Guardians."

Rajasta clasped his hands behind his back. He noticed that Riveda had not invited him to be seated, or even, really, to enter. The omission annoyed him, so that he spoke with a little more force than he had originally intended; if Riveda intended to discard the pretense of courtesy, he would meet the Adept half-way.

"There is more restlessness in the Temple precinct than that of your Order," Rajasta warned. "Day by day, the Priests grow more resentful. Rumors grow, daily, that you are a negligent leader who has allowed debased and decadent forms to creep into your ritual, so that it has become a thing of distortion. The women of your order—"

"I had wondered when we would come to them," Riveda interrupted in an undertone.

Rajasta scowled and continued, "—they are put to certain uses which frequently defy the laws even of your Order. It is known that you mask the Black-robes among yourselves—"

Riveda held up his hand. "Am I suspected of sorcery?"

The Guardian shook his head. "I have made no accusations. I repeat only the common talk."

"Does Rajasta, the Guardian, listen to the cackle of gate-gossip? That is not my idea of pleasant conversation—nor of a Priest's duty!" As Rajasta was silent, Riveda went on, the crackle of thunder in his deep voice. "Go on! Surely there is more of this! Who but the Grey-robes work with the magic of nature? Have we not been accused of blasting the harvests? What of my Healers who are the only men who dare to go into the cities when they are rotting with plague? Have they not yet been accused of poisoning the wells?"

Rajasta said tiredly, "There is no swarm that does not start with a single bee."

Riveda chuckled. "Then where, Lord Guardian, is the stinger?"

"That you care nothing for these things," Rajasta retorted sharply. "Yours is the responsibility for all these men. Accept it—or delegate it to another who will keep closer watch on the Order! Neglect it not—" Rajasta's voice deepened in impressive admonition: "—or their guilt may shape your destiny! The responsibility of one who leads others is frightful. See that you lead wisely."

Riveda, about to speak, instead swallowed the reproof in silence, staring at the brick floor; but the line of his jaw was insolent. At last he said, "It shall be seen to, have no fear of that."

In the silence which followed this, a faint, off-key whistling could be heard somewhere down the hall. Riveda glanced briefly at his open door, but his expression revealed little of his annoyance.

Rajasta tried another tack. "Your search for the Black-robes—?"

Riveda shrugged. "At present, all those of my Order can account for themselves—save one."

Rajasta started. "Indeed? And that one—?"

Riveda spread his hands. "A puzzle, in more ways than one. He wears chela's habit, but none claim him as their disciple; nor has he named anyone his master. I had never seen him before, yet there he was among the others, and, when challenged, he gave the right responses. Otherwise, he seemed witless."

"Micon's brother, perhaps?" Rajasta suggested.

Riveda snorted derision. "A halfwit? Impossible! Some runaway slave would be more like it."

Rajasta asked, using his privilege as Guardian of the Temple, "What have you done with him?"

"As yet, nothing," Riveda replied slowly. "Since he can pass our gates and knows our ritual, he is entitled to a place among our Order, even if his teacher is unknown. For the present, I have taken him as my own disciple. Although his past is a blanked slate, and he seems not to know even his own name, he has intervals of sanity. I think I can do much with him, and for him." A short space of silence passed. Rajasta said nothing, but Riveda burst out defensively, "What else could I have done? Forgetting for the moment that my vows pledge me to the aid of anyone who can give the Signs of my Order, should I have loosed the boy to be stoned and tormented, seized and put in a cage for fools to gape at as a madman—or taken again for evil uses?"

Rajasta's steady stare did not waver. "I have not accused you," he reminded Riveda. "It is your affair. But if Black-robes have tainted his mind—"

"Then I shall see that they make no evil use of him," Riveda promised grimly, and his face relaxed a little; "He has not the wit to be evil."

"Ignorance is worse than evil intent," Rajasta warned, and Riveda sighed.

"See for yourself, if you will," he said, and stepped to the open door, speaking in a low voice to someone in the court. After a moment, a young man came noiselessly into the room.

II

He was slight and small and looked very young, but on a second glance it could be seen that the features, though smooth as a boy's, were devoid of eyelashes as well as of beard. His brows were but the thinnest, light line, yet his hair was heavy and black, falling in lank locks which had been trimmed squarely at his shoulders. Light grey eyes gazed at Rajasta, unfocussed as if he were blind; and he was darkly tanned, although some strange pallor underlying the skin gave him a sickly look. Rajasta studied the haggard face intently, noting that the chela held himself stiffly erect, arms away from his body, thin hands hanging curled like a newborn child's at his sides. He had moved so lightly, so noiselessly, that Rajasta wondered, half-seriously, if the creature had pads like a cat's on his feet.

He beckoned the chela to approach, and asked kindly, "What is your name, my son?"

The dull eyes woke suddenly in an unhealthy glitter. He looked about and took a step backward, then opened his mouth once or twice. Finally, in a husky voice—as if unaccustomed to speaking—he said, "My name? I am . . . only a fool."

"Who are you?" Rajasta persisted. "Where are you from?"

The chela took another step backward, and the furtive swivelling of his sick eyes intensified. "I can see you are a Priest," he said craftily. "Aren't you wise enough to know? Why should I twist my poor brain to remember, when the High Gods know, and bid me be silent, be silent, sing silent when the stars glow, mooning driftward in a surge of light. . . ." The words slid off into a humming croon.

Rajasta could only stare, thunderstruck.

Riveda gestured to the chela in dismissal. "That will do," he said; and as the boy slipped from the room like a mumbling fog-wraith, the Adept added, in explanation to Rajasta, "Questions always excite him—as if at some time he'd been questioned until he—withdrew."

Rajasta, finding his tongue, exclaimed, "He's mad as a seagull!"

Riveda chuckled wryly. "I'm sorry. He does have intervals when he's reasonably lucid, and can talk quite rationally. But if you question—he slips back into madness. If you can avoid anything like a question—"

"I wish you had warned me of that,' Rajasta said, in genuine distress. "You told me he gave the correct responses—"

Riveda shrugged this off. "Our Signs and counter-Signs are not in the form of questions," he remarked, "at least he can betray none of my secrets! Have you no secrets in the Temple of Light, Rajasta?"

"Our secrets are available to any who will seek sincerely."

Riveda's frigid eyes glittered with offense. "As our secrets are more dangerous, so we conceal them more carefully. The harmless secrets of the Temple of Light, your pretty ceremonies and rites—no man could harm anyone even if he meddled with the knowledge unworthily! But we work with dangerous powers—and if one man know them and be unfit to trust with such secrets, then such things come as befell young Micon of Ahtarrath!" He turned savagely on Rajasta. "You of all men should know why we have cause to keep our secrets for those who are fit to use them!"

Rajasta's lips twisted. "Such as your crazy chela?"

"He knows them already; we can but make sure he does not misuse them in his madness." Riveda's voice was flat and definite. "You are no child to babble of ideals. Look at Micon . . . you honor him, I respect him greatly, your little Acolyte—what is her name? Domaris—adores him. Yet what is he but a broken reed?"

"Such is accomplishment," from Rajasta, very low.

"And at what price? I think my crazy boy is happier. Micon, unfortunately—" Riveda smiled, "is still able to think, and remember."

Sudden anger gusted up in Rajasta. "Enough! The man is my guest, keep your mocking tongue from him! Look you to your Order, and forbear mocking your betters!" He turned his back on the Adept, and strode from the room, his firm tread echoing and dying away on stone flooring; and never heard Riveda's slow-kindled laughter that followed him all the way.

CHAPTER THREE
✠ THE UNION ✠

I

The sacred chamber was walled with tall windows fretted and overlaid with intricate stone-work casements. The dimmed moonlight and patterns of shadow bestowed an elusive, unreal quality upon the plain chairs and the very simple furnishings. A high-placed oval window let the silvery rays fall full on the altar, where glowed a pulsing flame.

Micon on one side, Rajasta on the other, Domaris passed beneath the softly shadowed archway; in silence, the two men each took one of the woman's hands, and led her to a seat, one of three facing the altar.

"Kneel," said Rajasta softly, and Domaris, with the soft sibilance of her robes, knelt. Micon's hand withdrew from hers, and was laid upon the crown of her head.

"Grant wisdom and courage to this woman, O Great Unknown!" the Atlantean prayed, his voice low-pitched, yet filling the chamber with its controlled resonances. "Grant her peace and understanding, O Unknowable!" Stepping back a pace, Micon permitted Rajasta to take his place.

"Grant purity of purpose and true knowledge to this woman," said the Priest of Light. "Grant her growth according to her needs, and the fortitude to do her duty in the fullest measure. O Thou which Art, let her be in Thee, and of Thee." Rajasta took his hand from her head and himself withdrew.

The silence was complete. Domaris felt herself oddly alone upon the raised platform before the altar, though she had not heard the rustlings of robes, the slapping of sandals which would have accompanied Micon and Rajasta out of the room. Her heartbeats sounded dully in her ears, a muffled throbbing that slowed to a long drawn-out rhythm, a deep pulsing that seemed to take its tempo from the quivering flame upon the altar. Then, without warning, the two men raised her up and seated her between them.

Her hands resting in theirs, her face stilled to an unearthly beauty, Domaris felt as if she were rising, expanding to touch the far-flung stars. Even there a steady beat, a regular cadence that was both sound and light fused, filled and engulfed her. Domaris's senses shifted, rapidly reversing, painlessly twisting and contorting into an indescribable blending in which all past experience was suddenly quite useless. It was around her and in her and of her, a sustenance that, somehow, she herself fed, and slowly, very slowly, as if over centuries, the pulsing bright static of the stars gave way to the hot darkness of the beating heart of the earth. Of this, too, she was a part: it was she; she *was.*

With this realization, as if borne upward by the warm tides of the waters of life, Domaris came back to the surface of existence. About her, the sacred chamber was silent; to either side of her, she could see the face of a man transfigured even as Domaris had been. As one, the three breathed deeply, rose, and went forth in silence from that place, newly consecrated to a purpose that, for a little time, they could almost understand.

CHAPTER FOUR
⚜ STORM WARNINGS ⚜

I

A cool breeze stirred the leaves, and what light penetrated the branches was a shimmering, shifting dance of golden and green. Rajasta, approaching along a shrubbery-lined path, thought the big tree and the trio beneath it made a pleasing picture: Deoris, with her softly curling hair, looked shadowy and very dark as she sat on her scribe's stool, reading from a scroll; before her, in contrast, Micon's pallor was luminous, almost translucent. Close by the Atlantean's side, yet not much more distant from her little sister, Domaris was like a stilled flame, the controlled serenity of her face a pool of quiet.

Because Rajasta's sandals had made no noise on the grass, he was able to stand near them unnoticed a little while, half-listening to Deoris as she read; yet it was Domaris and Micon on whom his thoughts focussed.

As Deoris paused in her reading, Micon abruptly raised his head and turned toward Rajasta, the twisted smile warm with welcome.

Rajasta laughed. "My brother, you should be Guardian here, and not I! No one else noticed me." There was a spreading ripple of laughter beneath the big tree as the Priest of Light moved closer. Gesturing to both girls to keep their seats, Rajasta stopped a moment, to touch Deoris's tumbled curls fondly. "This breeze is refreshing."

"Yes, but it is the first warning of the coming storm," said Micon.

There was a brief silence then, and Rajasta gazed thoughtfully upon

Micon's uptilted face. *Which sort of storm, I wonder, does he refer to? There is more trouble ahead of us than bad weather.*

Domaris, too, was disturbed. Always sensitive, her new relationship with Micon had given her an awareness of him that was uncanny in its completeness. She could, with inevitable instinct, enter into his feelings; the result was a devotion that dwarfed all other relationships. She loved Deoris as much as ever, and her reverence for Rajasta had not altered in intensity or degree—but Micon's desperate need came first, and drew on every protective instinct in her. It was this which threatened to absorb her; for Domaris, of them all, had the faculty for an almost catastrophic self-abnegation.

Rajasta had, of course, long known this about his Acolyte. Now it struck him with renewed force that, as her Initiator, it was his duty to warn her of this flaw in her character. Yet Rajasta understood all too well the love that had given rise to it.

Nevertheless, he told himself sternly, *it is not healthy for Domaris to so concentrate all her forces on one person, however great the need!* But, before he had even quite completed this thought, the Priest of Light smiled, ruefully. *It might be well for me to learn that lesson, too.*

Settling on the grass beside Micon, Rajasta laid his hand over the Atlantean's lax and twisted one in a gently reassuring clasp. Scarcely a moment passed before his skilled touch found the slight, tell-tale trembling, and Rajasta shook his head sadly. Although the Atlantean seemed to have quite recovered his health, the truth was far otherwise.

But for the moment, the trembling lessened, then stilled, as if a door had slammed shut on sullen fury. Micon allowed the Guardian's strength to flow through his tortured nerves, comforting and reinforcing him. He smiled gratefully, then his face sobered.

"Rajasta—I must ask—make no further effort to punish on my behalf. It is an effort that will bear no, or bitter, fruit."

Rajasta sighed. "We have been over this so often," he said, but not impatiently. "You must know by now, I cannot let this rest as things stand; the matter is too grave to go unpunished."

"And it will not, be assured," said Micon, his blind eyes bright and almost glowing after the flow of new vitality. "But take heed that punishment for punishment not follow!"

"Riveda must cleanse his Order!" Domaris's voice was as brittle as ice. "Rajasta is right—"

"My gracious lady," Micon admonished gently, "when justice becomes an instrument of vengeance, its steel is turned to blades of grass. Truly, Rajasta must protect those to come—but he who takes vengeance will suffer! The Laws of Karma note first the act, and *then*—if at all—the intention!" He paused, then added, with emphasis, "Nor should we involve Riveda overmuch. He stands already at the crossroads of danger!"

Rajasta, who had been prepared to speak, gasped. Had Micon also been vouchsafed some vision or revelation such as Rajasta had had on the Night of Zenith?

The Priest of Light's reaction went unnoticed as Deoris raised her head, suddenly impelled to defend Riveda. Hardly had she spoken a word, though, before it struck her that no one had accused the Adept of anything, and she fell silent again.

Domaris's face changed; the sternness grew tender. "I am ungenerous," she acknowledged. "I will be silent until I know it is a love for justice, not revenge, that makes me speak."

"Flame-crowned," said Micon in softly ringing tones, "thou wouldst not be woman, wert thou otherwise."

Deoris's eyes were thunderclouds: Micon used the familiar "thou," which Deoris herself rarely ventured—and Domaris did not seem offended, but pleased! Deoris felt she would choke with resentment.

Rajasta, his misgivings almost forgotten, smiled now on Domaris and Micon, vast approval in his eyes. How he loved them both! On Deoris, too, he turned affectionate eyes, for he loved her well, and only awaited the ripening of her nature to ask her to follow in her sister's footsteps as his Acolyte. Rajasta sensed unknown potentialities in the fledgling woman, and, if it were possible, he greatly desired to guide her; but as yet Deoris was far too young.

Domaris, sensitive to his thought, rose and went to her sister, to drop with slender grace at her side. "Put up thy work, little sister, and listen," she whispered, "and learn. I have. And—I love thee, puss—very dearly."

Deoris, comforted, snuggled into the clasp of her sister's arm; Domaris was rarely so demonstrative, and the unexpected caress filled her with joy. Domaris thought, with self-reproach, *Poor baby, she's lonely, I've been neglecting her so! But Micon needs me now! There will be time for her later, when I am sure . . .*

"—and still you know nothing of my half-brother?" Micon was asking, unhappily. "His fate is heavy on me, Rajasta; I feel that he still lives, but I know, I *know* that all is not well with him, wherever he may be."

"I shall make further inquiries," Rajasta promised, and loosed Micon's quiet hands at last, so that the Atlantean would not sense the half-deception in the words. Rajasta would ask—but he had little hope of learning anything about the missing Reio-ta.

"If he be but half-brother to thee, Micon," Domaris said, and her lovely voice was even softer than usual, "then he must find the Way of Love."

"I find that way not easy," Micon demurred gently. "To think always and only with compassion and understanding is—a difficult discipline."

Rajasta murmured, "Thou art a Son of Light, and hast attained—"

"Little!" An undertone of rebellion sounded clear in the Atlantean's resonant voice. "I was to be—Healer, and serve my fellows. Now I am nothing, and the service remains to be met."

For a long moment, all were silent, and Micon's tragedy stood stark in the forefront of every mind. Domaris resolved that every comfort of mind and body, every bit of service and love that was hers to give, should be given, no matter what the cost.

Deoris spoke at last, quietly but aggressively. "Lord Micon," she said, "you show us all how a man may bear misfortune, and be more than man. Is that wasted, then?"

Her temerity made Rajasta frown; at the same time, he inwardly applauded her sentiment, for it closely matched his own.

Micon pressed her small fingers lightly in his. "My little Deoris," he said gravely, "fortune and misfortune, worth and waste, these values are not for men to judge. I have set many causes in motion, and all men reap as they have sown. Whether a man meets good or evil lies with the Gods who have determined his fate, but every man—" His face twisted briefly in a smile. "And every woman, too, is free to make fortune or misfortune of the stuff that has been allotted him." The Atlantean's full, glorious smile came back, and he turned his head from Rajasta to Domaris in that odd gesture that gave almost the effect of sight. "You can say whether there is no good thing that has come of all this!"

Rajasta bowed his head. "My very great good, Son of Light."

"And mine, also," said Micon softly.

Deoris, surprise shadowed in her eyes, watched with vague discontent, and a jealousy even more vague. She drew her hand from Micon's light clasp, saying, "You don't want me any more today, do you, Lord Micon?"

Domaris said instantly, "Run along, Deoris, I can read if Micon wishes it." Jealousy never entered her head, but she resented anything which took Micon from her.

"But I must have a word with you, Domaris," Rajasta interposed firmly. "Leave Micon and the little scribe to their work, and you, Domaris, come with me."

II

The woman rose, sobered by the implied rebuke in Rajasta's tone, and went silently along the path at his side. Her eyes turned back for a moment to seek her lover, who had not moved; only now his bent head and his smile were for Deoris, who curled up at his feet: Domaris heard the clear ripple of her little sister's laughter.

Rajasta looked down at the shining crown of Domaris's hair, and sighed. Before he had made up his mind how to speak, Domaris felt the Priest's eyes, grave and kind but more serious than usual, bent upon her, and raised her face.

"Rajasta, I love him," she said simply.

The words, and the restraint of the emotion behind them, almost unmanned the Priest, disarming his intended rebuke. He laid his hands on her shoulders and looked down into her face, not with the severity he had planned, but with fatherly affection. "I know, daughter," he said softly. "I am glad. But you are in danger of forgetting your duty."

"My duty?" she repeated, perplexed. As yet she had no duties within the Priest's Caste, save for her studies.

Rajasta understood her confusion, but he knew also that she was evading self-knowledge. "Deoris, too, must be considered," he pointed out. "She, too, has need of you."

"But—Deoris knows I love her," Domaris protested.

"Does she, my Acolyte?" He spoke the term deliberately, in an attempt to recall her position to her mind. "Or does she feel that you have pushed her away, let Micon absorb all your attention?"

"She can't—she wouldn't—oh, I never meant to!" Reviewing in her mind the happenings of the last few weeks, Domaris found the reproof just. Characteristically, she responded to her training and gave her mentor's words strict attention, emblazoning them upon her mind and heart. After a time, she raised her eyes again, and this time they were shadowed with deep remorse. "Acquit me, at least, of intentional selfishness," she begged. "She is so dear and close that she is like a part of myself, and I forget her concerns are not always as my own. . . . I have been negligent; I shall try to correct—"

"If it be not already too late." A shadow of deep trouble darkened the Priest's eyes. "Deoris may love you never the less, but will she ever trust you as much?"

Domaris's lovely eyes were clouded. "If Deoris no longer trusts me, I must accept the fault as mine," she said. "The Gods grant it be not too late. I have neglected my first responsibility."

And yet she knew she had been powerless to do otherwise, nor could she truly regret her exclusive concern with Micon. Rajasta sighed again as he followed her thoughts. It was hard to reprove her for a fault which was equally his own.

CHAPTER FIVE
✠ THE SECRET CROWN ✠

I

The rains were almost upon them. On one of the last sunny days they might reasonably expect, Domaris and Elis, with Deoris and her friend Ista, a scribe like herself, went to gather flowers; the House of the Twelve was to be decorated by the Acolytes for a minor festival that night.

They found a field of blossoms atop a hill overlooking the seashore. Faintly, from afar, came the salt smell of rushes and seaweed left by the receding tide; the scent of sweet grass, sun-parched, hung close about them, intermingled with the heavy, heady, honey-sweet of flowers,

Elis had Lissa with her. The baby was over a year old now, and scampering everywhere, to pull up flowers and trample in them, tumble the baskets and tear at skirts, until Elis grew quite exasperated.

Deoris, who adored the baby, snatched her up in her arms. "I'll keep her, Elis, I've enough flowers now."

"I've enough, too," said Domaris, and laid down her fragrant burden. She brushed a hand over her damp forehead. The sun was near-blinding even when one did not look toward it, and she felt dizzy with the heavy sickishness of breathing the mixed salt and sweet smells. Gathering her baskets of flowers together, she sat down in the grass beside Deoris, who had Lissa on her knees and was tickling her as she murmured some nonsensical croon.

"You're like a little girl playing with a doll, Deoris."

97

Deoris's small features tightened into a smile that was not quite a smile. "But I never liked dolls," she said.

"No." Her sister's smile was reminiscent, her eyes turned fondly on Lissa more than Deoris. "You wanted your babies alive, like this one."

Slender, raven-haired Ista dropped cross-legged on the grass, jerked at her brief skirts, and began delicately to plait the flowers from her basket. Elis watched for a minute, then tossed an armful of white and crimson blooms into Ista's basket. "My garlands are always coming untied," Elis explained. "Weave mine, too, and ask me any favor you will."

Ista's dexterous fingers did not hesitate as she went on tying the stems. "I will do it, and gladly, and Deoris will help me—won't you, Deoris? But scribes work only for love, and not for favors."

Deoris gave Lissa a final squeeze and put her into Domaris's arms; then, drawing a basket toward her, began weaving the flowers into dainty festoons. Elis bent and watched them. "Shameful," she murmured, laughing, "that I must learn the Temple laws from two scribes!"

She threw herself down in the grass beside Domaris. From a nearby bush, she plucked a handful of ripe golden berries, put one into her own mouth, then fed the others, one by one, to the bouncing, crowing Lissa, who sat on Domaris's knees, plastering them both with juicy kisses and staining Domaris's light robe with berry juice. Domaris snuggled Lissa close to her, with a queer hungriness. *But my baby will be a son,* she thought proudly, *a straight little son, with dark-blue eyes. . . .*

Elis looked sharply at her cousin. "Domaris, are you ill—or only daydreaming?"

The older woman pulled her braid of coppery hair free from Lissa's fat, insistent fingers. "A little dizzy from the sun," she said, and gave Lissa to her mother. Once again she made a deliberate effort to stop thinking, to give up the persistent thought that the form of words, even in her own mind, might make untrue. *Perhaps this time, though, it is true. . . .* For weeks, she had secretly suspected that she now bore Micon's son. And yet, once before, her own wish and her own hope had betrayed her into mentioning a false suspicion which had ended in disappointment. This time she was resolved to be silent, even to Micon, until she was sure beyond all possible doubt.

Deoris, glancing up from her flowers, dropped her garland and leaned toward Domaris, her eyes wide and anxious. The change in Domaris had struck the world from under Deoris's feet. She knew she had lost her sister, and was ready to blame everyone: she was jealous of Arvath, of Elis, of Micon, and above all at times of Rajasta. Domaris, wrapped in the profound anesthesia of her love, saw nothing, really, of the child's misery; she only knew that Deoris was exasperatingly dependent these days. Her causeless childish clinging drove Domaris almost frantic. Why couldn't Deoris behave sensibly and leave her alone? Sometimes, without meaning it—for Domaris, although quick to irritation, and now tense with nervous strain, was never deliberately unkind—she wounded Deoris to the quick with a single careless word, only seeing what she had done when it was too late, if at all.

This time the tension slackened: Elis had taken Lissa, and the baby was pulling insistently at her mother's dress. Elis laughed, wrinkling her nose in pretended annoyance. "Little greedy pig, I know what she wants. I'm glad there are only a few months more of this nonsense!" She was unfastening her robe as she spoke, and gave Lissa a playful spank as the baby caught at her breast. "Then, little Mistress Mine, you must learn to eat like a lady!"

Deoris averted her eyes in something like disgust. "How do you endure it?" she asked.

Elis laughed merrily without troubling to answer; her complaints had been only in jest, and she thought Deoris's question equally frivolous. Babies were always nursed for two full years, and only an overworked slave-woman or a prostitute would have dreamed of shirking the full time of suckling.

Elis leaned back, cradling Lissa on her arm, and picked another handful of berries. "You sound like Chedan, Deoris! I sometimes think he hates my poor baby! Still—" She made a comical face and thrust another berry between her lips. "Sometimes I wonder, when she *bites* me—"

"And you will no sooner wean her," Ista remarked with gleeful gravity, "than she will begin to shed her baby teeth."

Domaris frowned: she alone knew that Deoris had not been joking. Lissa's eyes were closed, now, in sleepy contentment, and her face, a pink petal framed in sunny curls, lay like a curled bud on her mother's breast. Domaris felt a sudden stab of longing so great that it was almost pain. Elis, raising her eyes, met Domaris's glance; the intuitive wisdom of their caste was especially strong in Elis, and the girl guessed at a story that closely paralleled her own. Reaching her free hand to her cousin, Elis gave the narrow fingers a little squeeze; Domaris returned the pressure, furtively, grateful for the implied understanding.

"Little nuisance," crooned Elis, rocking the sleepy baby. "Fat little elf . . ."

The sun wavered, hiding itself behind a bank of cloud. Deoris and Ista nodded over their flower-work, still drowsily tying stems. Domaris suddenly shivered; then her whole body froze, tense, in an attitude of stilled, incredulous listening. And once again it came, somewhere deep inside her body, a faint and indescribable fluttering like nothing she had ever felt before, but unmistakable, like the beating of prisoned wings—it came and went so swiftly that she was hardly sure what she had felt. And yet she *knew*.

"What's the matter?" Elis asked in a low voice, and Domaris realized that she was still holding Elis's hand, but that her fingers had tightened, crushing her cousin's fingers together painfully. She let go of Elis, drawing back her hand quickly and in apology—but she did not speak, and her other hand remained resting lightly and secretly against her body, where once again that little instantaneous fluttering came and went and then was stilled. Domaris remembered to breathe; but she stayed very still, unable to think beyond that final, unmistakable surety that the concealed secret was now a confirmable truth, that there within her womb Micon's son—she dared not think that it was other than a son—stirred to life.

Deoris's eyes, large and somewhat afraid, met her sister's, and the expression in them was too much for the taut Domaris. She began to laugh, at first softly, then uncontrollably—because she dared not cry, she *would not* cry. . . . The laughter became hysterical, and Domaris scrambled to her feet and fled down the hill toward the seashore, leaving the three girls to stare at one another.

Deoris half rose, but Elis, on an intuitive impulse, pulled her back. "She would rather be alone for a while, I think. Here, hold Lissa for me, won't you, while I fasten my dress!" She plumped the baby into Deoris's lap, and carefully knotted the fastenings of her dress, taking her time, to avert a minor crisis.

II

At the edge of the salt-marshes, Domaris flung herself full-length into the long grass and lay hidden there, her face against the pungent earth, her hands clasped across her body in a wonder that was half fright. She lay motionless, feeling the long grasses wavering with the wind, her thoughts trembling as they did, but without stirring the surface of her mind. She was afraid to think clearly.

Noon paled and retreated, and Domaris, raising herself as if by instinct, saw Micon walking slowly along the shore. She got to her feet, her hair tumbling loose about her waist, her dress billowing in the wind, and began to run toward him on impatient feet. Hearing the quick, uneven steps, he stopped.

"Micon!"

"Domaris—where are you?" His blind face turned to follow the sound of her voice, and she darted to him, pausing—no longer even regretful that she could not throw herself into his arms—a careful step away, and lightly touching his arm, raised her face for his kiss.

His lips lingered an instant longer than usual; then he withdrew his face a little and murmured, "Heart of flame, you are excited. You bring news."

"I bring news." Her voice was softly triumphant, but failed her. She took the racked hands lightly in her own and pressed them softly against her body, begging him to understand without being told. . . . Perhaps he read her thoughts; perhaps he only guessed from the gesture. Whichever it may have been, his face grew bright with an inner brilliance, and his arms went out to gather her close.

"You bring light," he whispered, and kissed her again.

She hid her face on his breast. "It is sure now, beloved. This time it is sure! I have guessed it for weeks, and I would not speak of it, for fear that—but now there is no doubt! He—*our son*—stirred today!"

"Domaris—beloved—"

The man's voice choked, and she felt burning tears drop from the blind eyes onto her face. His hands, usually so sternly controlled, trembled so violently that he could not raise them to hers, and as she held herself to him, loving him and almost drowning in the intensity of this love so closely akin to worship, she felt Micon's trembling as even a strong tree will tremble a little before a hurricane.

"My beloved, my blessed one . . ." With a reverence that hurt and frightened the girl, Micon dropped to his knees, in the sand, and managed to clasp her two hands, pressing them to his cheeks, his lips. "Bearer of Light, it is my life you hold, my freedom," he whispered.

"Micon! I love you, I love you," the girl stammered incoherently—because there was nothing else that she could possibly have said.

The Initiate rose, his control somewhat regained, though still trembling slightly, and gently dried her tears. "Domaris," he said, with tender gravity, "I—there is no way to tell you—I mean, I will try, but—" His mouth took on an even greater seriousness, and the twist of pain and regret and uncertainty there was like knives in Domaris's heart.

"Domaris," he said, and his voice rang in the deep and practiced tones that she recognized as the Atlantean's oath-voice. "I will—try," he promised solemnly, "to stay with you until our son is born."

And Domaris knew that she had pronounced the beginning of the end.

CHAPTER SIX
✠ IN THE SISTERHOOD ✠

I

The Temple of Caratra, which overlooked the Shrine and the holy pool, was one of the most beautiful buildings of the entire Temple precinct. It was fashioned of milky stone, veined with shimmering, opalescent fires in the heart of the rock. Long gardens, linked by palisaded arbors covered with trailing vines, surrounded pool and Temple; cool fountains splashed in the courts where a profusion of flowers bloomed the year round.

Within these white and glistening walls, every child of the Temple was born, whether child to slave-maiden or to the High Priestess. Here, also, every young girl within the Temple was sent to render service in her turn (for all women owed service to the Mother of All Men); in assisting the Priestesses, in caring for the mothers and for the newly born, even (if she was of a satisfactory rank in the Priest's Caste) in learning the secrets of bringing children to birth. And every year thereafter she spent a certain assigned period—ranging from a single day for slave women and commoners, to an entire month for Acolytes and Priestesses—living and serving in the Temple of the Mother; and from this assigned yearly service, not the humblest slave nor the highest Initiate was ever exempted.

Over a year before, Deoris had been adjudged old enough to enter upon her time of service; but a severe, though brief, attack of fever had intervened, and somehow her name had been passed over. Now her name was called again; but although most of the young girls of the Priest's Caste looked on this service rather eagerly, as a sign of their own oncoming womanhood, it was with reluctance bordering on rebellion that Deoris made her preparations.

Once—almost two years earlier, at the time of her first approach to the Shrine—she had been given her initial lesson in the delivery of a baby. The experience had bewildered her. She dreaded a recurrence of the questions it raised in her mind. She had seen the straining effort, and the agony, and had been revolted at the seeming cruelty of it all—though she had also witnessed, after all that, the ecstatic welcome that the mother had given the tiny mite of humanity. Beyond the puzzlement she had felt at this contradictory behavior, Deoris had been dismayed at her own feelings: the bitter hurt that she too must one day be woman and lie there in her turn, struggling to bring forth life. The eternal "*Why?*" beat incessantly at her brain. Now, when she had almost managed to forget, it would be before her again.

"I can't, I won't," she burst out in protest to Micon. "It's cruel—horrible—"

"Hush, Deoris." The Atlantean reached for her nervously twisting hands, catching and holding them despite his blindness. "Do you not know that to live is to suffer, and to bring life is to suffer?" He sighed, a feint and restrained sound. "I think pain is the law of life . . . and if you can help, dare you refuse?"

"I don't dare—but I wish I did! Lord Micon, you don't know what it's like!"

Checking his first impulse to laugh at her naivete, Micon reassured her, gently, "But I do know. I wish I could help you to understand, Deoris; but there are things everyone must learn alone—"

Deoris, flushed and appalled, choked out the question, "But how *can* you know—that?" In the world of the Temple, childbirth was strictly an affair for women, and to Deoris, whose whole world was the Temple, it seemed impossible that a man could know anything of the complexities of birth. Was it not everywhere a rigid, unalterable custom that no man might approach a childbed? No one, surely, could imagine this ultimate indecency! How could Micon, fortunate enough to have been born a man, even guess at it?

Micon could no longer restrain himself; his laughter only served to bruise Deoris's feelings even more. "Why, Deoris," he said, "men are not so ignorant as you think!" As her hurt silence dragged on, he tried to amend his statement. "Our customs in Atlantis are not like yours, child—you must remember—" He let an indulgent, teasing tone creep into his voice. "You must remember what barbarians we are in the Sea Kingdoms! And believe me, not all men are in ignorance, even here. And—my child, do you think I know nothing of pain?" He hesitated for a moment; could this be the right moment to tell Deoris that her sister bore his child? Instinct told him that Deoris, wavering on the balance between acceptance and rejection, might be swayed in the right direction by the knowledge. Yet it seemed to him it was Domaris's right, not his, to speak or be silent. His words blurred in sudden weariness. "Darling, I wish I could help you. Try to remember this: to live, you need every experience. Some will come in glory and in beauty, and some in pain and what seems like ugliness. But—they *are*. Life consists of opposites in balance."

Deoris sighed, impatient with the pious repetition—she had heard it before. Domaris, too, had failed her. She had tried, really tried, to make Domaris understand; Domaris had only looked at her, uncomprehending, and said, "But every woman must do that service."

"But it's so awful!" Deoris had wailed.

Domaris, stern-eyed, advised her not to be a silly little girl; that it was the way of nature, and that no one could change it. Deoris had stammered on, inclined to beg, cry, plead, convinced that Domaris *could* change it, if she only would.

Domaris had been greatly displeased: "You are being very childish! I've spoilt you, Deoris, and tried to protect you. I know now that I did wrong. You are not a child any longer. You must learn to take a woman's responsibilities."

II

Deoris was now fifteen. The Priestesses took it for granted that she had, like most girls of that age, completed the simpler preliminary tasks allotted to those who were serving for the first or second time. Too shy and too miserable to correct their mistake, Deoris found herself assigned an advanced task: as befitted a girl of her age who was the daughter of a Priest, she was sent to assist one of the midwife-Priestesses, a woman who was also a Healer of Riveda's Order; her name was Karahama.

Karahama was not of the Priest's Caste. She was the daughter of a Temple servant who, before her daughter was born, had claimed to be with child by Talkannon himself. Talkannon, then recently married to the highly-born Priestess who later became the mother of Deoris and Domaris, had most uncharacteristically refused to acknowledge the child. He admitted intimacy with the woman, but claimed that it was by no means sure that he was the father of her unborn child, and produced other men who had, in his opinion and theirs, a better claim.

Under such flagrant proofs of misconduct, the Elders had admitted that no one could be forced to acknowledge the child. The woman, stripped of her privileges as a Temple servant, was given only a minimum of shelter until the birth of her daughter, and then dismissed from the Temple altogether. Man and woman were free to live as they would before marriage, but promiscuity could not be tolerated.

The child Karahama, casteless and nameless, had been taken into the Grey-robe sect as one of their *saji*—and had grown up the very image of Talkannon. Eventually, of course, the Arch-Priest became aware of the jeers of the Temple slaves, the concealed gossip of his juniors. It was indeed a choice bit of scandal that the Temple's Arch-Priest should have a small replica of himself among the worst outcasts in the Temple. In self-defense, he at last succumbed to popular opinion. After doing lengthy penance for his error, he legally adopted Karahama.

As the Grey-robes had no caste laws, Karahama had been accepted by Riveda as a Healer-Priestess. Restored by Talkannon to her rightful caste and name, she had chosen to enter the Temple of Caratra, and was now an Initiate, entitled to wear the blue robe—a dignity as high as any in the Temple. No one could scorn or spit on the "nameless one" any more, but Karahama's uncertain beginnings had made her temperament a strange and uncertain thing.

At the realization that this girl assigned to her guidance was her own half-sister, Karahama felt oddly mixed emotions, which were soon resolved in Deoris's favor. Karahama's own children, born before her reclamation, were outcasts, nameless as she herself had been, and for them nothing could be done. Perhaps this was why Karahama tried to be particularly kind and friendly to this young and almost unknown kinswoman. But she knew that sooner or later she would have trouble with this child, whose sullen rebellion smouldered unspoken behind scared violet eyes, and whose work was carefully deliberate, as if Deoris made every movement against her will. Karahama thought this a great pity, for Deoris obviously had all the qualities of a born Healer: steady hands and a keen observation, a deft sure gentleness, a certain instinct for pain. Only the will was lacking—and Karahama quickly resolved that somehow she must make it her duty to find the hidden thing in Deoris which would win her over to the service of the Mother.

She thought she had found it when Arkati came to the House of Birth.

Arkati was the girl-wife of one of the Priests, a pretty thing scarcely out of childhood; younger, in fact, than Deoris herself. A fair-skinned, fair-haired, diminutive girl with sweet pleading eyes, Arkati had been brought to the Temple of Caratra a few weeks before the proper time, because she was not well; her heart had been damaged by a childhood illness, and they wished to strengthen her before her child was born. All of them, even the stern Karahama, treated the girl with tenderness, but Arkati was weak and homesick and would cry at nothing.

She and Deoris, it soon turned out, had known one another since childhood. Arkati clung to Deoris like a lost kitten.

Karahama used influence, and Deoris was given what freedom she wished to spend with Arkati. She noticed with pleasure that Deoris had a good instinct for caring for the sick girl; she followed Karahama's instructions with good sense and good judgment, and it seemed as if Deoris's hard rebellion gave the girl-mother strength. But there was restraint in their friendship, born of Deoris's fear.

More than fear, it was a positive horror. Wasn't Arkati afraid at all? She never tired of dreaming and making plans and talking about her baby; she accepted all the inconveniences, sickness and weariness, unthinkingly, even with laughter. How could she? Deoris did not know, and was afraid to ask.

Once, Arkati took Deoris's hand in hers, and put it against her swollen body, hard; and Deoris felt under her hand an odd movement, a sensation which filled her with an emotion she could not analyze.

Not knowing whether what she felt was pleasure or acute annoyance, she jerked her hand roughly away.

"What's wrong?" Arkati laughed. "Don't you like my baby?"

Somehow this custom, speaking of an unborn child as if already a person, made Deoris uncomfortable. "Don't be foolish," she said roughly—but for the first time in her entire life, she was consciously thinking of her own mother, the mother they said had been gentle and gracious and lovely, and very like Domaris, and who had died when Deoris was born. Drowned in guilt, Deoris remembered that she had killed her mother. Was that why Domaris resented her now?

She said nothing of all this, only attended to what she was taught with a determination born of anger; and within a few days Karahama saw, with surprise, that Deoris was already beginning to show something like skill, a deftness and intuitive knowledge that seemed to equal years of experience. When the ordinary term of service was ended, Karahama asked her—rather diffidently, it is true—to stay on for another month in the Temple, working directly with Karahama herself.

Somewhat to her own surprise, Deoris agreed, telling herself that she had simply promised Arkati to remain with her as long as possible. Not even to herself would she admit that she was beginning to enjoy the feeling of mastery which this work gave her.

III

Arkati's child was born on a rainy night when will-o'-the-wisps flitted on the seashore, and the wind wailed an ominous litany. Karahama had no cause to complain of Deoris, but somewhere in the dark hours the injured heart ceased to beat, and the fight—pitifully brief, after all—ended in tragedy. At sunrise, a newborn child wailed without knowing why, in an upper room of the Temple, and Deoris, sick to the bone, lay sobbing bitterly in her own room, her head buried in her pillows, trying to shut out memory of the sounds and sights that would haunt her in nightmares for the rest of her life.

"You mustn't lie here and cry!" Karahama bent over her, then sat down at her side, gathering up Deoris's hands in hers. Another girl came into the little dormitory, but Karahama curtly motioned her to leave them alone, and continued, "Deoris, listen to me, child. There was nothing we could have done for—"

Deoris's sobs mixed with incoherent words.

Karahama frowned. "That is foolishness. The child did not kill her! Her heart stopped; you know she has never been strong. Besides—" Karahama bent closer and said, in her gently resolute voice, so like Domaris's and yet so different, "You are a daughter of the Temple. We know Death's true face, a doorway to further life, and not something to be feared—"

"Oh, leave me alone!" Deoris wailed miserably.

"By no means," said Karahama firmly. Self-pity was not in her category of permitted emotions, and she had no sympathy with the involved reasoning that made Deoris curl herself up into a forlorn little huddle and want to be left alone. "Arkati is not to be pitied! So stop crying for yourself. Get up; bathe and dress yourself properly, and then go and tend Arkati's little daughter. She is your responsibility until her father may claim her, and also you must say protective spells over her, to guard her from the imps who snatch motherless children—"

Rebelliously, Deoris did as she was told, assuming the dozen responsibilities which must be taken: arranging for a wet-nurse, signing the child with protective runes, and—because a child's true name was a sacred secret, written on the rolls of the Temple but never spoken aloud except in ritual—Deoris gave the child the "little name" by which she would be called until she was grown: *Miritas.* The baby squirmed feebly in her arms, and Deoris thought, with unhappy contempt, *Protective spells! Where was the spell that could have saved Arkati?*

Karahama watched stoically, more grieved than she would say. They had all known that Arkati would not live; she had been warned, when she married, that she should not attempt to bear a child, and the Priestesses had given her runes and spells and arcane teachings to prevent this. Arkati had willfully disobeyed their counsel, and had paid for this disobedience with her life. Now there was another motherless child to be fostered.

But Karahama had known something else, for she understood Deoris better even than Domaris. Unlike as they were, both Deoris and Karahama had inherited from Talkannon a rugged and stubborn determination. Resentment, more than triumph, would spur Deoris on; hating pain and death, she would vow to conquer it. Where being forced to witness such a tragedy might have lost another neophyte, driving her away in revulsion, Karahama felt that this would place a decisive hand on Deoris.

Karahama said nothing more, however; she was wise enough to let the knowledge ripen slowly. When all had been done for the newborn child, Karahama told Deoris that she might be excused from other duties for the remainder of the day. "You have had no sleep," she added dryly, when Deoris would have thanked her. "Your hands and eyes would have no skill. Mind that you rest!"

Deoris promised, in a strained voice; but she did not ascend the stairway to the dormitory reserved for the women who were serving their season in the Temple. Instead, she slipped out by a side entrance, and ran toward the House of the Twelve, with only one thought in her mind—the lifelong habit of carrying all her sorrows to Domaris. Her sister would certainly understand her now, she *must!*

A summer wind was blowing, moist with the promise of more rain; Deoris hugged her scarf closely about her neck and shoulders, and ran wildly across the lawns. Turning a sharp corner she almost tumbled against the stately form of Rajasta, who was coming from the House. Barely pausing to recover her balance, Deoris stammered breathless words of apology and would have run on, but Rajasta detained her gently.

"Look to your steps, dear child, you will injure yourself," he cautioned, smiling. "Domaris tells me you have been serving in Caratra's Temple. Have you finished with your service there?"

"No, I am only dismissed for the day." Deoris spoke civilly, but twitched with impatience. Rajasta did not seem to notice.

"That service will bring you wisdom and understanding, little daughter," he counselled. "It will make a woman of a child." He laid his hand for a moment, in blessing, on the tangled, feathering curls. "May peace and enlightenment follow thy footsteps, Deoris."

IV

In the House of Twelve, men and women mingled almost

promiscuously, in a brother-and-sisterly innocence, fostered by the fact that all Twelve had been brought up together. Deoris, whose more impressionable years had been spent in the stricter confines of the Scribe's School, was not yet accustomed to this freedom, and when, in the inner courtyard, she discovered some of the Acolytes splashing in the pool, she felt confused and—in her new knowledge—annoyed. She did not want to seek her sister among them. But Domaris had often cautioned her, with as much sternness as Domaris ever showed, that while Deoris lived among the Acolytes she must conform to their customs, and forget the absurd strictures forced upon the scribes.

Chedan saw Deoris first, and shouted for her to strip and bathe with them. A merry boy, the youngest of the Acolytes, he had from the first treated Deoris with a special friendliness and indulgence. Deoris shook her head, and the boy splashed her until her dress was sopping and she ran out of reach. Domaris, standing under the fountain, saw this exchange and called to Deoris to wait; then, wringing the water from her drenched hair, Domaris went toward the edge of the pool. Passing Chedan, his bare shoulders and turned back tempted her to mischief; she scooped up a handful of water and dashed it into his eyes. Before the retaliating deluge, she dodged and squealed and started to run—then, remembering that it was hardly wise to risk a fall just now, slowed her steps to a walk.

The water fell away in shallows, and Deoris, waiting, looked at her sister—and her eyes widened in amazement. She didn't believe what she saw. Abruptly, Deoris turned and fled, and did not hear Domaris cry out as Chedan and Elis, screaming with mirth, caught Domaris at the very edge of the pool and dragged her back into the water, ducking her playfully, threatening to fling her into the very center of the fountain. They thought she was playing when she struggled to free herself of their rough hands. Two or three of the girls joined in the fun, and their shrieks of laughter drowned her pleas for mercy, even when, genuinely scared, Domaris began to cry in earnest.

They had actually swung her free of the water when Elis suddenly seized their hands and cried out harshly, "Stop it, stop it, Chedan, Riva! Let her go—take your hands from her, now, at once!"

The tone of her voice shocked them into compliance: they lowered Domaris to her feet and released her, but they were still too wild with mirth to realize that Domaris was sobbing. "She started it," Chedan protested, and they stared in disbelief as Elis encircled the shaken girl with a protecting arm, and helped her to the rim of the pool. Always before, Domaris had been a leader in their rough games.

Still crying a little, Domaris clung helplessly to Elis as her cousin helped her out of the water. Elis picked up a robe and tossed it to Domaris. "Put this on before you take a chill," she said, sensibly. "Did they hurt you? You should have told us—stop shaking, Domaris, you're all right now."

Domaris wrapped herself obediently in the white woolen robe, glancing down ruefully at the contours emphasized so strongly by the crude drapery. "I wanted to keep it to myself just a little longer . . . now I suppose everyone will know."

Elis slid her wet feet into sandals, knotting the sash of her own robe. "Haven't you even told Deoris?"

Domaris shook her head silently as they arose and went toward the passageway leading to the women's apartments. In retrospect, Deoris's face, shocked and disbelieving, was sharp in her memory. "I meant to," Domaris murmured, "but—"

"Tell her, right away," Elis ventured to advise, "before she hears it as gossip from someone else. But be gentle, Domaris. Arkati died last night."

They paused before Domaris's door, Domaris whispering distractedly, "Oh, what a pity!" She herself had barely known Arkati, but she knew Deoris loved her, and now—now, in such sorrow, Deoris could not come to see her without receiving a further shock,

Elis turned away, but over her shoulder she flung back, "Yes, and have a little more care for yourself! We could have hurt you badly— and suppose Arvath had been there?" Her door slammed.

V

While Elara dried and dressed her, and braided her wet hair, Domaris sat lost in thought, staring at nothing. There might be trouble with Arvath—no one knew that better than Domaris—but she could not spare any worry about that now. She had, as yet, no duty toward him; she acted within her rights under the law. Deoris was a more serious matter, and Domaris reproached herself for neglect. Somehow she must make Deoris understand. Warm and cozy after Elara's ministrations, she curled up on a divan and awaited her sister's return.

It was, in fact, not very long before Deoris returned, sullen fires burning a hectic warning in her cheeks. Domaris smiled at her joyously. "Come here, darling," she said, and held out her arms. "I have something wonderful to tell you."

Deoris, wordless, knelt and caught her sister close, in such a violent embrace that Domaris was dismayed, feeling the taut trembling of the thin shoulders. "Why, Deoris, Deoris," she protested, deeply distressed; and then, although she hated to, she had to add, "Hold me not so tightly, little sister—you'll hurt me—you can hurt us both, now." She smiled as she said it, but Deoris jerked away as if Domaris had struck her.

"It's true, then!"

"Why, yes—yes, darling, you saw it when I came from the pool. You are a big girl now, I felt sure you would know without being told."

Deoris gripped her sister's wrist in a painful grasp, which Domaris endured without flinching. "No, Domaris! It can't be! Tell me you are jesting!' Deoris would disbelieve even the evidence of her own eyes, if Domaris would only deny it.

"I would not jest of a sacred trust, Deoris," the woman said, and a deep sincerity gave bell-tones to the reproach in her voice, and the near-disappointment.

Deoris knelt, stricken, gazing up at Domaris and shaking as if with intense cold. "Sacred?" she whispered, choking. "You, a student, an Acolyte, under discipline—you gave it all up for *this?*"

Domaris, with her free hand, reached down and unclasped Deoris's frantic grip from her wrist. The white skin showed discolorations where the girl's fingers had almost met in the flesh.

Deoris, looking down almost without comprehension, suddenly lifted the bruised wrist in her palm and kissed it. "I didn't mean to hurt you, I—I didn't know what I was doing," she said, her breath catching with contrition. "Only I—I can't stand it, Domaris!"

The older girl touched her cheek gently. "I don't understand you, Deoris. What have I given up? I am still student, still discipline; Rajasta knows and has given his blessing."

"But—but this will bar you from Initiation—"

Domaris looked down at her in absolute bewilderment. Taking Deoris's resisting hand in hers, by main force she pulled her up on the divan, saying, "Who has put these bats into your brain, Deoris? I am still Priestess, still Acolyte, even if—no, because I am a woman! You have served in Caratra's Temple a month or more now, you should know better than that! Surely they have taught you that the cycles of womanhood and of the universe itself are attuned, that—" Domaris broke off, shaking her head with a light laugh. "You see, I even *sound* like Rajasta sometimes! Deoris, dear, as a woman—and even more as an Initiate—I must know fulfillment. Does one offer an empty vessel to the Gods?"

Deoris retorted hysterically, "Or one soiled by use?"

"But that's absurd!" Domaris smiled, but her eyes were sober. "I must find my place, to go with life and—" She laid her slender, ringed hands across her body with a protective gesture, and Deoris saw again, with a shudder, the faint, almost negligible rounding there. "—accept my destiny."

Deoris twisted away from her. "So does a cow accept destiny!"

Domaris tried to laugh, but it came out as a sob.

Deoris moved close to her again and threw her arms around her sister. "Oh, Domaris, I'm hateful, I know it! All I do is hurt you, and I don't want to hurt you, I love you, but, this, this desecrates you! It's awful!"

"Awful? Why?" Domaris smiled, a little mournfully. "Well, it does not seem so to me. You needn't be afraid for me, darling, I have never felt stronger or happier. And as for desecration—" The smile was not so sad now, and she took Deoris's hand in hers again, to hold it once more against her body. "You silly child! As if *he* could desecrate me—Micon's son!"

"Micon?" Deoris's hand dropped away and she stared at Domaris in absolute bewilderment, repeating stupidly, "Micon's *son?*"

"Why, yes, Deoris—didn't you know? What did you think?"

Deoris did not answer, only staring at Domaris with a stunned fixity. Domaris felt the sob trembling at her lips again as she tried to smile, saying, "What's the matter, Deoris? Don't you like my baby?"

"*OH!*" Stung by a twinge of horrified memory, Deoris wailed again, "Oh *no!*" and fled, sobbing, hearing the grieved cries of her sister follow her.

CHAPTER SEVEN
✠ WHAT THE ✠ STARS REVEALED

I

On a couch in her room, Domaris lay watching the play of the rainclouds across the valley. Long, low waves of cloud, deep grey tipped with white vapor like foam capping the waves of the sea, shifted in the wild winds as they drove across the sky, scattering arrows of sunshine across the face of Micon, who half reclined on a heap of cushions nearby, his useless hands in his lap, his dark quiet face at peace. The silence between them was charged with restfulness; the distant rumble of thunder and the faraway drumming of the stormy surf seemed to accentuate the shadowy comfort and coolness within the room.

They both sighed at the knock on the door, but as the tall shadow of Rajasta crossed the threshold, Domaris's annoyance vanished. She rose, still slender, still moving as lightly as a dancing palm, but the Priest detected a new dignity in her bearing as she crossed the room.

"Lord Rajasta, you have read the stars for my child!"

He smiled kindly as she drew him toward a seat by the windows. "Do you wish me to speak before Micon, then, my daughter?"

"I most certainly do wish it!"

At her emphatic tone, Micon raised his head inquiringly. "What means this, heart-of-flame? I do not understand—what will you tell us of our child, my brother?"

"I see that *some* of our customs are unknown in Atlantis." Rajasta smiled pleasantly, and he added, lightly, "Forgive my satisfaction that I can, for a change, make you *my* disciple."

"You teach me much, Rajasta," Micon murmured soberly.

"You honor me, Son of the Sun." Rajasta paused a moment. "Briefly, then—among the Priest's Caste, before your son can be acknowledged—and this must be done as soon as possible—the hour of his conception must be determined, from your stars and those of his mother. In this way, we shall know the day and the hour of his birth, and we may give your coming child a suitable name."

"Before even being born?" Micon asked in astonishment.

"Would you have a child born *nameless?*" Rajasta's own amazement verged on the scandalized. "As the Initiator of Domaris, this task is mine—just as, before Domaris was born, I read the stars for her mother. She, too, was my Acolyte, and I knew that her daughter, although fathered by Talkannon, would be the true daughter of my own soul. It was I who gave her the name of Isarma."

"Isarma?" Micon frowned in confusion. "I don't—"

Domaris laughed gleefully. "Domaris is but my baby name," she explained. "When I marry—" Her face changed abruptly, but she went on, in an even voice, "I shall use my true Temple name, Isarma. In our language that means *a doorway to brightness.*"

"So you have been to me, beloved," Micon murmured. "And Deoris?"

"Deoris means only—*little kitten.* She seemed no bigger than a kitten, and I called her so." Domaris glanced at Rajasta; to discuss one's own true name was permissible, but it was not common practice to speak of another's. The Priest of Light only nodded, however, and Domaris continued, "Her true name on the rolls of the Temple is Adsartha: *child of the Warrior Star.*"

Micon shuddered, a convulsive shiver that seemed to tear at his whole body. "In the name of all the Gods, why such a name of cruel omen for your sweet little sister?"

Rajasta's aspect was grave. "I do not know, for I did not read her stars; I was in seclusion at the time. I always meant to confer with Mahaliel, but—" Rajasta broke off. "This I know," he said, after a moment. "She was conceived upon the Nadir-night, and her mother, dying only a few hours after Deoris was born, told me almost with her last breath, that Deoris was foredoomed to much suffering." Rajasta paused again, regretful that in the rush of events following Deoris's birth he had not made time to inquire of Mahaliel, who had been greatly skilled; but the old Priest was many years dead now, and could be of no help any more. Drawing a deep breath, Rajasta resumed, "And so we guard our little Deoris so tenderly, that her sorrows may be lessened by our love, and her weakness nurtured by our strength— although I sometimes think too much care does not diminish weakness enough—"

Domaris cried out impatiently, "Enough of all these omens and portents! Rajasta, tell me, shall I bear my lord a son?"

Rajasta smiled and forbore to rebuke her impatience, for indeed it was a subject he was happy to set aside. He drew from his robes a scroll covered with figures which Domaris could not read, although he had taught her to count and to write the sacred numbers. For everyday counting, everyone but the very highest Initiates reckoned on their fingers; numbers were the most sacredly guarded mystery, and were never used lightly or for any frivolous purpose, for by them Priests read the movements of the stars and reckoned the days and years on their great calendar-stones—even as the Adepts, through the sacred numbers, manipulated the natural forces which were the source of their power. In addition to the cryptic figures and their permutations, Rajasta had drawn the simpler symbols of the Houses of the Sky—and with these Domaris, as an Acolyte of the Twelve, was familiar; to these, therefore, he referred as he spoke.

"At such a time, in the Sign of the Scales, were you born, Domaris. Here, under the House of the Carrier, is Micon's day of birth. I will not read all of this now," Rajasta said, in an aside to the Atlantean, who stirred with interest, "but if you truly wish, I will read it to you later. At present, I am sure, the primary interest to you both is the date upon which your child will be born."

He went on, pedantically, to give himself opportunity to ignore the overtones in their voices as they murmured happily to one another, "In such an hour, so your stars tell me, under the signs of the moon which regulate these things in women, your womb must have received the seed of life—and on such a day," he tapped the chart, "in the sign of the Scorpion, you will be brought to bed of a son—if my calculations are perfectly correct."

"A son!" Domaris cried out in triumph.

But Micon looked troubled.

"Not—on the Nadir-night?"

"I trust not," Rajasta reassured him, "but surely soon thereafter. In any case, remember that the Nadir-night brings not only evil. As I have told you, Deoris was conceived upon the Nadir-night, and she is as clever and dear a child as one could desire. With the balancing effects of your child's conception date falling so closely between your birthdate and that of Domaris—"

Rajasta rattled on soothingly like this for a little while, and Micon showed definite signs of relief which, in truth, Rajasta did not altogether share. The Priest of Light had puzzled over this chart for many hours, troubled by the knowledge that Micon's son might, indeed, be born on that night of evil omen. Try as he had, though, Rajasta had been unable to wholly exclude this possibility, for it had proven impossible to fix the time of conception with any exactness. *Had I only instructed Domaris more completely,* he now thought, not for the first time, *she herself would have been able to determine the proper time!*

"In fact," Rajasta ended, with just the proper note of amused tolerance for parental worryings, "I should say the worst thing you have to fear for your son-to-be is that he will be perhaps over-fond of contests and strifes, and be sharp-tongued, as Scorpions often are." He put the chart aside, deliberately. "Nothing that proper instruction during his youth cannot correct. I have other news, as well, my daughter," he said, smiling at Domaris. She was, he thought, lovelier than ever; something of the glow and sanctity of motherhood was already in her face, a radiant joy undimmed by the shadow of grief. Yet that shadow lay there already, a menace formless as yet, but discernible even to the relatively unimaginative Rajasta, and the Priest felt a surge of protectiveness.

"The time has come when I may give thee work for the Temple," Rajasta said. "Thou art woman, no longer incomplete." Catching the expression of fleeting disquiet in Micon's face, he hastened to reassure him. "Have no fear, my brother. I will not permit her to exhaust herself. She is safe with me."

"Of that I have no doubt," said Micon, quietly.

Rajasta returned his attention to Domaris, whose thoughtful

expression was tinged with a great curiosity. "Domaris—what know you of the Guardians?"

She hesitated to answer, considering. Rajasta himself, Guardian of the Outer Gates, was the only Guardian ever named in public. There were others, of course, but no one in the Temple knew their names, or even for certain that there were no more than the seven who sat veiled in Council on high occasions. A sudden suspicion widened her eyes.

Rajasta went on, without waiting for her answer, "My beloved daughter, you yourself have been chosen Guardian of the Second Circle, successor to Ragamon the Elder—who will remain at his post to teach and instruct thee until thou art mature in wisdom. You will be pledged to this duty as soon as your child has been acknowledged—although," he added, with another smile in Micon's direction, "this will entail no arduous duties until you have fulfilled your responsibilities to the coming child. And, as I know women—" His face was filled with tender indulgence as he regarded his young Acolyte. "—the acknowledgment of your son will take precedence over the greater ceremony!"

Domaris lowered her eyes, color staining her cheeks. She knew that if she had received this high honor at any other time, she would have been almost overcome by the thought; now it seemed remote, a vague secondary consideration beside the thought of the ceremony which would admit her child into the life of the Temple. "It is even so," she admitted.

Rajasta's smile was a benediction. "No woman would have it otherwise."

CHAPTER EIGHT
✠ THE NAMING OF ✠ THE NAME

I

It was the responsibility of the Vested Five to keep the records of the Priest's Caste and, as Temple Elders, to investigate and ascertain all matters pertaining to the place assigned each child born within the precinct. Their voluminous robes were embroidered and imprinted with cryptic symbols of such antiquity that only the highest Initiates had even a foggy conception of their meanings.

Side by side, Domaris and Micon stood before them in meditative silence as the ceremonial sprinkling of incense burnt itself out in the ancient filigreed bowl, filling the air with its perfume. As the last smoky tendrils curled up and were gone, an Acolyte stepped forward to softly shut the bowl's metal lid.

For the first time, Domaris was robed in blue, the color sacred to the Mother; her beautiful hair was braided and bound into a fillet of blue. Her heart pounded with a vast joy, touched with pride, as Micon, alerted by the faint sound of the incense burner's closing, stepped forward to address the Vested Five. Robed in simple white, with a fine golden band about his head, the Atlantean took his place before them with a sureness of step that belied his blindness.

His trained tones filled the room proudly, without being loud.

"Fathers, I am come here with this woman, my beloved, to announce and acknowledge that my chosen lady is with child, and that this child of her body is sole son of my begetting, my firstborn, and the inheritor of my name, station, and estate. I make solemn declaration of the purity of this woman, and I now swear, by the Central Fire, the Central Sun, and the Three Wings Within the Circle, that the law has been observed."

The Atlantean now took a step back, turned, and with a deliberation and economy of movement which told the Vested Five much, he knelt at Domaris's feet. "This mother and this child," Micon said, "are acknowledged under the law, in gratitude and in reverence; this, that my love not be wasted, nor my life unblessed, nor my duty unfinished. This, that I may give all honor where honor is due."

Domaris placed her hand lightly upon the crown of Micon's head. "I am come," she said, her voice ringing defiantly clear in that centuried chamber, "to announce and acknowledge my coming child as the son of this man. I, Domar—Isarma, daughter of Talkannon, declare it." She paused, coloring, abashed at having stumbled in the ritual; but the Elders did not move an eyelash, and she continued, "I further make declaration that this is the child of virginity, and the child of love; in reverence, I declare this." She now knelt beside Micon. "I act within my right under the law."

The Elder who sat at the center of the Five asked gravely, "The child's name?"

Rajasta presented the scroll with a formal gesture. "This to be placed in the archives of the Temple; I, Rajasta, have read the stars for the daughter of Talkannon, and I name her son thus: O-si-nar-men."

"What means it?" whispered Micon to Domaris, almost inaudibly, and she returned, in an undertone, "Son of Compassion."

The Elders stretched forth their hands in a gesture older than humanity, and intoned, "The budding life is acknowledged and welcome, under the law. Son of Micon and Isarma, O-si-nar-men. Be thou blessed!"

Rising slowly, Micon put out his hand to Domaris, who clasped it in her own and rose. They stood together with bent heads, as the low-voiced cadenced blessing flowed on: "Giver of Life—Bearer of Life—be thou blessed. Now and ever, blessed thou art, and blessed thy seed. Go in peace."

Domaris raised her hand in the ancient Sign of honor, and after a moment Micon followed her lead, hearing the rustling of her sleeve and remembering the instructions he had received from Rajasta. Together, with quiet humility, they left the council room—but Rajasta remained behind, for the Vested Five would wish to question him regarding specifics of the unborn child's horoscope.

In the outer vestibule, Domaris leaned against Micon's shoulder for a moment. "It is done," she whispered. "And even as I spoke, our child stirred again within me! I—I would be much with you now!"

"Beloved, thou shalt be," Micon promised tenderly; yet a wistful note shadowed his voice as he bent to kiss her. "Would that I might see thy coming glory!"

CHAPTER NINE
✠ A QUESTION OF ✠ SENTIMENT

I

Karahama, Priestess of Caratra, had judged Deoris well. In the days after Arkati's death, Deoris had indeed concentrated all her facilities upon this work she had formerly despised. Her intuitive knowledge grew into a deft sureness and skill and at the conclusion of her extra term of service, it was almost with reluctance that she prepared to leave the Temple.

Having completed the ritual purification, she went to Karahama to bid her goodbye. In the last weeks they had drawn as close as the older woman's reserve would allow, and in spite of Karahama's severe mannerisms, Deoris suddenly realized that she would miss Karahama.

After they had exchanged the usual formal exchanges, the Priestess detained Deoris a little longer. "I shall miss you," she said. "You have become skillful, my child." And while Deoris stood speechless with surprise—Karahama's praise was rare and difficult to earn—the Priestess took up a small silver disk on a fine chain. This ornament, inscribed with the sigil of Caratra, was a badge of service and achievement given eventually to every woman who served the Goddess—but it was rarely bestowed on anyone as young as Deoris. "Wear it in wisdom," said Karahama, and herself fastened the clasp about the girl's wrist. This done, she stood regarding Deoris as if she would speak further.

Karahama was a big woman, tall and deep-breasted, and imposing, with yellow cat-eyes and tawny hair. Like Talkannon, she gave the impression of an animal ferocity held in stern control; the blue robes of her rank added a certain arrogance to her natural dignity. "You are in the Scribe's school?" she asked at last.

"I left it many months ago. I have been assigned as a scribe to the Lord Micon of Ahtarrath."

Karahama's scorn withered Deoris's pride. "Any girl can do that work of reading and writing! Have you chosen to make *that* your life's work, then? Or is it your intention to follow the Lady Domaris into the Temple of Light?"

Until that very moment, Deoris had never seriously doubted that she would one day seek initiation into the Temple of Light, following in her sister's footsteps. Now, all at once, she knew that this was impossible, that it had always been impossible for her, and she said, with the first real decisiveness of her life, "No. I do not wish either of those things."

"Then," Karahama said quietly, "I believe your true place is here, in Caratra's Temple—unless you choose to join with Riveda's sect."

"The Grey-robes?" Deoris was shocked. "I, a *saji?*"

"Caratra guard you!" Karahama's hands wove a swift rune. "All Gods forbid I should send any child into that! No, my child—I meant as a Healer."

Deoris paused again, considering. She had not realized that women were admitted into the Healer sect. She said, tentatively, "I might—ask Riveda—"

Karahama chuckled lightly. "Riveda is not a very approachable man, child. Your own kinsman Cadamiri is a Healer-Priest, and it would be far easier to take up the matter with him. Riveda never troubles himself with the novices."

Her smile, for some reason, annoyed Deoris, who said, "Riveda himself once asked me whether I wished to enter the Grey Temple!"

This did have the desired effect, for Karahama's expression altered considerably, and she regarded Deoris in a curious silence before saying, "Very well then. If you wish, you may tell Riveda that I have pronounced you capable. Not that my word will carry much weight with him, but he knows my judgment to be sound on such matters."

Their talk turned to other matters; faltered and soon died away.

But, watching Deoris go, Karahama began to be disturbed. *Is it really well,* she asked herself, *to send this child in Riveda's path?* The Priestess of Caratra knew Riveda better, perhaps, than his own novices did; and she knew his motives. But Karahama threw off the disturbing thought. Deoris was nearly grown up, and would not take it kindly if Karahama were to meddle, even with the best of intentions. Riveda aroused strong feelings.

II

In the House of the Twelve, Deoris put away the bracelet and wandered idly through her rooms, feeling lonely and neglected. She wanted to make up the quarrel with Domaris, slip back into her old life, forget—for a while, at least—everything that had happened in the last few months.

The emptiness of the rooms and courts bothered her obscurely. Suddenly she stopped, staring at the cage which held her red bird. The bird lay in a queer still heap on the floor of the cage, its crimson plumage matted and crumpled. With a gasp Deoris ran to unfasten the cage door and took up the tiny corpse, cradling it in her palm with a little cry of pain.

She turned the bird helplessly on her hand, nearly crying. She had loved it, it was the last thing Domaris had given her before she began to change so—but what had happened? There was no cat to tear it— and anyhow, the tiny thing had not been mauled. Looking into the now-empty cage, she saw that the little pottery bowl inside was empty of water and there were only one or two scattered husks of seeds in the dirty litter at the bottom.

The sudden entrance of Elara startled her and Deoris, turning around, flew at the little woman in a fury. "You forgot my bird and now it's dead, dead!" she charged passionately.

Elara took a fearful step backward. "What bird do you mean? Why—I did not know—"

"Don't lie to me, you miserable slut!" Deoris cried out, and in an uncontrollable rage, she slapped Elara across the face.

"Deoris!" Shock and anger were in the voice, and Deoris, with a catch of breath, whirled to see Domaris standing, white and astonished in the doorway. "Deoris, what is the meaning of this—this performance?"

She had never spoken so roughly to Deoris before, and the girl put her hand to her mouth in sudden guilt and fear, and stood scarlet and speechless as Domaris repeated, "What is going on? Or must I ask Elara?"

Deoris burst into a flood of angry tears. "She forgot my bird, and it's dead!" she stammered, choking.

"That is neither a reason nor an excuse," Domaris said, still angry, her voice taut. "I am very sorry, Elara. My sister will apologize to you."

"To her?" Deoris said incredulously. "I will not!"

Domaris made her words come steadily, with an effort. "If you were my own child and not my sister, you should be beaten! I have never been so ashamed in my life!" Deoris turned to flee, but before she had taken more than a few steps, Domaris had grasped her wrist and held it in a tense grip. "You stay here!" she commanded. "Do you think I am going to let you disobey me?"

Deoris twisted free, white and furious; but she did stammer out the required apology.

Elara raised her serene face, the print of fingers already reddening on the tanned cheek. Her voice had its own dignity, the unshakable poise of the humble. "I am truly sorry about your bird, little mistress, but its care was not entrusted to me; I knew nothing of it. Have I ever forgotten anything you asked of me?"

When Elara had left them alone, Domaris looked at her sister almost in despair. "What has come over you, Deoris?" she said at last. "I don't know you any more."

Deoris's eyes remained sullenly fixed on the paving-stones; she had not moved since muttering her "apology" to Elara.

"Child, child," Domaris said, "I am sorry about your bird, too, but you could have a dozen for the asking. Elara has never been anything but kind to you! If she were your equal it would be bad enough, but to strike a servant!" She shook her head. "What am I going to do with you?"

Still Deoris made no reply, and Domaris looked into the open cage, with a shake of her head. "I do not know who is responsible," she said quietly, glancing back at Deoris, "but if there was negligence here, you have no one to blame but yourself."

Deoris muttered sulkily, "I haven't been here."

"That does not lessen your fault." There was no mercy in the older woman's voice. "Why did you not delegate its care directly to one of the women? You cannot blame them for neglecting a duty which no one had assigned to any one of them. Your own forgetfulness cost your pet its life! Have you no sense of responsibility?"

"Haven't I had enough to think about?" Pitiful tears began to trickle down the girl's face. "If you really cared about me, *you'd* have remembered!"

"Must I shoulder your responsibilities all your life?" Domaris retorted, in so furious a tone that Deoris actually stopped crying. Seeing her sister's shocked face, Domaris relented a little, taking the dead bird from Deoris's hands and laying it aside. "I meant what I said; you may have all the birds you wish," she promised.

"Oh, I don't care about the bird! It's *you!*" Deoris wailed, and flung her arms around Domaris, crying harder than ever. Domaris held her tight, feeling that Deoris was finally giving way to the frozen resentment she had been unable to speak before; that now perhaps they could cross that barrier which had lain between them since the night in the Star Field . . . but, finally, she had to remind her: "Gently, Deoris. Hold me not so tightly, you must not hurt us—"

Abruptly, Deoris's arms dropped to her sides and she turned away without a word.

Domaris stretched out her hand, pleading. "Deoris, don't draw away like that, I didn't mean—Deoris, can I say *nothing* that does not wound you?"

"You don't want me!" Deoris accused miserably. "You don't have to pretend."

"Oh, Deoris!" The grey eyes were misted now with tears. "How can you be jealous? How can you? Deoris, don't you know that Micon is dying? Dying! And I must stand between him and death!" Her hands clasped again, with that strange gesture, across her body. "Until our son is born—"

Blindly, Deoris caught her sister in her arms, hugging her close, anything to shut out that terrible, naked grief. Her self-pity fell away, and for the first time in her life she tasted a sorrow that was more than personal, knowing she could only try to comfort where there clearly could be no comfort, vainly try to say what she knew to be untrue . . . and for the first time, her own rebellion fell away, unimportant before her sister's tragedy.

CHAPTER TEN
✠ MEN OF PURPOSE ✠

I

With a definiteness that left no room for argument, Riveda at last informed Rajasta that his house had been set in order. Rajasta complimented him on work well done, and the Adept bowed and took his leave, a faintly derisive smile behind his heavy-lidded eyes.

The investigation into forbidden sorceries by members of his Order had lasted half a year. It had resulted in a round dozen of merited floggings for rather minor blasphemies and infringements: misuse of ceremonial objects, the wearing or display of outlasted symbols, and other similar offenses. There had also been two serious cases—not clearly connected—involving lesser Adepts who had been beaten and then expelled from the rolls of the Grey-robe sect. One had made use of certain alchemical potions to induce various otherwise blameless neophytes and *saji* to take part in acts of excessive sexual cruelty which, afterward, the victims could not even remember. In the other of these two cases, the culprit had broken into a locked shelf of the Order's private library and stolen some scrolls. This alone would have been bad enough, but it turned out that the man had been growing contagious disease cultures in his rooms. Decontamination procedures were still going on, so far with good hopes of a satisfactory outcome.

Still, all this had warned the undetected that Riveda was alert to their existence, and further progress was not likely to be easy.

For Riveda himself, the greatest reward, in some ways, was the discovery of a new field of experiment with tremendous potentials, which the Adept intended to test. The key to it was the stranger he had taken on as chela. Under hypnosis the lad revealed strange knowledge, and a stranger power—though hypnosis was necessary to make any impression on the odd apathy of the unknown, who existed (one could not say he lived) as in a shell of dark glass over which events passed as shadowy reflections, holding attention only a moment. His mind was locked away, as if from some recent horror and shame that had frozen him; but in his rare ravings he burst forth with oddly coherent words that sometimes gave Riveda clues to great things—long vistas of knowledge which Riveda himself could only glimpse were hidden in that seemingly damaged mind.

Whether the man was Micon's brother, Riveda did not know, nor did he care. He felt, quite sincerely, that any attempt to confront the two could only harm them both. Scrupulously he refrained from making serious inquiry into the chela's origin, or into the mystery of his coming to the Grey Temple.

However, Riveda did watch Micon—always casual, as became a Magician among Priests of Light; always detached, barely hovering on the edges of the Atlantean's circle of acquaintances, but studying them intently. Riveda quickly saw that for Domaris all had ceased to exist, save only Micon; he also discerned Rajasta's preoccupation with the blind Initiate, a relationship which transcended that of fellow-Priests and approached, at times, that of father and son. It was with somewhat less casualness that he watched Deoris.

Riveda did not very often agree with Rajasta, but in this case, both sensed strange potentialities in the young girl. With the coming of her womanhood, Deoris might be powerful, if she were properly taught. Yet, though he had spent much time in meditation over the question, Riveda could not quite determine exactly what potentialities he saw in her—possibly because they were many, and varied.

She seemed to be, Riveda noticed, Micon's pupil as well as his scribe. Somehow this enraged the Adept, as if Micon were usurping a privilege which should be Riveda's own. The Atlantean's impersonal and diffident guidance of the girl's thoughts impressed Riveda as fumbling, overcautious, and incompetent. In his opinion, they were holding Deoris back, where she should be allowed—even, if necessary, compelled—to open and unfold.

He watched, with detached humor, the growth of her interest in him; and, with even more amusement, the childish and stormy progress of her relationship with Chedan, an Acolyte and the pledged husband of Elis. Temple gossip (to which Riveda was not as deaf as he tried to seem) often made reference to the strained relations between Elis and Chedan. . . .

Chedan's infatuation with Deoris may have begun as an attempt, pure and simple, to spite Elis. In any case, it was now more serious than that. Whether Deoris really cared for Chedan or not—and not even Domaris pretended to know that—she accepted his attentions with gravely mischievous pleasure. Micon and Domaris watched and welcomed this new state of affairs, believing that it might bring Deoris some understanding of their own predicament, and alleviate her hostility to their love.

Riveda happened upon them one morning in an outdoor garden: Deoris, seated on the grass at Micon's feet, was sorting and caring for her writing instruments; Chedan, a slender brown-eyed stripling in the robes of an Acolyte, bent over her, smiling. Riveda was too far away to hear their words, but the two children—they were hardly more, especially in Riveda's eyes—disagreed on something. Deoris sprang up, indignant; Chedan fled in pretended terror, and Deoris raced after him, laughing.

Micon looked up at Riveda's approaching steps, and stretched out his hand in welcome—but he did not rise, and Riveda was struck anew by the ravages of pain in the blind Initiate's face. As always, because he was smitten by devastating pity, he took refuge in the mocking deference with which he masked his deepest emotions.

"Hail, Lord of Ahtarrath! Have your disciples fled from teachings over-wise? Or are you ready with a birchen rod for your neophytes?"

Micon, sensing the sarcasm, was wearily perplexed. He had genuinely tried to conquer his first wariness of Riveda, and his own failure dismayed him. Superficially, of course, Riveda was an easy man to like; yet Micon thought he could almost as easily hate this man, if he would permit himself to do so.

Now, sternly disciplining himself, Micon shrugged off Riveda's sardonic mood and instead spoke of the fevers that regularly decimated the coastal hills, and of the famine that might rage if too many men were disabled by disease and could not harvest the crops.

"It is your Healers who can do most to remedy that," he complimented, sincerely and deliberately. "I have heard of the fine work which you have done among them, Lord Riveda. These same Healers were, if I recall rightly, hardly more than corrupt charlatans, not ten years ago—"

"That would be something of an exaggeration." Riveda smiled, with the grim enjoyment of the reformer. "Yet it is true, there was much decadence in the Grey Temple when I came here. I am not of the Priest's Caste—as I would guess Rajasta has told you—I am a northman of Zaiadan; my people were common fisher folk, sea-farers after their fashion. In my land, we know that the right drugs are more efficient than the most earnest prayers, unless the illness be all in the brain. As a boy I learned the care of wounds, because I was lame in one leg and my family thought me fit for nothing else."

Micon seemed startled by this statement, and Riveda chuckled. "Oh, I was healed—never mind how—but I had learned by then there was more to the body than most Priests will ever admit—except in their cups." He chuckled again; then, sobering, went on, "And I had also learned just how much stronger the mind can be when the body is harnessed and brought under the discipline of the will. As, by that time, I had little fondness for the village of my birth, I took up my staff and wandered abroad, as they say. So I came to know of the Magicians; you call them Grey-robes here." Expressively, he shrugged, forgetful for a moment that Micon could not see him. "At last I came here, an Adept, and found among the local Order of Magicians a cult of lazy-minded mystics who masqueraded as Healers. They were not, as I have said, utter charlatans, for they had on their shelves most of the methods we employ today, but they had become decadent and careless, preferring chants and spells to honest work. So I threw them out."

"In anger?" Micon murmured, with a hint of deprecation.

"In good solid wrath," Riveda returned, with a laugh and a relishing grin. "Not to mention a few well-placed kicks. Some, in fact, I threw out bodily, only stopping to talk about it afterward . . ." He paused a moment in reflection. "Then I gathered together the few who felt as I did—both Priests of Light and Grey-robes—men who believed, like me, that the mind has healing powers of a kind, but that the body needs its treatments, too. The greatest help I had was from the Priestesses of Caratra, for they work with living women, not souls and ideals, and it is not so easy for them to forget that great truth, that bodies must be treated simply as suffering bodies. They have been using the correct methods for centuries; and now I have managed to return them to the world of men, where they are equally, if not more needed."

Micon smiled, somewhat sorrowfully. As a physician, at least, he knew he must admire Riveda; and the mental daring of Micon's own nature saluted like qualities in the Adept. *What a pity*, Micon thought, *that Riveda did not apply his high intelligence and his supreme good sense to his own life . . . what a pity that such a man must be wasted on the empty conquest of Magic!*

"Lord Riveda," he said suddenly, "your Healers are above all reproach, but some of your Grey-robes still practice self-torture. How can a man of your intelligence countenance that?"

Riveda countered, "You are of Ahtarrath; surely you know the value of—certain austerities?"

Micon's answer was to form a certain Sign with his right hand. Riveda pondered the value of returning this gesture to one who could not see—but went on, less guardedly, "Then you will know the value of sharpening the senses, raising certain mental and physical factors to a high level of awareness—without completing the pattern or releasing the tension. There are, of course, less extreme methods available, but in the end, you must concede that a man is his own master, and that which harms no one else—well, in the last analysis, there is not much one can do about it."

The Initiate's face betrayed his dissent; the thin lips seemed uncharacteristically stern. "I know that—results may be had from such procedures," he said, "but such results I call valueless. And—there is the question of your women, and the—uses—you make of them." He hesitated, trying to phrase his words in such a way as to give the least offense. "Perhaps what you do brings development, of a kind—but it can only be unbalanced, a violence to nature. You must always guard against madness within your walls, as a result."

"Madness has many causes," Riveda observed. "Yet, we Grey-robes spare our women the brutality of bearing children to satisfy our pride!"

The Atlantean ignored the insult, only asking quietly, "Have you no sons, Riveda?"

There was an appreciable pause. Riveda lowered his head, unable to rid himself of the absurd notion that this man's blind eyes saw more than his own good ones.

"We believe," Micon continued quietly, "a man shirks duty who leaves no son to follow his name. And as for your Magicians, it may be that the good they do others shall at last outmeasure the harm they do themselves. Yet one day they may set in motion causes which they themselves cannot control or set right." The twisted grin came back to Micon's face. "Yet that is but a possibility. I would not quarrel with you, Lord Riveda."

"Nor I with you," the Adept returned, and there was more than courtesy in his emphatic tone. He knew that Micon did not altogether trust him, and had no wish to make an enemy in so high a place as the Atlantean currently occupied. A word from Micon could bring the Guardians down upon the Grey Temple, and no one knew better than Riveda that certain of his Order's practices would not bear dispassionate investigation. Forbidden sorcery they might not be—but they would not meet with the approval of the stern Guardians. No, he did not want to quarrel with Micon. . . .

Deoris and Chedan, walking side by side and sedately now, rejoined them. Riveda greeted Deoris with a deference that made Chedan stare, his jaw suddenly loose and useless.

"Lord Micon," the Adept said, "I am going to take Deoris from you."

Micon's dark sightless features went rigid with displeasure, and as he turned his face toward Riveda, some ominous instinct touched the Atlantean. Tightly, he said, "Why do you say that, Riveda?"

Riveda laughed loudly. He knew very well what Micon meant, but it pleased him to misunderstand. "Why, what think you I meant?" he asked. "I must speak with the little maiden for a few minutes, for Karahama of Caratra's Temple gave me her name for admission into the Healers." Riveda laughed again. "If you think so ill of me, I will gladly speak in your presence, Prince Micon!"

A deathly weariness crept into Micon, supplanting his anger by degrees. His shoulders sagged. "I—know not what I meant. I—" He broke off, still nervous but unable to justify it even to himself. "Yes, I had heard that Deoris was to seek Initiation. I am very glad. . . . Go, my Deoris."

II

Thoughtful, Riveda drew the girl along the pathway. Deoris was sensitive, fine-grained, all nerves; instinctively he felt she belonged, not among the Healers but among the Grey-robes themselves. Many of the women of the Grey Temple were only *saji*, despised or ignored—but now and then a woman might be accepted on the Magician's Path. A few, only a few, could seek attainment on the same footing as a man, and it would be hard to make a place for Deoris among them.

"Tell me, Deoris," said Riveda suddenly, "have you served long in the House of the Mother?"

She shrugged. "Only the preliminary services which all women must do." She glanced briefly into the Adept's eyes, but looked away again as she murmured, "I worked for a month with Karahama."

"She spoke of your skill." Riveda paused. "Perhaps you are not learning this for the first time, but recovering something which you once knew, in a previous life."

Deoris raised her eyes to his once more, wonder clear to read in her face. "What do you mean?"

"I am not permitted to speak of it to a daughter of Light," said Riveda, smiling, "but you will learn of this, as you rise in the Temple. Let us talk for a minute about practical things." Aware that her shorter legs were not accustomed to his own swift stride, Riveda turned aside onto a little plaza that overlooked one of the rivulets that ran through the Temple precinct. "Karahama," the Adept continued, "tells me that you wish admission into the Healers, but there are many reasons why I do not wish to accept you at this time." He watched her out of the corner of his eye as he said this, and was vaguely gratified at her discomfort. "As a Healer," he went on, "you would remain only a child of the Temple, not a Priestess. . . . Tell me, have you yet been bound into the Path of Light?"

So rapidly had Deoris's emotions vacillated in the last minutes that at first she could only shake her head, speechless. Then, recovering her composure, she clarified, "Rajasta has said I am still too young. Domaris took no vows until she was past seventeen."

"I would not have you wait so long," Riveda demurred, "but it is true that there is no need of haste—" He fell silent again, gazing off across the plaza and into the distances beyond. At last, turning to Deoris, he said, "This is what I advise you: first, to seek initiation into the lowest grade of the Priestesses of Caratra. As you grow older, you may decide that your true place is among the Magicians—" Riveda checked her question with an imperative gesture. "I know, you do not wish to be *saji*, nor do I suggest it. However, as an Initiated Priestess of Caratra, you could rise in Her service to the highest levels—or enter the Grey Temple. Most women are not fit to attain the grade of Adept, but I believe you have inborn powers." He smiled down at her and added, "I only hope you will use them as you should."

She returned his gaze earnestly. "I don't know how—"

"But you will learn." He laid one of his hands on her shoulder. "Trust me."

"I do," she said confidingly, with the sudden realization that it was true.

In perfect seriousness, Riveda warned her, "Your Micon puts no faith in me, Deoris. Perhaps I'm not a good man to trust."

Deoris looked unhappily down at the flagstones. "Micon—Lord Micon has been so cruelly treated—perhaps he trusts no one any more," she hazarded, unable to face the idea that Micon might be right. She didn't want to believe anything unpleasant of Riveda.

The Adept let his hand fall away from her. "I will ask Karahama, then, to take you under her personal guidance," he said, with an air of dismissal. Deoris, accepting it, thanked him rather timidly and departed. Riveda stood watching her go, his arms folded on his chest, and though there was a trace of an ironic smile upon his lips, his eyes were thoughtful. Could Deoris be the woman he had visualized? No one knew better than he that the random memories of previous lives sometimes appear to one as presentiments of the future. . . . If he read this girl's character rightly, she was eager—over-eager, perhaps, even impetuous. Did she have any caution at all?

Unwilling to let his thoughts drift too far from current realities, Riveda turned on his heel and began to walk once more, his stride swiftly carrying him from the plaza. Deoris was still a little girl, and he must wait, perhaps for years, to be sure he was not mistaken—but he had made a beginning.

The Adept Riveda was not accustomed to waiting for what he wanted—but this once, it might prove worth the waiting!

CHAPTER ELEVEN
✠ OF BLESSINGS ✠ AND CURSES

I

Her hands folded meekly before her, her hair simply braided, Deoris stood before the assembled Priestesses of Caratra. She wore, for the last time, her scribe's frock, and already it felt strange.

Even while she listened with serious attention to the grave admonitions of Karahama, Deoris was scared, even panicky, her thoughts running in wistful counterpoint to the Priestess's words. From this day and hour, she would no longer be "little Deoris," but a woman who had chosen her life's work—although for years to come she would be no more than an apprenticed Priestess, even this conferred upon her the responsibilities of an adult. . . .

And now Karahama beckoned her forward. Deoris stretched forth her hands, as she had been bidden.

"Adsartha, daughter of Talkannon, called Deoris, receive from my hands these ornaments it is now thy right to wear. Use them wisely, and profane them never," Karahama adjured. "Daughter thou art to the Great Mother; daughter and sister and mother to every other woman." Into the outstretched hands Karahama placed the sacred ornaments which Deoris must wear for the rest of her life. "May these hands be blessed for the Mother's work; may they be consecrated," said Karahama, and closed Deoris's small fingers over the ritual gems, holding them closed for a moment, then Signing them with a protective gesture.

Deoris did not consider herself in any way a superstitious person, and yet she half-expected to feel the touch of some great, warm, and mystic power flowing into her—or else, that the very walls would denounce her as unworthy. But she felt nothing, only a continuing nervous tension and a slight trembling in her calves from standing almost motionless throughout the long ceremony—which, clearly, was not yet ended.

Karahama raised her arms in yet another ritual gesture, saying, "Let the Priestess Deoris be invested as befits her rank."

Mother Ysouda, the old Priestess who had brought both Domaris and Deoris into the world and who had cared for them after the death of their mother, led her away; Domaris, in the place of her mother, accompanied them into the antechamber.

First the scribe's flaxen frock was taken from her and cast into the fire; Deoris stood naked, shivering on the stones. In prescribed silence, Mother Ysouda's face too forbidding to reassure either of them, Domaris unbraided her sister's heavy hair, and the ancient Priestesses sheared it off and cast the heavy dark ringlets into the flames. Deoris blinked back tears of humiliation as she watched them burn, but she did not utter a sound; it would have been unthinkable to weep during such a ceremony. While Mother Ysouda performed the elaborate rites of purification, and of dressing the shorn and chastened Deoris in the garments of a Priestess of the lowest grade, Domaris looked on with eyes shining. She was not sorry that Deoris had chosen a different service than herself; all were aspects of the hierarchy into which they had been born, and it seemed right that Deoris should choose the service of humanity, rather than her own choice of the esoteric wisdom of Light. Seeing Deoris in the simple novice's garments, Domaris's eyes filled and spilled over with tears of joy; she felt a mother's pride in a grown child, without a mother's sorrow that the child is grown past her control.

Once Deoris had been robed in the straight sleeveless garment of blue, cross-woven with white, they bound a plain blue girdle about her waist and fastened it with a single pearl—the stone of the Great Deep, brought from the womb of earth in danger and death, and thus symbolic of childbirth. About Deoris's throat was hung an amulet of carven crystal, which she would later learn to use as both hypnotic pendulum and psychic channel when this became necessary in her work.

Thus clothed and thus adorned, she was led back to the assembled Priestesses, who had broken their solemn circle and now crowded around the girl to welcome her to their order, kissing and embracing her, congratulating her, even teasing her a little about her shorn hair. Even Mother Ysouda, stern and bony, unbent enough to reminisce with the delighted Domaris—who stood apart from the throng of blue-clad women crowding about the newcomer.

"It hardly seems that it can have been fifteen years since I first laid her in your arms!"

"What was I like?" Deoris asked curiously.

Mother Ysouda straightened herself with a dignified air. "Very much like a little red monkey," she returned, but she smiled at Deoris and Domaris lovingly. "You have lost your little one, Domaris—but soon now I shall lay another child in your arms, shall I not?"

"In only a few months," Domaris said shyly, and the old lady pressed her hand with warm affection.

II

Since Deoris's formal duties would not begin until the next day, the sisters walked back together toward the House of the Twelve. Domaris put a hand to her sister's close-cropped head with hesitant compassion. "Your lovely hair," she mourned.

Deoris shook her head, sending the short ringlets flying. "I like it," she lied recklessly. "Now I need not spend all my time plaiting and combing it—Domaris, is it so very ugly?"

Domaris saw the tremble of her sister's mouth and laughed, reassuring her quickly, "No, no, little Deoris, you grow very lovely. I think the style suits you, really—but it does make you look very little," she teased. "Chedan may ask proof that you are a woman!"

"He is welcome to such proofs as he has had already," Deoris said negligently, "but I shall not imperil my friendship with Elis for the sake of that overgrown baby!"

Domaris laughed. "You might win Elis's undying gratitude if you took Chedan from her altogether!" Her mirth evaporated as an annoyingly recurrent little thought came to trouble her again: she still did not know how Arvath really felt about the fact that she had invoked her legal freedom. Already there had been some unpleasantness, and Domaris anticipated more. She had seen how Chedan behaved when Elis had done the same thing. She hoped Arvath would be more generous, more understanding—but more and more she suspected that hope was only wishful thinking.

Frowning slightly, Domaris gave a little impatient shrug. She had made her choice, and if it involved unpleasantness, well, she would face it when the time came. Deliberately, she turned her thoughts to more immediate concerns. "Micon wished to see you after the ceremonies, Deoris. I will go and take off these tapestries," she joked, shaking the cumbersome robes which she had had to wear for the ritual, "and join you both afterward."

Deoris started. Inexplicably, the idea of confronting Micon without Domaris nearby disturbed her. "I'll wait for you," she offered.

"No," said Domaris lightly, "I think he wanted to see you alone."

III

Micon's Atlantean servants conducted her into a room which opened on a great series of terraced gardens, green with flowering trees and filled with the sound of falling waters and of the songs of many birds. These rooms were spacious and cool, as befitted apartments reserved for visitors of rank and dignity; Rajasta had spared no pains to insure the comfort of his guest.

Outlined against the window, Micon's luminous robes gave his erect, emaciated form an almost translucent look in the afternoon sunlight. As he turned his head, smiling brilliantly, Deoris caught a flash of radiant color, like an aura of sparkling, exploding brightness around his head—then it was gone, so swiftly that Deoris could only doubt the evidence of her own eyes. The instant of clairvoyant sight had made her a little dizzy, and she halted in the doorway; then regretted the pause, for Micon heard her and moved painfully toward her.

"Is it you, my little Deoris?"

At hearing his voice, her lingering nervousness vanished; she ran and knelt before him. He grinned down at her crookedly. "And I must not call you *little Deoris* now, they have told me," he teased, and laid his hand, thin and blue-veined, on her head; then moved it in surprise. "They have cut off your pretty hair! Why?"

"I don't know," she said shyly, rising. "It is the custom."

Micon smiled in puzzlement. "How odd," he murmured. "I have always wondered—are you like Domaris? Is your hair fiery, like hers?"

"No, my hair is black as night. Domaris is beautiful, I am not even pretty," said Deoris, without subterfuge.

Micon laughed a little. "But Domaris has said the same of you, child—that you are lovely and she is quite plain!" He shrugged. "I suppose sisters are always so, if they love one another. But I find it hard to picture you to myself, and I feel I have lost my little scribe— and indeed I have, for you will be far too busy to come to me!"

"Oh, Micon, truly I am sorry for that!"

"Never mind, puss. I am glad—not to lose you, but that you have found the work which will lead you to Light."

She corrected him hesitantly. "I am not to be a Priestess of Light, but of the Mother."

"But you are yourself a daughter of Light, my Deoris. There is Light in you, more than you know, for it shines clearly. I have seen it, though these eyes are blind." Again he smiled. "But enough of this; I am sure you have heard quite enough vague exhortations for one day! I know you may not wear ornaments while you are only an apprentice Priestess, but I have a gift for you . . ." He turned, and from a table beside him took up a tiny statuette: a little cat, carved from a single piece of green jade, sitting back on sleek haunches, topaz eyes winking comically at Deoris. About his neck was a collar of green stones, beautifully cut and polished. "The cat will bring you luck," he said, "and when you are the Priestess Adsartha, and no longer forbidden to wear gems and ornaments—" Deftly, Micon unclasped the collar of gems. "See, Master Cat will lend you his collar for a bracelet, if your wrist be still as dainty as now." Taking her slim hand in his, he slipped the circlet of stones for a moment over her wrist; then removed it, laughing. "But I must not tempt you to break your vow," he added, and clasped the ornament about the cat's throat again.

"Micon, it's lovely!" Deoris cried, enchanted.

"And therefore, it could only belong to you, little one—my beloved little sister," he repeated, his voice lingering for a moment on the words; then he said, "Until Domaris comes, let us walk in the garden."

The lawns were shadowy and cool, although the summer greens were parched now and yellow. The great tree where they had so often sat during the summer was dry, with clusters of hard bright berries among the branches—but the fine gritty dust did not penetrate to there, and the trees filtered out the burning glare of the sun somewhat. They found their old seat, and Deoris dropped to the dry grass, letting her head rest lightly against Micon's knees as she looked up at him. Surely the bronzed face was thinner—more drawn with pain.

"Deoris," he said, his odd smile coming and going like summer lightning, "your sister has missed you." His tone was not reproachful, but Deoris felt guilty crimsons bannering her cheeks.

"Domaris doesn't need me now," she muttered.

Micon's touch on her shorn curls was very tender. "You are wrong, Deoris, she needs you now more than ever—needs your understanding, and—your love. I would not intrude on what is personal between you—" He felt her stir jealously beneath his hand. "No, wait, Deoris. Let me tell thee something." He shifted restlessly, as if he would have preferred to speak standing; but an odd look crossed his mobile features, and he remained where he was. "Deoris, listen to me. I shall not live much longer."

"Don't say that!"

"I must, little sister." A shadow of regret deepened the Atlantean's resonant voice. "I shall live—perhaps—until my son is born. But I want to know that—afterward—Domaris will not be altogether alone." His mutilated hands, scarred but thin and gentle, touched her wet eyes. "Darling, don't cry—I love you very dearly, little Deoris, and I do feel I can trust Domaris to you. . . ."

Deoris could not force herself to speak, or move, but only gazed up into Micon's sightless eyes as if transfixed.

With a ghastly emphasis, the Atlantean went on, "I am not so much in love with life that I could not bear to leave it!" Then, as if conscious that he had frightened her, the terrible self-mockery slowly faded from his face. "Promise me, Deoris," he said, and touched her lips and breast in a curious symbolic gesture she did not understand for many years.

"I promise," she whispered, crying.

The man closed his eyes and leaned back against the great tree's broad trunk. Speaking of Domaris had weakened the fiercely-held control to which he owed his life, and he was human enough to be terrified. Deoris saw the shadow that crossed his face and gasping, sprang up.

"Micon!" she cried out, fearfully bending close to him. He raised his head, perspiration breaking out upon his brow, and choked out a few words in a language Deoris could not comprehend. "Micon," she said gently, "I can't understand—"

"Again it comes!" he gasped. "I felt it on the Night of Nadir, reaching for me—some deadly evil—" He leaned against her shoulder, heavy, limp, breathing with a forced endurance. "*I will not!*" he shrieked, as if in reply to some unseen presence—and the words were harsh, rasping, utterly unlike his usual tone, even in extremity.

As Deoris drew him into her arms, unable to think of anything else to do, she suddenly found herself supporting all of his weight. He slipped down, almost insensible but holding to consciousness with what seemed must be his last wisps of strength.

"Micon! What shall I do?"

He tried to speak again, but his command of her language had deserted him again, and he could only mutter broken phrases in the Atlantean tongue. Deoris felt very young, and terrified: she had had some training, of course, but nothing that prepared her for this—and the wisdom of love was not in her arms; the very strength of her frightened embrace was cruel to Micon's pain-wracked body. Moaning, he twitched away from her, or tried to; swaying, he would have fallen precipitously had the girl not held him upright. She tried to support him more gently, but fingers of freezing panic were squeezing at her throat; Micon looked as if he were dying, and she dared not even leave him to summon aid! The feeling of helplessness only added to her terror.

She uttered a little scream as a shadow fell across them, and another's arms lifted the burden of Micon's weight abruptly from her young shoulders.

"Lord Micon," said Riveda firmly, "how can I assist you?"

Micon only sighed, and went limp in the Grey-robe's arms. Riveda glanced at Deoris, his stern, sharp face appraising her coolly, as if to make certain she was not about to faint.

"Good Gods," the Adept murmured, "has he been this way for long?" He did not wait for her answer, but easily rose to his feet, bearing the wasted form of the blind man without apparent effort. "I had better take him at once to his rooms. Merciful Gods, the man weighs no more than you! Deoris, come with me; he may need you."

"Yes," Deoris said, the flush of her embarrassment at her previous terror fading. "I will show you the way," she said, rushing ahead of Riveda and up the path.

Behind them, Riveda's chela sought his master with dull, empty eyes. A flicker of life momentarily brightened their flatness as they observed Micon. Moving noiselessly at Riveda's heels, the chela's face was a troubled emptiness, like a slate wiped imperfectly with a half-dampened sponge.

As they entered Micon's suite, one of the Atlantean servants cried out, running to help Riveda lay the unconscious man upon his bed. The Grey-robe Adept gave a swift succession of low-voiced orders, then set about applying restoratives.

Mute and frightened, Deoris stood at the foot of the bed. Riveda had forgotten her existence; the Adept's whole intense attention was concentrated on the man he was tending. The chela ghosted into the room on feet more silent than a cat's, and stood uncertainly by the doorway.

The blind man stirred on the bed, moaned deliriously, and muttered something in the Atlantean tongue; then, quite suddenly, in a low and startlingly clear voice, he said, "Do not be afraid. They can only kill us, and if we submit to them we would be better dead—" He emitted another groan of agony, and Deoris, sickened, clutched at the high bed-frame.

The chela's staring eyes found Micon, and the dulled glance widened perceptibly. He made an odd sound, half gasp, half whimper.

"Be quiet!" Riveda snarled, "or get out!"

Beneath the Grey-robe's gently restraining hands, Micon moved: first a stir, as of returning consciousness—then he writhed, groping, his head jerking backward in a convulsive movement, his whole body arching back in horror as the twisted hands made terrible clutching movements; suddenly Micon screamed, a high shrill scream of agonized despair.

"*Reio-ta! Reio-ta!* Where are you? What are you? *They have blinded me!*"

The chela stood twitching, as if blasted by lightning and unable to flee. "Micon!" he shrieked. His hands lifted, clenched, and he took one step—then the impulse died, the spark faded, and the chela's hands fell, lax-fingered, to his sides.

Riveda, who had raised his head in sharp question, saw that the chela's face was secret with madness, and with a shake of his head, the Adept bent again to his task.

Micon stirred again, but this time less violently. After a moment he murmured, "Rajasta—"

"He will come," said Riveda, with unwonted gentleness, and raised his head to the Atlantean servant, who stood staring at the chela with wide, unbelieving eyes. "Find the Guardian, you fool! I don't care where or how, *go and find him!*" The words left no room for argument or hesitation; the servant turned and went at a run, only pausing to cast a furtive quick look at the chela.

Deoris, who had stood motionless and rigid throughout, suddenly swayed, clutching with wooden hands at the high bed-frame, and would have fallen—but the chela stepped swiftly forward and held her upright, his arm about her waist. It was the first rational action anyone had yet seen from him.

Riveda covered his start of surprise with harsh asperity. "Are you all right, Deoris? If you feel faint, sit down. I have no leisure to attend to you, too."

"Of course I am all right," she said, and pulled herself away from the grey-clad chela in fastidious disgust. How dared this half-wit touch her!

Micon murmured, "My little Deoris—"

"I am here," she assured him softly. "Shall I send Domaris to you?"

He gave a barely perceptible nod, and Deoris went quickly before Riveda could make a move to prevent her; Domaris must be warned, she must not come unexpectedly upon Micon when he was like this!

Micon gave a restless sigh. "Is that—Riveda? Who else is here?"

"No one, Lord of Ahtarrath," Riveda lied compassionately. "Try to rest."

"No one else?" The Atlantean's voice was weak, but surprised. "I—I don't believe it. I felt—"

"Deoris was here, and your servant. They have gone now," said Riveda with quiet definiteness. "You were wandering in your mind, I think, Prince Micon."

Micon muttered something incomprehensible before the weary voice faded again, and the lines of pain around his mouth reappeared, as if incised there by words he could not utter. Riveda, having done all he could, settled himself to watch—glancing, from time to time, at the blank-faced chela.

It was not long before the rustling of stiff robes broke into the near silence, and Rajasta practically brushed Riveda aside as he bent over Micon. His face had a look no one else ever saw. Wonder and question mingled in his voice as he spoke the Adept's name.

"I would that I might do more," Riveda answered, with grave emphasis, "but no living man can do that." Rising to his feet, the Grey-robe added softly, "In his present state, he does not seem to trust me." He looked down at Micon regretfully, continuing, "But at any hour, night or day, I am at your service—and his."

Rajasta glanced up curiously, but he was already alone with Micon. Casting all other thoughts from his mind, the Priest of Light knelt by the bedside, taking Micon's thin wrists carefully in his hands, gently infusing his own strengthening energies into the depleted and flickering spirit of the half-sleeping Atlantean. . . . Hearing steps, Rajasta came out of his meditation, and motioned for Domaris to approach and take his place.

As Rajasta lifted one hand, however, Micon stirred again, whispering with an effort, "Was—someone else—here?"

"Only Riveda," said Rajasta in surprise, "and a half-wit he calls his chela. Rest, my brother—Domaris is here."

At Rajasta's answer to his question, a frown had crossed Micon's face—but at mention of Domaris, all other thoughts fled. "Domaris!" he sighed, and his hand groped for hers, his taut features relaxing.

Yet Rajasta had seen that frown, and immediately divined its significance. The Priest of Light's nostrils flared wide in disdain. There was something very wrong about Riveda's chela, and Rajasta resolved to find out what it was at the earliest opportunity.

IV

Micon slept, at last, and Domaris slipped down on the floor beside his bed in a careful, listening stillness—but Rajasta bent and gently raised her up, drawing her a little distance away, where his whispered words would not disturb the sleeping man.

"Domaris, you must go, daughter. He would never forgive me if I let you spend your strength."

"You—you will send for me if he wakes?"

"I will not promise even that." He looked in her eyes, and saw exhaustion there. "For his son's sake, Domaris. Go!"

Thus admonished, the girl obediently departed; it was growing late, and the moon had risen, silvering the dried foliage and wrapping the fountains in a luminous mist. Domaris went carefully and slowly, for her body was heavy now, and she was not altogether free of pain.

Abruptly a pale shadow darkened the pathway, and the girl drew a frightened breath as Riveda's tall broad figure barred her way; then let it out, in foolish relief, as the Adept stepped aside to let her pass. She bowed her head courteously to him, but the man did not respond; his eyes, cold with the freezing fire of the Northern lights, were searching her silently and intently. Then, as if compelled, he uncovered his head and bent before her in a very ancient gesture of reverence.

Domaris felt the color drain from her face, and the pounding of her heart was very loud against her ribs. Again the Grey-robe inclined his head—this time in casual courtesy—and drew the long skirt of his cowled robe aside so that she might pass him with more ease. When she remained standing, white and shaken, in the middle of the pathway, the ghost of a smile touched Riveda's face, and he moved past her, and was gone.

It was perfectly clear to Domaris that the Adept's reverence had been directed, not toward her personally, nor even to the rank betrayed by her Initiate's robes, but to the fact of her incipient maternity. Yet this raised more questions than it answered: what had prompted Riveda to bestow upon her this high and holy salutation? It occurred to Domaris that she would have been less frightened if the Adept of the Grey-robes had struck her.

Slowly, thoughtfully, she continued on her way. She knew very little of the Grey Temple, but she had heard that its Magicians worshipped the more obvious manifestations of the life-force. Perhaps, standing like that in the moonlight, she had resembled one of their obscenely fecund statues! Ugh, what a thought! It made her laugh wildly, in the beginnings of hysteria, and Deoris, crossing the outer corridor of the House of the Twelve, heard the strained and unnatural laughter, and hurried to her in sudden fright.

"Domaris! What's wrong, why are you laughing like that?"

Domaris blinked, the laughter choking off abruptly. "I don't know," she said, blankly.

Deoris looked at her, distressed. "Is Micon—"

"Better. He is sleeping. Rajasta would not let me stay," Domaris explained. She felt tired and depressed, and longed for sympathetic companionship, but Deoris had already turned away. Tentatively, Domaris said, "Puss—"

The girl turned around and looked at her sister. "What is it?" she inquired, with a shade of impatience. "Do you want something?"

Domaris shook her head. "No, nothing, kitten. Good night." She leaned forward and kissed her sister's cheek, then stood watching as Deoris, released, darted lightly away. Deoris was growing very fast in these last weeks . . . it was only natural, Domaris thought, that she should grow away from her sister. Still she frowned a little, wondering, as Deoris disappeared down the passageway.

At the time when Deoris had made known her decision to seek initiation into Caratra's Temple, she had also been assigned—as befitted a girl her age—separate apartments of her own. Since she was still technically under the guardianship of Domaris, those apartments were here, in the House of the Twelve, and near those of Domaris, but not adjacent to them. Domaris took it for granted that all the Acolytes mingled casually, without considering the strictures usually accepted outside: there was an excellent reason for this freedom, and it really meant very little. Nothing could be kept secret from the Acolytes, and everyone knew that Chedan slept sometimes in Deoris's rooms. How little that meant, Domaris knew; since her thirteenth year Domaris had passed many nights, quite innocently, with Arvath, or some other boy at her side. It was acceptable behaviour, and Domaris detested herself for the malice of her suspicion. After all, Deoris was now fifteen . . . if the two *were* actually lovers, well, that too was permissible. Elis had been even younger when her daughter was born.

As if their minds ran along similar paths, Elis herself suddenly joined Domaris in the hallway. "Is Deoris angry with me?" Elis asked. "She passed me without a word just now."

Domaris, dismissing her worries, laughed. "No—but she does take growing up very seriously! I am sure that tonight she feels older than Mother Lydara herself!"

Elis chuckled in sympathy. "I had forgotten, her ceremony was today. So! Now she is a woman, and a postulant of Caratra's Temple; and perhaps Chedan—" At the look on her cousin's face, Elis sobered and said, "Don't look like that, Domaris. Chedan won't do her any harm, even if—well, you and I would have no right to criticize."

Domaris's face, in its halo of coppery hair, was pale and strained. "But Deoris is so very young, Elis!"

Elis snorted lightly. "You have always babied her much too much, Domaris. She is grown up! And—we both chose for ourselves. Why deny her that privilege?"

Domaris looked up, with a heartbreaking smile. "You do understand, don't you," she said; and it was not a question.

Brusquely, to hide her feelings (Elis did not often display emotion), she took Domaris by the wrist and half pulled, half pushed her cousin into her room, propelled Domaris to a divan and sat down beside her. "You don't have to tell me anything," she said. "Remember, I know what you are living through." Her gentle face recalled humiliation and tenderness and pain. "I have known it all, Domaris. It does take courage, to be a complete person. . . ."

Domaris nodded. Elis *did* understand.

A woman had this right, under the Law, and indeed, in the old days it had been rare for a woman to marry before she had proven her womanhood by bearing a child to the man of her choice. The custom had gradually fallen into disuse; few women these days invoked the ancient privilege, disliking the inevitable accompaniment of curious rumors and speculations.

Elis asked, "Does Arvath know yet?"

Domaris shivered unexpectedly. "I don't know—he hasn't spoken of it—I suppose he must," she said, with a nervous smile. "He's not stupid."

Arvath had maintained a complete and stony silence in the last weeks, whenever he came into the presence of his pledged wife. They appeared together when custom demanded, or as their Temple duties brought them into contact; otherwise he let her severely alone. "But I haven't told him in so many words—Oh, Elis!"

The dark girl, in a rare gesture of affection, laid her soft hand over Domaris's. "I—am sorry," she said shyly. "He can be cruel. Domaris . . . forgive me for asking. Is it Arvath's child?"

Silently, but indignantly, Domaris shook her head. That *was* forbidden. A woman might choose a lover, but if she and her affianced husband possessed one another before marriage, it was considered a terrible disgrace; such haste and precipitancy would be cause enough for dismissing both from the Acolytes.

Elis's lovely face showed both relief and a residual disturbance. "I could not have believed it of you," she said, then added softly, "I know it to be untrue, but I have heard whispers in the courts—forgive me, Domaris, I know you detest such gossip, but—but they believe it is Rajasta's child!"

Domaris's mouth worked soundlessly for a moment before she covered her face with her hands and rocked to and fro in misery. "Oh, Elis," she wept, "how could they!" *That,* then, was the reason for the cold looks and the whispers behind her back. Of course! Such a thing would have been shame unutterable and unspeakable; of all the forbidden relationships in the Temple, the spiritual incest with one's Initiator was the most unthinkable. The bond of Priest and disciple was fixed as immutably as the paths of the stars. "How can they think such a thing?" Domaris sobbed, desolately. "My son's name, and the name of his father, have been acknowledged before the Vested Five, and the entire Temple!"

Elis turned furiously crimson, shamed at the turn their conversation had taken. "I know," she whispered, "but—he who acknowledges a child is not always the true father. . . . Chedan acknowledged my Lissa, when we had never shared a single couch. I have heard it said—that—it is only because Rajasta is Guardian that he has not been scourged from the Temple, because he seduced you—"

Domaris's sobs became hysterical.

Elis regarded her cousin, frightened. "You must not cry like that, Domaris! You will make yourself ill, and injure your child!"

Domaris made an effort to control herself, and said helplessly, "How can they be so cruel?"

"I—I—" Elis's hands twisted nervously, fluttering like caged wild birds. "I should not have told you, it is only filthy gossip, and—"

"No! If there is more, tell me! It is best I should hear it from you." Domaris wiped her eyes and said, "I know you love me, Elis. I would rather hear it all from you."

It took a little while, but at last Elis relented. "Arvath it was who said this—that Micon was Rajasta's friend, and would take on himself the burden—that it was a deception so transparent that it was rotten. He said Micon was only a wreck of a man, and—and could not have fathered your child—" She stopped again, appalled, for Domaris's face was white even to the lips, except for two spots of hectic crimson which seemed painted on her cheeks.

"Let him say that to me," said Domaris in a low and terrible voice. "Let him say that honestly to my face, instead of sneaking behind me like the craven filth he is if he can think such rottenness! Of all the filthy, foul, disgusting—" She stopped herself, but she was shaking.

"Domaris, Domaris, he meant it not, I am sure," Elis protested, frightened.

Domaris bent her head, feeling her anger die, and something else take its place. She knew Arvath's sudden, reckless jealousies—and he had had some provocation. Domaris hid her face in her hands, feeling soiled by the touch of tongues, as if she had been stripped naked and pelted with manure. She could hardly breathe under the weight of shame. What she had . . . discovered, with Micon, was sacred! This, *this* was defilement, disgrace.

Elis looked at her in helpless, pained compassion. "I did wrong to tell you, I knew I should not."

"No, you did right," said Domaris steadily. Slowly she began once more to recover her self-control. "See? I will not let it trouble me." She would confess it to Rajasta, of course; he could help her bear it, help her to learn to live with this shameful thought—but no word or breath of this should ever reach Micon's ear. Dry-eyed now, she looked into Elis's eyes and said softly, "But warn Arvath to guard his tongue; the penalty for slander is not light!"

"So I have reminded him already," Elis murmured; then looked away from Domaris, biting her lip. "But—if he is too cruel—or if he makes a scene which embarrasses you—ask one question of him." She paused, drawing breath, as if afraid of what she was about to say. "Ask Arvath why he left me to throw myself on Chedan's mercy, to face the Vested Five alone, lest my Lissa be born one of the *no people.*"

In shocked silence, Domaris slowly took Elis's hand and pressed it. So *Arvath* was Lissa's father! That explained many things; his insane jealousy was rooted deep in guilt. Only the fact that everyone knew for a certainty that Chedan had not truly fathered Elis's child had allowed him to honorably acknowledge the child—and even so, it could not have been an easy decision for him to have made. And that Arvath had let this happen!

"Elis, I never guessed!"

Elis smiled ever so slightly. "I made sure you would not," she said coolly.

"You should have told me," Domaris murmured distractedly. "Perhaps I could have—"

Elis stood up to move restlessly about the room. "No, you could have done nothing. There was no need to involve you. Actually, I'm almost sorry I told you now! After all, you will have to marry the—the worthless fool, someday!" There was wrath and shadowy regret in Elis's eyes, and Domaris said no more. Elis had confided in her, she had given Domaris a powerful weapon which might, one day, serve to protect her child against Arvath's jealousy—but that gave Domaris no right to pry.

Nevertheless, she could not help wishing that she had known of this before. At one time, she had had influence enough with Arvath that she could have persuaded him to accept his responsibility. Elis had humiliated herself to give her child caste—and Chedan had not been pleasant about the matter, for they had risked much.

Domaris knew herself well enough to realize that only the greatest extremity could bring her to use this powerful weapon against Arvath's malice. But her new understanding of his underlying cowardice helped her to regain her perspective in the matter.

They talked of other things, until Elis clapped her hands softly and Simila brought Lissa to her. The child was now past two, and beginning to talk; in fact, she chattered and babbled incessantly, and at last Elis gave her a tiny exasperated shake. "Hush, mistress tongue-loose," she admonished, and told Domaris acidly, "What a nuisance she is!"

Domaris was not fooled, however, noting the tenderness with which Elis handled the tiny girl. A vagrant thought came to trouble her: did Elis still love Arvath? After all that had happened, it seemed extremely unlikely—but there was, beyond any imaginable denial, an unbreakable bond between them . . . and always would be.

Smiling, Domaris held out her arms to Lissa. "She grows more like you every day, Elis," she murmured, taking the little girl up and holding the small, wriggling, giggling body to her breast.

"I hope she is a finer woman," Elis retorted, half speaking to herself.

"She could not be more understanding," said Domaris, and released the heavy child, smiling tiredly. Leaning back, with a gesture now familiar, Domaris pressed one hand against her body.

"Ah, Domaris!" With an excess of tenderness, Elis caught Lissa to her. "*Now* you know!"

And Domaris bowed her head before the dawning knowledge.

V

All through the quiet hours of the night Rajasta sat beside Micon, rarely leaving his side for more than the briefest moment. The Atlantean slept fitfully, twitching and muttering in his native tongue as if the pains that sleep could ease were only replaced with other pains, deeper and less susceptible of treatment, a residue of anguish that gnawed its way deeper into Micon's tortured spirit with every passing moment. The pallor of false dawn was stealing across the sky when Micon moved slightly and said in a low, hoarse voice, "Rajasta—"

The Priest of Light bent close to him. "I am here, my brother."

Micon struggled to raise himself, but could not summon the strength. "What hour is it?"

"Shortly before dawn. Lie still, my brother, and rest!"

"I must speak—" Micon's voice, husky and weak as it was, had a resoluteness which Rajasta recognized, and would brook no argument. "As you love me, Rajasta, stop me not. Bring Deoris to me."

"*Deoris?*" For a moment Rajasta wondered if his friend's reason had snapped. "At this hour? Why?"

"Because I ask it!" Micon's voice conceded nothing. Rajasta, looking at the stubborn mouth, felt no desire to argue. He went, after encouraging Micon to lie back, and hoard his strength.

Deoris returned with him after a little delay, bewildered and disbelieving, dressed after a fashion; but Micon's first words banished her drowsy confusion, for he motioned her close and said, without preliminaries, "I need your help, little sister. Will you do something for me?"

Hardly hesitating, Deoris replied at once, "Whatever you wish."

Micon had managed to raise himself a little on one elbow, and now turned his face full toward her, with that expression which gave the effect of keen sight. His face seemed remote and stern as he asked, "Are you a virgin?"

Rajasta started. "Micon," he began.

"There is more here than you know!" Micon said, with unusual force. "Forgive me if I shock you, *but I must know;* I have my reason, be sure of that!"

Before the Atlantean's unexpected vehemence, Rajasta retreated. For her part, Deoris could not have been more surprised if everyone in the room had turned into marble statuary, or removed their heads to play a game of ball with them.

"I am, Lord," she said, shyness and curiosity mixing in her tone.

"The Gods be praised," said Micon, pulling himself more upright on his bed. "Rajasta, go you to my travel chest; within you will find a bag of crimson silk, and a bowl of silver. Fill that bowl with clear water from a spring. Spill no drop upon the earth, and be sure that you return before the sun touches you."

Rajasta stared at him stiffly a moment, surprised and highly displeased, for he guessed Micon's intention; but he went to the chest, found the bowl, and departed, his mouth tightly clenched with disapproval; *for no one else,* he told himself, *would I do this thing!*

They awaited the Priest of Light's return in nearly complete silence, for though Deoris at first pressed him to tell her his intentions, Micon would only say that she would soon know, and that if she did not trust him, she was not bound to do as he asked.

At last Rajasta returned, and Micon directed, in a low voice, "Place it here, on this little table—good. Now, take from the chest that buckle of woven leather, and give it to Deoris—Deoris, take it from his hand, but touch not his fingers!" Once this had been done, and Micon had in his own hands the bag of crimson silk, the Atlantean went on, "Now, Deoris, kneel at my side; Rajasta, go you and stand afar from us—*let not ever your shadow touch Deoris!*"

Micon's mutilated fingers were unsteady as he fumbled with the knot, unfastening the red silk. There was a short pause, and then, holding his hands so that Rajasta could not see what was between them, he said quietly, "Deoris—look at what I have in my hands."

Rajasta, watching in stiff disapproval, caught only a momentary but almost blinding flash of something bright and many-coloured. Deoris sat motionless, no longer fidgeting, her hands quiet on the hand-woven leather buckle—a clumsily-made thing, obviously the work of an amateur in leatherwork. Gently, Micon said, "Look into the water, Deoris. . . ."

The room was very still. Deoris's pale blue dress fluttered a little in the dawn breeze. Rajasta continued to fight back an unwonted anger; he disliked and distrusted such magic—such games were barely permissible when practiced by the Grey-robes, but for a Priest of Light to dabble in such manipulations! He knew he had no right to prevent this, but much as he loved Micon, in that moment, had the Atlantean been a whole man, Rajasta might have struck him and walked out, taking Deoris with him. The Guardian's severe code, however, allowed no such interference; he merely tightened his shoulders and looked forbidding—which, of course, had no effect whatever upon the Atlantean Prince.

"Deoris," Micon said softly, "what do you see?"

The girl's voice sounded childish, unmodulated. "I see a boy, dark and quick . . . dark-skinned, dark-haired, in a red tunic . . . barefoot . . . his eyes are grey—no, they are yellow. He is weaving something in his hands . . . it is the buckle I am holding."

"Good," Micon said quietly, "you have the Sight. I recognize your vision. Now put down the buckle, and look into the water again . . . *where is he now, Deoris?*"

There was a long silence, during which Rajasta gritted his teeth and counted slowly to himself the passing seconds, keeping silence by force of will.

Deoris sat still, looking into the basin of silvery water, surprised and a little scared. She had expected some kind of magical blankness; instead, Micon was just talking in an ordinary voice, and she—she was seeing pictures. They were like daydreams; was that what he wanted? Uncertain, she hesitated, and Micon said, with a little impatience, "Tell me what you see!"

Haltingly, she said, "I see a little room, walled in stone . . . a cell—no, just a little grey room with a stone floor and stone half way to the ceiling. He—he lies on a blanket, asleep . . ."

"Where is he? *Is he in chains?*"

Deoris made a startled movement. The pictures dissolved, ran before her eyes. Only rippling water filled the bowl. Micon breathed hard and forced his impatience under control. "Please, look and tell me where his is now," he asked gently.

"He is not in chains. He is asleep. He is in the—he is turning. His face—ah!" Deoris's voice broke off in a strangled cry. "Riveda's chela! The madman, the apostate—oh, send him away send him—" The words jerked to a stop and she sat frozen, her face a mask of horror. Micon collapsed weakly, fighting to raise himself again.

Rajasta could hold himself aloof no longer. His pent-up emotion suddenly exploded into violence; he strode forward, wrenched the bowl from Deoris's hands and flung its contents from the window, hurling the bowl itself into a corner of the room, where it fell with a harsh musical sound. Deoris slid to the floor, sobbing noiselessly but in great convulsive spasms that wrenched her whole body, and Rajasta, stooping over her, said curtly, "Stop that!"

"Gently, Rajasta," Micon muttered. "She will need—"

"I know what she will need!" Rajasta straightened, glanced at Micon, and decided that Deoris's need was more imperative. He lifted the girl to her feet, but she drooped on his arm. Rajasta, grimly angry, signalled to his slave and commanded, "Summon the Priest Cadamiri, at once!"

It was not more than a minute or two before the white-robed form of a Priest of Light, spare and erect, came with disciplined step from a nearby room; Cadamiri had been readying himself for the Ceremony of Dawn. Tall and gaunt, the Priest Cadamiri was still young: but his severe face was lined and ascetic. His stern eyes immediately took in the scene: the fainting child, the fallen silver bowl, Rajasta's grim face.

Rajasta, in a voice so low that even Micon's sharp ears could not hear, said, "Take Deoris to her room, and tend her."

Cadamiri raised a questioning eyebrow as he took the swooning girl from Rajasta's arms. "Is it permitted to ask—?"

Rajasta glanced toward Micon, then said slowly, "Under great need, she was sent out over the Closed Places. You will know how to bring her back to herself."

Cadamiri hefted the sagging, half-lifeless weight of Deoris, and turned to carry her from the room, but Rajasta halted him. "Speak not of this! I have sanctioned it. Above all—say no word to the Priestess Domaris! Speak no falsehood to her, but see that she learns not the truth. Refer her to me if she presses you."

Cadamiri nodded and went, Deoris cradled in his arms like a small child—but Rajasta heard him mutter sternly, "What need could be great enough to sanction *this?*"

And to himself, Rajasta murmured, "I wish I knew!" Turning back to the racked figure of the Atlantean, he stood a moment, thoughtful. Micon's desire to learn the fate of his brother Reio-ta was understandable, but to put Deoris at hazard thus!

"I know what you are thinking," Micon said, tiredly. "You ask yourself why, if I had this method at my disposal, I did not use it earlier—or under more closely guarded auspices."

"For once," said Rajasta, his tone still curt, biting back anger, "you misread my thoughts. I am in fact wondering why you dabble in such things at all!"

Micon eased himself back against his cushions, sighing. "I make no excuses, Rajasta. I had to know. And—and your methods had failed. Do not fear for Deoris. I know," he said, waving a hand weakly as Rajasta began to speak again, "I know, there is some danger; but no more than she was in before, no more than you or Domaris are in— no more than my own unborn child, or any other who is near to me. Trust me, Rajasta. I know full well what I did—better than you, or you would not feel as you do."

"Trust you?" Rajasta repeated. "Yes, I trust you; else I would not have permitted this at all. Yet it was not for such a purpose that I became your disciple! I will honor my vow to you—but you must make compact with me, too, for as Guardian I can permit no more of this—this *sorcery!* Yes, you are right, we were all in danger merely by keeping you among us—but now you have given that danger a clearer focus! You have learned what you sought to know, and so I will forgive it; but had I known beforehand exactly what you intended—"

Micon laughed suddenly, unexpectedly. "Rajasta, Rajasta," he said, calming himself, "you say you trust me, and yet at the same time that you do not! But you say nothing of Riveda!"

CHAPTER TWELVE
✠ LIGHTS HOSTAGE ✠

I

Only the comparatively few high Initiates of the Priesthood of Light were admitted to this ceremony, and their white mantles made a ghostly gleaming in the shadowed chamber. The seven Guardians of the Temple were gathered together, but the sacred regalia upon their breasts was shrouded in swathes of silvery veilings, and all save Rajasta were hooded, their mantles drawn so closely over their heads that it was impossible to ascertain whether men or women stood there. As Guardian of the Outer Gate, Rajasta alone wore his blazoning clear to see on his breast, the symbol gleaming visible about his brow.

Laying his hand on Micon's arm, Rajasta said softly, "She comes."

Micon's haggard face became radiant, and Rajasta felt—not for the first time—the stab of an almost painful hope, as Micon asked eagerly, "How looks she?"

"Most beautiful," Rajasta returned, and his eyes dwelt on his Acolyte. "Robed in stainless white, and crowned with that flaming hair—as if in living light."

Indeed, Domaris had never seemed more beautiful. The shimmering robes lent her a grace and dignity that was new and yet wholly her own, and her coming motherhood, perfectly noticeable, was not yet a disfigurement. Her loveliness seemed such a visible radiance that Rajasta murmured softly, "Aye, Micon: light-crowned in truth."

The Atlantean sighed. "If I might—only once—behold her," he said, and Rajasta touched his arm in sympathy; but there was no time for further speech, for Domaris had advanced, and knelt before the high seat of the Guardians.

At the foot of the altar the eldest of the Guardians, Ragamon, now aged and grey but still erect with a serene dignity, stood with his hands outstretched to bless the kneeling woman. "Isarma, Priestess of Light, Acolyte to the Holy Temple; Isarma, daughter of Talkannon; vowed to the Light and to the Life that is Light, do you swear by the Father of Light and the Mother of Life, ever to uphold the powers of Life and of Light?" The old Guardian's voice, thin now, almost quavering, still held a vibrant power that clanged around the hewn rock of the chamber, and his narrowed eyes were clear and sharp as they studied the uplifted face of the white-clad woman. "Do you, Isarma, swear that, fearing nothing, you will guard the Light, and the Temple of Light, and the Life of the Temple?"

"I do so swear," she said, and stretched her hands toward the altar—and at that moment a single ray of sunlight lanced the gloom, kindling the pulsing golden light upon the altar. Even Rajasta was always impressed by this part of the rite—although he knew that a simple lever, operated by Cadamiri, had but caused some water to run through a pipe, altering the pipe's balance of weight and setting in motion a system of pulleys that opened a tiny aperture exactly overhead. It was a deception, but a sensible one: those who took their vows honestly were reassured by that beam of sunlight, while those who knelt and swore falsely were chastened, even terrified; more than once this little deception had saved the Guardians from undesirable infiltrations.

Domaris, her face aglow and reverent, laid her hands over her heart. "By the Light, by the Life, I so swear," she said again.

"Be watchful, vigilant, and just," charged the ancient. "Swear it now not by yourself alone, not by the light within you and above you, but also by that Life you bear; pledge you now, as your surety and hostage, the child you carry in your womb; this lest you hold your task lightly."

Domaris rose to her feet. Her face was pallid and solemn, but her voice did not hesitate. "I do pledge the child of my body as hostage," she said, and both hands curved themselves about her body, then stretched again toward the altar, with a gesture of supplication, as if offering something to the light that played there.

Micon stirred a little, unquietly. "I like not that," he murmured.

"It is customary, that pledge," Rajasta reassured him, softly.

"I know, but—" Micon shrank, as if with pain, and was silent.

The old Guardian spoke again. "Then, my daughter, these be thine." At his signal, a mantle of white was laid about the woman's shoulders; a golden rod and a gold-hilted dagger were placed in her folded hands. "Use these justly. My mantle, my rod, my dagger, pass to you; punish, spare, strike, or reward, but above all, Guard; for the Darkness eats ever at the Light." Ragamon stepped forward to touch her two hands. "My burden upon thee." He touched her bowed shoulders, and they straightened. "Upon thee, the seal of Silence." He drew up the hood of the mantle over her head. "Thou art Guardian," he said, and with a final gesture of blessing, vacated the raised space, leaving Domaris alone in the central place before the altar. "Fare thee well."

CHAPTER THIRTEEN
✠ THE CHELA ✠

I

The garden was dry now; leaves crackled underfoot, and blew about aimlessly with the night wind. Micon paced, slowly and silently, along the flagstoned walk. As he halted near the fountain, a lurking shadow sprang up noiselessly before him.

"Micon!" It was a racking whisper; then the shadow darted forward and Micon heard the sound of heavy breathing.

"Reio-ta—it is you?"

The shadow bowed his head, then sank humbly to his knees. "Micon . . . my Prince!"

"My brother," said Micon, and waited.

The chela's smooth face was old in the moonlight; no one could have known that he was younger than Micon.

"They betrayed me!" the chela said, raspily. "They swore you would go free—and unhurt! Micon—" His voice broke in agony. "Do not condemn me! I did not submit to them from cowardice!"

Micon spoke with the weariness of dead ages. "It is not for me to condemn you. Others will do that, and harshly."

"I—I could not bear—it was not for myself! It was only to stop your torture, to save you—"

For the first time, Micon's controlled voice held seeds of wrath. "Did I *ask* for life at your hands? Would I buy my freedom at such a price? That one who knows—what *you* know—might turn it to a—

spiritual whoredom? *And you dare to say it was for my sake?*" His voice trembled. "I might have—forgiven it, had you broken under torture!"

The chela started back a little. "My Prince—my brother—forgive me!" he begged.

Micon's mouth was a stern line in the pallid light. "My forgiveness cannot lighten your ultimate fate. Nor could my curses add to it. I bear you no malice, Reio-ta. I could wish you no worse fate than you have brought upon yourself. May you reap no worse than you have sown. . . ."

"I—" The chela inched closer once more, still half crouching before Micon. "I would strive to hold it worthily, our power . . ."

Micon stood, straight, stiff, and very still. "That task is not for you, not now." He paused, holding himself immobile, and in the silence the fountain gushed and spattered echoingly behind them. "Brother, fear not: *you shall betray our house not twee!*"

The figure at Micon's feet groaned, and turned his face away, hiding it in his hands.

Inflexibly, Micon went on, "That much I may prevent! Nay—say no more of it! You cannot, you know you cannot use our powers while I live—and I hold death from me, until I *know* you cannot so debase our line! Unless you kill me here and now, my son will inherit the power I hold!"

Reio-ta's grovelling figure sank lower still, until the prematurely old face rested against Micon's sandalled feet. "My Prince—I knew not of this—"

Micon smiled faintly. "This?" he repeated. "I forgive you this—and that I see not. But your apostasy I cannot forgive, for it is a cause that you, yourself, set in motion, and its effect *will* reach you; you will be ever incomplete. Thus far, and not further, can you go. My brother—" His voice softened. "I love you still, but our ways part here. Now go— before you rob me of what poor strength remains to me. Go—or end my life now, take the power and try to hold it. *But you will not be able to!* You are not ready to master the storm-wrack, the deep forces of earth and sky—and now you shall never be! Go!"

Reio-ta groaned in anguished sorrow, clasping Micon's knees. "I cannot bear—"

"Go!" said Micon again, sternly, steadily. "Go—while I may yet hold back your destiny, as I hold back my own. Make what restitution you may."

"I cannot bear my guilt . . ." The voice of the chela was broken now, and sadder than tears. "Say one kind word to me—that I may know you remember that we were once brothers. . . ."

"You *are* my brother," Micon acknowledged gently. "I have said that I love you still. I do not abandon you utterly. But this must be our parting." He bent and laid a wasted hand upon the chela's head.

Crying out sharply, Reio-ta cringed away. "Micon! Your pain— burns!"

Slowly and with effort, Micon straightened and withdrew. "Go quickly," he commanded, and added, as if against his own will, in a voice of raw torture, "*I can bear no more!*"

The chela sprang to his feet and stood a moment, gazing haggardly at the other, as if imprinting Micon's features upon his memory for all time; then turned and ran, with stumbling feet, from his brother's presence.

The blind Initiate remained, motionless, for many minutes. The wind had risen, and dry leaves skittered on the path and all about him; he did not notice. Weakly, as if forcing his steps through quicksand, he turned at last and went toward the fountain, where he sank down upon the dampened stone rim, fighting the hurricane clamor of the pain that he refused to give mental lease. Finally, his strength all but gone, he lay huddled on the flagstones amid the windblown leaves, victoriously master of himself, but so spent that he could not move.

In response to some inner uneasiness, Rajasta came—and the face of the Guardian was a terrible thing to see as he gathered Micon up into his strong arms, and bore him away.

The next day, the whole force of the Temple gathered for the search. Riveda, suspected of connivance, was taken into custody for many hours, while they sought throughout the Temple precincts, and even in the city below, for the unknown chela who had once been Reio-ta of Ahtarrath.

But he had disappeared—and the Night of the Nadir was one day closer to them all.

CHAPTER FOURTEEN
✠ THE UNREVEALED GOD ✠

I

About three months after Deoris had been received into the Temple of Caratra, Riveda encountered her one evening in the gardens. The last rays of the setting sun turned the young Priestess into a fairy shape of mystery, and Riveda studied her slim, blue-garbed form and grave, delicate young face with a new interest as he carefully phrased his request. "Who would forbid you, if I should invite you to visit the Grey Temple with me, this evening?"

Deoris felt her pulses twitch. To visit the Grey Temple—in the company of their highest Adept! Riveda did her honor indeed! Still she asked, warily, "Why?"

The man laughed. "Why not? There is a ceremony this evening. It is beautiful—there will be some singing. Many of our ceremonials are secret, but to this one I may invite you."

"I will come," Deoris said. She spoke demurely, but inwardly she danced with excitement: Karahama's guarded confidences had awakened her curiosity, not only about the Grey-robes, but about Riveda himself.

They walked silently under the blossoming stars. Riveda's hand was light on her shoulder, but Deoris was intensely aware of the touch, and it made her too shy to speak until they neared the great windowless loom of the Temple. As Riveda held aside the heavy bronze doors for her to pass, Deoris shrank in amazed terror from the bent wraith that slipped past them—the chela!

Riveda's hand tightened on her arm until Deoris almost cried out. "Say nothing of this to Micon, child," he warned sternly. "Rajasta has been told that he lives; but it would kill Micon to be confronted with him again!"

Deoris bent her head and promised. Since that night when Cadamiri had carried her, senseless, from Micon's rooms, her awareness of Micon had been almost as complete as that of Domaris; the Atlantean's undercurrents of emotion and thought were clear to her, except where they concerned herself. Her broadened perceptions had gone almost unnoticed, except for her swift mastery of work far beyond her supposed skill in the Temple; not even Domaris had guessed at Deoris's wakening awareness. Domaris was now wholly absorbed in Micon, and in their coming child. And the waiting, Deoris knew—and there was still more than a month to wait—was an unbearable torment to both, a joy and yet an insufferable pain.

The bronze doors clamored shut. They stood in a narrow corridor, dimly dark, that stretched away between rows of closed stone doors. The haggard, haunted figure of the chela was nowhere to be seen.

Their footsteps were soundless, muffled in the dead air, and Deoris, moving in the silence, felt some electric tension in the man beside her, a coiled strength that was almost sensible to her nerves. At the end of the corridor was an arched door bound about with iron. Riveda knocked, using a curious pattern of taps, and from nowhere a shrill, high, bodiless voice challenged in unfamiliar syllables. Riveda spoke equally cryptic words in response; an invisible bell sounded in midair, and the door swung inward.

They passed into—greyness.

There was no lack of light, but warmth or color there was none; the illumination was serene and cold, a mere shimmer, a pallor, an absence of darkness rather than a positive light. The room was immense, lost above their heads in a grey dimness like a heavy fog, or solidified smoke. Beneath their feet, the floor was grey stone, cold and sprinkled with chips of crystal and mica; the walls, too, had a translucent glitter, like winter moonlight. The forms that moved tenuously, like wraiths of mist in the wan radiance, were grey as well; tenebrous shadows, cloaked and cowled and mantled in sorcerer's grey—and there were women among them, women who moved restlessly like chained flames, robed in shrouding veils of saffron color, dull and lightless. Deoris glanced guardedly at the women, in the moment before Riveda's strong hands turned her gently about so that she faced—

A Man.

He might have been man or carven idol, corpse or automaton. He *was*. That was all. He existed, with a curious sort of finality. He sat on the raised dais at one end of the huge Hall, on a great throne-like chair, a grey bird of carven stone poised above his head. His hands lay crossed on his breast. Deoris found herself wondering whether He were really there, or if she dreamed Him there. Involuntarily, she whispered, "Where sits the Man with Crossed Hands. . . ."

Riveda bent and whispered, "Remain here. Speak to no one." Straightening, he walked away. Deoris, watching him wistfully, thought that his straight figure, grey-robed and cowled in grey though he was, had a kind of sharpness, as if he were in focus whereas the others were shadowy, like dreams within a dream. Then she saw a face she knew.

Standing tautly poised, half-hidden by one of the crystal pillars, a young girl watched Deoris shyly; a child, tall but slight, her slim body still straight between the saffron veils, her small pointed face lifted a little and shadowed by the translucent light. Frost-pale hair lay whitely around her shoulders, and the suppressed glitter of the Northern lights dwelt in her intent, colorless eyes. The diaphanous gauze about her body fluttered lightly in an invisible breeze; she seemed weightless, a wraith of frost, a shimmer of snowflakes in the chilly air.

But Deoris had seen her outside this eerie place, and knew she was real; this silver-haired girl slipped sometimes like a ghost in or out of Karahama's rooms. Karahama never spoke of the child, but Deoris knew that this was the nameless girl, the child of the *no people*, born to the then-still-outcast Karahama. Her mother, it was said, called her Demira, but she had no real name. By law, she did not exist at all.

No man, however willing, could have acknowledged Demira as his daughter; no man could have claimed or adopted her. Even Karahama had only a debatable legal existence—but Karahama, as the child of a free Temple woman, had a certain acknowledged, if illegitimate, status. Demira, under the strict laws of the Priest's Caste, was not even illegitimate. She was nothing. She was covered by no law, protected by no statute, recorded in no Temple writing; she was not even a slave.

She quite simply *did not exist.* Only here, among the lawless *saji,* could she have found shelter and sustenance.

The stern code of the Temple forbade Deoris, Priest's daughter and Priestess, to recognize the nameless girl in any way—but although they had never exchanged a single word, Deoris knew that Demira was her own near kinswoman, and the child's strange, fantastic beauty excited Deoris's pity and interest. She now raised her eyes and smiled timidly at the outcaste girl, and Demira smiled back—a quick, furtive smile.

Riveda returned, his eyes abstracted and vague, and Demira slipped behind a pillar, out of sight.

II

The Temple was crowded now, with men in grey robes and the saffron-shrouded *saji,* some of whom held curious stringed instruments, rattles, and gongs. There were also many chelas in grey kilts, their upper bodies bare except for curious amulets; none were very old, and most of them were approximately Deoris's own age. Some were only little boys of five or six. Looking about the room, Deoris counted only five persons in the full grey robe and cowl of Adeptship—and realized, startled, that one of these was a woman; the only woman there, except Deoris herself, who was not wearing the *saji* veils.

Gradually, the Magicians and Adepts formed a roughly circular figure, taking great pains about their exact positions. The *saji* with their musical instruments, and the smaller chelas, had withdrawn toward the translucent walls. From their ranged ranks came the softest of pipings, a whimper of flutes, the echo of a gong touched with a steel-clad fingertip.

Before each Magician stood either a chela or one of the *saji;* sometimes three or four clustered before one of the Adepts or one of the oldest Magicians—but the chelas were in the majority, only four or five of those in the inner ring being women. One of these was Demira, her veils thrown back so that her silver hair glittered like moonlight on the sea.

Riveda motioned Reio-ta to take his place in the forming Ring, then paused and asked, "Deoris, have you the courage to stand for me in the Chela's Ring tonight?"

"Why, I—" Domaris stuttered with astonishment. "I know nothing of it, how could I—?"

Riveda's stern mouth held the shadow of a smile. "No knowledge is necessary. In fact the less you know of it, the better. Try to think of nothing—and let it come to you." He signalled Reio-ta to guide her, and, with a final look of appeal, Deoris went.

Flutes and gongs broke suddenly into a dissonant, harsh chord, as if tuning, readying. Adepts and Magicians cocked their heads, listening, testing something invisible and intangible. Deoris, the chord elusive in her skull, felt herself drawn into the Ring between Reio-ta and Demira. A spasm of panic closed her throat; Demira's small steely fingers clutched hers like torturer's implements. In a moment she must scream with horror. . . .

The flattened impact of Riveda's hand struck her clenched finger, and her frenzied grasp loosened and fell free. He shook his head at her briefly and, without a word, motioned her out of the Ring. He did not do it as if the failure meant anything to him; he seemed absolutely abstracted as he beckoned to a *saji* girl with a face like a seagull to take her place.

Two or three other chelas had been dismissed from the Ring; others were being placed and replaced. Twice more the soft but dissonant chords sounded, and each time positions and patterns were altered. The third time, Riveda held up his hand, looking angry and annoyed, and stepped from his place, glaring around the Chela's Ring. His eyes fell upon Demira, and roughly, with a smothered monosyllable, he grasped the girl's shoulder and pushed her violently away. She reeled and almost fell—at which the woman Adept stepped out of line and caught the staggering child. She held Demira for a minute; then, carefully, her wrinkled hands encircling the child's thin wrist, she re-guided her into the Ring, placing her with a challenging glance at Riveda.

Riveda scowled darkly. The woman Adept shrugged, and gently moved Demira once more, and then again, changing her position until suddenly Riveda nodded, immediately taking his eyes from Demira and apparently forgetting her existence.

Again the dissonant whimper of flutes and strings and gongs sounded! This time there was no interruption. Deoris stood watching, faintly bewildered. The chelas answered the music with a brief chanting, beautifully timed but so alien to Deoris's experience that it seemed meaningless. Accustomed to the exalted mysticism of the Temple of Light, and the sparse simplicity of their rituals, this protracted litany of intonation and gesture, music and chant and response, was incomprehensible.

This is silly, Deoris decided, *it doesn't mean anything at all.* Or did it? The face of the woman Adept was thin and lined and worn, although she seemed young, otherwise; Riveda's aspect, in the pitiless light, gave the impression almost of cruelty, while Demira's fantastic, frosty beauty seemed unreal, illusive, with something hard and vicious marring the infantile features. All at once, Deoris could understand why, to some, the ceremonies of the Grey Temple might seem tinged with evil.

The chanting deepened, quickened, pulsed in strange monodies and throbbing cadences. A single whining, wailing dissonance was reiterated; the muffled piping came behind her like a smothered sob; a shaken drum rattled weirdly.

The Man with Crossed Hands was watching her.

Neither then nor ever did Deoris know whether the Man with Crossed Hands was idol, corpse, or living man, demon, god, or image. Nor was she able—then or ever—to determine how much of what she saw was illusion . . .

The eyes of the Man were grey. Grey as the sea; grey as the frosty light. She sank deep into their compelling, compassionate gaze, was swallowed up and drowned there.

The bird above his chair flapped grey stone wings and flew, with a harsh screech, into a place of grey sands. And then Deoris was running after the bird, among needled rocks and the shadows of their spires, under skies split by the raucous screaming of seagulls.

Far away, the booming of surf rode the winds; Deoris was near the sea, in a place between dawn and sunrise, coldly grey, without color in sands or sea or clouds. Small shells crunched beneath her sandals, and she smelled the rank stench of salt water and seaweed and marshy reeds and rushes. To her left, a cluster of small conical houses with pointed grey-white roofs sent a pang of horror through Deoris's breast.

The Idiots' Village! The awful stab of recognition was so sharp a shock that she thrust aside a briefly flickering certainty that she had never seen this place before.

There was a deathly silence around and between and over the screeching of the seagulls. Two or three children, large-headed and white-haired with red eyes and mouths that drooled above swollen pot-bellied torsos squatted, listless, between the houses, mewling and muttering to one another. Deoris's parched lips could not utter the screams that scraped in her throat. She turned to flee, but her foot twisted beneath her and she fell. Struggling to rise, she caught sight of two men and a woman coming out of the nearest of the chinked pebble-houses; like the children, they were red-eyed and thick-lipped and naked. One of the men tottered with age; the other groped, his red eyes caked blots of filth and blood; the woman moved with a clumsy waddling, hugely swollen by pregnancy into an animal, primal ugliness.

Deoris crouched on the sands in wildly unreasoning horror. The half-human idiots were mewling more loudly now, grimacing at her; their fists made scrabbling noises in the colorless sands. Scrambling fearfully to her feet, Deoris looked madly around for a way of escape. To one side, a high wall of needled rock bristled her away; to the other, a quicksand marsh of reeds and rushes stretched on to the horizon. Before her the idiots were clustering, staring, blubbering. She was hemmed in.

But how did I come here? Was there a boat?

She spun around, and saw only the empty, rolling sea. Far, far in the distance, mountains loomed up out of the water, and long streaks of reddening clouds, like bloody fingers, scraped the skies raw.

And when the sun rises . . . when the sun rises . . . The vagrant thought slipped away. More of the huge-headed villagers were crowding out of the houses. Deoris began to run, in terror-stricken panic.

Ahead of her, lancing through the greyness and the bloody outstretched streaks of sullen light, a sudden spark flared into a glowing golden gleam. *Sunlight!* She ran even faster, her footsteps a thudding echo of her heart; behind her the groping pad-pad-pad of the pursuit was like a merciless incoming tide.

A stone sailed past her ears. Her feet splashed in the surf as she turned, whirling like a cornered animal. Someone rose up before her, red hideous eyes gleaming emptily, lips drawn back over blackened and broken teeth in a bestial snarl. Frantically, she struck the clutching hands away, kicked and twisted and struggled free—heard the creature shrieking its mindless howling cries as she stumbled, ran on, stumbled again—and fell.

The light on the sea exploded in a burst of sunshine, and she stretched her hands toward it, sobbing, crying out no more coherently than the idiots behind her. A stone struck her shoulder; another grazed her skull. She struggled to rise, scratching at the wet sands, clawing to free herself from groping, scrabbling hands. Someone was screaming, a high, wild ululation of anguish. Something hit her hard in the face. Her brain exploded in fire and she sank down . . . and down . . . and down . . . as the sun burst in her face and she died.

III

Someone was crying.

Light dazzled her eyes. A sharp-sweet, dizzying smell stung her nostrils.

Elis's face swam out of the darkness, and Deoris choked weakly, pushed away the hand that held the strong aromatic to her nostrils.

"Don't, I can't breathe—Elis!" she gasped.

The hands on her shoulders loosened slightly, laid her gently back in a heap of pillows. She was lying on a couch in Elis's room in the House of the Twelve, and Elis was bending over her. Behind Elis, Elara was standing, wiping her eyes, her face looking drawn and worried.

"I must go now to the lady Domaris," Elara said shakily.

"Yes, go," Elis said without looking up.

Deoris struggled to sit up, but pain exploded blindingly in her head and she fell back. "What happened?" she murmured weakly. "How did I get here? Elis, what *happened?*"

To Deoris's horror, Elis, rather than answering, began to cry, wiping her eyes with her veil.

"Elis—" Deoris's voice quavered, little-girlish. "*Please* tell me. I was—in the Idiots' Village, and they threw stones—" Deoris touched her cheek, her skull. Though she fancied she felt a stinging sensation, there were no lacerations, no swellings. "Oh, my head!"

"You're raving again!" Elis grabbed Deoris's shoulders and shook her, hard. It brought a sudden flash of horror; then the vague half-memory closed down again as Elis snapped, "Don't you even remember what you did?"

"Oh, Elis, stop! Please don't, it hurts my head so," Deoris moaned. "Can't you tell me what happened? How did I get here?"

"You don't remember!" Shock and disbelief were in Elis's voice. As Deoris struggled to sit up again, Elis supported her cousin with an arm around her shoulders. Still touching her head, Deoris looked toward the window. It was late afternoon, the sun just beginning to lengthen the shadows. *Yet it had been before moonrise when she went with Riveda—*

"I don't remember anything," Deoris said shakily. "Where is Domaris?"

Elis's mouth, which had softened, became set and angry again. "In the House of Birth."

"*Now?*"

"They were afraid—" A strained fury tightened Elis's voice; she swallowed hard and said, "Deoris, I swear that if Domaris loses her child because of this, I will—"

"Elis, let me come in," someone outside the door said; but before any reply could be made, Micon entered, leaning heavily on Riveda's arm. Unsteadily, the Atlantean moved to the bedside. "Deoris," he said, "can you tell me—"

Hysterical laughter mixed with sobs in Deoris's throat. "What can I tell *you?*" she cried. "*Doesn't anybody know what's happened to me!*"

Micon sighed deeply, slumping noticeably where he stood. "I feared this," he said, with a great bitterness. "She knows nothing, remembers nothing. Child—my dear child! You must never allow yourself to be—used—like that again!"

Riveda looked tense and weary, and his grey robe was crumpled and darkly stained. "Micon of Ahtarrath, I swear—"

Abruptly, Micon pulled away from the support of Riveda's arm. "I am not yet ready for you to swear!"

At this, Deoris somehow got to her feet and stood swaying, sobbing with pain and fright and frustration. Micon, with that unerring sense that served him so well instead of sight, reached toward her clumsily—but Riveda drew the girl into his own arms with a savage protectiveness. Gradually her trembling stilled, and she leaned against him motionless, her cheek resting against the rough material of his robe.

"You shall not blame *her!*" Riveda said harshly. "Domaris is safe—"

"Nay," said Micon, conciliatingly, "I meant not to blame, but only—"

"I know well that you hate me, Lord of Ahtarrath," Riveda interrupted, "though I—"

"I hate no one!" Micon broke in, sharply. "Do you insinuate—"

"Once for all, Lord Micon," Riveda snapped, "I do not *insinuate!*" With a great gentleness that contrasted strangely with his harsh words, Riveda helped Deoris to return to the couch. "Hate me if you will, Atlantean," the Grey-robe said, "you and your Priestess leman—and that unborn—"

"*Have a care!*" said Micon, ominously.

Riveda laughed, scornful—but his next words died in his throat, for out of the clear and cloudless sky outside the window came the rolling rumble of impossible thunder as Micon's fists clenched. Elis, forgotten, cowered in the corner, while Deoris began to shiver uncontrollably. Micon and Riveda faced each other, Adepts of vastly different disciplines, and the tension between them was like an invisible, but tangible, force, quivering in the room.

Yet it lasted only a moment. Riveda swallowed, and said, "My words were strong. I spoke in anger. But what have I done to merit your insults, Micon of Ahtarrath? My beliefs are not yours—none could fail to see that—but you know my creed as I know yours! By the Unrevealed God, would *I* harm a childing woman?"

"Am I then to believe," Micon asked savagely, "that a Priestess of Caratra would—*of her own will*—harm the sister she adores?"

Deoris's hands went to her mouth in a wordless shriek and she ran to Elis, clinging to her cousin and sobbing in nightmarish disbelief.

"I invited the child," Riveda stated, coldly, "to witness a ceremony in the Grey Temple. Believe, if you will, that it was with malice and forethought—that I invoked Dark Powers. But I give you my word, the pledged word of an Adept, that I meant no more than courtesy! A

courtesy it is my privilege to extend to any regularly pledged Priest or
Priestess."

Save for the muted snuffling of Deoris, still huddled against Elis,
the room was quite silent. The late afternoon light had vanished, as if
night had come, while the skies continued to fill with sudden, heavy
clouds. The two women dared not even so much as look at the
wrangling Adepts.

Yet at last the awful tensions in the room abated somewhat; the
very stones of the walls seemed to sigh in relief as Micon half-turned
away from Riveda, who, had any been watching, could have been seen
to blink several times, and wipe a cold sweat from his forehead.

"During the ceremony," the Grey-robe resumed, in a quiet voice,
"Deoris became giddy and fell to the floor; one of the girls took her
into the open air. Afterward, it did not seem serious. She spoke to me
quite normally. I conducted her to the gates of the House of the
Twelve. That is all that I know of this. All." Riveda spread his hands,
then looked around at Deoris and asked her gently, "Do you truly
remember nothing?"

Deoris shuddered as the terror she had been thought closed in
again, squeezing her heart with icy talons. "I was watching the—the
Man with Crossed Hands," she whispered. "The—the bird on his
throne flew! And then I was in the Idiots' Village—"

"Deoris!" Micon's cry was a strained and hoarse shout. The
Atlantean drew a deep breath that was almost a sob. "What mean you
by—the Idiots' Village?"

"Why, I—" Deoris's eyes grew wide, and with growing horror, she
whispered, "I don't know, I never—I never heard of—"

"Gods! Gods!" Micon's haggard face was suddenly like that of a
very old man, and he staggered where he stood; gone now was the
inner strength that had called on the powers of Ahtarrath, as he
stumbled and groped his way into a nearby chair. "I feared that! And
it has come!" He bent his head, covered his face with gaunt and
twisted hands.

Deoris, at seeing Micon's sudden weakness, had left Elis and
rushed to the Atlantean's side. Half-kneeling before him, she pleaded,
"Micon, tell me! *What did I do?*"

"Pray that you never remember!" Micon said, his voice muffled
behind his hands. "But by the mercy of the Gods, Domaris is unhurt!"

"But—" Deoris found herself oddly unable to speak that name which had so upset Micon, and so instead said only, "But that place—what—how could I have—?" Her voice broke down utterly.

Micon, regaining control of himself, stretched one trembling hand to the crown of her head and drew the sobbing girl to him. "An old sin," he murmured, in a quavery old man's voice, "an all-but-forgotten shame of the House of Ahtarrath . . . enough! This attack was not aimed at you, Deoris, but at—at one of the Ahtarrath yet unborn. Do not torture yourself, child."

Silent, Riveda stood, unmoving as stone, his arms crossed tight upon his chest, his lips tightly set and his bright blue eyes half-closed. Elis sat shivering on the couch, staring at the floor, alone with her thoughts.

"Go to Domaris, my darling," said Micon softly; and after a moment, Deoris wiped away her tears, kissed the Atlantean's hand reverently, and went. Elis rose and followed her from the room on tiptoe. Behind them was silence.

Riveda broke the stillness, saying roughly, "I will never rest easy until I know who has done this!"

Micon dragged himself heavily to his feet. "What I said was the truth; this was an attack on me, through my son. I personally am not now worth attacking."

Riveda chuckled—a low-pitched rumble of cynical amusement. "I wish I had known that a few minutes ago, when the very thunders of heaven came to your defense!" The Grey-robe paused, then asked, softly, "Or is it that you do not trust me?"

Micon answered sharply, "You are in part to blame; though you took Deoris into danger unknowing, nonetheless—"

Riveda's fury exploded, spilled over, "I to blame? What of you? Had you managed to pocket your damnable pride long enough to testify against these devils, they would have been flogged to death long ago, and this could not have happened! Lord of Ahtarrath, I intend to cleanse my Order! Not now for your sake, nor even to preserve my own reputation—that has never been so good! But the health of my Order requires—" He suddenly realized he was shouting, and lowered his voice. "He who allows sorcery is worse than he who commits it. Men may sin from ignorance or folly—but what of a wise man, pledged to cleave to Light, whose charity is so great that he refuses even to protect the innocent, for fear of injuring the guilty? If that is the path of Light, I say, let Darkness fall!" Riveda, looking down at the collapsed Micon, felt his last anger fading. He put his hand on the Atlantean's thin shoulder and said gravely, "Prince of Ahtarrath, I swear that I will find who has done this, though it cost me my own life!"

Micon said, in a voice whose very shrillness revealed the edge of exhaustion, "Seek not too far, Riveda! Already you are too deeply involved in this. Look to yourself, lest it cost you more than your life!"

Riveda emitted a little snort of ugly, mirthless laughter. "Keep your dooms and prophecies, Prince Micon! I have no less love for life than any other—but it is my task to find the guilty, and take steps to prevent another such—incident. Deoris, too, must be guarded—and it is my right to guard her, even as it is yours to guard Domaris."

Micon said, in a quick, low voice, "What mean you?"

Riveda shrugged. "Nothing, perhaps. It may be your prophecy carries its own contagion, and I see my own karma reflected in yours." He stared at Micon, his eyes wide and bleak and blue. "I don't know quite why I said that. But you will not bid me spare punishment to those responsible!"

Micon sighed, and his emaciated hands twitched slightly. "No, I will not," he murmured. "That, too, is karma!"

CHAPTER FIFTEEN
✠ THE SIN ✠
THAT QUICKENS

I

Only in extreme emergency or death were men allowed within the boundaries of the Temple of Caratra; however, the circumstances were unusual, and after certain delays Mother Ysouda conducted Micon to the rooftop court where Domaris had been taken, for coolness, once they knew that her child would not be prematurely born.

"You must not stay long," the old Priestess cautioned, and left them alone.

Micon waited until her receding footsteps were lost on the stairs, then said with a mirthful sternness that mocked its own anxiety, "So, you have terrified us all for nothing, my Lady!"

Domaris smiled wanly. "Blame your son, Micon, not his mother! Already he thinks himself lord of his surroundings!"

"Well, and is he not?" Micon seated himself beside her and asked, "Has Deoris been to you?"

She looked away. "Yes. . . ."

Micon's hand closed gently on hers and he said lovingly, "Heart-of-flame, be not resentful. Our child is safe—and Deoris is as innocent as you, beloved!"

"I know—but your son is very precious to me!" Domaris whispered; then, with implacable vehemence: "That—damned—Riveda!"

"*Domaris!*" In surprise and displeasure, Micon covered her lips with his hand. She kissed the palm, and he smiled, then went on gently, "Riveda knew nothing of this. His only fault was that he suspected no evil." He touched her eyes, lightly, with his gaunt fingers. "You must not cry, beloved—" Then, half-hesitant, his hand lingered. "May I—?"

"Of course." Divining his wish, Domaris took his hand lightly in hers, guiding it gently across her swollen body. Suddenly, all of Micon's senses coalesced; past and present fell together in a single coherent moment of sensation so intense that it seemed almost as if he saw, as if every sense combined to bring the meaning of life home to him. He had never been so keenly alive as in that moment when he smelled the sharpsweet odor of drugs, the elusive perfume of Domaris's hair, and the clean fragrance of linens; the air was moist with the cool and salty sting of the sea, and he heard the distant boom of surf and the gurgle of the fountain, the muted sounds of women's voices in distant rooms. Under his hand he felt the fine textures of silk and linen, the pulsing warmth of the woman-body, and then, through the refined sensitivity of his fingers, he felt a sharp little push, a sudden slight bulging, elusive as a butterfly beneath his hand.

With a quick movement, Domaris sat up and stretched her arms to Micon, holding herself to him in an embrace so light that she barely touched the man. She had learned caution, where a careless touch or caress could mean agony for the man she loved—and Domaris, young and passionately in love, had not easily learned that lesson! But for once Micon forgot caution. His arms tightened about her convulsively. Once, once only he should have had the right to see this woman he loved with every atom, every nerve of his whole being. . . .

The moment passed, and he admonished gently, "Lie still, beloved. They made me promise not to disturb you." He loosed her, and she lay back, watching him with a smile so resigned that Domaris herself did not know it was sorrowful. "And yet," said Micon, his voice troubled, "we have been too cowardly to speak of many things. . . . There is your duty to Arvath. You are bound by law to—to what, exactly?"

"Before marriage," Domaris murmured, "we are free. So runs the law. After marriage—it is required that we remain constant. And if I should fail, or refuse, to give Arvath a son—"

"Which you must not," said Micon with great gentleness.

"I shall not refuse," Domaris assured him. "But if I should fail, I would be dishonoured, disgraced . . ."

"This is my karma," Micon said sorrowfully, "that I may never see my son, that I may not live to guide him. I sinned against that same law, Domaris."

"Sin?" Domaris's voice betrayed her shock, "You?"

He bent his head in shamed avowal. "I desired the things of the spirit, and so I am—Initiate. But I was too proud to recall that I was a man, too, and so under the law." The blind face brooded, distantly. "In my pride I chose to live as an ascetic and deny my body, under the false name of worthy austerity—"

Domaris whispered, "That is necessary to such accomplishment—"

"You have not heard all, beloved. . . ." Micon drew a shaky breath. "Before I entered the Priesthood, Mikantor required me to take a wife, and raise up a son to my house and my name." The stern mouth trembled a little, and his rigid self-control faltered. "As my father commanded, so I allowed myself to be wedded by the law. She was a young girl, pure and lovely, a princess; but I was—I was blind to her as I am—" Micon's voice broke altogether, and he covered his face with his hands. At last he spoke, in a suffocated voice. "And so it is my fate that I may never look on your face—you that I love more than life and more than death! I was blind to her, I told her coldly and—and cruelly, Domaris—that I was vowed a Priest, and—and she left my marriage-bed as virgin as she came to me. And in that, I humiliated her and sinned, against my father and against myself and against our whole House! Domaris—knowing this—can you still love me?"

Domaris had turned deathly white; what Micon had confessed was regarded as a crime. But she only whispered, "Thou hast paid the price, thrice over, Micon. And—and it brought thee to me. And I love thee!"

"I do not regret that." Micon's lips pressed softly against her hand. "But—can you understand this? Had I had a son, I could have died, and my brother been spared his apostasy!" The dark face was haunted and haggard. "Thus I carry the blame for his sin; and other evil shall follow—for evil plants evil, and reaps and harvests a hundredfold, and sows evil yet again . . ." He paused and said, "Deoris too may need protection. Riveda is contaminated with the Black-robes."

At her quick gasp of horror, he added quickly, "No, what you are thinking is not true. He is no Black-robe, he despises them; but he is intelligent, and seeks knowledge, and he is not too fastidious where he acquires it. . . . Never underrate the power of intellectual curiosity, Domaris! It leads to more trouble than any other human motive! If Riveda *were* malicious, or deliberately cruel, he would be less dangerous! But he serves only one motive: the driving force of a powerful mind which has never been really challenged. He is entirely devoid of any personal ambition. He seeks and serves knowledge for its own sake. Not for service, not for self-perfection. If he were a more selfish man, I would feel easier about him. And—and Deoris loves him, Domaris."

"*Deoris?* Loves that detestable old—?"

Micon sighed. "Riveda is not so old. Nor does Deoris love him as— as you and I understand love. If it were only that, I would feel no concern. Love is not to be compelled. He is not the man I should have chosen for her, but I am not her guardian." He sensed something of the woman's confusion and added quietly, "No, this is something other. And it disturbs me. Deoris is barely old enough to feel *that* kind of love, or to know it exists. Nor—" He paused. "I hardly know how to say this . . . She is not a girl who will grow easily to know passion. She must ripen slowly. If she should be too soon awakened, I would fear for her greatly! And she loves Riveda! She adores him—although I do not think she knows it herself. To give Riveda his due, I do not believe he has fostered it. But understand me: he could violate her past the foulest prostitution and leave her virgin—or he could keep her in innocence, though she bore him a dozen children!"

Domaris, troubled and even a little dazed by Micon's unusual vehemence, bit her lip and said, "I *don't* understand!"

Reluctantly, Micon said, "You know of the *saji*—"

"Ah, no!" It was a cry of horror. "Riveda would not dare!"

"I trust not. But Deoris may not be wise in loving." He forced a weary smile. "You were not wise, to be sure! But—" Again he sighed. "Well, Deoris must follow her karma, as we follow ours." Hearing Domaris's sigh, an echo of his own, Micon accused himself. "I have tired you!"

"No—but he is heavy now, and—your son hurts me."

"I am sorry—if only I could bear it for you!"

Domaris laughed a little, and her hands, feather-soft, stole into his. "You are Prince of Ahtarrath," she said gaily, "and I am your most obedient handmaiden and slave. But this one privilege you cannot have! I know my rights, my Prince!"

The grave sternness of his face relaxed again, and a delighted grin took its place as he bent to kiss her. "That would indeed be magic of an extraordinary sort," he admitted. "We of Ahtarrath have certain powers over nature, it is true. But alas, all my powers could not encompass even such a little miracle!"

Domaris relaxed; the moment of danger was past. Micon would not break again.

But the Night of the Nadir was almost upon them.

CHAPTER SIXTEEN
✠ THE NIGHT ✠
OF THE NADIR

I

These months have not been kind to Micon, Rajasta thought, sad and puzzled by the Atlantean's continuing failure to heal to any significant degree.

The Initiate stood before the window now, his gaunt and narrow body barely diminishing the evening light. With a nervousness of motion that was becoming less and less foreign to him, Micon fingered the little statuette of Nar-inabi, the Star-Shaper.

"Where got you this, Rajasta?"

"You recognize it?"

The blind man bent his head, half-turning away from Rajasta. "I cannot say that—now. But I—know the craftsmanship. It was made in Ahtarrath, and I think it could belong only to my brother, or to me." He hesitated. "Such works as this are—extremely costly. This type of stone is very rare." He half-smiled. "Still, I suppose I am not the only Prince of Ahtarrath ever to travel, or have something stolen. Where did you find it?"

Rajasta did not reply. He had found it in this very building, in the servants' quarters. He told himself that this did not necessarily implicate any of the residents, but the implications dismayed and sickened him, for it was by the same token impossible, now, to eliminate any of them as suspects. Riveda might be truly as innocent as he claimed, and the true guilt lie elsewhere, perhaps among the very Guardians themselves—Cadamiri, or Ragamon the Elder, even Talkannon himself! These suspicions shook Rajasta's world to the very foundations.

A haunting sadness drifted across Micon's face as, with a lingeringly gentle touch, he set the exquisitely carven, opalescent figurine carefully on a little table by the window. "My poor brother," he whispered, almost inaudibly—and Rajasta, hearing, could not be quite sure that Micon referred to Reio-ta.

Realizing that he had to say something, the Priest of Light took refuge in pleasantries. "Already it is the Nadir-night, Micon, and you need have no fear; your son will surely not be born tonight. I have just come from Domaris; she and those who tend her assure me of that. She will sleep soundly in her own rooms," Rajasta went on, "without awakening and without fear of any omens or portents. I have asked Cadamiri to give her a sleeping drug. . . ."

Yet, as he had spoken, the Priest of Light had stumbled slightly over the name of Cadamiri, as his newfound apprehension conflicted with his desire to assure Micon. The Atlantean, sensing this without knowing the precise reason for Rajasta's nervousness, grew rigid with tension.

"The Nadir-night?" Micon half-whispered. "Already? I had lost count of the days!"

A fitful gust of wind stirred in the room, bringing a faint echo; a chant, in a strange wailing minor key, weirdly cadenced and prolonged. Rajasta's brows lifted and he inclined his head to listen, but Micon turned and went, not swiftly but with a concentrated intention, to the window again. There was deep trouble on his features, and the Priest came to stand beside him.

"Micon?" he said, with a questioning unhappiness.

"I know that chant!" the Atlantean gasped. "And what it forebodes—" He raised his thin hands and laid them gropingly on Rajasta's shoulders. "Stay thou with me, Rajasta! I—" His voice faltered. "*I am afraid!*"

The older man stared at him in ill-concealed horror, glad Micon could not see him. Rajasta had been with Micon through times of what seemed the ultimate of human extremity—yet never had the Initiate betrayed fear like this!

"I will not leave you, my brother," he promised—and the chant sounded again, ragged phrases borne eerily on the wind as the sun sank into the dusk. The Priest felt Micon grow tense, the wracked hands clutching on Rajasta's shoulders, the noble face ashen and trembling, a shivering that gradually crept over the man's entire body until every nerve seemed to quiver with a strained effort.... And then, despite the visible dread in Micon's bearing and features, the Atlantean released his hold on Rajasta and turned again to the window, to stare sightlessly at the gathering darkness, his face listening avidly.

"My brother lives," Micon said at last, and his words fell like drumbeats of doom, slow-paced in the falling night. "Would that he did not! None of the line of Ahtarrath chants thus, unless—unless—" His voice trailed away again, giving way to that listening stillness.

Suddenly Micon turned, letting his forehead fall against the older man's shoulder, clutching at him in the grip of emotions so intense that they found a mirror in Rajasta's mind, and both men trembled with unreasoning fear; nameless horrors flickered in their thoughts.

Only the wind had steadied: the broken cadences were more sustained now, rising and falling with a nightmarish, demanding, monotonous, aching insistence that kept somehow a perfect rhythm with the pounding of blood in their ears.

"They call on *my power!*" Micon gasped brokenly. "This is black betrayal! Rajasta!" He raised his head, and the unseeing features held a desperation that only increased the terror of the moment. "*How shall I survive this night?* And I must! I must! If they succeed—if that which they invoke—be summoned—only my single life stands between it and all of mankind!" He paused, gasping for breath, shivering uncontrollably. "If that link be made—then even I cannot be sure I can stay the evil!" He stood, half-swaying, at once twisted and yet utterly erect, clinging to Rajasta; his words fell like dropped stones. "Only three times in all our history has Ahtarrath summoned thus! And thrice that power has been harnessed but hardly."

Rajasta gently raised his own hands to echo Micon's, so that they stood with their hands upon each other's shoulders. "Micon!" said Rajasta sharply. "*What must we do?*"

The Atlantean's clutching hands relaxed a little, tightened, and then fell to his sides. "You would help me?" he said, in a broken, almost childish voice. "It means—"

"Do not tell me what it means," said Rajasta, his own voice quaking a little. "*But I will help you.*"

Micon drew a shaky breath; the least bit of color returned to his face. "Yes," he murmured, and then, his voice becoming stronger, "yes, we have not much time."

II

Groping in the chest where he kept his private treasures, Micon took out a flexible cloak of some metallic fabric and drew it about his shoulders. Next he removed a sword wrapped in sheer, filmy cloth, which he set down close beside him. Muttering to himself in his native tongue, Micon rummaged in the chest for no little while until he at last brought out a small bronze gong, which he handed to Rajasta with the admonition that it must not touch the floor or walls.

All the time the awful chant rose and fell, rose and fell, with eerie wailing overtones and sobbing, savage cadences; a diapason of sonic minors that beat on the brain with boneshaking reiteration. Rajasta stood holding the gong, concentrating his attention fully on Micon as he bent over the chest again, shutting his mind and ears to that sound.

The Atlantean's angry mutterings turned to a sigh of relief, and he brought forth a final object—a little brazier of bronze, curiously worked with embossed figures that bulged and intertwined in a fashion that confused the eye into thinking they moved. After a moment Rajasta recognized them for what they were, a representation of fire-elementals.

With the sparse economy of movement so characteristically his, Micon rose to his feet, the wrapped sword in one hand. "Rajasta," he said, "give me the gong." When this was done, the Atlantean went on, "Move the brazier to the center of the room, and build thou a fire— pine and cypress and ultar." His words were clipped and brief, as if he recited a lesson learned well.

Rajasta, ignoring the second thoughts that already besieged him, set about the task resolutely. Micon went to the window again, and placed the sword upon the little table next to the figurine of Nar-inabi. Unwrapping the cloth, he exposed the decorated blade and the bejewelled hilt of the ceremonial weapon, and grasped it firmly again, to stand facing the window in a strained, listening attitude; Rajasta could almost see the Initiate gathering strength to himself; in sudden sympathy, he laid his hand on Micon's arm.

Micon stirred, impatiently. "Is the fire ready?"

Rebuked, the Priest bent to the brazier; kindling the slivers of fragrant wood, scattering the grains of incense over the thin blaze. Clouds of misty white smoke billowed upward; the smouldering woods were tiny sullen eyes glaring through the smoke.

Far away the chant rose and fell, rose and fell, gathering strength and volume. The thin column of fire rolled narrowly upward through the smoke, and subsided.

"It is ready," Rajasta said—and the chanting swelled, a rising flood of sound; and around the sound crept silence, as if the very pulses of the living were hushed and slow and heavy.

Almost majestic of aspect, quite changed from the Micon Rajasta knew so well, the Atlantean Initiate moved slowly to the room's center, placed the very tip of the ceremonial blade upon the brazier's metal rim, and half-circled so that again he faced the window. The sword's point still touching the brazier, Micon raised the gong, and held it before him at arm's length a moment; the smoking incense rose to writhe about the gong, as metal filings to a magnet.

"Rajasta!" Micon said, commandingly. "Stand by me, your arm across my shoulders." He winced as the Priest of Light complied. "Gently, my brother! Good. And now—" He drew a deep breath. "We wait."

The keening wail deepened, a rushing crescendo of sonic vibrations that ranged away and above the audible tones. Then— silence.

They waited. The sudden quiet lengthened, dripped and shadowed, crept back and welled up, suggesting the starless vastnesses of the universe, drowning all sounds in a dead, immense weight of stillness that crushed them like the folds of burial robes.

Rajasta could feel Micon's body, straight and stiff and real beneath the metallic cloak, and it was somehow the only real thing in all that empty deadened stillness. With a rasping whisper a wind blew through the window, and the lights grew dim; the air about them quivered, and a prickling came and crawled over Rajasta's skin. He felt, rather than saw, a misty shivering in the gloom, sensed faint distortions in the outlines of the familiar room.

The trained resonance of the Initiate's voice rang through the weight of the silence: "I have not summoned! By the Gong—" Moving suddenly, he struck the gong a sharp, hard blow with the sword's pommel; the brazen clamor sounded dashingly through the deadness. "By the Sword—" Again Micon raised the sword and held it outstretched, the point toward the window. "And by the Word on the Sword—by iron and bronze and fire—" He plunged the sword down, into the flame, and there was a crackling and sputtering of sparks.

Then the Word came slowly from Micon's throat, almost visible, in long tremolos of slow vibration that echoed and reechoed through octave over octave, thrilling and reverberating, sounding on . . . and on . . . and on, into some unimaginable infinity of time and space, quivering through universe after universe, into a stirring and a quickening that had neither place nor moment, but encompassed beginning and end and all between.

The shimmering distortion swirled and sparkled, faster and faster as if the masonry walls spun around and closed in upon them. Once more Micon raised the sword and sounded the gong with its pommel; again he thrust the blade's point into the brazier. There came a dull, distant roaring as the fire flared and tongued its way up the embedded blade. The distortions continued to twist around them, closer but less dizzyingly swift now; no longer did the room seem about to collapse.

Red and sullen orange, the hot light glowed in a streak across the Initiate's dark face. Slowly, slowly, the shimmerings wrapped themselves around the sword-blade, and for a moment lingered, a blue-white corona pulsing, before flowing down the blade into the flickering fire—which, with a hiss and a whisper, extinguished itself. The floor beneath them quaked and rattled. Then all was quiet.

Micon let himself lean against Rajasta, shivering, the aura of power and majesty quite gone from him. The sword remained, still upright in the burnt-out coals of the brazier. Rajasta was about to speak when there was a final, ear-splitting boom from far away.

"Fear not," Micon whispered, harshly. "The power returns through those who sought to use it, unsanctioned. Our work is—ended, now.

And I—" He sagged suddenly and went limp, a dead weight in the Priest's arms.

Rajasta lifted the Atlantean bodily and carried him to the bed. He laid Micon down, gently loosed and removed the leather thong about the Initiate's wrist, from which the gong had hung suspended. Setting the instrument aside, Rajasta dampened a bit of cloth he found nearby and bathed the beaded sweat from the unconscious man's face. Micon stirred and moaned.

Rajasta frowned sternly, his lips pursed with worry. The Atlantean had a white and death-like pallor, a waxen quality that boded no good. *This,* Rajasta reflected, *is exactly what I do not like about magic! It weakens the strong, enervates the weak! It would be a fine thing,* he thought angrily, *if Micon drove away one danger, only to succumb to this!*

The Atlantean groaned again, and Rajasta rose up, to stride to the door with a sudden decision. Summoning a slave, the Priest said only, "Send for the Healer Riveda."

III

For Domaris, drugged but tense with half-waking, formless shadows and horrors, the Nadir-night was a confused nightmare. It was almost a relief to struggle to awareness and find imperative physical pain substituted for dreams of dread; her child's birth, she suddenly realized, was imminent. On a fatalistic impulse, she sent no word to Micon or Rajasta. Deoris was nowhere to be found, and only Elara knew when she went, alone and afoot as the custom required, to the House of Birth.

And then there was the long waiting, more tiresome at first than painful. She submitted to the minor irritations of the preliminary stages with good grace, for Domaris was too well-disciplined to waste her strength in resentment: answering questions, giving all sorts of intimate information, being handled and examined like some animal (*like a kittening cat,* she told herself, trying to be amused instead of annoyed) kept her mind off her discomfort.

She was not exactly afraid: in common with all Temple women, she had served in Caratra's Temple many times, and the processes of birth held no mysteries for her. But her life had been one of radiant health, and this was almost her first experience with pain and its completely personal quality.

Moreover, and worse, she felt sorry for the little girl they had left with her during this first time of waiting. It was all too obviously the child's first attendance at a confinement, and she acted frightened. This did not add to Domaris's assurance, for she hated blundering of any sort, and if she had one deep-rooted fear, it was of being placed in unskilled hands when she could not help herself. And yet, irrationally, her annoyance grew, rather than lessening, when little Cetris told her, by way of reassurance, that the Priestess Karahama had chosen to attend her confinement.

Karahama! thought Domaris. *That daughter-to-the-winds!*

It seemed a long time, although it was barely past noon, when Cetris sent for the Priestess. To Domaris's complete astonishment, Deoris came into the room with her. It was the first time since the ceremony that Domaris had seen her sister robed as a Priestess of Caratra, and for a moment she hardly recognized the little white face beneath the blue veil. It seemed to her that Deoris's face was the most welcome thing she had ever seen in her life.

She turned toward her little sister—they had kept her on her feet—and held out her arms. But Deoris stood, stricken, in the doorway, making no move to come near her.

Domaris's knuckles were white as she clenched her hands together. "Deoris!" she pleaded. With frozenly reluctant steps, Deoris went to her sister's side and stood beside Domaris, while Karahama took Cetris to a far corner and questioned her in an undertone.

Deoris felt sick, seeing the familiar agony seize on Domaris. Domaris! Her sister, always to Deoris a little more than human. The realization shook something which lay buried in Deoris's heart; somehow, she had thought it would have to be different with Domaris. Ordinary things could not touch *her!* All that—the pain and the danger and the blood—it couldn't happen to Domaris!

And yet it could, it would. It was happening now, before her eyes.

Karahama dismissed Cetris—the little girls of twelve and thirteen were allotted only these simple tasks of waiting, of fetching and carrying and running errands—and came to Domaris, looking down at her with a reassuring smile. "You may rest now," she remarked, good-humouredly, and Domaris sank gratefully down on the couch. Deoris, steadying her with quick, strong hands, felt that Domaris was trembling, and sensed—with a terrible sensitivity—the effort Domaris was making not to struggle, or cry out.

Domaris made herself smile at Deoris and whisper, "Don't look like that, you silly child!" Domaris felt quite bewildered: what was the matter with Deoris? She had seen Deoris's work, had made a point of informing herself, for personal reasons, about her sister's progress. She knew that Deoris was already permitted to work without supervision, even to go unattended into the city to deliver the wives of such commoners or merchant women as might request the attendance of a Priestess; a token of skill which not even Elis had won as yet.

Karahama, noticing the smile and the rigid control, nodded with satisfaction. *Good! This Domaris has courage!* She felt kindly disposed toward her more fortunate half-sister, and now, bending above her, said pleasantly, "You will find the waiting easier now, I think. Deoris, the rule has not yet been broken—only bent a little." Karahama smiled at her own tiny joke as she added in dismissal, "You may go now."

Domaris heard the sentence with her heart sinking. "Oh, please let her stay with me!" she begged.

Deoris added her own plea: "I will be good!"

Karahama only smiled tolerantly and reminded them of the law: both women must surely know that in Caratra's House it was forbidden for a woman's sibling sister to attend the birth of her child. "Moreover," Karahama added, with a deferential movement of her head, "as an Initiate of Light, Domaris must be attended only by her equals."

"How interesting," Domaris murmured dryly, "that my own sister is not my equal."

Karahama said, with a little tightening of her mouth, "The rule does not refer to equality of birth. True, you are both daughters to the Arch-Priest—but you are Acolyte to the Guardian of the Gate, and an Initiate-Priestess. You must be attended by Priestesses of equivalent achievement."

"Has not the Healer-Priest Riveda, as well as yourself, pronounced Deoris capable?" Domaris argued, persisting despite the inner knowledge that it would serve no purpose.

Karahama deferentially repeated that the law was the law, and that if an exception was made now, exception would pile upon exception until the law crumbled away completely. Deoris, afraid to disobey, bent miserably to kiss her sister goodbye. Domaris's lips thinned in anger; this bastard half-sister presumed to lecture them on law, and speak of equals—either of birth or achievement! But a sudden wrench of pain stopped the protests on her tongue; she endured the pain for a moment, then cried out, clutching at Deoris's hands, twisting in sudden torment. Deoris could not have freed herself if she had tried, and Karahama, watching not unsympathetically for all her icy reserve, made no motion to interfere.

At last the spasm passed, and Domaris raised her face; sweat glistened on her forehead and her upper lip. Her voice had a knife's edge: "As an Initiate of Light," she said, throwing Karahama's words back to her, "I have the right to suspend that law! Deoris stays! Because *I wish it!*" She added the indomitable formula—As I have said it."

It was the first time Domaris had used her new rank to command. A queer little glow thrilled through her, to be drowned in the recurring pain. An ironical reflection stirred in the back of her mind: she had power over pain for others, but she was powerless to save herself any of this. Men's laws she might suspend almost as she willed; but she might not abrogate Nature so much as a fraction for her own sake, whatever her power, for she must experience fully, to her own completion. She endured.

Deoris's small hands were marked red when Domaris released them, and the older girl raised them remorsefully to her lips and kissed them. "Do I ask too much, puss?"

Deoris shook her head numbly. She couldn't refuse anything Domaris asked—but in her heart she wished that Domaris had not asked this, wished that Domaris had not the power to set aside those laws. She felt lost, too young, totally unfitted to take this responsibility.

Karahama, indignant at this irrefutable snubbing of herself and her authority, departed. Domaris's pleasure at this development was short-lived, for Karahama returned minutes later with two novice pupils.

Domaris raised herself, her face livid with fury. "This is intolerable!" she protested, her wrath driving out pain for a moment.

Temple women were supposed to be exempt from being the objects of lessons; Domaris, as a Priestess of Light, had the right to choose her own attendants, and she certainly was not subject to this—this humiliation!

Karahama paid not the slightest attention, but went on calmly lecturing to her pupils, indirectly implying that women in labor sometimes developed odd notions. . . . Domaris, smouldering with resentment, submitted. She was angry still, but there were intervals now, more and more often, when she was unable to express herself— and it is not effective to vent one's wrath in broken phrases. The most humiliating fact was that with each paroxysm she lost the thread of her invective.

Karahama's retaliation was not entirely heartless, however. Before long, she concluded her remarks, and began to dismiss her pupils.

Domaris summoned enough concentrated coherence to command, "You too may go! You have said yourself that I must be attended by my equals—so—leave me!"

It was biting dismissal: it repaid, in full and in kind, the indignity offered to Domaris. Spoken to an equal, without witnesses, it would have been cruel and insulting enough; said to Karahama, before her pupils, a blow in the face would have been less offensive.

Karahama drew herself erect, half inclined to protest; then, forcing a smile, only shrugged. Deoris *was* capable, after all; and Domaris was not in the slightest danger. Karahama could only demean herself further by argument. "So be it," she said tersely, and went.

Domaris, conscious that she violated the spirit if not the letter of the law, was almost moved to call her back—but still, not to have Deoris with her! Domaris was not perfect; she was very human, and very angry. Also, she was torn again by a hateful wave of pain that seemed to tear her protesting body in a dozen different directions. She forgot Karahama's existence. "Micon!" she moaned, writhing, "Micon!"

Deoris quickly bent over her, speaking soothing words, holding her, quieting the restless rebellion with a skillful touch. "Micon will come, if you ask it, Domaris," she said, when her sister had calmed a little. "Do you want that?"

Domaris dug her hands convulsively into the bedding. Now at last she understood this—which was not law but merely custom—which decreed that a woman should bear her child apart and without the knowledge of the father. "No," she whispered, "no, I will be quiet." Micon should not, must not know the price of his son! If he were in better health—but Mother Caratra! Was it like this for everyone?

Although she tried to keep her mind on the detailed instructions Deoris was giving, her thoughts slid away again and again into tortured memories. *Micon,* she thought, *Micon! He has endured more than this! He did not cry out! At last I begin to understand him!* She laughed then, more than a little hysterical, at the thought that, once, she had prayed to the Gods that she might share some of his torments. *Let no one say the Gods do not answer our prayers! And yes, yes! I would endure gladly worse than this for him!* Here her thoughts slid off into incoherence again. *The rack must be like this, a body broken apart on a wheel of pain . . . and so I share what he endured, to free him of all pain forever! Do I give birth, or death? Both, both!*

Grim, terrible laughter shook her with hysterical frenzies until mere movement became agony unbearable. She heard Deoris protesting angrily, felt hands restraining her, but none of Deoris's coaxing and threatening could quiet her hysteria now. She went on and on, laughing deliriously until it became more than laughter and she sobbed rackingly, unconscious to all except pain and its sudden cessation. She lay weeping in absolute exhaustion, unknowing, uncaring what was going on.

"Domaris." The strained, taut voice of her sister finally penetrated her subsiding sobs. "Domaris, darling, please try to stop crying, *please.* It's over. Don't you want to see your baby?"

Limp and worn with the aftermath of hysteria, Domaris could hardly believe her ears. Languidly she opened her eyes. Deoris looked down, with a weary smile, and turned to pick up the child—a boy, small and perfectly formed, with a reddish down that covered lightly the small round head, face tightly-screwed and contorted, squalling lustily at the need to live and breathe apart from his mother.

Domaris's eyes had slipped shut again. Deoris sighed, and set about wrapping the baby in linen cloths. *Why should such an indefinite scrap of flesh be allowed to cause such awful pain?* she asked herself, not for the first time. Something was gone irrevocably from her feeling for her sister. Domaris never knew quite how close Deoris came to hating her then, for having put her through this. . . .

When Domaris's eyes opened again, reason dwelt behind them, though they looked dark and haunted. She moved an exploring hand. "My baby," she whispered fearfully.

Deoris, afraid her sister would break into that terrible sobbing again, held the swaddled infant where Domaris could see him. "Can't you hear?" she asked gently. "He screams loud enough for twins!"

Domaris tried to raise herself, but fell back with weariness. She begged hungrily, "Oh, Deoris, give him to me!"

Deoris smiled at the unfailing miracle and bent to lay the baby boy on his mother's arm. Domaris's face was ecstatic and shining as she snuggled the squirming bundle close—then, with sudden apprehension, she fumbled at the cloths about him. Deoris bent and prevented her, smiling at this, too—further proof that Domaris was no different from any other woman. "He is perfect," she assured. "Must I count every finger and toe for you?"

With her free hand, Domaris touched her sister's face. "Little Deoris," she said softly, and stopped. She would never have wanted to endure that without Deoris at her side, but there was no way to tell her sister that. She only murmured, so very low that Deoris could, if she chose, pretend not to hear: "Thank you, Deoris!" Then, laying her head wearily beside the baby, "Poor mite! I wonder if he is as tired as I am?" Her eyes flickered open again. "Deoris! Say nothing of this to Micon! I must myself lay our son in his arms. That is my duty—" Her lips contracted, but she went on, steadily, "and my very great privilege."

"He shall not hear it from me," Deoris promised, and lifted the baby from his mother's reluctant arms.

Domaris almost slept, dreaming, although she was conscious of cool water on her hot face and bruised body. Docilely, she ate and drank what was put to her lips, and knew, sleepily, that Deoris—or someone—smoothed her tangled hair, covered her with clean fresh garments that smelled of spices, and tucked her between smooth fragrant linens. Twilight and silence were cool in the room; she heard soft steps, muted voices. She slept, woke again, slept.

Once, she became conscious that the baby had been laid in her arms again, and she cuddled him close, for the moment altogether happy. "My little son," she whispered tenderly, contentedly; then, smiling to herself, Domaris gave him the name he would bear until he was a man. "My little Micail!"

IV

The door swung open silently. The tall and forbidding form of Mother Ysouda stood at the threshold. She beckoned to Deoris, who motioned to her not to speak aloud; the two tiptoed into the corridor.

"She sleeps again?" Mother Ysouda murmured. "The Priest Rajasta waits for you in the Men's Court, Deoris. Go at once and change your garments, and I will care for Domaris." She turned to enter the room, then halted and looked down at her foster daughter and asked in a whisper, "What happened, girl? How came Domaris to anger Karahama so fearfully? Were there angry words between them?"

Timidly with much prompting, Deoris related what had happened.

Mother Ysouda shook her grey head. "This is not like Domaris!" Her withered face drew down in a scowl.

"What will Karahama do?" Deoris asked apprehensively.

Mother Ysouda stiffened, conscious that she had spoken too freely to a mere junior Priestess. "You will not be punished for obeying the command of an Initiate-Priestess," she said, with austere dignity, "but it is not for you to question Karahama. Karahama is a Priestess of the Mother, and it would indeed be unbecoming in her to harbor resentment. If Domaris spoke thoughtlessly in her extremity, doubtless Karahama knows it was the anger of a moment of pain and will not be offended. Now go, Deoris. The Guardian waits."

The words were rebuke and dismissal, but Deoris pondered them, deeply troubled, while she changed her garments—the robes she wore within the shrine of the Mother must not be profaned by the eyes of any male. Deoris could guess at much that Mother Ysouda had not wanted to say: Karahama was not of the Priest's Caste, and her reactions could not accurately be predicted.

In the Men's Court, a few minutes later, Rajasta turned from his pacing to hasten toward Deoris.

"Is all well with Domaris?" he asked. "They say she has a son."

"A fine healthy son," Deoris answered, surprised to see the calm Rajasta betraying such anxiety. "And all is well with Domaris."

Rajasta smiled with relief and approval. Deoris seemed no longer a spoilt and petulant child, but a woman, competent and assured within her own sphere. He had always considered himself the mentor of Deoris as well as of Domaris, and, though a little disappointed that she had left the path of the Priesthood of Light and thus placed herself beyond his reach as a future Acolyte or Initiate, he had approved her choice. He had often inquired about her since she had been admitted to the service of Caratra, and it pleased him greatly that the Priestess praised her skill.

With genuine paternal affection he said, "You grow swiftly in wisdom, little daughter. They tell me you delivered the child. I had believed that was contrary to some law. . . ."

Deoris covered her eyes with one hand. "Domaris's rank places her above that law."

Rajasta's eyes darkened. "That is true, but—did she ask, or command?"

"She—commanded."

Rajasta was disturbed. While a Priestess of Light had the privilege of choosing her own attendants, that law had been made to allow leniency under certain unusual conditions. In wilfully invoking it for her own comfort, Domaris had done wrong.

Deoris, sensing his mood, defended her sister. "*They* violated the law! A Priest's daughter is exempt from having pupils or voices beside her, and Ka—"

She broke off, blushing. In the heat of the moment, she had forgotten that she spoke to a man. Moreover, it was unthinkable to argue with Rajasta; yet she felt impelled to add, stubbornly, "If anyone did wrong, it was Karahama!"

Rajasta checked her with a gesture. "I am Guardian of the Gate," he reminded her, "not of the Inner Courts!" More gently, he said, "You are very young to have been so trusted, my child. Command or no command—no one would have dared leave the Arch-Priest's daughter in incompetent hands."

Shyly, Deoris murmured, "Riveda told me—" She stopped, remembering that Rajasta did not much like the Adept.

The Priest said only, "Lord Riveda is wise; what did he tell thee?"

"That—when I lived before—" She flushed, and hurried on, "I had known all the healing arts, he said, and had used them evilly. He said that—in this life, I should atone for that. . . ."

Rajasta considered, heavy-hearted, recollecting the destiny written in the stars for this child. "It may be so, Deoris," he said, noncommittally. "But beware of becoming proud; the dangers of old lives tend to recur. Now tell me: did it go hard for Domaris?"

"Somewhat," Deoris said, hesitantly. "But she is strong, and all should have been easy. Yet there was much pain that I could not ease. I fear—" She lowered her eyes briefly, then met Rajasta's gaze bravely as she went on, "I am no High Priestess in this life, but I very much fear that another child might endanger her greatly."

Rajasta's mouth became a tight line. Domaris had indeed done ill, and the effect of her wilfulness was already upon her. Such a recommendation, from one of Deoris's skill, was a grave warning— but her rank in the Temple was not equivalent to her worth, and she had, as yet, no authority to make such a recommendation. Had Domaris been properly attended by a Priestess of high rank, even one of lesser skill, her word, when properly sworn and attested, would have meant that Domaris would never again be allowed to risk her life; a living mother to a living child was held, in the Temple of Light, as worth more than the hope of a second child. Now Domaris must bear the effect of the cause she had herself set in motion.

"It is not your business to recommend," he said, as gently as possible. "But for now, we need not speak of that. Micon—"

"Oh, I almost forgot!" Deoris exclaimed. "We are not to tell him, Domaris wants to—" She broke off, seeing the immense sadness that crossed Rajasta's face.

"You must think of something to tell him, little daughter. He is gravely ill, and must not be allowed to worry about her."

Deoris suddenly found herself unable to speak, and her eyes stared wide.

Brokenly, Rajasta said, "Yes, it is the end. At last—I think it is the end."

CHAPTER SEVENTEEN
✠ DESTINY AND DOOM ✠

I

Micail was three days old when Domaris rose and dressed herself with a meticulous care unusual with her. She used the perfume Micon loved, the scent from his homeland—his first gift to her. Her face was still, but not calm, and although Domaris kept from crying as Elara made her lovely for this ordeal, the servant woman herself burst into tears as she put the wiggling, clean-scented bundle into his mother's arms.

"Don't!" Domaris begged, and the woman fled. Domaris held her son close, thinking dearly, *Child, I bore you to give your father death.*

Remorsefully she bent her face over the summer softness of his. Grief was a part of her love for this child, a deep bitter thing twisting into her happiness. She had waited three days, and still she was not sure that either her body or her mind would carry her through this final duty to the man she loved. Lingering, still delaying, she scanned the miniature indeterminate features of Micail, seeking some strong resemblance to his father, and a sob twisted her throat as she kissed the reddish down on his silken forehead.

At last, raising her face proudly, she moved to the door and went forth, Micail in her arms. Her step was steady; her reluctant feet did not betray her dread.

Guilt lay deep on her. Those three days were, she felt, a selfishness that had held a tortured man to life. Even now she moved only under the compulsion of sworn duty, and her thoughts were barbed whips of self-scorn. Micail whimpered protestingly and she realized that she was clutching him far too tightly to her breast.

She walked on, slowly, seeing with half her eyes the freshening riot of color in the gardens; though she pulled the swaddlings automatically closer about her child's head, Domaris saw only Micon's dark haggard face, felt only the bitterness of her own pain.

The way was not long, but to Domaris it was the length to the world's end. With every step, she left the last of her youth a little further behind. Yet after a time, an indefinite period, the confusion of thought and feeling gradually cleared and she found herself entering Micon's rooms. She swayed a little with the full realization: *Now there is no return.* Dimly she knew that for her there had never been.

Her eyes swept the room in unconscious appeal, and the desperation in her young face brought choking grief to Deoris's throat. Rajasta's eyes became even more compassionate, and even Riveda's stern mouth lost some of its grimness. This last Domaris saw, and it gave her a new strength born of anger.

Proudly she drew herself erect, clasping the child. Her eyes resting on Micon's wasted face; she put the others out of her mind. This was the moment of her giving; now she could give more than herself, could surrender—and by her own act—her hopes of any personal future. Silently she moved to stand beside him, and the change which but a few days had wrought in him smote her like a blow.

Until this moment, Domaris had allowed herself to cling to some faint hope that Micon might still be spared to her, if only a little longer. . . . Now she saw the truth.

Long she looked upon him, and every feature of Micon's darkly noble frame etched itself forever across her life with the bitter acid of agony.

Finally Micon's sightless eyes opened, and it seemed that at last he saw, with something clearer than sight, for—although Domaris had not spoken, and her coming had been greeted with silence—he spoke directly to her. "My lady of Light," he whispered, and there was that in his voice which defied naming. "Let me hold—our son!"

Domaris knelt, and Rajasta moved to unobtrusively support Micon as the Atlantean drew himself upright. Domaris laid the child in the thin outstretched arms, and murmured words in themselves unimportant, but to the dying man, of devastating significance: "Our son, beloved—our perfect little son."

Micon's attenuated fingers ran lightly, tenderly across the little face. His own face, like a delicate waxen death-mask, bent over the child; tears gathered and dropped from the blind eyes, and he sighed, with an infinite wistfulness. "If I might—only once—behold my son!"

A harsh sound like a sob broke the silence, and Domaris raised wondering eyes. Rajasta was as silent as a statue, and Deoris's throat could never have produced that sound . . .

"My beloved—" Micon's voice steadied somewhat. "One task remains. Rajasta—" The Atlantean's ravaged face turned to the Priest. "It is yours to guide and guard my son." So saying, he allowed Rajasta to take the baby in his hands, and quickly Domaris cradled Micon's head against her breast. Weakly smiling, he drew away from her. "No," he said with great tenderness. "I am weary, my love. Let me end this now. Begrudge not your greatest gift."

He rose slowly to his feet, and Riveda, shadow-swift, was there to put his strong arm under Micon's. With a little knowing smile, Micon accepted the Grey-robe's support. Deoris reached to clasp her sister's icy hand in her tiny warm one, but Domaris was not even aware of the touch.

Micon leaned his face over the child, who lay docile in Rajasta's arms, and with his racked hands, lightly touched the closed eyes.

"See—what I give you to see, Son of Ahtarrath!"

The twisted fingers touched the minute, curled ears as the Initiate's trained voice rang through the room: "Hear—what I give you to hear!"

He drew his hands slightly over the downy temples. "Know the power I know and bestow upon you, child of Ahtarrath's heritage!"

He touched the rosy seeking mouth, which sucked at his finger and spat it forth again. "Speak with the powers of the storm and the winds—of sun and rain, water and air, earth and fire! Speak only with justice, and with love."

The Atlantean's hand now rested over the baby's heart. "Beat only to the call of duty, to the powers of love! Thus I, by the Power I bear—" Micon's voice thinned suddenly. "By the—the Power I bear, I seal and sign you to—to that Power . . ."

Micon's face had become a drained and ghastly white. Word by word and motion by motion, he had loosed the superb forces which alone had held him from dissolution. With what seemed a tremendous effort, he traced a sign across the baby's brow; then leaned heavily on Riveda.

Domaris, with hungry tenderness, rushed to his side, but Micon, for a moment, paid her no heed as he gasped, "I knew this would—I knew—Lord Riveda, you must finish—finish the binding! I am—" Micon drew a long, labored breath. "Seek not to play me false!" And his words were punctuated by a distant clap of thunder.

Grim, unspeaking, Riveda let Domaris take Micon's weight, freeing him for the task. The Grey-robe knew well why he, and not Rajasta or some other, had been chosen to do this thing. The apparent sign of the Atlantean's trust was, in feet, the exact opposite: by binding Riveda's karma with that of the child, even in this so small way, Micon sought to ensure that Riveda, at least, would not dare attack the child, and the Power the baby represented. . . .

Riveda's ice-blue eyes burned beneath his brows as, with a brusque voice and manner, he took up the interrupted ritual: "To you, son of Ahtarrath, Royal Hunter, Heir-to-the-Word-of-Thunder, the Power passes. Sealed by the Light—" The Adept undid, with his strong skillful hands, the swaddlings about the child, and exposed him, with a peculiarly ceremonious gesture, to the flooding sunlight. The rays seemed to kiss the downy skin, and Micail stretched with a little cooing gurgle of content.

The solemnity of the Magician's face did not lighten, but his eyes now smiled as he returned the child to Rajasta's hands, and raised his arms as for invocation. "Father to son, from age to age," Riveda said, "the Power passes; known to the true-begotten. So it was, and so it is, and so it shall ever be. Hail Ahtarrath—and to Ahtarrath, farewell!"

Micail stared with placid, sleepy gravity at the circle of faces which ringed him in—but not for long. The ceremony ended now, Rajasta hastily placed the baby in Deoris's arms, and took Micon from Domaris's embrace, laying him gently down. Still the Atlantean's hands groped weakly for Domaris, and she came and held him close again; the naked grief in her eyes was a crucifixion.

Deoris, the baby clasped to her breast, sobbed noiselessly, her face half-buried in Rajasta's mantle; the Priest of Light stood with his arm around her, but his eyes were fixed upon Micon. Riveda, his arms crossed on his chest, stared somberly upon the scene, and his massive shadow blotted the sunlight from the room.

The Prince was still, so still that the watchers, too, held their breath. . . . At last he stirred, faintly. "Lady—clothed with Light," he whispered. "Forgive me." He waited, and drops of sweat glistened on his forehead. "*Domaris.*" The word was a prayer.

It seemed that Domaris would never speak, that speech had been dammed at its fountainhead, that all the world would go silent to the end of eternity. At last her white lips parted, and her voice was clear and triumphant in the stillness. "It is well, my beloved. Go in peace."

The waxen face was immobile, but the lips stirred in the ghost of Micon's old radiant smile. "Love of mine," he whispered, and then more softly still, "Heart—of flame—" and a breath and a sigh moved in the silence and faded.

Domaris bent forward . . . and her arms, with a strange, pathetic little gesture, fell to her sides, empty.

Riveda moved softly to the bedside, and looked into the serene face, closing the dead eyes. "It is over," the Adept said, almost tenderly and with regret. "What courage, what strength—and what waste!"

Domaris rose, dry-eyed, and turned toward Riveda. "That, my Lord, is a matter of opinion," she said slowly. "It is our triumph! Deoris—give me my son." She took Micail in her arms, and her face shone, unearthly, in the sublimity of her sorrow. "Behold our child— and our future. Can you show me the like, Lord Riveda?"

"Your triumph, Lady, indeed," Riveda acknowledged, and bent in deep reverence.

Deoris came and would have taken the baby once more, but Domaris clung to him, her hands trembling as she caressed her little son. Then, with a last, impassioned look at the dark still face that had been Micon's, she turned away, and the men heard her whispered, helpless prayer: "Help me—O Thou Which Art!" Deoris led her sister, resistless, away.

II

That night was cold. The full moon, rising early, flooded the sky with a brilliance that blotted out the stars. Low on the horizon, sullen flames glowed at the sea-wall, and ghost-lights, blue and dancing, flitted and streamed in the north.

Riveda, for the first and last time in his life robed in the stainless white of the Priest's Caste, paced with stately step backward and forward before Micon's apartments. He had not the faintest idea why he, rather than Rajasta or one of the other Guardians, had been chosen for this vigil—and he was no longer so certain why Micon had suffered his aid at the last! Had trust or distrust been the major factor in Micon's final acceptance of him?

It was clear that the Atlantean had, in part at least, feared him. But why? He was no Black-robe! The twists and turns of it presented a riddle far beyond his reading—and Riveda did not like the feeling of ignorance. Yet without protest or pride he had divested himself tonight of the grey robe he had worn for so many years, and clothed himself in the ritual robes of Light. He felt curiously transformed, as if with the robes he had also slipped on something of the character of these punctilious Priests.

Nonetheless he felt a deeply personal grief, and a sense of defeat. In Micon's last hours, his weakness had moved Riveda as his strength could never have done. A grudged and sullenly yielded respect had given way to deep and sincere affection.

It was seldom, indeed, that Riveda allowed events to disturb him. He did not believe in destiny—but he knew that threads ran through time and the lives of men, and that one could become entangled in them. *Karma.* It was, Riveda thought grimly, like the avalanches of his own Northern mountains. A single stone rattled loose by a careless step, and all the powers of the world and nature could not check an inch of its motion. Riveda shuddered. He felt a curious certainty that Micon's death had brought destiny and doom on them all. He didn't like the thought. Riveda preferred to believe that he could master destiny, pick a path through the pitfalls of karma, by his will and strength alone.

He continued his pacing, head down. The Order of Magicians, known here as Grey-robes, was ancient, and elsewhere held a more honored name. In Atlantis were many Adepts and Initiates of this Order, among whom Riveda held high place. And now Riveda knew something no one else had guessed, and felt it was legitimately his own.

Once, in mad raving, a word and a gesture had slipped unaware, from his chela, Reio-ta. Riveda had noted both, meaningless as they had seemed at the moment. Later, he had seen the same gesture pass between Rajasta and Cadamiri when they thought themselves unobserved; and Micon, in the delirium of agony which had preceded the quiet of his last hours, had muttered Atlantean phrases—one a duplicate of Reio-ta's. Riveda's brain had stored all these things for future reference. Knowledge, to him, was something to be acquired; a thing hidden was something to be sought all the more assiduously.

Tomorrow, Micon's body was to be burned, the ashes returned to his homeland. That task he, Riveda, should undertake. Who had a better right than the Priest who had consecrated Micon's son to the power of Ahtarrath?

III

At daybreak, Riveda ceremoniously drew back the curtains, letting sunlight flood in and fill the apartment where Micon lay. Dawn was a living sea of ruby and rose and livid fire; the light lay like dancing flames on the dark dead face of the Initiate, and Riveda, frowning, felt that Micon's death had ended nothing.

This began in fire, Riveda thought, *it will end in fire . . . but will it be only the fire of Micon's funeral? Or are there higher flames rising in the future . . . ? He* frowned, shaking his head. *What nonsense am I dreaming? Today, fire will burn what the Black-robes left of Micon, Prince of Ahtarrath . . . and yet, in his own way, he has defeated all the elements.*

With the sun's rise, white-robed Priests came and took Micon up tenderly, bearing him down the winding pathway into the face of the morning. Rajasta, his face drawn with grief, walked before the bier; Riveda, with silent step and bent head, walked after. Behind them, a long procession of white-mantled Priests and Priestesses in silver fillets and blue cloaks followed in tribute to the stranger, the Initiate who had died in their midst . . . and after these stole a dim grey shadow, bowed like an old man shaken with palsied sobbing, grey cloak huddled over his face, his hands hidden within a patched and threadbare robe. But no man saw how Reio-ta Lantor of Ahtarrath followed his Prince and brother to the flames.

Also unseen, high on the summit of the great pyramid, a woman stood, tall and sublime, her face crimsoned with the sunrise and the morning sky ablaze with the fire of her hair. In her arms a child lay cradled, and as the procession faded to black shadows against the radiant light in the east, Domaris held her child high against the rising sun. In a steady voice, she began to intone the morning hymn:

> *O beautiful upon the Horizon of the East,*
> *Lift up the light unto day, O eastern Star.*
> *Day-star, awaken, arise!*
> *Joy and giver of light, awake.*
> *Lord and giver of life,*
> *Lift up thy light, O Star of Day,*
> *Day-star, awaken, arise!*

Far below, the flames danced and spiralled up from the pyre, and the world was drowned in flame and sunlight.

BOOK THREE
✠ DEORIS ✠

CHAPTER ONE
✠ THE PROMISE ✠

I

"Lord Rajasta," Deoris greeted the old Priest anxiously. "I am glad you are come! Domaris is so—so strange!"

Rajasta's lined face quirked into an enquiring glance.

Deoris rushed on impetuously, "I can't understand—she does everything she should, she isn't crying all the time any more, but—" The words came out as a sort of wail: "She isn't *there!*"

Nodding slowly, Rajasta touched the child's shoulder in a comforting caress. "I feared this—I will see her. Is she alone now?"

"Yes, Domaris wouldn't look at them when they came, wouldn't answer when they spoke, just sat staring at the wall—" Deoris began to cry.

Rajasta attempted to soothe her, and after a few moments managed to discover that "they" referred to Elis and Mother Ysouda. His wise, old eyes looked down into Deoris's small face, white and mournful, and what he saw there made him stroke her hair lingeringly before he said, with gentle insistence, "You are stronger than she, now, though it may not seem so. You must be kind to her. She needs all your love and all your strength, too." Leading the still sniffling Deoris to a nearby couch, and settling her upon it, he said, "I will go to her now."

In the inner room, Domaris sat motionless, her eyes fixed on distances past imagining, her hands idle at her sides. Her face was as a statue's, still and remote.

"Domaris," said Rajasta softly. "My daughter."

Very slowly, from some secret place of the spirit, the woman came back; her eyes took cognizance of her surroundings. "Lord Rajasta," she acknowledged, her voice little more than a ripple in the silence.

"Domaris," Rajasta repeated, with an oddly regretful undertone. "My Acolyte, you neglect your duties. This is not worthy of you."

"I have done what I must," Domaris said tonelessly, as if she did not even mean to deny the accusation.

"You mean, you make the gestures," Rajasta corrected her. "Do you think I do not know you are willing yourself to die? You can do that, if you are coward enough. But your son, and Micon's—" Her eyes winced, and seeing even this momentary reaction, Rajasta insisted, "Micon's son needs you."

Now Domaris's face came alive with pain. "No," she said, "even in that I have failed! My baby has been put to a wet nurse!"

"Which need not have happened, had you not let your grief master you," Rajasta charged. "Blind, foolish girl! Micon loved and honored and trusted you above all others—and you fail him like this! You shame his memory, if his trust was misplaced—and you betray yourself—and you disgrace me, who taught you so poorly!"

Domaris sprang to her feet, raising protesting hands, but at Rajasta's imperative gesture she stilled the words rising in her throat, and listened with bent head.

"Do you think you are alone in grieving, Domaris? Do you not know that Micon was more than friend, more than brother to me? I am lonely since I can no longer walk at his side. But I cannot cease to live because one I loved has gone beyond my ability to follow!" He added, more gently, "Deoris, too, grieves for Micon—and she has not even the memory of his love to comfort her."

The woman's head drooped, and she began to weep, stormily, frantically; and Rajasta, his austere face kind again, gathered her in his arms and held her close until the crisis of desolate sobbing worked itself out, leaving Domaris exhausted, but alive.

"Thank you, Rajasta," she whispered, with a smile that almost made the man weep too. "I—I will be good."

II

Restlessly, Domaris paced the floor of her apartments. The weary hours and days that had worn away had only brought the unavoidable nearer, and now the moment of decision was upon her. Decision? No, the decision had been made. Only the time of action had come, when she must grant the fulfillment of her pledged word. What did it matter that her promise to Arvath had been given when she was wholly ignorant of what it entailed?

With a tight smile, she remembered words spoken many years ago: *Yes, my Lords of the Council, I accept my duty to marry. As well Arvath as another—I like him somewhat.* That had been long ago, before she had dreamed that love between man and woman was more than a romance of pretty words, before birth and death and loss had become personal to her. She had been, she reflected dryly, thirteen years old at the time.

Her face, thinner than it had been a month ago, now turned impassive, for she recognized the step at the door. She turned and greeted Arvath, and for a moment Arvath could only stand and stammer her name. He had not seen her since Micon's death, and the change in her appalled him. Domaris was beautiful—more beautiful than ever—but her face was pale and her eyes remote, as if they had looked upon secret things. From a gay and laughing girl she had changed to a woman—a woman of marble? Or of ice? Or merely a stilled flame that burned behind the quiet eyes?

"I hope you are well," he said banally, at last.

"Oh, yes, they have taken good care of me," Domaris said, and looked at him with tense exasperation. She knew what he wanted (she thought with a faint sarcasm that was new to her); why didn't he come to the point—why evade the issue with courtesies?

Arvath sensed that her mood was not entirely angelic, and it made him even more constrained. "I have come to ask—to claim—your promise. . . ."

"As is your right," Domaris acknowledged formally, stifling with the attempt to control her breathing.

Arvath's impetuous hands went out and he clasped her close to him. "O beloved! May I claim you tonight before the Vested Five?"

"If you wish," she said, almost indifferently. One time was no worse than another. Then the old Domaris came back for a moment in a burst of impulsive sincerity. "O Arvath, forgive me that I—that I bring you no more than I can give," she begged, and briefly clung to him.

"That you give yourself is enough," he said tenderly.

She looked at him, with a wise sorrow in her eyes but said nothing.

His arms tightened around her demandingly. "I will make you happy," he vowed. "I swear it!"

She remained passive in his embrace; but Arvath knew, with a nagging sense of futility, that she was unstirred by the torment that swept him. He repeated, and it sounded like a challenge, "I swear it— that I will make you forget!"

After an instant, Domaris put up her hands and freed herself from him; not with any revulsion, but with an indifference that filled the man with apprehension . . . Quickly he swept the disturbing thought aside. He would awaken her to love, he thought confidently—and it never occurred to him that she was far more aware of love's nature than he.

Still, he had seen the momentary softening of pity in her eyes, and he knew enough not to press his advantage too far. He whispered, against her hair, "Be beautiful for me, my wife!" Then, brushing her temple with a swift kiss, he left her.

Domaris stood for a long minute, facing the closed door, and the deep pity in her eyes paled gradually to a white dread. "He's—he's *hungry*," she breathed, and a hidden trembling started and would not be stilled through her entire body. "How can I—I can't! I can't! Oh. Micon, *Micon!*"

CHAPTER TWO
✠ THE FEVER ✠

I

That summer, fever raged in the city called the Circling Snake. Within the Temple precincts, where the Healers enforced rigid sanitary laws, it did not strike; but in the city itself it worked havoc, for a certain element of the population was too lazy or too stupid to follow the dictates of the priests.

Riveda and his Healers swept through the city like an invading army, without respect for plague or persons. They burned the stinking garbage heaps and the festering, squalid tenements; burned the foetid slave-huts of cruel or stupid owners who allowed men to live in worse filth than beasts. Invading every home, they fumigated, cleaned, nursed, isolated, condemned, buried, or burned, daring even to enter homes where the victims were already rotten with the stink of death. They cremated the corpses—sometimes by force, where caste enjoined burial. Wells suspected of pollution were tested and often sealed, regardless of bribes, threats. and sometimes outright defiance. In short, they made themselves an obnoxious nuisance to the rich and powerful whose neglect or viciousness had permitted the plague to spread in the first place.

Riveda himself worked to exhaustion, nursing cases whom no one else could be persuaded to approach, out-bullying fat city potentates who questioned the value of his destructive mercy, sleeping in odd moments in houses already touched by death. He seemed to walk guarded by a series of miracles.

Deoris, who had served her novitiate in the Healers sponsored by her kinsman Cadamiri, met Riveda one evening as she stepped out for a moment from a house where she, with another Priestess, had been caring for the sick of two families. The woman of the house was out of danger, but four children had died, three more lay gravely ill, and another was sickening.

Seeing her, Riveda crossed the street to give her a greeting. His face was lined and very tired, but he looked almost happy, and she asked why.

"Because I believe the worst is over. There are no new cases in the North Quarter today, and even here—if the rains hold off three days more, we have won." The Adept looked down at Deoris; effort had put years into her face, and her beauty was dimmed by tiredness. Riveda's heart softened, and he said with a gentle smile, "I think you must be sent back to the Temple, my child; you are killing yourself."

She shook her head, fighting temptation. It would be heavenly comfort to be out of this! But she only said, stubbornly, "I'll stay while I'm needed."

Riveda caught her hands and held them. "I'd take you myself, child, but I'd not be allowed inside the gates, for I go where contagion is worst. I can't return until the epidemic is over, but you . . ." Suddenly, he caught her against him in a hard, rough embrace. "Deoris, you must go! I won't have you ill, I won't take the chance of losing you too!"

Startled and confused, Deoris was stiff in his arms; then she loosened and clung to him and felt the tickly stubble of his cheek against her face.

Without releasing her, he straightened and looked down, his stern mouth gentle. "There is danger even in this. You will have to bathe and change your clothing now—but Deoris, you're shivering, you can't be cold in this blistering heat?"

She stirred a little in his arms. "You're hurting me," she protested.

"Deoris!" said Riveda, in swift alarm, as she swayed against him.

The girl shivered with the violent cold that crawled suddenly around her. "I—I am all right," she protested weakly—but then she whispered. "I—I do want to go home," and slipped down, a shivering, limp little huddle in Riveda's arms.

II

It was not the dreaded plague. Riveda diagnosed marsh-fever, aggravated by exhaustion. After a few days, when they were certain there was no danger of contagion, they allowed her to be carried to the Temple in a litter. Once there, Deoris spent weeks that seemed like years, not dangerously ill, but drowsily delirious; even when the fever finally abated, her convalescence was very gradual, and it was a long time before she began to take even the most languid interest in living again.

The days flickered by in brief sleeps and half-waking dreams. She lay watching the play of shadows and sunlight on the walls, listening to the babble of the fountains and to the musical trilling of four tiny blue birds that chirped and twittered in a cage in the sunlight—Domaris had sent them to her. Domaris sent messages and gifts nearly every day, in fact, but Domaris herself did not come near her, though Deoris cried and begged for her for days during her delirium. Elara, who tended Deoris night and day, would say only that Arvath had forbidden it. But when the delirium was gone, Deoris learned from Elis that Domaris was already pregnant, and far from well; they dared not risk the contagion of even this mild fever. At learning this, Deoris turned her face to the wall and lay without speaking for a whole day, and did not mention her sister again.

Arvath himself came often, bringing the gifts and the loving messages Domaris sent. Chedan paid brief, shy, tongue-tied visits almost every day. Once Rajasta came, bearing delicate fruits to tempt her fastidious appetite, and full of commendation for her work in the epidemic.

When memory began to waken in her, and the recollection of Riveda's curious behavior swam out of the bizarre dreams of her delirium, she asked about the Adept of the Grey-robes. They told her Riveda had gone on a long journey, but secretly Deoris believed they lied, that he had died in the epidemic. Grief died at the source; the well-springs of her emotions had been sapped by the long illness and longer convalescence, and Deoris went through the motions of living without much interest in past, present, or future.

It was many weeks before they allowed her to leave her bed, and months before she was permitted to walk about in the gardens. When, finally, she was well enough, she returned to her duties in the Temple of Caratra—more or less, for she found them all conspiring to find easy and useless tasks which would not tax her returning strength. She devoted much of her time to study as she grew stronger, attending lectures given to the apprentice healers even though she could not accompany them in their work. Often she would steal into a corner of the library to listen from afar to the discussions of the Priests of Light. Moreover, as the Priestess Deoris, she was now entitled to a scribe of her own; it was considered more intelligent to listen than to read, or the hearing could be more completely concentrated than the sight.

On the evening of her sixteenth birthday, one of the Priestesses had sent Deoris to a hill overlooking the Star Field, to gather certain flowers of medicinal value. The long walk had taxed her strength, and she sat down for a moment to rest before beginning the task when, suddenly, raising her head, she saw the Adept Riveda walking along the sunlit path in her direction. For a moment she could only stare. She had been so convinced of his death that she thought momentarily that the veil had thinned, that she saw not him but his spirit . . . then, convinced she was not having hallucinations after all, she cried out and ran toward him.

Turning, he saw her and held out his arms. "Deoris," he said, and clasped her shoulders with his hands. "I have been anxious about you, they told me you had been dangerously ill. Are you quite recovered?" What he saw as he looked down into her face evidently satisfied him.

"I—I thought you were dead."

His rough smile was warmer than usual. "No, as you can see, I am very much alive. I have been away, on a journey to Atlantis. Perhaps some day I will tell you all about it . . . I came to see you before I left, but you were too ill to know me. What are you doing here?"

"Gathering *shaing* flowers."

Riveda snorted. "Oh, a most worthy use of your talents! Well, now I have returned, perhaps I can find more suitable work for you. But at the moment I have errands of my own, so I must return you to your blossoms." He smiled again. "Such an important task must not be interrupted by a mere Adept!"

Deoris laughed, much cheered, and on an impulse Riveda bent

and kissed her lightly before going on his way. He could not himself have explained the kiss—he was not given to impulsive actions. As he hastened toward the Temple, Riveda felt curiously disturbed, remembering the lassitude in the girl's eyes. Deoris had grown taller in the months of her illness, although she would never be very tall. Thin and frail, and yet beautiful with a fragile and wraithlike beauty, she was no longer a child, and yet she was hardly a woman. Riveda wondered, annoyed with himself for the direction his thoughts took, how young Chedan stood with his lovemaking. *No,* he decided, *that is not the answer.* Deoris had not the look of a girl mazed by the wakening of passion, nor the consciousness of sex that would have been there in that case. She had *permitted* his kiss, as innocently as a small child.

Riveda did not know that Deoris followed him with her eyes until he was quite out of sight, and that her face was flushed and alive again.

CHAPTER THREE
✠ CHOICE AND KARMA ✠

I

The night was falling, folding like soft and moonless wings of indigo over the towered roofs of the Temple and the ancient city which lay beneath it, smothered in coils of darkness. A net of dim lights lay flung out over the blackness, and far away a pale phosphorescence hung around the heavier darkness of the sea-harbor. Starlight, faint and faulty, flickered around the railings which outlined the roof-platform of the great pyramid and made a ghostly haze around the two cloaked figures who stood there.

Deoris was shivering a little in the chilly breeze, holding, with lifted hands, the folds of her hooded cloak. The wind tugged at them, and finally she threw back the hood and let the short heavy ringlets of her hair blow as they would. She felt a little scared, and very young.

Riveda's face, starkly austere in the pallid light, brooded with a distant, inhuman calm. He had not spoken a single word since they had emerged onto the rooftop, and her few shy attempts to speak had been choked into silence by the impassive quiet of his eyes. When he made an abrupt movement, she started in sudden terror.

He leaned on the railing, one clenched hand supporting the leaning blackness of his body and said, in tones of command, "Tell me what troubles you, Deoris."

"I don't know," Deoris murmured. "So many new things are coming at once." Her voice grew hard and tight. "My sister Domaris is going to have another baby!"

Riveda stared a moment, his eyes narrowing. "I knew that. What did you expect?"

"Oh, I don't know. . . ." The girl's shoulders drooped. "It was different, somehow, with Micon. He was . . ."

"He was a Son of the Sun," Riveda prompted gently, and there was no mockery in his voice.

Deoris looked up, almost despairing. "Yes. But Arvath—and so soon, like animals—Riveda, *why?*"

"Who can say?" Riveda replied, and his voice dropped, sorrowful and confiding. "It is a great pity. Domaris could have gone so far. . . ."

Deoris lifted her eyes, eager, mute questions in them.

The Adept smiled, a very little, over her head. "A woman's mind is strange, Deoris. You have been kept in innocence, and cannot yet understand how deeply the woman is in subjugation to her body. I do not say it is wrong, only that it is a great pity." He paused, and his voice grew grim. "So. Domaris has chosen her way. I expected it, and yet. . . ." He looked down at Deoris. "You asked me, *why.* It is for the same reason that so many maidens who enter the Grey Temple are *saji,* and use magic without knowing its meaning. But we of the Magicians would rather have our women free, make them *SA#kti SidhA#na*—know you what that is?"

She shook her head, dumbly.

"A woman who can use her powers to lead and complement a man's strength. Domaris had that kind of strength, she had the potentiality . . ." A significant pause. "Once."

"Not now?"

Riveda did not answer directly, but mused, "Women rarely have the need, or the hunger, or the courage. To most women, learning is a game, wisdom a toy—attainment, only a sensation."

Timidly, Deoris asked, "But is there any other way for a woman?"

"A woman of your caste?" The Adept shrugged. "I have no right to advise you—and yet, Deoris . . .

Riveda paused but a moment—yet the mood was shattered by a woman's cry of terror. The Adept whirled, swift as a hunting-cat; behind him Deoris started back, her hands at her throat. At the corner of the long stairway, she made out two white-robed figures and a crouching, grey and ghostly form which had suddenly risen before them.

Riveda rapped out several words in an alien tongue, then spoke ceremoniously to the white robes: "Be not alarmed, the poor lad is harmless. But his wits are not in their seat."

Clinging to Rajasta's arm, Domaris murmured in little gasps. "He rose out of the shadows—like a ghost."

Riveda's strong warm laughter filled the darkness. "I give you my word he is alive, and harmless." And this last, at least, was proven, for the grey-clad chela had scuttled away into the darkness once again and was lost to their sight. Riveda continued, his voice holding a deep deference exaggerated to the point of mockery, "Lord Guardian, I greet you; this is a pleasure I had ceased to expect!"

Rajasta said with asperity, "You are too courteous, Riveda. I trust we do not interrupt your meditations?"

"No, for I was not alone," Riveda retorted suavely, and beckoned Deoris to come forward. "You are remiss, my lady," he added to Domaris, "your sister has never seen this view, which is not a thing to be missed on a clear night."

Deoris, holding her hood about her head in the wind, looked sullenly at the intruders, and Domaris slipped her arm free of Rajasta's and went to her. "Why, if I had thought, I would have brought you up here long ago," Domaris murmured, her eyes probing her sister's closely. In the instant before the chela had risen up to terrify her, she had seen Riveda and Deoris standing very close together, in what had looked like an embrace. The sight had sent prickles of chill up her spine. Now, taking her sister's hand, she drew Deoris to the railing. "The view from here is truly lovely, you can see the pathway of the moon on the sea. . . ." Lowering her voice almost to a whisper, she murmured, "Deoris, I do not want to intrude on you, but what were you talking about?"

Riveda loomed large beside them. "I have been discussing the Mysteries with Deoris, my lady. I wished to know if she has chosen to walk in the path which her sister treads with such great honor." The Adept's words were courteous, even deferential, but something in their tone made Rajasta frown.

Clenching his fists in almost uncontrollable anger, the Priest of Light said curtly, "Deoris is an apprenticed Priestess of Caratra."

"Why, I know that," Riveda said, smiling. "Have you forgotten, it was I who counselled her to seek Initiation there?"

Forcing his voice to a deliberate calm, Rajasta answered, "Then you showed great wisdom, Riveda. May you always counsel as wisely." He glanced toward the chela, who had reappeared some distance away. "Have you found as yet any key to what is hidden in his soul?"

Riveda shook his head. "Nor found I anything in Atlantis which could rouse him. Yet," he paused and said, "I believe he has great knowledge of magic. I had him in the Chela's Ring last night."

Rajasta started. "With empty mind?" he accused. "Without awareness?" His face was deeply troubled. "Permit me this once to advise you, Riveda, not as Guardian but as a kinsman or a friend. *Be careful*—for your own sake. He is—emptied, and a perfect channel for danger of the worst sort."

Riveda bowed, but Deoris, watching, could see the ridge of muscle tighten in his jaw. The Grey-robe bit off his words in little pieces and spat them at Rajasta. "My Adeptship, cousin, is—suitable and sufficient—to guard that channel. Do me the courtesy—to allow me to manage my own affairs—friend!"

Rajasta sighed, and said, with a quiet patience, "You could wreck his mind."

Riveda shrugged. "There is not much left to wreck," he pointed out. "And there is the chance that I might rouse him." He paused, then said, with slow and deadly emphasis, "Perhaps it would be better if I consigned him to the Idiots' Village?"

There was a long and fearful silence. Domaris felt Deoris stiffen, every muscle go rigid, her shoulders taut with trembling horror. Eager to comfort, Domaris held her sister's hand tightly in her own, but Deoris wrenched away.

Riveda continued, completely calm. "Your suspicions are groundless, Rajasta. I seek only to restore the poor soul to himself. I am no black sorcerer; your implication insults me, Lord Guardian."

"You know I meant no insult," Rajasta said, and his voice was weary and old, "but there are those within your Order on whom we cannot lay constraint."

The Grey-robe stood still, the line of his lifted chin betraying an unusual self-doubt; then Riveda capitulated, and joined Rajasta at the railing. "Be not angry," he said, almost contritely. "I meant not to offend you."

The Priest of Light did not even glance at him. "Since we cannot converse without mutual offense, let us be silent," he said coldly. Riveda, stung by the rebuff, straightened and gazed in silence over the harbor for some minutes.

The full moon rose slowly, like a gilt bubble cresting the waves, riding the surf in a fairy play of light. Deoris drew a long wondering breath of delight, looking out in awe and fascination over the moon-flooded waves, the rooftops . . . She felt Riveda's hand on her arm and moved a little closer to him. The great yellow-orange globe moved slowly higher and higher, suspended on the tossing sea, gradually illuminating their faces: Deoris like a wraith against the darkness, Domaris pale beneath the hood of her loose frost-colored robes; Rajasta a luminescent blur against the far railing, Riveda like a dark pillar against the moonlight. Behind them, a dark huddle crouched against the cornice of the stairway, unseen and neglected.

Deoris began to pick out details in the moonlit scene: the shadows of ships, their sails furled, narrow masts lonesome against a phosphorescent sea; nearer, the dark mass of the city called the Circling Snake, where lights flickered and flitted in the streets. Curiously, she raised one hand and traced the outline made by the city and the harbor; then gave a little exclamation of surprise.

"Lord Riveda, look here—to trace the outline of the city from here is to make the Holy Sign!"

"It was planned so, I believe," Riveda responded quietly. "Chance is often an artist, but never like that."

A low voice called, "Domaris?"

The young Priestess stirred, her hand dropping from her sister's arm. "I am here, Arvath," she called.

The indistinct white-robed figure of her husband detached itself from the shadows and came toward them. He looked around, smiling. "Greetings, Lord Rajasta—Lord Riveda," he said. "And you, little Deoris—no, I should not call you that now, should I, kitten? Greetings to the Priestess Adsartha of Caratra's Temple!" He made a deep, burlesque bow.

Deoris giggled irrepressibly, then tossed her head and turned her back on him.

Arvath grinned and put an arm around his wife. "I thought I would find you here," he said, his voice shadowed with concern and reproach as he looked down at her. "You look tired. When you have finished your duties, you should rest, not weary yourself climbing these long steps."

"I am never tired," she said slowly, "not really tired."

"I know, but . . ." The arm around her tightened a little.

Riveda's voice, with its strangely harsh overtones, sounded through the filtered shadows. "No woman will accept sensible advice."

Domaris raised her head proudly. "I am a person before I am a woman."

Riveda let his eyes rest on her, with the strange and solemn reverence which had once before so frightened Domaris. Slowly, he answered, "I think not, Lady Isarma. You are woman, first and always. Is that not altogether evident?"

Arvath scowled and took an angry step forward, but Domaris caught this arm. "Please," she whispered, "anger him not. I think he meant no offense. He is not of our caste, we may ignore what he says."

Arvath subsided and murmured, "It is the woman in you I love, dear. The rest belongs to you. I do not interfere with that."

"I know, I know," she soothed in an undertone.

Rajasta, with an all-embracing kindliness, added, "I have no fear for her, Arvath. I know that she is woman, too, as well as priestess."

Riveda glanced at Deoris, with elaborate mockery. "I think we are two too many here," he murmured, and drew the girl along the railing, toward the southern parapet, where they stood in absorbed silence, looking down into the fires that flickered and danced at the sea-wall.

Arvath turned to Rajasta, half in apology. "I am all too much man where she is concerned," he said, and smiled in wry amusement.

Rajasta returned the smile companionably. "That is readily understood, my son," he said, and looked intently at Domaris. The clear moonlight blurred the wonderful red mantle of her hair to an uneven shining, and softened, kindly, the tiredness in her young face; but Rajasta needed no light to see that. *And why*, he asked himself, *was she so quick to deny that she might be primarily woman?* Rajasta turned away, staring out to sea, reluctantly remembering. *When she bore Micon's son, Domaris was all woman, almost arrogantly so, taking pride and deep joy in that. Why, now, does she speak so rebelliously, as if Riveda had insulted her—instead of paying her the highest accolade he knows?*

With a sudden smile, Domaris flung one arm around her husband

and the other around Rajasta, pulling them close. She leaned a little on Arvath, enough to give the effect of submission and affection. Domaris was no fool, and she knew what bitterness Arvath so resolutely stifled. No man would ever be more to Domaris—save the memory she kept with equal resoluteness apart from her life. No woman can be altogether indifferent to the man whose child she carries.

With a secret, wise little smile that did much to reassure the Guardian, Domaris leaned to touch her lips to her husband's cheek. "Soon, now, Rajasta, I shall ask to be released from Temple duties, for I will have other things to think of," she told them, still smiling. "Arvath, take me home, now. I am weary, and I would rest."

Rajasta followed the young couple as Arvath, with tender possessiveness, escorted his wife down the long stairway. He felt reassured: Domaris was safe with Arvath, indeed.

II

As the others disappeared into the shadows, Riveda turned and sighed, a little sorrowfully. "Well, Domaris has chosen. And you, Deoris?"

"No!" It was a sharp little cry of revulsion.

"A woman's mind is strange," Riveda went on reflectively. "She is sensitive to a greater degree; her very body responds to the delicate influence of the moon and the tidewaters. And she has, inborn, all the strength and receptivity which a man must spend years and his heart's blood to acquire. But where man is a climber, woman tends to chain herself. Marriage, the slavery of lust, the brutality of childbearing, the servitude of being wife and mother—and all this without protest! Nay, she seeks it, and weeps if it is denied her!"

A far-off echo came briefly to taunt Deoris—Domaris, so long ago, murmuring, *Who has put these bats into your brain?* But Deoris, hungry for his thoughts, was more than willing to listen to Riveda's justification for her own rebellion, and made only the faintest protest: "But there *must* be children, must there not?"

Riveda shrugged. "There are always more than enough women who are fit for nothing else," he said. "At one time I had a dream of a woman with the strength and hardness of a man but with a woman's sensitivity; a woman who could set aside her self-imposed chains. At one time, I had thought Domaris to be such a woman. And believe me, they are rare, and precious! But she has chosen otherwise." Riveda turned, and his eyes, colorless in the moonlight, stabbed into the girl's uplifted face. His light speaking voice dropped into the rich and resonant baritone in which he sang. "But I think I have found another. Deoris, are you . . . ?"

"What?" she whispered.

"Are *you* that woman?"

Deoris drew a long breath, as fear and fascination tumbled in her brain.

Riveda's hard hands found her shoulders, and he repeated, softly persuasive, "Are you, Deoris?"

A stir in the darkness—and Riveda's chela suddenly materialized from the shadows. Deoris's flesh crawled with revulsion and horror—fear of Riveda, fear of herself, and a sort of sick loathing for the chela. She wrenched herself away and ran, blindly ran, to get away and alone; but even as she fled, she heard the murmur of the Adept's words, re-echoing in her brain.

Are you that woman?

And to herself, more than terrified now, and yet still fascinated, Deoris whispered, "Am I?"

CHAPTER FOUR
✠ THE SUMMIT ✠
AND THE DEPTHS

I

The opened shutters admitted the incessant flickers of summer lightning. Deoris, unable to sleep, lay on her pallet, her thoughts flickering as restlessly as the lightning flashes. She was afraid of Riveda, and yet, for a long time she had admitted to herself that he roused in her a strange, tense emotion that was almost physical. He had grown into her consciousness, he was a part of her imagination. Naive as she was, Deoris realized indistinctly that she had reached, with Riveda, a boundary of no return: their relationship had suddenly and irrevocably changed.

She suspected she could not bear to be closer to him, but at the same time the thought of putting him out of her life—and this was the only alternative—was unbearable. Riveda's swift clarity made even Rajasta seem pompous, fumbling . . . Had she ever seriously thought of following in Domaris's steps?

A soft sound interrupted her thoughts, and Chedan's familiar step crossed the flagstones to her side. "Asleep?" he whispered.

"Oh, Chedan—you?"

"I was in the court, and I could not . . ." He dropped to the edge of the bed. "I haven't seen you all day. Your birthday, too—how old?"

"Sixteen. You know that." Deoris sat up, wrapping her thin arms around her knees.

"And I would have a gift for you, if I thought you would take it from me," Chedan murmured. His meaning was unmistakable, and Deoris felt her cheeks grow hot in the darkness while Chedan went on, teasingly, "Or do you guard yourself virgin for higher ambition? I saw you when Cadamiri carried you, unconscious, from the seance in the Prince Micon's quarters last year! Ah, how Cadamiri was angry! For all of that day, anyone who spoke to him caught only sharp words. *He* would advise you, Deoris—"

"I am not interested in his advice!" Deoris snapped, flicked raw by his teasing.

Again, two conflicting impulses struggled in her: to laugh at him, or to slap him. She had never accepted the easy customs and the free talk of the House of the Twelve; the boys and girls in the Scribes' School were more strictly confined, and Deoris had spent her most impressionable years there. Yet her own thoughts were poor company, confused as they were, and she did not want to be alone.

Chedan bent down and slid his arms around the girl. Deoris, in a kind of passive acquiescence, submitted, but she twisted her mouth away from his.

"Don't," she said sulkily. "I can't breathe."

"You won't have to," he said, more softly than usual, and Deoris made no great protest. She liked the warmth of his arms around her, the way he held her, gently, like something very fragile . . . but tonight there was an urgency in his kisses that had never been there before. It frightened her a little. Warily, she shifted herself away from him, murmuring protesting words—she hardly knew what.

Silence again, and the flickering of lightning in the room, and her own thoughts straying into the borderland of dreams. . . .

Suddenly, before she could prevent him, Chedan was lying beside her and his arms slowly forced themselves beneath her head; then all the strength of his hard young body was pressing her down, and he was saying incoherent things which made no sense, punctuated by frightening kisses. For a moment, surprise and a sort of dreamy lassitude held her motionless . . . then a wave of revulsion sent every nerve in her body to screaming.

She struggled and pulled away from him, scrambling quickly to her feet; her eyes burned with shock and shame. "How dare you," she stammered, "how dare you!"

Chedan's mouth dropped open in stupefaction. He raised himself, slowly, and his voice was remorseful. "Deoris, sweet, did I frighten you?" he whispered, and held out his arms.

She jerked away from him with an incongruous little jump. "Don't touch me!"

He was still kneeling on the edge of the bed; now he rose to his feet, slowly and a little bewildered. "Deoris, I don't understand. What have I done? I am sorry. Please, don't look at me like that," he begged, dismayed and shamed, and angry with himself for a reckless, precipitous fool. He touched her shoulder softly. "Deoris, you're not crying? Don't, please—I'm sorry, sweet. Come back to bed. I promise, I won't touch you again. See, I'll swear it." He added, puzzled. "But I had not thought you so unwilling."

She was crying now, loud shocked sobs. "Go away," she wept, "go away!"

"*Deoris!*" Chedan's voice, still uncertain, cracked into falsetto. "Stop crying like that. Somebody will hear you, you silly girl! I'm not going to touch you, ever, unless you want me to! Why, what in the world did you think I was going to do? I never raped anyone in my life and I certainly wouldn't begin with you! Now stop that, Deoris, stop that!" He put his hand on her shoulder and shook her slightly, "If someone hears you, they'll . . ."

Her voice was high and hysterical. "Go away! Just go away, away!"

Chedan's hands dropped, and his cheeks flamed with wrathful pride. "Fine, I'm going," he said curtly, and the door slammed behind him.

Deoris, shaking with nervous chill, crept to her bed and dragged the sheet over her head. She was ashamed and unhappy and her loneliness was like a physical presence in the room. Even Chedan's presence would have been a comfort.

Restless, she got out of bed and wandered about the room. What had happened? One moment she had been contented, lying in his arms and feeling some emptiness within her heart solaced and filled by his closeness—and in the next instant, a fury of revolt had swept through her whole body. Yet for years she and Chedan had been moving, slowly and inexorably, toward such a moment. Probably everyone in the Temple believed they were already lovers! Why, faced with the prospect itself, had she exploded into this storm of passionate refusal?

Obeying a causeless impulse, she drew a light cape over her night-dress, and went out on the lawn. The dew was cold on her bare feet, but the night air felt moist and pleasant on her hot face. She moved into the moonlight, and the man who was slowly pacing up the path caught his breath, in sharp satisfaction.

"Deoris," Riveda said.

She whirled in terror, and for an instant the Adept thought she would flee; then she recognized his voice, and a long sigh fluttered between her lips.

"Riveda! I was frightened . . . it *is* you?"

"None other," he laughed, and came toward her, his big lean body making a blackness against the stars, his robes shimmering like frost; he seemed to gather the darkness about himself and pour it forth again. She put out a small hand, confidingly, toward his; he took it.

"Why, Deoris, your feet are bare! What brought you to me like this? Not that I am displeased," he added.

She lowered her eyes, returning awareness and shame touching her whole body. "To—you?" she asked, rebellious.

"You always come to me," Riveda said. It was not a statement made in pride, but a casual statement of fact; as if he had said, *the sun rises to the East.* "You must know by now that I am the end of all your paths—you must know that now as I have known it for a long time. Deoris, will you come with me?"

And Deoris heard herself say, "Of course," and realized that the decision had been made long ago. She whispered, "But where? Where are we going?"

Riveda gazed at her in silence for a moment. "To the Crypt where the God sleeps," he said at length.

She caught her hands against her throat. Sacrilege this, for a Daughter of Light—she knew this, now. And when last she had accompanied Riveda to the Grey Temple, the consequences had been frightening. Yet Riveda—he said, and she believed him—had not been responsible for what had happened then. *What had happened then* . . . she fought to remember, but it was fogged in her mind. She whispered, "Must I—?" and her voice broke.

Riveda's hands fell to his sides, releasing her.

"All Gods past, present, and future forbid that I should ever constrain you, Deoris."

Had he commanded, had he pleaded, had he spoken a word of persuasion, Deoris would have fled. But before his silent face she could only say, gravely, "I will come."

"Come, then." Riveda took her shoulder lightly in his hand, turning her toward the pyramid. "I took you tonight to the summit; now I will show you the depths. That, too, is a Mystery." He put his hand on her arm, but the touch was altogether impersonal. "Look to your steps, the hill is dangerous in the dark," he cautioned.

She went beside him, docile; he stopped for a moment, turned to her, and his arm moved; but she pulled away, panicky with denial.

"So?" Riveda mused, almost inaudibly. "I have had my question answered without asking."

"What do you mean?"

"You really don't know?" Riveda laughed shortly, unamused. "Well, you shall learn that, too, perhaps; but at your own will, always at your own will. Remember that. The summit—and the depths. You shall see."

He led her on toward the raised square of darkness.

II

Steps—uncounted, interminable steps—wound down, down, endlessly, into dim gloom. The filtered light cast no shadows. Cold, stone steps, as grey as the light; and the soft pad of her bare feet followed her in echoes that re-echoed forever. Her breathing sounded with harsh sibilance, and seemed to creep after her with the echoes, hounding at her heels. She forced herself on, one hand thrusting at the wall. . . . Her going had the feeling of flight, although her feet refused to change their tempo, and the echoes had a steady insistence, like heartbeats.

Another turn; more steps. The grayness curled around them, and Deoris shivered with a chill not born altogether of the dank cold. She waded in grey fog beside grey-robed Riveda, and the fear of closed places squeezed her throat; the knowledge of her sacrilege knifed her mind.

Down and down, through eternities of aching effort.

Her nerves screamed at her to run, run, but the quicksand cold dragged her almost to a standstill. Abruptly the steps came to an end. Another turn led into a vast, vaulted chamber, pallidly lighted with flickering greyness. Deoris advanced with timid steps into the catacomb and stood frozen.

She could not know that the simulacrum of the Sleeping God revealed itself to each seeker in different fashion. She knew only this: Long and long ago, beyond the short memory of mankind, the Light had triumphed, and reigned now supreme in the Sun. But in the everlasting cycles of time—so even the Priests of Light conceded—the reign of the Sun must end, and the Light should emerge back into Dyaus, the Unrevealed God, the Sleeper . . . and he would burst his chains and rule in a vast, chaotic Night.

Before her strained eyes she beheld, seated beneath his carven bird of stone, the image of the Man with Crossed Hands . . .

She wanted to scream aloud; but the screams died in her throat. She advanced slowly, Riveda's words fresh in her mind; and before the wavering Image, she knelt in homage.

III

At last she rose, cold and cramped, to see Riveda standing nearby, the cowl thrown back from his massive head, his silvered hair shining like an aureole in the pale light. His face was lighted with a rare smile.

"You have courage," he said quietly. "There will be other tests; but for now, it is enough." Unbending, he stood beside her before the great Image, looking up toward what was, to him, an erect image, faceless, formidable, stern but not terrible, a power restricted but not bound. Wondering how Deoris saw the Avatar, he laid a light hand on her wrist, and with a moment of Vision, he caught a brief glimpse in which the God seemed to flow and change and assume, for an instant, the figure of a seated man with hands crossed upon his breast. Riveda shook his head slightly, with a dismissing gesture, and, tightening his grasp upon the girl's wrist, he led her through an archway into a series of curiously furnished rooms which opened out from the great Crypt.

This underground maze was a Mystery forbidden to most of the

Temple folk. Even the members of the Grey-robe sect, though their Order and their ritual served and guarded the Unrevealed God, came here but rarely.

Riveda himself did not know the full extent of these caverns. He had never tried to explore more than a little way into the incredible labyrinth of what must, once, have been a vast underground temple in daily use. It honeycombed the entire land beneath the Temple of Light; Riveda could not even guess when or by whom these great underground passages and apartments had been constructed, or for what purpose.

It was rumored that the hidden sect of Black-robes used these forbidden precincts for their secret practice of sorcery; but although Riveda had often wished to seek them out, capture them and try them for their crimes, he had neither the time nor the resources to explore the maze more than a little way. Once, indeed, on the Nadir-night when someone unsanctioned—Black-robes or others—had sought to draw down the awesome thunder-voiced powers of the Lords of Ahtarrath and of the Sea Kingdoms, Riveda had come into these caverns; and there, on that ill-fated night, he had found seven dead men, lying blasted and withered within their black robes, their hands curled and blackened and charred as with fire, their faces unrecognizable, charred skulls. But the dead could neither be questioned nor punished; and when he sought to explore further into the labyrinthine mazes of the underground Temple, he had quickly become lost; it had taken him hours of weary wandering to find his way back to this point, and he had not dared it again. He could not explore it alone, and there was, as yet, no one he could trust to aid him. Perhaps now . . . but he cut off the thought, calling years of discipline to his aid. That time had not come. Perhaps it would never come.

He led Deoris into one of the nearer rooms. It was furnished sparsely, in a style ancient beyond belief, and lighted dimly with one of the ever-burning lamps whose secret still puzzled the Priests of Light. In the flickering, dancing illumination, furniture and walls were embellished with ancient and cryptic symbols which Riveda was grateful the girl could not read. He himself had learned their meaning but lately, after much toil and study, and even his glacial composure had been shaken by the obscenity of their meaning.

"Sit here beside me," he bade her, and she obeyed like a child.

Behind them the chela ghosted like a wraith through the doorway and stood with empty, unseeing eyes. Riveda leaned forward, his head in his hands, and she looked upon him, a little curious but trusting.

"Deoris," he said at last, "there is much a man can never know. Women like you have certain—awarenesses, which no man may gain; or gain only under the sure guidance of such a woman." He paused, his cold eyes pensive as they met hers. "Such a woman must have courage, and strength, and knowledge, and insight. You are very young, Deoris, you have much to learn but more than ever I believe you could be such a woman." Once again he paused, that pause that gave such a powerful emphasis to his words. His voice deepened as he said, "I am not young, Deoris, and perhaps I have no right to ask this of you, but you are the first I have felt I could trust—or follow." His eyes had flickered away from hers as he said this; now he looked again directly into her face. "Would you consent to this? Will you let me lead you and teach you, and guide you to awareness of that strength within you, so that some day you might guide me along that pathway where no man can walk alone, and where only a woman may lead?"

Deoris clasped her hands at her breast, sure that the Adept could hear the pounding of her heart. She felt dazed, sick and weightless with panic—but more, she felt the true emptiness of any other life. She felt a wild impulse to scream, to burst into shattering, hysterical laughter, but she forced her rebellious lips to speak and obey her. "I will, if you think I am strong enough," she whispered, and then emotion choked her with the clamor of her adoration for this man. It was all she desired, all she ever desired, that she might be closer to him, closer than Acolyte or chela, closer than any woman might ever be—but she trembled at the knowledge of what she committed herself to; she had some slight knowledge of the bonds the Grey-robes put on their women. She would be—close—to Riveda. What was he like, beneath that cynical, derisive mask he wore? The mask had slipped a little, tonight—

Riveda's mouth moved a little, as if he struggled with strong emotion. His voice was hushed, almost gentle for once. "Deoris," he said, then smiled faintly, "I cannot call you my Acolyte—the bonds of that relationship are fixed, and what I wish lies outside those bonds. You understand this?"

"I—think so."

"For a time—I impose obedience on you—and surrender. There must be complete knowledge of one another, and—" He released her hand, and looked at the girl, with the slight, stern pause that gave emphasis to his words, "—and complete intimacy."

"I—know," Deoris said, trying to make her voice steady. "I accept that, too."

Riveda nodded, in curt acknowledgement, as if he took no especial notice of her words—but Deoris sensed that he was unsure of himself now; and, in truth, Riveda was unsure, to the point of fear. He was afraid to snap, by some incautious word or movement, the spell of fascination he had, almost without meaning to, woven around the girl. Did she really understand what he demanded of her? He could not guess.

Then, with a movement that startled the Adept, Deoris slid to her knees before him, bending her head in surrender so absolute that Riveda felt his throat tighten with an emotion long unfamiliar.

He drew her forward, gently raising her, until she stood within the circle of his arms. His voice was husky: "I told you once that I am not a good man to trust. But Deoris, may the Gods deal with me as I deal with you!"

And the words were an oath more solemn than her own.

The last remnant of her fear quickened in a protest that was half-instinctive as his hands tightened on her, then died. She felt herself lifted clear of the floor, and cried out in astonishment at the strength in his hands. She was hardly conscious of movement, but she knew that he had laid her down and was bending over her, his head a dark silhouette against the light; she remembered, more than saw, the cruel set of his jaw, the intent strained line of his mouth. His eyes were as cold as the northern light, and as remote.

No one—certainly not Chedan—had ever touched her like this, no one had ever touched her except gently, and she sobbed in an instant of final, spasmodic terror. *Domaris—Chedan—the Man with Crossed Hands—Micon's death-mask*—these images reeled in her mind in the short second before she felt the roughness of his face against hers, and his strong and sensitive hands moving at the fastenings of her nightdress. Then there was only the dim dancing light, and the shadow of an image—and Riveda.

The chela, muttering witlessly, crouched upon the stone floor until dawn.

CHAPTER FIVE
✠ WORDS ✠

I

Beneath a trellised arbor of vines, near the House of the Twelve, lay a deep clear pool which was known as the Mirror of Reflection. Tradition held that once an oracle had stood here; and even now some believed that in moments of soul-stress the answer one's heart or mind most sought might be mirrored in the limpid waters, if the watcher had eyes to see.

Deoris, lying listlessly under the leaves, gazed into the pool in bitter rebellion. Reaction had set in; with it came fear. She had done sacrilege; betrayed Caste and Gods. She felt dreary and deserted, and the faint stab of pain in her body was like the echo and shadow of a hurt already half forgotten. Sharper than the memory of pain was a vague shame and wonder.

She had given herself to Riveda in a dreamy exaltation, not as a maiden to her lover, but in a surrender as complete as the surrender of a victim on the altar of a god. And he had taken her—the thought came unbidden—as a hierophant conducting an Acolyte into a sacred secret; not passion, but a mystical initiatory rite, all-encompassing in its effect on her.

Reviewing her own emotions, Deoris wondered at them. The physical act was not important, but close association with Domaris had made Deoris keenly conscious of her own motives, and she had been taught that it was shameful to give herself except in love. Did she

245

love Riveda? Did he love her? Deoris did not know—and she was never to have more assurance than she had had already.

Even now she did not know whether his mystical and cruel initiatory passion had been ardent, or merely brutal.

For the time, Riveda had blotted out all else in her thoughts—and that fact accounted for the greater part of Deoris's shame. She had counted on her own ability to keep her emotions aloof from his domination of her body. *Still,* she told herself sternly, *I must discipline myself to accept complete dominance; the possession of my body was only a means to that end—the surrender of my will to his.*

With all her heart, she longed to follow the path of psychic accomplishment which Riveda had outlined to her. She knew now that she had always desired it; she had even resented Micon because he had tried to hold her back. As for Rajasta—well, Rajasta had taught Domaris, and she could see the result of *that*!

She did not hear the approaching steps—for Riveda could move as noiselessly as a cat when he chose—until he bent and, with a single flexing of muscular arms, picked her up and set her on her feet.

"Well, Deoris? Do you consult the Oracle for your fate or mine?"

But she was unyielding in his arms, and after a moment he released her, puzzled.

"What is it, Deoris? Why are you angry with me?"

The last flicker of her body's resentment flared up. "I do not like to be mauled like that!"

Ceremoniously, the Adept inclined his head. "Forgive me. I shall remember."

"Oh, Riveda!" She flung her arms about him then, burrowing her head into the rough stuff of his robes, gripping him with a desperate dread. "Riveda, I am afraid!"

His arms tightened around her for a moment, strong, almost passionate. Then, with a certain sternness, he disengaged her clinging clasp. "Be not foolish, Deoris," he admonished. "You are no child, nor do I wish to treat you as one. Remember—I do not admire weakness in women. Leave that for the pretty wives in the back courts of the Temple of Light!"

Stung, Deoris lifted her chin. "Then we have both had a lesson today!"

Riveda stared at her a moment, then laughed aloud. "Indeed!" he exclaimed. "That is more like it. Well then. I have come to take you to the Grey Temple." As she hung back a little, he smiled and touched her cheek. "You need not fear—the foul sorcerer who threw you into illusion that previous time has been exorcized; ask, if you dare, what befell him! Be assured, no one will dare to meddle with the mind of my chosen novice!"

Reassured, she followed him, and he continued, abridging his long stride to correspond with her steps, "You have seen one of our ceremonies, as an outsider. Now you shall see the rest. Our Temple is mostly a place of experiment, where each man works separately, as he will, to develop his own powers."

Deoris could understand this, for in the Priest's Caste great emphasis was placed on self-perfection. But she wondered for what sins the Magicians strove. . . .

He answered her unspoken question. "For absolute self-mastery, first of all; the body and mind must be harnessed and brought into subjugation by—certain disciplines. Then each man works alone, to master sound, or color, or light, or animate things—whatever he chooses—with the powers inherent in his own body and mind. We call ourselves Magicians, but there is no magic; there is only vibration. When a man can attune his body to any vibration, when he can master the vibrations of sound so that rock bursts asunder, or think one color into another, that is not magic. He who masters himself, masters the Universe."

As they passed beneath the great archway which spanned the bronze doors of the Grey Temple, he motioned to her to precede him; the bodiless voice challenged in unknown syllables, and Riveda called back. As they stepped through the doors, he added, in an undertone, "I will teach you the words of admission, Deoris, so that you will have access here even in my absence."

II

The great dim room seemed more vast than before, being nearly empty. Instinctively, Deoris looked for the niche where she had seen the Man with Crossed Hands—but the recess in the wall was hidden with grey veils Nevertheless she recalled another shrine, deep in the bowels of the earth, and could not control a shudder.

Riveda said in her ear, "Know you why the Temple is grey, why we wear grey?"

She shook her head, voiceless.

"Because," he went on, "color is in itself vibration, each color having a vibration of its own. Grey allows vibration to be transmitted freely, without the interference of color. Moreover, black absorbs light into itself, and white reflects light and augments it; grey does neither, it merely permits the true quality of the light to be seen as it is." He fell silent again, and Deoris wondered if his words had been symbolic as well as scientific.

In one corner of the enormous chamber, five young chelas were grouped in a circle, standing in rigidly unnatural poses and intoning, one by one, sounds that made Deoris's head ache. Riveda listened for a moment, then said, "Wait here. I want to speak to them."

She stood motionless, watching as he approached the chelas and spoke to them, vehemently but in a voice pitched so low she could not distinguish a word. She looked around the Temple.

She had heard horrible tales about this place—tales of self-torture, the *saji* women, licentious rites—but there was nothing fearful here. At a little distance from the group of chelas, three young girls sat watching, all three younger than Deoris, with loose short hair, their immature bodies saffron-veiled and girdled with silver. They sat cross-legged, looking weirdly graceful and relaxed.

Deoris knew that the *saji* were recruited mostly from the outcastes, the nameless children born unacknowledged, who were put out on the city wall to die of exposure—or be found by the dealers in girl slaves. Like all the Priest's Caste, Deoris believed that the *saji* were harlots or worse, that they were used in rituals whose extent was limited only by the imagination of the teller. But these girls did not look especially vicious or degenerate. Two, in fact, were extremely lovely; the third had a hare-lip which marred her young face, but her body was dainty and graceful as a dancer's. They talked among themselves in low chirping tones, and they all used their hands a great deal as they spoke, with delicately expressive gestures that bespoke long training.

Looking away from the *saji* girls, Deoris saw the woman Adept she had seen before. From Karahama she had heard this woman's name: *Maleina.* In the Grey-robe sect she stood second only to Riveda, but it was said that Riveda and Maleina were bitter enemies for some reason still unknown to Deoris.

Today, the cowl was thrown back from Maleina's head; her hair, previously concealed, was flaming red. Her face was sharp and gaunt, with a strange, ascetic, fine-boned beauty. She sat motionless on the stone floor. Not an eyelash flickered, nor a hair stirred. In her cupped hands she held something bright which flickered light and dark, light and dark, as regularly as a heartbeat; it was the only thing about her that seemed to live.

Not far away, a man clad only in a loincloth stood gravely on his head. Deoris had to stifle an uncontrollable impulse to giggle, but the man's thin face was absolutely serious.

And not five feet from Deoris, a little boy about seven years old was lying on his back, gazing at the vaulted ceiling, breathing with deep, slow regularity. He did not seem to be doing anything except breathing; he was so relaxed that it made Deoris sleepy to look at him, although his eyes were wide-open and clearly alert. He did not appear to move a single muscle . . . After several minutes, Deoris realized that his head was several inches off the floor. Fascinated, she continued to watch until he was sitting bolt upright, and yet at no instant had she actually seen the fraction of an inch's movement, or seen him flex a single muscle. Abruptly, the little boy shook himself like a puppy and, bounding to his feet, grinned widely at Deoris, a gamin, little boyish grin very much at variance with the perfect control he had been exercising. Only then did Deoris recognize him: the silver-gilt hair, the pointed features were those of Demira. This was Karahama's younger child, Demira's brother.

Casually, the little boy walked toward the group of chelas where Riveda was still lecturing. The Adept had pulled his grey cowl over his head and was holding a large bronze gong suspended in midair. One by one, each of the five chelas intoned a curious syllable; each made the gong vibrate faintly, and one made it emit a most peculiar ringing sound. Riveda nodded, then handed the gong to one of the boys, and turning toward it, spoke a single deep-throated syllable.

The gong began to vibrate; then clamored a long, loud brazen note as if struck repeatedly by a bar of steel. Again Riveda uttered the bass syllable; again came the gong's metallic threnody. As the chelas stared, Riveda laughed, flung back his cowl and walked away, pausing a moment to put his hand on the small boy's head and ask him some low-voiced questions Deoris could not hear.

The Adept returned to Deoris. "Well, have you seen enough?" he asked, and drew her along until they were in the grey corridor. Many, many doors lined the hallway, and at the centers of several of them a ghostly light flickered. "Never enter a room where a light is showing," Riveda murmured; "it means someone is within who does not wish to be disturbed—or someone it would be dangerous to disturb. I will teach you the sound that causes the light; you will need to practice uninterrupted sometimes."

Finding an unlighted door, Riveda opened it with the utterance of an oddly unhuman syllable, which he taught her to speak, making her repeat it again and again until she caught the double pitch of it, and mastered the trick of making her voice ring in both registers at once. Deoris had been taught singing, of course, but she now began to realize how very much she still had to learn about sound. She was used to the simple-sung tones which produced light in the Library, and other places in the Temple precincts, but *this*—!

Riveda laughed at her perplexity. "These are not used in the Temple of Light in these days of decadence," he said, "for only a few can master them. In the old days, an Adept would bring his chela here and leave him enclosed in one of these cells—to starve or suffocate if he could not speak the word that would free him. And so they assured that no unfit person lived to pass on his inferiority or stupidity. But now—" He shrugged and smiled. "I would never have brought you here, if I did not believe you could learn."

She finally managed to approximate the sound which opened the door of solid stone, but as it swung wide, Deoris faltered on the threshold. "This—this room," she whispered, "it is horrible!"

He smiled, noncommittally. "All unknown things are fearful to those who do not understand them. This room has been used for the initiation of *saji* while their power is being developed. You are sensitive, and sense the emotions that have been experienced here. Do not be afraid, it will soon be dispelled."

Deoris raised her hands to her throat, to touch the crystal amulet there; it felt comfortingly familiar.

Riveda saw, but misinterpreted the gesture, and with a sudden softening of his harsh face he drew her to him. "Be not afraid," he said gently, "even though I seem at times to forget your presence. Sometimes my meditations take me deep into my mind, where no one else can reach. And also—I have been long alone, and I am not used to the presence of—one like you. The women I have known—and there have been many, Deoris—have been *saji,* or they have been— just women. While you, you are . . ." He fell silent, gazing at her intently, as if he would absorb her every feature into him.

Deoris was, at first, only surprised, for she had never before known Riveda to be so obviously at a loss for words. She felt her whole identity softening, pliant in his hands. A flood of emotion overwhelmed her and she began softly to cry.

With a gentleness she had never known he possessed, Riveda took her to him, deliberately, not smiling now. "You are altogether beautiful," he said, and the simplicity of the words gave them meaning and tenderness all but unimaginable. "You are made of silk and fire."

III

Deoris was to treasure those words secretly in her heart during the many bleak months that followed, for Riveda's moods of gentleness were more rare than diamonds, and days of surly remoteness inevitably followed. She was to gather such rare moments like jewels on the chain of her inarticulate and childlike love, and guard them dearly, her only precious comfort in a life that left her heart solitary and yearning, even while her questing mind found satisfaction.

Riveda, of course, took immediate steps to regularize her position in regard to himself. Deoris, who had been born into the Priest's Caste, could not formally be received into the Grey-robe sect; also she was an apprenticed Priestess of Caratra and had obligations there. The latter obstacle Riveda disposed of quite easily, in a few words with the High Initiates of Caratra. Deoris, he told them, had already mastered skills far beyond her years in the Temple of Birth; he suggested it might be well for her to work exclusively among the Healers for a time, until her competence in all such arts equalled her knowledge of midwifery. To this the Priestesses were glad to agree; they were proud of Deoris, and it pleased them that she had attracted the attention of a Healer of such skill as Riveda.

So Deoris was legitimately admitted into the Order of Healers, as even a Priest of Light might be, and recognized there as Riveda's novice.

Soon after this, Domaris fell ill. In spite of every precaution she went into premature labor and, almost three months too soon, gave painful birth to a girl child who never drew breath. Domaris herself nearly died, and this time, Mother Ysouda, who had attended her, made the warning unmistakable: Domaris must never attempt to bear another child.

Domaris thanked the old woman for her counsel, listened obediently to her advice, accepted the protective runes and spells given her, and kept enigmatic silence. She grieved long hours in secret for the baby she had lost, all the more bitterly because she had not really wanted this child at all. . . . She was privately certain that her lack of love for Arvath had somehow frustrated her child's life. She knew the conviction to be an absurd one, but she could not dismiss it from her mind.

She recovered her strength with maddening slowness. Deoris had been spared to nurse her, but their old intimacy was gone almost beyond recall. Domaris lay silent for hours, quiet and sad, tears sliding weakly down her white face, often holding Micail with a hungry tenderness. Deoris, though she tended her sister with an exquisite competence, seemed abstracted and dreamy. Her absentmindedness puzzled and irritated Domaris, who had protested vigorously against allowing Deoris to work with Riveda in the first place but had only succeeded in alienating her sister more completely.

Only once Domaris tried to restore their old closeness. Micail had fallen asleep in her arms, and Deoris bent to take him, for the heavy child rolled about and kicked in his sleep, and Domaris still could not endure careless handling. She smiled up into the younger girl's face and said, "Ah, Deoris, you are so sweet with Micail, I cannot wait to see you with a child of your own in your arms!"

Deoris started and almost dropped Micail before she realized Domaris had spoken more or less at random; but she could not keep back her own overflowing bitterness. "I would rather die!" she flung at Domaris out of her disturbed heart.

Domaris looked up reproachfully, her lips trembling. "Oh, my sister, you should not say such wicked things—"

Deoris threw the words at her like a curse: "On the day I know myself with child, Domaris, I will throw myself into the sea!"

Domaris cried out in pain, as if her sister had struck her—but although Deoris instantly flung herself to her knees beside Domaris, imploring pardon for her thoughtless words, Domaris said no more; nor did she again speak to Deoris except with cool, reserved formality. It was many years before the impact of those wounding, bitter words left her heart.

CHAPTER SIX
✠ CHILDREN OF THE ✠ UNREVEALED GOD

I

Within the Grey Temple, the Magicians were dispersing. Deoris, standing alone, dizzy and lightheaded after the frightening rites, felt a light touch upon her arm and looked down into Demira's elfin face.

"Did not Riveda tell you? You are to come with me. The Ritual forbids that they speak to, or touch, a woman for a night and a day after this ceremony; and you must not leave the enclosure until sundown tomorrow." Demira slipped her hand confidently into Deoris's arm and Deoris, too bewildered to protest, went with her. Riveda had told her this much, yes; sometimes a chela who had been in the Ring suffered curious delusions, and they must remain where someone could be summoned to minister to them. But she had expected to remain near Riveda. Above all, she had not expected Demira.

"Riveda told me to look after you," Demira said pertly, and Deoris recalled tardily that the Grey-robes observed no caste laws. She went acquiescently with Demira, who immediately began to bubble over, "I have thought about you so much, Deoris! The Priestess Domaris is your sister, is she not? She is so beautiful! You are pretty, too," she added as an afterthought.

Deoris flushed, thinking secretly that Demira was the loveliest little creature she had ever seen. She was very fair, all the same shade of silvery gold: the long straight hair, her lashes and level brows, even the splash of gilt freckles across her pale face. Even Demira's eyes looked silver, although in a different light they might have been grey, or even blue. Her voice was very soft and light and sweet, and she moved with the heedless grace of a blown feather and just as irresponsibly.

She squeezed Deoris's fingers excitedly and said, "You were frightened, weren't you? I was watching, and I felt so sorry for you."

Deoris did not answer, but this did not seem to disturb Demira at all. *Of course,* Deoris thought, *she is probably used to being ignored! The Magicians and Adepts are not the most talkative people in the world!*

The cold moonlight played on them like sea-spray, and other women, singly and in little groups, surrounded them on the path. But no one spoke to them. Several of the women, indeed, came up to greet Demira, but something—perhaps only the childlike way the two walked, hand in hand—prevented them. Or perhaps they recognized Deoris as Riveda's novice, and that fact made them a little nervous. Deoris had noted something of the sort on other occasions.

They passed into an enclosed court where a fountain spouted cool silver into a wide oval pool. All around, sheltering trees, silvery black, concealed all but the merest strips of the star-dusted sky. The air was scented with many flowers.

Opening on this court were literally dozens of tiny rooms, hardly more than cubicles, and into one of these Demira led her. Deoris glanced round fearfully. She wasn't used to such small, dim rooms, and felt as if the walls were squeezing inward, suffocating her. An old woman, crouched on a pallet in the corner, got wheezily to her feet and shuffled toward them.

"Take off your sandals," Demira said in a reproving whisper, and Deoris, surprised, bent to comply. The old woman, with an indignant snort, took them and set them outside the door.

Once more Deoris peered around the little room. It was furnished sparsely with a low, rather narrow bed covered with gauzy canopies, a brazier of metal that looked incredibly ancient, an old carved chest, and a divan with a few embroidered cushions; that was all.

Demira noted her scrutiny and said proudly, "Oh, some of the others have nothing but a straw pallet, they live in stone cells and practice austerities like the young priests, but the Grey Temple does not force such things on anyone, and I do not care. Well, you will know that later. Come along, we must bathe before we sleep; and you've been in the Ring! There are some things—I'll show you what to do." Demira turned to the old woman suddenly and stamped her foot. "Don't stand there staring at us! I can't stand it!"

The crone cackled like a hen. "And who is this one, my missy? One of Maleina's little pretties who grows lonely when the woman has gone to the rites with—" She broke off and ducked, with surprising nimbleness, as one of Demira's sandals came flying at her head.

Demira stamped her bare foot again furiously. "Hold your tongue, you ugly witch!"

The old woman's cackling only grew louder. "She's sure too old for the Priests to take in and—"

"I said hold your tongue!" Demira flew at the old woman and cuffed her angrily. "I will tell Maleina what you have said about her and she will have you crucified!"

"What I *could* say about Maleina," the old witch mumbled, unhumbled, "would make little missy turn to one big blush forever— if she has not already lost that talent here!" Abruptly she grasped Demira's shoulders in her withered claws and held the girl firmly for an instant, until the angry light faded from Demira's colorless eyes. Giggling, the girl slid free of the crone's hands.

"Get us something to eat, then take yourself off," Demira said carelessly, and as the hag hustled away she sank down languidly on the divan, smiling at Deoris. "Don't listen to her, she's old and half-witted, but phew! she should be more careful, what Maleina would do if she heard her!" The light laughter bubbled up again. "I'd not want to be the one to mock Maleina, no, not even in the deepest chambers of the labyrinth! She might strike me with a spell so I walked blind for three days, as she did to the priest Nadastor when he laid lewd hands on her." Suddenly she leaped to her feet and went to Deoris, who still stood as if frozen. "You look as if struck with a spell yourself!" she laughed; then, sobering, she said kindly, "I know you are afraid, we are all afraid at first. You should have seen me staring about and squalling like a legless cat when they first brought me here, five years ago! No one will hurt you, Deoris, no matter what you have heard of us! Don't be afraid. Come to the pool."

II

Around the edge of the great stone basin, women lounged, talking and splashing in the fountain. A few seemed preoccupied and solitary, but the majority were chirping about as heedlessly and sociably as a flock of winter sparrows. Deoris peered at them with frightened curiosity, and all the horror-tales of the *saji* flooded back into her mind.

They were a heterogenous group: some of the brown-skinned pygmy slave race, a few fair, plump and yellow-haired like the commoners of the city, and a very few like Deoris herself—tall and light-skinned, with the silky black or reddish curls of the Priest's Caste. Yet even here Demira stood out as unusual.

They were all immodestly stripped, but that was nothing new to Deoris except for the careless mingling of castes. Some wore curious girdles or pectorals on their young bodies, engraved with symbols that looked vaguely obscene to the still relatively innocent Deoris; one or two were tattooed with even older symbols, and the scraps of conversation which she caught were incredibly frank and shameless. One girl, a darker beauty with something about her eyes that reminded Deoris of traders from Kei-Lin, glanced at Deoris as she shyly divested herself of the saffron veils Riveda had asked her to wear, then asked Demira an indecent question which made Deoris want to sink through the earth; suddenly she realized what the old slave woman had meant by her taunts.

Demira only murmured an amused negative, while Deoris stared, wanting to cry, not understanding that she was simply being teased in the traditional fashion for all newcomers. *Why did Riveda throw me in with these—these harlots! Who are they to mock me?* She set her lips proudly, but she felt more like bursting into tears.

Demira, ignoring the teasing, bent over the edge of the pool and, dipping up water in her palms, with murmured words, began swiftly to go through a stylized and conventional ritual of purification, touching lips and breasts, in a ritual so formalized that the symbols had all but lost their original form and meaning, and done swiftly, as if from habit. Once finished, however, she led Deoris to the water and in an undertone explained the symbolic gestures.

Deoris cut her short in surprise: it was similar in form to the purification ceremonies imposed on a Priestess of Caratra—but the Grey-robe version seemed an adaptation so stylized that Demira herself did not seem to understand the meaning of the words and gestures involved. Still, the similarity did a great deal to reassure Deoris. The symbolism of the Grey-robe ceremonies was strongly sexual, and now Deoris understood even more. She went through the brief lustral rite with a thoroughness that somehow calmed and assuaged her feeling of defilement.

Demira looked on with respect, struck into a brief gravity by the evident deep meaning Deoris gave to what was, for Demira, a mere form repeated because it was required.

"Let's go back at once," Demira said, once Deoris had finished. "You were in the Ring, and that can exhaust you terribly. I know." With eyes too wise for her innocent-seeming face, she studied Deoris. "The first time I was in the Ring, I did not recover my strength for days. They took me out tonight because Riveda was there."

Deoris eyed the child curiously as the old slave woman came and wrapped Demira in a sheetlike robe; enveloped Deoris in another. Had not Riveda himself flung Demira out of the Ring, that first time, that faraway and disastrous visit to the Grey Temple? *What has Riveda to do with this nameless brat?* She felt almost sick with jealousy.

III

Demira smiled, a malicious, quirky smile as they came back into the bare little room. "Oho, now I know why Riveda begged me to look after you! Little innocent Priestess of Light, you are not the first with Riveda, nor will you be the last," she murmured in a mocking sing-song. Deoris angrily pulled away, but the child caught her coaxingly and hugged her close with an astonishing strength—her spindly little body seemed made of steel springs. "Deoris, Deoris," she crooned, smiling, "be not jealous of me! Why, I am of all women the *one* forbidden Riveda! Little silly! Has Karahama never told you that I am Riveda's daughter?"

Deoris, unable to speak, looked at Demira with new eyes—and now she saw the resemblance: the same fair hair and strange eyes; that impalpable, indefinable alienness.

"That is why I am placed so that I may never come near him in the rites," Demira went on. "He is a Northman of Zaiadan, and you know how they regard incest—or do you?"

Deoris nodded, slowly, understanding. It was well known that Riveda's countrymen not only avoided their sisters, but even their half-sisters, and she had heard it said that they even refused to marry their cousins, though Deoris found this last almost beyond belief.

"And with the symbols there—oh!" Demira bubbled on confidingly, "It has not been easy for Riveda to be so scrupulous!"

As the old woman dressed them and brought them food—fruits and bread, but no milk, cheese, or butter—Demira continued, "Yes, I am daughter to the great Adept and Master Magician Riveda! Or at least it pleases him to claim me, unofficially, for Karahama will almost never admit she knows my father's name . . . she was *saji* too, after all, and I am a child of ritual." Demira's eyes were mournful. "And now she is Priestess of Caratra! I wish—I wish . . ." She checked herself and went on swiftly, "I shamed her, I think, by being born nameless, and she does not love me. She would have had me exposed on the city wall, there to die or be found by the old women who deal in girl-brats, but Riveda took me the day I was born and gave me to Maleina; and when I was ten, they made me *saji*."

"*Ten!*" Deoris repeated, shocked despite her resolve not to be.

Demira giggled, with one of her volatile shifts of mood. "Oh, they tell some awful stories about us, don't they? At least we *saji* know everything that goes on in the Temple! More than some of your Guardians! We knew about the Atlantean Prince, but we did not tell. We never tell but a particle of what we know! Why should we? We are only the *no people*, and who would listen to us but ourselves, and we can hardly surprise one another any more. But I know," she said, casually but with a mischievous glance, "who threw the Illusion on you, when you first came to the Grey Temple." She bit into a fruit and chewed, watching Deoris out of the corner of her eye.

Deoris stared at her, frozen, afraid to ask but half desperate to know, even as she dreaded the knowledge.

"It was Craith—a Black-robe. They wanted Domaris killed. Not because of Talkannon, of course."

"Talkannon?" Deoris whispered in mute shock. What had her father to do with this?

Demira shrugged and looked away nervously. "Words, words, all of it—only words. I'm glad you didn't kill Domaris, though!"

Deoris was by now utterly aghast. "You know all this?" she said, and her voice was an unrecognizable, rasping whisper in her own ears.

Whatever slight malice had motivated Demira, it was vanished now. She put out a tiny hand and slipped it into Deoris's nerveless one. "Oh, Deoris, when I was only a little girl I used to steal into Talkannon's gardens and peep at you and Domaris from behind the bushes! Domaris is so beautiful, like a Goddess, and she loved you so much—how I used to wish I were you! I think—I think if Domaris ever spoke kindly to me—or at all!—I would die of joy!" Her voice was lonely and wistful, and Deoris, more moved than she knew, drew the blonde head down on her shoulder.

Tossing her feathery hair, Demira shook off the moment of soberness. The gleam came back to her eyes as she went on, "So I wasn't sorry for Craith at all! You don't know what Riveda was like before that, Deoris—he was just quiet and scholarly and didn't come among us for months at a time—but that turned him into a devil! He found out what Craith had done and accused him of meddling with your mind, and of a crime against a pregnant girl." She glanced quickly at Deoris and added, in explanation, "Among the Grey-robes, you know, that is the highest of crimes."

"In the Temple of Light, too, Demira."

"At least they have some sense!" Demira exclaimed.

"Well, Riveda said, 'These Guardians let their victims off too easily!' And then he had Craith scourged—whipped almost to death before he ever delivered him over to the Guardians. When they met to judge him, I slipped a grey smock over my *saji* dress, and went with Maleina—" She gave Deoris another wary little glance. "Maleina is an Initiate of some high order, I know not what, but none can deny her anywhere, I think she could walk into the chapel of Caratra and draw dirty pictures on the wall if she wanted to, and no one would dare to do anything! It was Maleina, you know, who freed Karahama from her bondage and arranged for her to enter the Mother's Temple. . . ." Demira shuddered suddenly. "But I was speaking of Craith. They judged him and condemned him to death; Rajasta was terrible! He held the mercy-dagger, but did not give it to Craith. And so they burned him alive to avenge Domaris—and Micon!"

Trembling, Deoris covered her face with her hands. *Into what world have I, by my own act, come?*

IV

But the world of the Grey Temple was soon familiar to Deoris. She continued, occasionally, to serve in the House of Birth, but most of her time was spent now among the Healers, and she soon began to think of herself almost exclusively as a Grey-robe priestess.

She was not accepted among them very soon, however, or without bitter conflict. Although Riveda was their highest Adept, the titular head of their Order, his protection hindered more than helped her. In spite of his surface cordiality, Riveda was not a popular man among his own sect; he was withdrawn and remote, disliked by many and feared by all, especially the women. His stern discipline was over-harsh; the touch of his cynical tongue missed no one, and his arrogance alienated all but the most fanatic.

Of the whole Order of Healers and Magicians, only Demira, perhaps, really loved him. To be sure, others revered him, respected him, feared him—and heartily avoided him when they could. To Demira, however, Riveda showed careless kindness—entirely devoid of paternal affection, but still the closest to it that the motherless and fatherless child had ever known. In return, Demira gave him a curious worshipping hate, that was about the deepest emotion she ever wasted on anything.

In the same mixed way, she championed Deoris among the *saji*. She quarrelled constantly and bitterly with Deoris herself, but would permit no one else to speak a disrespectful word. Since everyone was afraid of Demira's unpredictable temper and her wild rages—she was quite capable of choking a girl breathless or of clawing at her eyes in one of these blind fits of fury—Deoris won a sort of uneasy tolerance. Also, for some reason, Deoris became very fond of Demira in quite a short time, though she realized that the girl was incapable of any very deep emotion, and that it would be safer to trust a striking cobra than the volatile Demira at her worst.

Riveda neither encouraged nor disparaged this friendship. He kept Deoris near him when he could, but his duties were many and varied, and there were times when the Ritual of his Order forbade this; Deoris began to spend more and more time in the curious half-world of the *saji* women.

She soon discovered that the *saji* were not shunned and scorned without good reason. And yet, as Deoris came to know them better, she found them pathetic rather than contemptible. A few even won her deep respect and admiration, for they had strange powers, and these had not been lightly won.

Once, off-handedly, Riveda had told Deoris that she could learn much from the *saji*, although she herself was not to be given the *saji* training.

Asked why, he had responded, "You are too old, for one thing. A *saji* is chosen before maturity. And you are being trained for quite a different purpose. And—and in any case I would not risk it for you, even if I were to be your sole initiator. One in every four . . ." He broke off and shrugged, dismissing the subject; and Deoris recalled, with a start of horror, the tales of madness.

The *saji*, she knew now, were not ordinary harlots. In certain rituals they gave their bodies to the priests, but it was by rite and convention, under conditions far more strict, although very different, than the codes of more honored societies. Deoris never understood these conventions completely, for on this one subject Demira was reticent, and Deoris did not press her for details. In fact, she felt she would rather not be too certain of them.

This much Demira did tell her: in certain grades of initiation, a magician who sought to develop control over the more complex nervous and involuntary reactions of his body must practice certain rites with a woman who was clairvoyantly aware of these psychic nerve centers; who knew how to receive and return the subtle flow of psychic energy.

So much Deoris could understand, for she herself was being taught awareness like these magicians, and in much the same way. Riveda was an Adept, and his own mastery was complete; his full awareness worked like a catalytic force in Deoris, awakening clairvoyant powers in her mind and body. She and Riveda were physically intimate—but it was a strange and almost impersonal intimacy. Through the use of controlled and ritualistic sex, a catalyst in its effects on her nerves, he was awakening latent forces in her body, which in turn reacted on her mind.

Deoris underwent this training in full maturity, safeguarded by his concern for her, guarded also by his insistence on discipline, moderation, careful understanding and lengthy evaluation of every experience and sensation. Her early training as a Priestess of Caratra, too, had played no small part in her awakening; had prepared her for the balanced and stable acquisition of these powers. How much less and more this was than the training of a *saji,* she learned from Demira.

Saji were, indeed, chosen when young—sometimes as early as in their sixth year—and trained in one direction and for one purpose: the precocious and premature development along psychic lines.

It was not entirely sexual; in fact, that came last in their training, as they neared maturity. Still, the symbolism of the Grey-robes ran like a fiercely phallic undercurrent through all their training. First came the stimulation of their young minds, and excitement of their brains and spirits, as they were subjected to richly personal spiritual experiences which would have challenged a mature Adept. Music, too, and its laws of vibration and polarity, played a part in their training. And while these seeds of conflict flourished in the rich soil of their untrained minds—for they were purposely kept in a state little removed from ignorance—various emotions and, later, physical passions were skillfully and precociously roused in their still-immature minds and bodies. Body, mind, emotion, and spirit—all were roused and kept keyed to a perpetual pitch, restless, over-sensitized to a degree beyond bearing for many. The balance was delicate, violent, a potential of suppressed nervous energy.

When the child so trained reached adolescence, she became *saji.* Literally overnight, the maturing of her body freed the suppressed dynamic forces. With terrifying abruptness the latent potentials became awareness in all the body's reflex centers; a sort of secondary brain, clairvoyant, instinctive, entirely psychic, erupted into being in the complicated nerve ganglions which held the vital psychic centers: the throat, solar plexus, womb.

The Adepts, too, had this kind of awareness, but they were braced for the shock by the slow struggle for self-mastery, by discipline, careful austerities, and complete understanding. In the *saji* girls it was achieved by violence, and through the effort of others. The balance, such as it was, was forced and unnatural. One girl in four, when she reached puberty, went into raving madness and died in convulsive nerve spasms. The sudden awakening was an inconceivable thing, referred to, among those who had crossed it, as *The Black Threshold.* Few crossed that threshold entirely sane. None survived it unmarred.

Demira was a little different from the others; she had been trained not by a priest, but by the woman Adept Maleina. Deoris was to learn, in time, something of the special problems confronting a woman who travelled the Magician's path, and to discount as untrue most of the tales told of Maleina—untrue because imagination can never quite keep pace with a truth so fantastic.

The other girls trained by Maleina had exploded, at puberty, into a convulsive madness which soon lapsed into drooling, staring idiocy . . . but Demira, to everyone's surprise, had crossed The Black Threshold not only sane, but relatively stable. She had suffered the usual agonies, and the days of focusless delirium—but she had awakened sane, alert, and quite her normal self . . . on the surface.

She had not escaped entirely unscathed. The days of that fearful torment had made of her a fey thing set apart from ordinary womanhood. Close contact with Maleina, as well—and Deoris learned this only slowly, as the complexity of human psychic awareness, in its complicated psycho-chemical nervous currents, became clear to her— had partially reversed, in Demira, the flow of the life currents. Deoris saw traces of this return each month, as the moon waned and dwindled: Demira would grow silent, her volatile playfulness disappear; she would sit and brood, her catlike eyes veiled, and sometimes she would explode into unprovoked furies; other times she would only creep away like a sick animal and curl up in voiceless, inhuman torture. No one dared go near Demira at such times; only Maleina could calm the child into some semblance of reason. At such times, Maleina's face held a look so dreadful that men and women scattered before her; a haunted look, as if she were torn by some emotion which no one of lesser awareness could fathom.

Deoris, with the background of her intuitive knowledge, and what she had learned in the Temple of Caratra about the complexity of a woman's body, eventually learned to foresee and to cope with, and sometimes prevent these terrible outbursts; she began to assume responsibility for Demira, and sometimes could ward off or lighten those terrible days for the little girl—for Demira was not yet twelve years old when Deoris entered the Temple. She was hardened and precocious, a pitifully wise child—but for all that, only a child; a strange and often suffering little girl. And Deoris warmed to this little girl in a way that was eventually to prove disastrous for them all.

CHAPTER SEVEN
✠ THE MERCY OF ✠ CARATRA

I

A young girl of the *saji,* whom Deoris knew very slightly, had absented herself for many weeks from the rituals, and it finally became evident that she was pregnant. This was an exceedingly rare occurrence, for it was believed that the crossing of The Black Threshold so blighted the *saji* that the Mother withdrew from their spirit. Deoris, aware of the extremely ritualistic nature of the sexual rites of the Grey-robes, had become a bit more skeptical of this explanation.

It was a fact, however, that the *saji* women—alone in the whole social structure of the Temple-city—served not Caratra's temple; nor could they claim the privilege granted even to slaves and prostitutes— to bear their children within the Temple of Birth.

Outlawed from the rites of Caratra, the *saji* had to rely on the good graces of the women around them, or their slaves, or—in dire extremity—some Healer-priest who might take pity on them. But even to the *saji,* a man at a childbed was fearful disgrace; they preferred the clumsier ministrations of a slave.

The girl had a difficult time; Deoris heard her cries most of the night. Deoris had been in the Ring, she was exhausted and wanted to sleep, and the tortured moaning, interspersed with hoarse screams, rubbed her nerves raw. The other girls, half fascinated and half horrified, talked in frightened whispers—and Deoris listened, thinking guiltily of the skill Karahama had praised.

At last, maddened and exasperated by the tormented screaming, and the thought of the clumsy treatment the *saji* girl must be getting, Deoris managed to gain access to the room. She knew she risked terrible defilement—but had not Karahama herself been *saji* once?

By a combination of coaxing and bullying, Deoris managed to get rid of the others who had bungled the business, and after an hour of savage effort she delivered a living child, even contriving to correct some of the harm already done by the ignorant slave-women. She made the girl swear not to tell who had attended her, but somehow, either through the insulted and foolish talk of the slaves, or those invisible undercurrents which run deep and intractable within any large and closely-knit community, the secret leaked out.

When next Deoris went to the Temple of Caratra, she found herself denied admission; worse, she was confined and questioned endlessly about what she had done. After a day and a night spent in solitary confinement, during which time Deoris worked herself almost into hysteria, she was sternly informed that her case must be handled by the Guardians.

Word had reached Rajasta of what had happened. His first reaction had been disgust and shock, but he had rejected several plans which occurred to him, and many that were suggested; nor did Deoris ever become aware of what she so narrowly avoided. The most logical thing was to inform Riveda, for he was not only an Adept of the Grey-robe sect but Deoris's personal initiator, and could be relied upon to take appropriate action. This idea, too, Rajasta dismissed without a second thought.

Domaris was also a Guardian, and Rajasta might reasonably have referred the matter to her, but he knew that Domaris and Deoris were no longer friendly, and that such a thing might easily have done far more harm than good. In the end, he called Deoris into his own presence, and after talking to her gently of other matters for a little while, he asked why she had chanced such a serious violation of the laws of Caratra's Temple.

Deoris stammered her answer: "Because—because I could not bear her suffering. We are taught that at such a time all women are one. It might have been Domaris! I mean . . ."

Rajasta's eyes were compassionate. "My child, I can understand that. But why do you think the priestesses of Caratra's Temple are guarded with such care? They work among the women of the Temple and the entire city. A woman in childbirth is vulnerable, sensitive to the slightest psychic disturbance. Whatever bodily danger there may be to her is not nearly so grave as this; her mind and spirit are open to great harm. Not long ago, Domaris lost her child in great suffering. Would you expose others to such misery?"

Deoris stared mutely at the flagstoned floor.

"You yourself are guarded when you go among the *saji*, Deoris," said Rajasta, sensing her mood. "But you attended a *saji* woman at her most vulnerable moment—and had that *not* been discovered, *any pregnant girl you attended would have lost her child!*"

Deoris gasped, horrified but still half disbelieving.

"My poor girl," said Rajasta gently, shaking his head slowly. "Such things are generally not known; but the laws of the Temple are not mere superstitious prohibitions, Deoris! Which is why the Adepts and Guardians do not permit young Novices and Acolytes to use their own ignorant judgment; for you know not how to protect yourself from carrying contamination—and I do not mean physical contamination, but something far, far worse: a contamination of the life currents themselves!"

Deoris pressed her fingers over her trembling mouth and did not speak.

Rajasta, moved in spite of himself by her submission—for he had not looked forward to this interview, thinking back upon her younger days—went on, "Still, perhaps they were to blame who did not warn you. And as there was no malice in your infraction of the law, I am going to recommend that you not be expelled from Caratra's Temple, but only suspended for two years." He paused. "You yourself ran great danger, my child. I still think you are somewhat too sensitive for the Magician's Order, but—"

Passionately, Deoris interrupted, "So I am always to deny aid to a woman who needs it? To refuse the knowledge taught to me—to a sister woman—because of caste? Is that the mercy of Caratra? For lack of my skill a woman must scream herself to death?"

With a sigh, Rajasta took her small shaking hands into his own and held them. A memory of Micon came to him, and softened his reply. "My little one, there are those who forsake the paths of Light, to aid those who walk in darkness. If such a path of mercy is your karma, may you be strong in walking it—for you will need strength to defy the simple laws made for ordinary men and women. Deoris, Deoris! I do not condemn, yet I cannot condone, either. I only guard, that the forces of evil may not touch the sons and daughters of Light. Do what you must, little daughter. You are sensitive—but make that your servant, not your master. Learn to guard yourself, lest you carry harm to others." He laid one hand gently on her curls for a moment. "May you err always on the side of mercy! In your years of penance, my child, you can turn this weakness into your strength."

They sat in silence a few moments, Rajasta gazing tenderly on the woman before him, for he knew, now, that Deoris was a child no longer. Sadness and regret mingled with a strange pride in him then, and he thought again of the name she had been given: Adsartha, child of the Warrior Star.

"Now go," he said gently, when at last she raised her head. "Come not again into my presence until your penance is accomplished." And, unknown to her as she turned away, Rajasta traced a symbol of blessing in the air between them, for he felt that she would need such blessings.

II

As Deoris, miserable and yet secretly a little pleased, went slowly along the pathway leading down toward the Grey Temple, a soft, deep contralto voice came at her from nowhere, murmuring her name. The girl raised her eyes, but saw no one. Then there seemed a little stirring and shimmering in the air, and suddenly the woman Maleina stood before her. She might have only stepped from the shrubbery that lined the path, but Deoris believed, then and always, that she had simply appeared out of thin air.

The deep, vibrant voice said, "In the name of Ni-Terat, whom you call Caratra, I would speak with you."

Timidly, Deoris bent her head. She was more afraid of this woman than of Rajasta, Riveda, or any priest or priestess in the entire world of the Temple precincts. Almost inaudibly, she whispered, "What is your will, O Priestess?"

"My lovely child, be not afraid," said Maleina quickly. "Have they forbidden you the Temple of Caratra?"

Hesitantly, Deoris raised her eyes. "I have been suspended for two years."

Maleina took a deep breath, and there was a jewel-like glint in her eyes as she said, "I shall not forget this."

Deoris blinked, uncomprehending.

"I was born in Atlantis," Maleina said then, "where the Magicians are held in more honor than here. I like not these new laws which have all but prohibited magic." The Grey-robed woman paused again, and then asked, "Deoris—what are you to Riveda?"

Deoris's throat squeezed under that compelling stare, forbidding speech.

"Listen, my dear," Maleina went on, "the Grey Temple is no place for you. In Atlantis, one such as you would be honored; here, you will be shamed and disgraced—not this time alone, but again and again. Go back, my child! Go back to the world of your fathers, while there is still time. Complete your penance and return to the Temple of Caratra, while there is still time!"

Tardily, Deoris found her voice and her pride. "By what right do you command me thus?"

"I do not command," Maleina said, rather sadly. "I speak—as to a friend, one who has done me a great service. Semalis—the girl you aided without thought of penalty—she was a pupil of mine, and I love her. And I know what you have done for Demira." She laughed, a low, abrupt, and rather mournful sound. "No, Deoris, it was not I who betrayed you to the Guardians—but I would have, had I thought it would bring sense into your stubborn little head! Deoris, *look at me.*"

Unable to speak, Deoris did as she was told.

After a moment, Maleina turned away her compelling gaze, saying gently, "No, I would not hypnotize you. I only want you to see what I am, child."

Deoris studied Maleina intently. The Atlantean woman was tall and very thin, and her long smooth hair, uncovered, flamed above a darkly-bronzed face. Her long slim hands were crossed on her breast, like the hands of a beautiful statue; but the delicately molded face was drawn and haggard, the body beneath the grey robe was flat-breasted, spare and oddly shapeless, and there was a little sag of age in the poised shoulders. Suddenly Deoris saw white strands, cunningly combed, threading the bright hair.

"I too began my life in Caratra's Temple," Maleina said gravely, "and now when it is too late, I would I had never looked beyond. Go back, Deoris, before it is too late. I am an old woman, and I know of what I warn you. Would you see your womanhood sapped before it has fully wakened in you? Deoris, know you *yet* what I am? You have seen what I have brought on Demira! Go back, child."

Fighting not to cry, her throat too tight for speech, Deoris lowered her head.

The long thin hands touched her head lightly. "You cannot," Maleina murmured sadly, "can you? Is it already too late? Poor child!"

When Deoris could look up again, the sorceress was gone.

CHAPTER EIGHT
✠ THE CRYSTAL SPHERE ✠

I

Now, sometimes, for days at a time, Deoris never left the enclosure of the Grey Temple. It was a lazy and hedonistic life, this world of the Grey-robe women, and Deoris found herself dreamily enjoying it. She spent much of her time with Demira, sleeping, bathing in the pool, chattering idly and endlessly—sometimes childish nonsense, sometimes oddly serious and mature talk. Demira had a quick, though largely neglected intelligence, and Deoris delighted in teaching her many of the things she herself had learned as a child. They romped with the little-boy chelas who were too young for life in the men's courts, and listened avidly—and surreptitiously—to the talk of the older priestesses and more experienced *saji;* talk that often outraged the innocent Deoris, reared among the Priesthood of Light. Demira took a wicked delight in explaining the more cryptic allusions to Deoris, who was first shocked, then fascinated.

She got on well, all told, with Riveda's daughter. They were both young, both far too mature for their years, both forced into a rebellious awareness by tactics—though Deoris never realized this— almost equally unnatural.

She and Domaris were almost strangers now; they met rarely, and with constraint. Nor, strangely enough, had her intimacy with Riveda progressed much further; he treated Deoris almost as impersonally as Micon had, and rarely as gently.

273

Life in the Grey Temple was largely nocturnal. For Deoris these were nights of strange lessons, at first meaningless; words and chants of which the exact intonation must be mastered, gestures to be practiced with almost mechanical, mathematical precision. Occasionally, with a faintly humoring air, Riveda would set Deoris some slight task as his scribe; and he often took her with him outside the walls of the Temple precincts, for although he was scholar and Adept, the role of Healer was still predominant in Riveda. Under his tuition, Deoris developed a skill almost worthy of her teacher. She also became an expert hypnotist: at times, when a broken limb was to be splinted, or a deep wound opened and cleansed, Riveda would call upon her to hold the patient in deep, tranced sleep, so that he could work slowly and thoroughly.

He had not often allowed her to enter the Chela's Ring. He gave no reason, but she found it easy to guess at one: Riveda did not intend that any man of the Grey-robes should have the slightest excuse for approaching Deoris. This puzzled the girl; no one could have been less like a lover, but he exercised over her a certain jealous possessiveness, tempered just enough with menace that Deoris never felt tempted to brave his anger.

In fact, she never understood Riveda, nor caught a glimmering of the reasons behind his shifting moods—for he was changeable as the sky in raintime. For days at a time he would be gentle, even lover-like. These days were Deoris's greatest joy; her adoration, however edged with fear, was too innocent to have merged completely into passion—but she came close to truly loving him when he was like this, direct and simple, with the plainness of his peasant forefathers. . . . Still, she could never take him for granted. Overnight, with a change of personality so complete that it amounted to sorcery, it would become remote, sarcastic, as icy to her as to any ordinary chela. In these moods he rarely touched her, but when he did, ordinary brutality would have seemed a lover's caress; and she learned to avoid him when such a mood had taken him.

Nevertheless, on the whole, Deoris was happy. The idle life left her mind—and it was a keen and well-trained mind—free to concentrate on the strange things he taught her. Time drifted, on slow feet, until a year had gone by, and then another year.

II

Sometimes Deoris wondered why she had never had even the hope of a child by Riveda. She asked him why more than once. His answer was sometimes derisive laughter, or a flare of exasperated annoyance, occasionally a silent caress and a distant smile.

She was almost nineteen when his insistence on ritual gesture, sound, and intonation, grew exacting—almost fanatical. He had re-trained her voice himself, until it had tremendous range and an incredible flexibility; and Deoris was beginning, now, to grasp something of the significance and power of sound: words that stirred sleeping consciousness, gestures that wakened dormant senses and memories . . .

One night, toward the low end of the year, he brought her to the Grey Temple. The room lay deserted beneath its cold light, the grayness burning dimly like frost around the stone walls and floors. The air was flat and fresh and still, soundless and insulated from reality. At their heels the chela Reio-ta crept, a voiceless ghost in his grey robes, his yellow face a corpse-like mask in the icy light. Deoris, shivering in thin saffron veils, crouched behind a pillar, listening fearfully to Riveda's terse, incisive commands. His voice had dropped from tenor to resonant baritone, and Deoris knew and recognized this as the first storm-warning of the hurricane loose in his soul.

Now he turned to Deoris, and placed between her trembling hands a round, silvery sphere in which coiled lights moved sluggishly. He cupped the fingers of her left hand around it, and motioned her to her place within the mosaicked sign cut into the floor of the Temple. In his own hand was a silvered metal rod; he extended it toward the chela, but at its touch Reio-ta made a curious, inarticulate sound, and his hand, outstretched to receive it, jerked convulsively and refused to take the thing, as if his hand bore no relation to its owner's will. Riveda, with an exasperated shrug, retained it, motioning the chela to the third position.

They were standing by then in a precise triangle, Deoris with the shining sphere cradled in her raised hand, the chela braced defensively as if he held an uplifted sword. There was something defensive in Riveda's own attitude; he was not sure of his own motives. It was partly curiosity that had led him to this trial, but mainly a desire to test his own powers, and those of this girl he had trained—and those of the stranger, whose mind was still a closed book to Riveda.

With a slight shrug, the Adept shifted his own position somewhat, completing a certain pattern of space between them . . . instantly he felt an almost electric tension spring into being. Deoris moved the sphere a very little; the chela altered the position of only one hand.

The patterned triangle was complete!

Deoris began a low crooning, a chant, less sung than intoned, less intoned than spoken, but musical, rising and falling in rhythmic cadences. At the first note of the chant, the chela sprang to life. A start of recognition leaped in his eyes, although he did not move the fraction of an inch.

The chant went into a weird minor melody; stopped. Deoris bent her head and slowly, with a beautiful grace and economy of motion, her balanced gestures betraying her arduous practices, sank to her knees, raising the crystal sphere between her hands. Riveda elevated the rod . . . and the chela bent forward, automatic gestures animating his hands, so slowly, like something learned in childhood and forgotten.

The pattern of figures and sound altered subtly; changed. Amber lights and shadows drifted in the crystal sphere.

Riveda began to intone long phrases that rose and fell with a sonorous, pulsating rhythm; Deoris added her voice in subtle counterpoint. The chela, his eyes aware and alert for the first time, his motions automatic, like the jerky gestures of a puppet, was still silent. Riveda, tautly concentrated on his own part in the ritual, flickered only the corner of a glance at him.

Would he remember enough? Would the stimulus of the familiar ritual—and that it was familiar to him, the Adept had no doubts—be sufficient to waken what was dormant in the chela's memory? Riveda was gambling that Reio-ta actually possessed the secret.

The electric tension grew, throbbed with the resonance of sound in the high and vaulted archway overhead. The sphere glowed, became nearly transparent at the surface to reveal the play of coiled and jagged flickers of color; darkened; glowed again.

The chela's lips opened. He wet them, convulsively, his eyes haunted prisoners in the waxen face. Then he was chanting too, in a hoarse and gasping voice, as if his very brain trembled with the effort, rocking in its cage of bone.

No, Deoris reflected secretly, with the scrap of her consciousness not entirely submerged in the ceremonial, *this rite is not new to him.*

Riveda had gambled, and won. Two parts of this ritual were common knowledge, known to all; but Reio-ta knew the third and hidden part, which made it an invocation of potent power. Knew it—and, forced by Riveda's dominant will and the stimulus of the familiar chant on his beclouded mind, was using it—openly!

Deoris felt a little tingle of exultation. They had broken through an ancient wall of secrecy, they were hearing and witnessing what no one but the highest Initiates of a certain almost legendary secret sect had ever seen or heard—and then only under the most solemn pledges of silence until death!

She felt the magical tension deepen, felt her body prickling with it and her mind being wedged open to accept it. The chela's voice and movements were clearer now, as memory flooded back into his mind and body. The chela dominated now: his voice was clear and precise, his gestures assured, perfect. Behind the mask of his face his eyes lived and burned. The chant rushed on, bearing Deoris and Riveda along on its crest like two straws in a seething torrent.

Lightning flickered within the sphere; flamed out from the rod Riveda held. A vibrant force throbbed between the triangled bodies, an almost visible pulsing of power that brightened, darkened, spasmodically. Lightning flared above them; thunder snapped the air apart in a tremendous crashing.

Riveda's body arched backward, rigid as a pillar, and sudden terror flooded through Deoris. The chela was being *forced* to do this—this secret and sacred thing! And for what? It was sacrilege—it was black blasphemy—somehow it must be stopped! Somehow she must stop it—but it was no longer in her power even to stop herself. Her voice disobeyed her, her body was frozen, the restless sweep of tyrant power bore them all along.

The unbearable chanting slowly deepened to a single long Word— a Word no one throat could encompass, a Word needing three blended voices to transform it from a harmless grouping of syllables into a dynamic rhythm of space-twisting power. Deoris felt it on her tongue, felt it tearing at her throat, vibrating the bones of her skull as if to tear them to scattering atoms . . .

Red-hot fire lashed out with lightning shock. White whips of flame splayed out as the Word thundered on, and on, and on . . . Deoris shrieked in blind anguish and pitched forward, writhing. Riveda leaped forward, snatching her to him with a ferocious protectiveness; but the rod clung to his fingers, twisting with a life of its own, as if it had grown to the flesh there. The pattern was broken, but the fire played on about them, pallid, searing, uncontrollable; a potent spell unleashed only to turn on its blasphemers.

The chela, frozenly, was sinking, as if forced down by intense pressure. His waxen face convulsed as his knees buckled beneath him, and then he jumped forward, clutching at Deoris. With a savage yell, Riveda lashed out with the rod to ward him away, but with the sudden strength of a madman, Reio-ta struck the Adept hard in the face, narrowly avoiding the crackling nimbus of the rod. Riveda fell back, half-conscious; and Reio-ta, moving through the darting lights and flames as if they were no more than reflections in a glass, caught Deoris's chewed hands in his own and tore the sphere from them. Then, turning, he gave the staggering Riveda another swift blow and wrenched the rod from him, and with a single long, low, keening cry, struck rod and sphere together, then wrenched them apart and flung them viciously into separate ends of the room.

The sphere shattered. Harmless fragments of crystal patterned the stone tiles. The rod gave a final crackle, and darkened. The lightning died.

Reio-ta straightened and faced Riveda. His voice was low, furious—and sane. *"You filthy, damned, black sorcerer!"*

III

The air was void and empty, cold grey again. Only a faint trace of ozone hovered. Silence prevailed, save for Deoris's voice, moaning in delirious agony, and the heavy breathing of the chela. Riveda held the girl cradled across his knees, though his own shaking, seared hands hung limply from his wrists. The Adept's face had gone bone-white and his eyes were blazing as if the lightning had entered into them.

"I will kill you for that someday, Reio-ta."

The chela, his dark face livid with pain and rage, stared down darkly at the Adept and the insensible girl. His voice was almost too low for hearing. "You have killed me already, Riveda—and yourself."

But Riveda had already forgotten Reio-ta's existence. Deoris whimpered softly, unconsciously, making little clawing gestures at her breast as he let her gently down onto the cold stone floor. Carefully Riveda loosened the scorched veils, working awkwardly with the tips of his own injured hands. Even his hardened Healer's eyes contracted with horror at what he saw—then her moans died out; Deoris sighed and went limp and slack against the floor, and for a heart-stopping instant Riveda was sure that she was dead.

Reio-ta was standing very still now, shaken by fine tremors, his head bent and his mind evidently on the narrow horizon between continued sanity and a relapse into utter vacuity.

Riveda flung his head up to meet those darkly condemning eyes with his own compelling stare. Then the Adept made a brief, imperative gesture, and Reio-ta bent and lifted Deoris into Riveda's outstretched arms. She lay like a dead weight against his shoulder, and the Adept set his teeth as he turned and bore her from the Temple.

And behind him, the only man who had ever cursed Riveda and lived followed the Adept meekly, muttering to himself as idiots will . . . but there was a secret spark deep in his eyes that had not been there before.

CHAPTER NINE
✠ THE DIFFERENCE ✠

I

For the first two years of their marriage, Arvath had deceived himself into believing that he could make Domaris forget Micon. He had been kind and forbearing, trying to understand her inward struggle, conscious of her bravery, tender after the loss of their child.

Domaris was not versed in pretense, and in the last year a tension had mounted between them despite all their efforts. Arvath was not entirely blameless, either; no man can quite forgive a woman who remains utterly untouched by emotion.

Still, in all outward things, Domaris made him a good wife. She was beautiful, modest, conventional, and submissive; she was the daughter of a highly-placed priest and was herself a priestess. She managed their home well, if indifferently, and when she realized that he resented her small son, she arranged to keep Micail out of Arvath's sight. When they were alone, she was compliant, affectionate, even tender. Passionate she was not, and would not pretend.

Frequently, he saw a curious pity in her grey eyes—and pity was the one thing Arvath would not endure. It stung him into jealous, angry scenes of endless recrimination, and he sometimes felt that if she would but once answer him hotly, if she would ever protest, they would at least have some place for a beginning. But her answers were always the same; silence, or a quiet, half-shamed murmur—"I am sorry, Arvath. I told you it would be like this."

And Arvath would curse in frustrated anger, and look at her with something approaching hate, and storm out to walk the Temple precincts alone and muttering for hour after hour. Had she ever refused him anything, had she ever reproached him, he might in time have forgiven her; but her indifference was worse, a complete withdrawal to some secret place where he could not follow. She simply was not there in the room with him at all.

"I'd rather you made a cuckold of me in the court with a garden slave, where everyone could see!" he shouted at her once, in furious frustration. "At least then I could kill the man, and be satisfied!"

"*Would* that satisfy you?" she asked gently, as if she only awaited his word to pursue exactly the course of action he had outlined; and Arvath felt the hot bitter taste of hate in his mouth and slammed out of the room with fumbling steps, realizing sickly that if he stayed he would kill her, then and there.

Later he wondered if she were trying to goad him to do just that. . . .

He found that he could break through her indifference with cruelty, and he even began to take a certain pleasure in hurting her, feeling that her hot words and her hatred were better than the indifferent tolerance which was the most his tenderness had ever won. He came to abuse her shamefully, in fact, and at last Domaris, hurt past enduring, threatened to complain to the Vested Five.

"You will complain!" Arvath jeered. "Then I will complain, and the Vested Five will throw us out to settle it ourselves!"

Bitterly, Domaris asked, "Have I ever refused you anything?"

"You've never done anything else, you . . ." The word he used was one which had no written form, and hearing it from a member of the Priest's Caste made Domaris want to faint with sheer shame. Arvath, seeing her turn white, went on pouring out similar abuse with savage enjoyment. "Of course I shouldn't talk this way, you're an Initiate," he sneered. "You know the Temple secrets—one of which allows you to deliberately refuse to conceive my child!" He made a little mocking bow. "All the while protesting your innocence, of course, as befits one so elevated."

The injustice of this—for Domaris had hidden Mother Ysouda's warning in her heart and forgotten her counsel as soon as it was given—stung her into unusual denial. "You lie!" she said shakily, raising her voice to him for the first time. "You lie, and you know you lie! I don't know why the Gods have denied us children, but *my* child bears my name—and the name of his father!"

Arvath, raging, advanced to loom over her threateningly. "I don't see what that has to do with it! Except that you thought more of that Atlantean swine-prince than of me! Don't you think I know that you yourself frustrated the life of the child you almost gave me? And all because of that—that . . ." He swallowed, unable to speak, and caught her thin shoulders in his hands, roughly dragging her to her feet. "Damn you, tell me the truth! Admit what I say is true or I will kill you!"

She let herself go limp between his hands. "Kill me, then," she said wearily. "Kill me at once, and make an end of this."

Arvath mistook her trembling for fear; genuinely frightened, he lowered her gently, releasing her from his harsh clasp. "No, I didn't mean it," he said contritely; then his face crumpled and he flung himself to his knees before her, throwing his arms around her waist and burying his head in her breast. "Domaris, forgive me, forgive me, I did not mean to lay rough hands on you! Domaris, Domaris, Domaris . . ." He kept on saying her name over and over in incoherent misery, sobbing, the tight terrible crying of a man lost and bewildered.

The woman leaned over him at last, clasping him close, her eyes dark with heartbroken pity, and she, too, wept as she rocked his head against her breast. Her whole body, her heart, her very being ached with the wish that she could love him.

II

Later, full of dread and bitter conflict, she was tempted to speak at last of Mother Ysouda's warnings; but even if he believed her—if it did not start the whole awful argument over again—the thought that he might pity her was intolerable. And so she said nothing of it.

Shyly, wanting fatherly advice and comfort, she went to Rajasta, but as she talked with him, she began to blame herself: it had not been Arvath who was cruel, but she who shirked sworn duty. Rajasta, watching her face as she spoke, could find no comfort to offer, for he did not doubt that Domaris had made a deliberate display of her passivity, flaunted her lack of emotion in the man's face. What wonder if Arvath resented such an assault on his manhood? Domaris obviously did not enjoy her martyrdom; but, equally certainly, she took a perverse satisfaction in it. Her face was drawn with shame, but a soft light glowed in her eyes, and Rajasta recognized the signs of a self-made martyr all too easily.

"Domaris," he said sadly, "do not hate even yourself, my daughter." He checked her reply with a raised hand. "I know, you make the gestures of your duty. But are you *his wife*, Domaris?"

"What do you mean?" Domaris whispered; but her face revealed her suspicions.

"It is not I who ask this of you," said Rajasta, relentlessly, "but you who demand it of yourself, if you are to live with yourself. If your conscience were clean, my daughter, you would not have come to me! I know what you have given Arvath, and at what cost; *but what have you withheld?*" Pausing, he saw that she was stricken, unable to meet his gaze. "My child, do not resent that I give you the counsel which you, yourself, know to be right." He reached to her and picked up one of her tautly clenched and almost bloodlessly white hands in his own and stroked it gently, until her fingers relaxed a little. "You are like this hand of yours, Domaris. You clasp the past too tightly, and so turn the knife in your own wounds. Let go, Domaris!"

"I—I cannot," she whispered.

"Nor can you will yourself to die any more, my child. It is too late for that."

"Is it?" she asked, with a strange smile.

III

Rajasta's heart ached for Domaris; her stilled, bitter smile haunted him day after day, and at last he came to see things more as she did, and realized that he had been remiss. In his innermost self he knew that Domaris was widowed; she had been wife in the truest sense to Micon, and she would never be more than mistress to Arvath. Rajasta had never asked, but he *knew* that she had gone to Micon as a virgin.

Her marriage to Arvath had been a travesty, a mockery, a weary duty, a defilement—and for nothing.

One morning, in the library, unable to concentrate, Rajasta thought in sudden misery, *It is my doing. Deoris warned me that Domaris should not have another child, and I said nothing of it! I could have stopped them from forcing her into marriage. Instead I have sanctimoniously crushed the life from the girl who was child to me in my childless old age—the daughter of my own soul. I have sent my daughter into the place of harlots! And my own light is darkened in her shame.*

Throwing aside the scroll he had ineffectually been perusing, Rajasta rose up and went in search of Domaris, intending to promise that her marriage should be dissolved; that he would move heaven and earth to have it set aside.

He told her nothing of the kind—for before he could speak a word she told him, with a strange, secret, and not unhappy smile, that once again she was bearing Arvath a child.

CHAPTER TEN
✠ IN THE LABYRINTH ✠

I

Failure was, of all things, the most hateful to Riveda. Now he faced failure; and a common chela, his own chela, in fact, had had the audacity to protect him! The fact that Reio-ta's intervention had saved all their lives made no difference to Riveda's festering hate.

All three had suffered. Reio-ta had escaped most lightly, with blistering burns across shoulders and arms; easily treated, easily explained away. Riveda's hands were seared to the bone—maimed, he thought grimly, for life. But the *dorje* lightning had struck Deoris first with its searing lash; her shoulders, arms, and sides were blistered and scorched, and across her breasts the whips of fire had eaten deep, leaving their unmistakable pattern—a cruel sigil stamped with the brand of the blasphemous fire.

Riveda, with his almost-useless hands, did what he could. He loved the girl as deeply as it was in his nature to love anyone, and the need for secrecy maddened him, for he knew himself incapable now of caring for her properly; he lacked the proper remedies, lacked—with his hands maimed—the skill to use them. But he dared not seek assistance. The Priests of Light, seeing the color and the fearful form of her wounds, would know instantly what had made them—and then swift, sure, and incontrovertible, punishment would strike. Even his own Grey-robes could not be trusted in this; not even they would dare to conceal any such hideous tampering with the forces rightly locked in nature. His only chance of aid lay among the Black-robes; and if

Deoris were to live, he must take that chance. Without care, she might not survive another night.

With Reio-ta's assistance, he had taken her to a hidden chamber beneath the Grey Temple, but he dared not leave her there for long. To still her continual moans he had mixed a strong sedative, as strong as he dared, and forced her to swallow it; she had fallen into restless sleep, and while her fretful whimperings did not cease, the potion blurred her senses enough to dull the worst of the agony.

With a sting of guilt Riveda found himself thinking again what he had thought about Micon: *Why did they not confine their hell's play to persons of no importance, or having dared so far, at least make certain their victims did not escape to carry tales?*

He would have let Reio-ta die without compunction. As Prince of Ahtarrath, he had been legally dead for years; and what was one crazy chela more or less? Deoris, however, was the daughter of a powerful priest; her death would mean full and merciless investigation. Talkannon was not one to be trifled with, and Rajasta would almost certainly suspect Riveda first of all.

The Adept felt some shame at his weakness, but he still would not admit, even to himself, that he loved Deoris, that she had become necessary to him. The thought of her death made a black aching within him, an ache so strong and gnawing that he forgot the agonies in his seared hands.

II

After a long, blurred nightmare when she seemed to wander through flames and lightning and shadows out of half-forgotten awful legends, Deoris opened her eyes on a curious scene.

She was lying upon a great couch of carven stone, in a heap of downy cushions. Above was fixed one of the ever-burning lamps, whose flame, leaping and wavering, made the carved figures on the rails of the couch into shapes of grotesque horror. The air was damp and rather chilly, and smelled musty, like cold stone. She wondered at first if she were dead and laid in a vault, and then became aware that she was swathed in moist, cool bandages. There was pain in her body, but it was all far away, as if that swaddled mass of bandages belonged to someone else.

She turned her head a little, with difficulty, and made out the shape of Riveda, familiar even with his back to her; and before him a man Deoris recognized with a little shiver of terror—Nadastor, a Grey-robe Adept. Middle-aged, gaunt, and ascetic in appearance, Nadastor was darkly handsome and yet forbidding. Nor was he robed now in the grey robe of a Magician, but in a long black tabard, embroidered and blazoned with strange emblems; on his head was a tall, mitered hat, and between his hands he held a slight glass rod.

Nadastor was speaking, in a low, cultured voice that reminded Deoris vaguely of Micon's: "You say she is not *saji?*"

"Far from it," Riveda answered dryly. "She is Talkannon's daughter, and a Priestess."

Nadastor nodded slowly. "I see. That does make a difference. Of course, if it were mere personal sentiment, I would still say you should let her die. But . . ."

"I have made her *SA#kti SidhA#na.*"

"Within the restraints you have always burdened yourself with," Nadastor murmured, "you have dared much. I knew that you had a great power, of course; that was clear from the first. Were it not for the coward's restrictions imposed by the Ritual . . ."

"I am done with restraints!" Riveda said savagely. "I shall work as I, and I alone, see fit! I have not spared myself to gain this power and no one—now—shall curtail my right to use it!" He raised his left hand, red and raw and horribly maimed, and slowly traced a gesture that made Deoris gasp despite herself. There could be no return from that; that sign, made with the left hand, was blasphemy punishable by death, even in the Grey Temple. It seemed to hang in the air between the Adepts for a moment.

Nadastor smiled. "So be it," he said. "First we must save your hands. As for the girl—"

"Nothing about the girl!" Riveda interrupted violently.

Nadastor's smile had become mockery. "For every strength, a weakness," he said, "or you would not be here. Very well, I will attend her."

Deoris suddenly felt violently sick; Riveda had mocked Micon and Domaris just that way.

"If you have taught her as you say, she is too valuable to let her womanhood be sapped and blasted by—that which has touched her." Nadastor came toward the bed; Deoris shut her eyes and lay like death as the Black-robe drew away the clumsy bandages and skillfully dressed the hurts with a touch as cold and impersonal as if he handled a stone image. Riveda stood close by throughout, and when Nadastor had ended his ministrations, Riveda knelt and stretched one heavily bandaged hand to Deoris.

"Riveda!" she whispered, weakly.

His voice was hardly any stronger as he said, "This was not failure. We shall make it success, you and I—we have invoked a great power, Deoris, and it is ours to use!"

Deoris longed only for some word of tenderness. This talk of power sickened and frightened her; she had seen that power invoked and wished only to forget it. "An—an evil power!" she managed to whisper, dry-mouthed.

He said, with the old concentrated bitterness, "Always babbling of good and evil! Must everything come in ease and beauty? Will you run away the first time you see something which is not encompassed in your pretty dreams?"

Shamed and defensive as always, she whispered, "No. Forgive me."

Riveda's voice became gentle again. "No, I should not blame you if you are fearful, my own Deoris! Your courage has never failed when there was need for it. Now, when you are so hurt, I should not make things any worse for you. Try to sleep now, Deoris. Grow strong again."

She reached toward him, sick for his touch, for some word of love or reassurance—but suddenly, with a terrifying violence, Riveda burst into a fit of raving blasphemy. He cursed, shouting, straining with an almost rabid wrath, calling down maledictions in a foul litany in which several languages seemed to mix in a pidgin horrible to hear, and Deoris, shocked and frightened beyond her limits, began to weep wildly. Riveda only stopped when his voice failed him hoarsely, and he flung himself down on the couch beside her, his face hidden, his shoulders twitching, too exhausted to move or speak another word.

After a long time Deoris stirred painfully, curving her hand around his cheek which rested close to hers. The movement roused the man a little; he turned over wearily and looked at Deoris from wide, piteous eyes in which steaks of red showed where tiny veins had burst.

"Deoris, Deoris, what is it that I've done to you? How can I hold you to me, after this? Flee while you can, desert me if you will—I have no right to ask anything more of you!"

She tightened her clasp a little. She could not raise herself, but her voice was trembling with passion. "I gave you that right! *I go where you go!* Fear or no fear. Riveda, don't you know yet that I love you?"

The bloodshot eyes flickered a little, and for the first time in many months he drew her close and kissed her, with concentrated passion, hurting her in his fierce embrace. Then, recollecting himself, he drew carefully away—but she closed her weak fingers around his right arm, just above the bandage.

"I love you," she whispered weakly. "I love you enough to defy gods and demons alike!"

Riveda's eyes, dulled with pain and sorrow, dropped shut for a moment. When he opened them, his face was once again composed, a mask of unshakable calm. "I may ask you to do just that," he said, in a low, tense voice, "but I will be just one step behind you all the way."

And Nadastor, unseen in the shadows beyond the arched door of the room, shook his head and laughed softly to himself.

III

For some time Deoris alternated between brief lucid moments and days of hellish pain and delirious, drugged nightmares. Riveda never left her side; at whatever hour she awakened, he would be there, gaunt and impassive; deep in meditation, or reading from some ancient scroll.

Nadastor came and went, and Deoris listened to all they said to one another—but her intervals of consciousness were so brief and painful at first that she never knew where reality ended and dreams began. She remembered once waking to see Riveda fondling a snake which writhed around his head like a pet kitten—but when she spoke of it days later, he stared blankly and denied it.

Nadastor treated Riveda with courtesy and respect, as an equal;

but an equal whose education has been uncouthly remiss and must be remedied. After Deoris was out of danger and could stay awake for more than a few minutes undrugged, Riveda read to her—things that made her blood run cold. Now and again Riveda demonstrated his new skill with these manipulations of nature, and gradually Deoris lost her personal fear; never again would Riveda allow any rite to get out of control through lack of knowledge!

With only one thing was Deoris at odds: Riveda had suddenly become ambitious; his old lust for knowledge had somehow mutated into a lust for power. But she did not voice her misgivings over this, lying quiet and listening when he talked, too full of love to protest and sure in any case that if she protested he would not listen.

Never had Riveda been so kind to her. It was as if his whole life had been spent in some tense struggle between warring forces, which had made him stern and rigid and remote in the effort to cleave to a line of rectitude. Now that he had finally abandoned himself to sorcery, this evil and horror absorbed all his inborn cruelty, leaving the man himself free to be kind, to be tender, to show the basic simplicity and goodness that was in him. Deoris felt her old childlike adoration slowly merging into something deeper, different . . . and once, when he kissed her with that new tenderness, she clung to him, in sudden waking of an instinct as old as womanhood.

He laughed a little, his face relaxing into humorous lines. "My precious Deoris . . ." Then he murmured doubtfully, "But you are still in so much pain."

"Not much, and I—I want to be close to you. I want to sleep in your arms and wake there—as I have never done."

Too moved to speak, Riveda drew her close to him. "You shall lie in my arms tonight," he whispered at last. "I—I too would have you close."

He held her delicately, afraid to hurt by a careless touch, and she felt his physical presence—so familiar to her, so intimately known to her body, and yet alien, altogether strange, after all these years a stranger to her—so that she found herself shy of the lover as she had never been of the initiator.

Riveda made love to her softly, with a sensitive sincerity she had not dreamed possible, at first half fearful lest he bring her pain; then, when he was certain of her, drawing on some deep reserve of gentleness, giving himself up to her with the curious, rare warmth of a man long past youth: not passionate, but very tender and full of love. In all her time with Riveda she had never known him like this; and for hours afterward she lay nestled in his arms, happier than she had ever been in her life, or would ever be again, while in a muted, hoarse, hesitant voice he told her all the things every woman dreams of hearing from her lover, and his shaking scarred hands moved softly on her silky hair.

CHAPTER ELEVEN
✠ THE DARK SHRINE ✠

I

Deoris remained within the subterranean labyrinth for a month, cared for by Riveda and Nadastor. She saw no other person, save an old deaf-mute who brought her food. Nadastor treated Deoris with a ceremonious deference which astonished and terrified the girl— particularly after she heard one fragment of conversation . . .

She and Riveda had grown by degrees into a tender companionship like nothing the girl had ever known. He had no black, surly moods now. On this day he had remained near her for some time, translating some of the ancient inscriptions with an almost lewd gaiety, coaxing her to eat with all sorts of playful little games, as if she were an ailing child. After a time, for she still tired quickly, he laid her down and drew a blanket of woven wool over her shoulders, and left her; she slept until she was wakened by a voice, raised a little as if he had forgotten her in his annoyance.

"... *all my life* have I held that in abhorrence!"

"Even within the Temple of Light," Nadastor was saying, "brothers and sisters marry sometimes; their line is kept pure, they want no unknown blood which might bring back those traits they have bred out of the Priest's Caste. Children of incest are often natural clairvoyants."

"When they are not mad," said Riveda cynically.

Deoris closed her eyes again as the voices fell to a murmur; then Riveda raised his voice angrily again.

"*Which* of Talkannon's . . . ?"

"You will wake the girl," Nadastor rebuked; and for minutes they spoke so softly that Deoris could hear nothing. The next thing she caught was Nadastor's flat statement, "Men breed animals for what they want them to become. Should they scatter the seed of their own bodies?" The voice fell again, then surged upward: "I have watched you, Riveda, for a long time. I knew that one day you would weary of the restraints laid on you by the Ritual!"

"Then you knew more than I," Riveda retorted. "Well, I have no regrets—and whatever you may think, no scruples in that line. Let us see if I understand you. The child of a man past the age of passion, and a girl just barely old enough to conceive, can be—almost outside the laws of nature . . ."

"And as little bound by them," Nadastor added. He rose and left the room, and Riveda came to look down at Deoris. She shut her eyes, and after a moment, thinking her still sleeping, he turned away.

II

The burns on her back and shoulders had healed quickly, but the cruel brand on her breasts had bitten deep; even by the time she was able to be up again, they were still swathed in bandages which she could not bear to touch. She was growing restless; never had she been so long absent from the Temple of Light, and Domaris must be growing anxious about her—at the very least, she might make inquiries.

Riveda soothed her fear a little.

"I have told a tale to account for you," he said. "I told Cadamiri that you had fallen from the sea-wall and been burned at one of the beacon fires; that also explained my own hurt." He held out his hands, free now of bandages, but terribly scarred, too stiff even to recover their old skill.

"No one questions my ability as Healer, Deoris, so they did not protest when I said you must be left in peace. And your sister—" His eyes narrowed slightly. "She waylaid me today in the library. She is anxious about you; and in all truth, Deoris, I could give no reason why she should not see you, so tomorrow it would be well if you left this place. You must see her, and reassure her, else . . ." he laid a heavy hand on her arm, "the Guardians may descend on us. Tell Domaris—whatever you like, I care not, but—whatever you do, Deoris, unless you want me to die like a dog, let not even Domaris see the scars on your breasts until they are wholly healed. And Deoris, if your sister insists, you may have to return to the Temple of Light. I—I grieve to send you from me, and would not have it so, but—the Ritual forbids any maiden of the Light-born to live among Grey-robes. It is an old law, and seldom invoked; it has been ignored time and time again. But Domaris reminded me of it, and—I dare not endanger you by angering her."

Deoris nodded without speaking. She had known that this interlude could not last forever. In spite of all the pain, all the terror, her new dread of Riveda, this had been a sort of idyll, suspended in nothingness and wrapped in an unexpected certainty of Riveda's nearness and his love; and now, already it was part of the past.

"You will be safest under your sister's protection. She loves you, and will ask no questions, I think." Riveda clasped her hand in his own and sat without moving or speaking for a long time; at last, he said, "I told you, once, Deoris, that I am not a good man to trust. By now I imagine I have proved that to you." The bitter and despondent tone was back in his voice. Then, evenly and carefully, he asked, "Are you still—my Priestess? I have forfeited the right to command you, Deoris. I offer to release you, if you wish it."

As she had done years ago, Deoris let go of his hand, dropped to her knees and pressed her face to his robes in surrender. She whispered, "I have told you I will defy all for you. Why will you never believe me?"

After a moment, Riveda raised her gently, his touch careful and light. "One thing remains," he said in a low voice. "You have suffered much, and I—I would not force this on you, but—but if not tonight, a year's full cycle must go by before we can try again. This is the Night of Nadir, and the only night on which I can complete this."

Deoris did not hesitate even a moment, although her voice shook a little. "I am at your command," she whispered, in the ritual phrase of the Grey-robes.

III

Some few hours later, the old deaf-mute woman came. She stripped Deoris, bathed and purified her, and robed her in the curious garments Riveda had sent. First a long, full robe of transparent linen, and over this a tabard of stiffly embroidered silk, decorated with symbols of whose meaning Deoris was not wholly certain. Her hair, now grown thick and long, was confined in a silver fillet, and her feet stained with dark pigment. As the deaf-mute completed this final task, Riveda returned—and Deoris forgot her own unusual garb in amazement at the change in him.

She had never seen him clothed in aught but the voluminous grey robe, or a simpler grey smock for magical work. Tonight he blazed in raw colors that made him look crude, sinister—frightening. His silver-gilt hair shone like virgin gold beneath a horned diadem which partially concealed his face; he wore a tabard of crimson like her own, with symbols worked in black from which Deoris turned away shamed eyes: the emblems were legitimate magical symbols, but in company with the ornaments of her clothing they seemed obscene. Under the crimson surcoat, Riveda wore a close-fitting tunic dyed blue—and this to Deoris was the crowning obscenity, for blue was the color sacred to Caratra, and reserved for women; she found she could not look at it on his body, and her face was aflame. Over all, he wore the loose magician's cloak which could be drawn about him to form the Black Robe. Seeing her blushes slowly whiten, Riveda smiled sternly.

"You are not *thinking*, Deoris! You are reacting to your childhood's superstitions. Come, what have I taught you about vibration and color?"

She felt all the more shamed and foolish at the reminder. "Red vitalizes and stimulates," she muttered, reciting, "where blue produces calmness and peace, mediating all inflamed and feverish conditions. And black absorbs and intensifies vibrations."

"That's better," he approved, smilingly. He then surveyed her costume critically, and once satisfied, said, "One thing remains; will you wear this for me, Deoris?"

He held out a girdle to her. Carved of wooden links, it was bound with crimson cords knotted in odd patterns. Runes were incised in the wood, and for a moment some instinct surged up in Deoris, and her fingers refused to touch the thing.

Riveda, more sternly, said, "Are you afraid to wear this, Deoris? Must we waste time with a lengthy explanation?"

She shook her head, chastened, and began to fasten it about her body—but Riveda bent and prevented her. With his strong, scarred hands he cinctured it carefully about her waist, tying the cords into a firm knot and ending with a gesture incomprehensible to her.

"Wear this until I give you leave to take it off," he told her. "Now come."

She almost rebelled again when she saw where he was taking her—to the terrible shrouded Crypt of the Avatar, where the Man with Crossed Hands lay, continually bound. Once within, she watched, frozen, as Riveda kindled ritual fire upon the altar which had been dark for a million years.

In his deepest voice, blazing in his symbolic robes, he began to intone the invocatory chant and Deoris, recognizing it, knew in trembling terror what it invoked. Was Riveda mad indeed? Or splendidly, superbly courageous? This was blackest blasphemy—*or was it?* And for what?

Shivering, she had no real choice but to add her own voice to the invocation. Voice answered voice in dark supplication, strophe and antistrophe, summoning . . . entreating. . . .

Riveda turned abruptly to the high stone altar where a child lay, and with a surge of horror Deoris saw what Riveda held in his hands. She clasped her own hands over her mouth so that she would not scream aloud as she recognized the child: *Larmin.* Karahama's son, Demira's little brother—Riveda's own son . . .

The child watched with incurious drugged eyes. The thing was done with such swiftness that the child gave only a single smothered whimper of apprehension, then fell back into the drugged sleep. Riveda turned back to the terrible ceremony which had become, to Deoris, a devil's rite conducted by a maniac.

Nadastor glided from the shadows, unbound the little boy, lifted the small senseless figure from the altar-stone and bore it from the

Crypt. Deoris and Riveda were alone in the Dark Shrine—the very shrine where Micon had been tortured, alone with the Unrevealed God.

Her mind reeling with the impact of sound and sight, she began to comprehend if not the whole, then the drift of the blasphemous ritual: Riveda meant nothing less than to loose the terrible chained power of the Dark God, to bring the return of the Black Star. But there was something more, something she could not quite understand . . . or was it that she dared not understand?

She sank to her knees; a deathly intangible horror held her by the throat, and though her mind screamed *No! No-no-no-no!* in the grip of that hypnotic dream she could not move or cry out. With a single word or gesture of protest she could so distort and shatter the pattern of the ritual that Riveda must fail—but sound was beyond her power, and she could not raise a hand or move her head so much as a fraction to one side or the other . . . and because in this crisis she could not summon the courage to defy Riveda, her mind slid off into incoherence, seeking an escape from personal guilt.

She could not—she *dared* not understand what she was hearing and seeing; her brain refused to seize on it. Her eyes became blank, blind and though Riveda saw the last remnant of sanity fade from her wide eyes, it was with only the least of his attention; the rest of him was caught up in what he did.

The fire on the shrine blazed up.

The chained and faceless image stirred . . .

Deoris saw the smile of the Man with Crossed Hands leering from the distorted shadows. Then, for an instant, she saw what Riveda saw, a chained and faceless figure standing upright—but that too swam away. Where they had been a great and fearful form hulked, recumbent and swathed in corpse-windings—an image that stirred and fought its bonds.

Then Deoris saw only an exploding pinwheel of lights into which she fell headlong. She barely knew it when Riveda seized her; she was inert, half-conscious at best, her true mind drowned in the compassionate stare of the Man with Crossed Hands, blinded by the spinning wheel of lights that whirled blazing above them. She knew, dimly, that Riveda lifted and laid her on the altar, and she felt a momentary shock of chill awareness and fear as she was forced back onto the wet stone. Not here, not here, not on the stone stained with the child's blood . . .

But he isn't dead! she thought with idiotic irrelevance, *he isn't dead, Riveda didn't kill him, it's all right if he isn't dead . . .*

IV

As if breaking the crest of a deep dark wave, Deoris came to consciousness suddenly, sensible of cold, and of pain from her half-healed burns. The fire on the shrine was extinguished; the Man with Crossed Hands had become but a veiled darkness.

Riveda, the frenzy gone, was lifting her carefully from the altar. With his normal, composed severity, he assisted her to rearrange her robes. She felt bruised and limp and sick, and leaned heavily on Riveda, stumbling a little on the icy stones—and she guessed, rightly, that he was remembering another night in this crypt, years before.

Somewhere in the labyrinth she could hear a child's distant sobs of pain and fright. They seemed to blend with her own confusion and terror that she put her hands up to her face to be sure that she was not crying, whether the sounds came from within or without.

At the door of the room where she had lain all during her long illness, Riveda paused, beckoning the deaf-mute woman and giving her some orders in sign-language.

He turned to Deoris again, and spoke with a cold formality that chilled her to the bone: "Tomorrow you will be conducted above ground. Do not fear to trust Demira, but be very careful. Remember what I have told you, especially in regard to your sister Domaris!" He paused, for once at a loss for words; then, with sudden and unexpected reverence, the Adept dropped to his knees before the terrified girl and taking her icy hand in his, he pressed it to his lips, then to his heart.

"Deoris," he said, falteringly. "O, my love—"

Quickly he let go her hand, rose to his feet and was gone before the girl could utter a single word.

BOOK FOUR
✠ RIVEDA ✠

⊕ ⊕ ⊕

" . . . common wisdom has it that Good has a tendency to grow and preserve itself, whereas Evil tends to grow until it destroys itself. But perhaps there is a flaw in our definitions—for would it be evil for Good to grow until it crowded Evil out of existence?

" . . . everyone is born with a store of knowledge he doesn't know he possesses. . . . The human body of flesh and blood, which has to feed itself upon plants and their fruits, and upon animal meats, is not a fit habitation for the eternal spirit that moves us—and for this, we must die—but somewhere in the future is the assurance of a new body-type which can outlast the stones which do not die. . . . The things we learn strike sparks, and the sparks light fires; and the firelight reveals strange things moving in the darkness. . . . The darkness can teach you things that the light has never seen, and will never be able to see. . . .

"Unwilling to continue a merely mineral existence, plants were the first rebels; but the pleasures of a plant are limited to the number of ways in which it can circumvent the laws governing the mineral world. . . . There are poisonous minerals that can kill plants or animals or men. There are poisonous plants that can kill animals or men. There are poisonous animals (mostly reptiles) which can kill men—but man is unable to continue the poisonous chain, poison other creatures though he may, because he has never developed a means for poisoning the gods. . . ."
                    —from *The Codex of the Adept Riveda*

⊕ ⊕ ⊕

CHAPTER ONE
✠ A WORLD OF DREAMS ✠

I

"But Domaris, why?" Deoris demanded. "Why do you hate him so?"

Domaris leaned against the back of the stone bench where they sat, idly fingering a fallen leaf from the folds of her dress before casting it into the pool at their feet. Tiny ripples fanned out, winking in the sunlight.

"I don't believe that I do hate Riveda," Domaris mused, and shifted her swollen body awkwardly, as if in pain. "But I distrust him. There is—something about him that makes me shiver." She looked at Deoris, and what she saw in her sister's pale face made her add, with a deprecating gesture, "Pay not too much attention to me. You know Riveda better than I. And—oh, it may all be my imagination! Pregnant women have foolish fancies."

At the far end of the enclosed court, Micail's tousled head popped up from behind a bush and as quickly ducked down again; he and Lissa were playing some sort of hiding game.

The little girl scampered across the grass. "I see you, M'cail!" she cried shrilly, crouching down beside Domaris's skirt, "Pe-eep!"

Domaris laughed and petted the little girl's shoulder, looking with satisfaction at Deoris. The last six months had wrought many changes in the younger girl; Deoris was not now the frail, huge-eyed wraith bound in bandages and weak with pain, whom Domaris had brought from the Grey Temple. Her face had begun to regain its color, though she was still paler than Domaris liked, if no longer so terribly thin . . . Domaris frowned as another, persistent suspicion came back to her. *That change I can recognize!* Domaris never forced a confidence, but she could not keep herself from wondering, angrily, just *what* had been done to Deoris. That story of falling from the sea-wall into a watch-fire . . . did not ring true, somehow.

"You don't have foolish fancies, Domaris," the girl insisted. "Why do you distrust Riveda?"

"Because—because he doesn't feel *true* to me; he hides his mind from me, and I think he has lied to me more than once." Domaris's voice hardened to ice. "But mostly because of what he is doing to you! The man is using you, Deoris . . . Is he your lover?" she asked suddenly, her eyes searching the young face.

"No!" The denial was angry, almost instinctive.

Lissa, forgotten at Domaris's knee, stared from one sister to the other for a moment, confused and a little worried; then she smiled slightly, and ran to chase Micail. Grown-ups had these exchanges. It didn't usually mean anything, as far as Lissa could tell, and so she rarely paid attention to such talk—though she had learned not to interrupt.

Domaris moved a little closer to Deoris and asked, more gently, "Then—who?"

"I—I don't know what you mean," Deoris said; but the look in her eyes was that of a trapped and frightened creature.

"Deoris," her sister said kindly, "be honest with me, kitten; do you think you can hide it forever? I have served Caratra longer than you—if not as well."

"I am *not* pregnant! It isn't possible—I *won't!*" Then, controlling her panic, Deoris took refuge in arrogance. "I have no lover!"

The grave grey eyes studied her again. "You may be sorceress," Domaris said deliberately, "but all your magic could not compass *that* miracle." She put her arm around Deoris, but the girl flung it petulantly away.

"Don't! I'm not!"

The response was so immediate, so angry, that Domaris only stared, open-mouthed. How could Deoris lie with such conviction, unless—unless . . . *Has that damned Grey-robe, then, taught her his own deceptive skills?* The thought troubled her. "Deoris," she said, half-questioning, "it *is* Riveda?"

Deoris edged away from her, sullenly, scared. "And if it were so—which it is not!—it is my right! You claimed yours!"

Domaris sighed; Deoris was going to be tiresome. "Yes," the older woman said tiredly, "I have no right to blame. Yet—" She looked away across the garden to the tussling children, her brows contracting in a half-troubled smile. "I *can* wish it were any other man."

"You do hate him!" Deoris cried, "I think you're—I hate *you!*" She rose precipitately to her feet, and ran from the garden, without a backward glance. Domaris half rose to follow her, then sank back heavily, sighing.

What's the use? She felt weary and worn, not at all inclined to soothe her sister's tantrums. Domaris felt unable to deal with her own life at present—how could she handle her sister's?

When she had carried Micon's child, Domaris had felt an odd reverence for her body; not even the knowledge that Micon's fate followed them like a shadow had dimmed her joy. Bearing Arvath's was different; this was duty, the honoring of a pledge. She was resigned, rather than rejoicing. Vised in pain, she walked with recurrent fear, and Mother Ysouda's words whispering in her mind. Domaris felt a guilty, apologetic love for Arvath's unborn son—as if she had wronged him by conceiving him.

And now—why is Deoris like that? Perhaps it isn't Riveda's child, and she's afraid of what he'll do . . . ? Domaris shook her head, unable to fathom the mystery.

From certain small but unmistakable signs, she was certain of her sister's condition; the girl's denial saddened and hurt Domaris. The lie itself was not important to her, but the reason for it was of great moment.

What have I done, that my own sister denies me her confidence?

She got up, with a little sigh, and went heavily toward the archway leading into the building, blaming herself bitterly for her neglect. She had been lost in grief for Micon—and then had come her marriage, and the long illness that followed the loss of her other child—and her Temple duties were onerous. Yet, somehow, Deoris's needs should have been met.

Rajasta warned me, years ago, Domaris thought sadly. *Was it this he foresaw? Would that I had listened to him! If Deoris has ceased to trust me—*Pausing, Domaris tried to reassure herself. *Deoris is a* *strange girl; she has always been rebellious. And she's been so ill, perhaps she wasn't really lying; maybe she really doesn't know, hasn't bothered to think about the physical aspects of the thing. That would be just like Deoris!*

For a moment, Domaris saw the garden rainbowed through sudden tears.

II

In the last months, Deoris had abandoned herself to the moment, not thinking ahead, not letting herself dwell on the past. She drifted on the surface of events; and when she slept, she dreamed obsessively of that night in the Crypt—so many terrifying nightmares that she almost managed to convince herself that the bloodletting, the blasphemous invocation, all that had transpired there, had been only another, more frightening dream.

This had been reinforced by the ease with which she had been able to pick up most of the broken threads of her life. Riveda's story had been accepted without question.

At her sister's insistence, Deoris had returned to Domaris's home. It was not the same. The House of the Twelve now contained a new group of Acolytes; Domaris and Arvath, with Elis and Chedan and another young couple, occupied pleasant apartments in a separate dwelling. Into this home Deoris had been welcomed, made a part of their family life. Until this moment, Domaris had never once questioned the past years.

But I should have known! Deoris thought superstitiously, and shivered. Only last night, very late, Demira had stolen secretly into the courts and into her room, whispering desperately, "Deoris—oh, Deoris, I shouldn't be here, I know, but don't send me away, I'm so terribly, terribly frightened!"

Deoris had taken the child into her bed and held her until the scared crying quieted, and then asked, incredulously, "But what is it, Demira, what's happened? I won't send you away, darling, no matter what it was, you can tell me what's the matter!" She looked at the thin, huddled girl beside her with troubled eyes, and said, "It's not likely

Domaris would come into my rooms at this hour of the night, either;
but if she did, I'll tell her—tell her something."

"Domaris," said Demira, slowly, and smiled—that wise and sad
smile which always saddened Deoris; it seemed such an old smile for
the childlike face. "Ah, Domaris doesn't know I exist, Deoris. Seeing
me wouldn't change that." Demira sat up then, and looked at Deoris
a moment before her silvery-grey eyes slid away again, blank and
unseeing, the white showing all around the pupil. "*One of us three will
die very soon,*" she said suddenly, in a strange, flat voice as unfocussed
as her eyes. "One of us three will die, and her child with her. The
second will walk beside Death, but it will take only her child. And the
third will pray for Death to come for herself and her child, and both
will live to curse the very air they breathe."

Deoris grabbed the slim shoulders and shook Demira, hard.
"Come out of it!" she commanded, in a high, scared voice. "*Do you
even know what you are saying?*"

Demira smiled queerly, her face lax and distorted. "Domaris, and
you, and I—Domaris, Deoris, Demira; if you say the three names very
quickly it is hard to tell which one you are saying, no? We are bound
together by more than that, though, we are all three linked by our
fates, all three with child."

"No!" Deoris cried out, in a denial as swift as it was vehement. *No,
no, not from Riveda, not that cruelty, not that betrayal . . .*

She bent her head, troubled and afraid, unable to face Demira's
wise young eyes. Since the night when she and Riveda and the chela
had been trapped in the ritual which had loosed the Fire-spirit on
them, scarring her with the blasting seal of the *dorje,* Deoris had not
once had to seclude herself for the ritual purifications . . . She had
thought about that, remembering horror-tales heard among the *saji,*
of women struck and blasted barren, remembering Maleina's
warnings long ago. Secretly, she had come to believe that, just as her
breasts were scarred past healing, so she had been blasted in the citadel
of her womanhood and become a sapped and sexless thing, the mere
shell of a woman. Even when Domaris had suggested a simpler
explanation—that she might be pregnant—she could not accept it.
Surely if she were capable of conception, she would have borne
Riveda's child long before this time!

Or would she? Riveda was versed in the mysteries, able to prevent conception if it pleased him. With a flash of horrified intuition, the thought came, to be at once rejected. *Oh no, not from that night in the Crypt—the mad invocation—the girdle, even now concealed beneath my nightdress . . .*

With a desperate effort, she snapped shut her mind on the memory. *It never happened, it was a dream . . . except for the girdle. But if that's real—no. There must be some explanation . . .*

Then her mind caught up with the other thing Demira had said, seizing on it almost with relief. "*You!*"

Demira looked up plaintively at Deoris. "You'll believe me," she said pitifully. "You will not mock me?"

"Oh, no, Demira, no, of course not." Deoris looked down into the pixyish face that now laid itself confidingly on her shoulder. Demira, at least, had not changed much in these three years; she was still the same, strange, suffering, wild little girl who had excited first Deoris's distrust and fear, and later her pity and love. Demira was now fifteen, but she seemed essentially the same, and she looked much as she had at twelve: taller than Deoris but slight, fragile, with the peculiar, deceptive appearance of immaturity and wisdom intermingled.

Demira sat up and began to reckon on her fingers. "It was like an awful dream. It happened, oh, perhaps one change of the moon after you left us."

"Five months ago," Deoris prompted gently.

"One of the little children had told me I was wanted in a sound-chamber. I thought nothing of it. I had been working with one of Nadastor's chelas. But it was empty. I waited there and then—and then a priest came in, but he was—he was masked, *and in black,* with horns across his face! He didn't say anything, he only—caught at me, and—*oh Deoris!*" The child collapsed in bitter sobbing.

"Demira, no!"

Demira made an effort to stifle her tears, murmuring, "You do believe me—you will not mock me?"

Deoris rocked her back and forth like a baby. "No, no, darling, no," she soothed. She knew very well what Demira meant. Outside the Grey Temple, Demira and her like were scorned as harlots or worse; but Deoris, who had lived in the Grey Temple, knew that such as Demira were held in high honor and respect, for she and her kind were sacred, indispensable, under protection of the highest Adepts.

The thought of a *saji* being raped by an unknown was unthinkable, fantastic . . . Almost unbelieving, Deoris asked, "Have you *no* idea who he was?"

"No—oh, I should have told Riveda, I should have told, but I couldn't, I just couldn't! After the—the Black-robe went away, I—I just lay there, crying and crying, I couldn't stop myself, I—it was Riveda who heard me, he came and found me there. He was . . . for once he was kind, he picked me up and held me, and—and scolded me until I stopped crying. He—he tried to make me tell him what had happened, but I—I was afraid he wouldn't believe me . . ."

Deoris let Demira go, remaining as still as if she had been turned to a statue. Scraps of a half-heard conversation had returned to float through her mind; her intuition now turned them to knowledge, and almost automatically she whispered the invocation, "*Mother Caratra! Guard her,*" for the first time in years.

It couldn't be, it simply was not possible, not thinkable . . .

She sat motionless, afraid her face would betray her to the child.

At last Deoris said, frozenly, "But you have told Maleina, child? Surely you know she would protect you. I think she would kill with her own hands anyone who harmed you or caused you pain."

Demira shook her head mutely; only after several moments did she whisper, "I am afraid of Maleina. I came to you because—because of Domaris. She has influence with Rajasta . . . When last the Black-robes came into our temple, there was much terror and death, and now, if they have returned—the Guardians should know of it. And Domaris is—is so kind, and beautiful—she might have pity, even on me—"

"I will tell Domaris when I can," Deoris promised, her lips stiff; but conflict tore at her. "Demira, you must not expect too much."

"Oh, you are good, Deoris! Deoris, how I love you!" Demira clung to the older girl, her eyes bright with tears. "And Deoris, if Riveda must know—will you tell him? He will allow you anything, but no one else dares approach him now, since you left us no one dares speak to him unless he undresses them, and even then . . . " Demira broke off. "He was kind, when he found me, but I was so afraid."

Deoris stroked the little girl's shoulder gently, and her own face grew stern. Her last shred of doubt vanished. *Riveda heard her crying? In a sealed sound-chamber? That I'll believe taken the sun shines at midnight!*

"Yes," said Deoris grimly, "I will talk to Riveda."

III

"She did not even guess, Deoris. I did not mean that you should know, either, but since you are so shrewd, yes, I admit it." Riveda's voice was as deep and harsh as winter surf; in the same icy bass he went on, "Should you seek to tell her, I—Deoris, much as you mean to me, I think I would kill you first!"

"Take heed lest you be the one killed," Deoris said coldly. "Suppose Maleina makes the same wise guess I did?"

"Maleina!" Riveda practically spat the woman Adept's name. "She did what she could to ruin the child—nevertheless, I am not a monster, Deoris. What Demira does not know will not torment her. It is—unfortunate that she knows I am her father; fool that I was to let it be guessed even in the Grey Temple. I will bear the responsibility; it is better that Demira know nothing more than she does now."

Sickened, Deoris cried out, "And this you will confess to me?"

Slowly, Riveda nodded. "I know now that Demira was begotten and reared for this one purpose alone. Otherwise, why should I have stretched out my hand to save her from squalling to death on the city wall? I knew not what I did, not then. But is it not miraculous, you see, how all things fall together to have meaning? The girl is worthless for anything else—she made Karahama hate me, just by being born." And for the first time Deoris sensed a weak spot in the Adept's icy armor, but he went on swiftly, "But now you see how it all makes a part of the great pattern? I did not know when she was born, but Karahama's blood is one with yours, and so is Demira's, that strain of the Priest's Line, sensitive—and so even this unregarded nothing shall serve some part in the Great work."

"Do you care for nothing else?" Deoris looked at Riveda as if he were a stranger; at this moment he seemed as alien as if he had come from far beyond the unknown seas. This talk of patterns, as if he had planned that Demira should be born for this . . . was he mad, then? Always Deoris had believed that the strangeness of his talk hid some great and lofty purpose which she was too young and ignorant to understand. But this, this she *did* understand for the corrupt madness it was, and of this he spoke as if it were more of the same high purpose. Was it all madness and illusion then, had she been dragged into insanity and corruption under the belief that she was the chosen of the great Adept? Her mouth was trembling; she fought not to break down.

Riveda's mouth curved in a brutal smile. "Why, you little fool, I believe you're jealous!"

Mutely, Deoris shook her head. She did not trust herself to speak. She turned away, but Riveda caught her arm with a strong hand. "Are you going to tell Demira this?" he demanded.

"To what purpose?" Deoris asked coldly, "To make her sick, as I am? No, I will keep your secret. Now take your hands from me!"

His eyes widened briefly, and his hand dropped to his side. "Deoris," he said in a more persuasive voice, "you have always understood me before."

Tears gathered at her eyelids. "Understood you? No, never. Nor have you been like this before! This is—sorcery, distortion—black magic!"

Riveda bit off his first answer unspoken, and only muttered, rather despondently, "Well, call me Black Magician then, and have done with it." Then, with the tenderness which was so rare, he drew her stiff and unresponsive form to him. "Deoris," he said, and it was like a plea, "you have always been my strength. Don't desert me now! Has Domaris so quickly turned you against me?"

She could not answer; she was fighting back tears.

"Deoris, the thing is done, and I stand by it. It is too late to crawl out of it now, and repentance would not undo it in any case. Perhaps it was—unwise; it may have been cruel. *But it is done.* Deoris, you are the only one I dare to trust: make Demira your care, Deoris, let her be your child. Her mother has long forsworn her, and I—I have no rights any more, if ever I did." He stopped, his face twisted. Lightly he touched the fearful scars hidden by her clothing; then his hands strayed gently to her waist, to touch the wooden links of the carved symbolic girdle with a curiously tentative gesture. He raised his eyes, and she saw in his face a painful look of question and fear which she did not yet understand as he murmured, "You do not yet know—the Gods save you, the Gods protect you all! I have forfeited their protection; I have been cruel to you—Deoris, help me! Help me, help me—"

And in a moment the melting of his icy reserve was complete—and with it fled all Deoris's anger. Choking, she flung her arms about him, saying half incoherently, "I will, Riveda, always—I will!"

CHAPTER TWO
✠ THE BLASPHEMY ✠

I

Somewhere in the night the sound of a child's sudden shrill wailing shredded the silence into ribbons, and Deoris raised her head from the pillow, pressing her hands to her aching eyes. The room was filled with heavy blackness barred by shuttered moonlight. She was so used to the silence of the *saji* courts—she had been dreaming—then memory came back. She was not in the Grey Temple, nor even in Riveda's austere habitation, but in Domaris's home; it must be Micail crying . . .

She slid from the bed, and barefoot, crossed the narrow hall into her sister's room. At the sound of the opening door, Domaris raised her head; she was half-clad, her unbound hair a coppery mist streaming over the little boy who clung to her, still sobbing.

"Deoris, darling, did he wake you? I'm sorry." She stroked Micail's tangled curls as she rocked the child gently against her shoulder. "There now, there now, hush, hush you," she murmured.

Micail hiccoughed sleepily with the subsidence of his sobs. His head dropped onto Domaris's shoulder, then perked up momentarily. "De'ris," he murmured.

The younger girl came quickly to him. "Domaris, let me take Micail, he's too heavy for you to lift now," she rebuked softly. Domaris demurred, but gave the heavy child into her sister's arms. Deoris looked down at the drooping eyes, darkly blue, and the smudge of freckles across the turned-up nose.

"He will be very like . . ." she murmured; but Domaris put out her hands as if to ward off a physical blow, and the younger woman swallowed Micon's name. "Where shall I put him?"

"Into my bed; I'll take him to sleep with me, and perhaps he will be quiet. I am sorry he woke you, Deoris. You look—so tired." Domaris gazed into her sister's face, pale and pinched, with a strange look of weary lethargy. "You are not well, Deoris."

"Well enough," said Deoris indifferently. "You worry too much. You're not in the best health yourself," she accused, suddenly frightened. With the eyes of a trained Healer-priestess, Deoris now saw what her self-absorption had hidden: how thin Domaris was in spite of her pregnancy; how the fine bones of her face grew sharp beneath the white skin, how swollen and blue the veins in her forehead were, and those in her thin white hands . . .

Domaris shook her head, but the weight of her unborn child was heavy on her, and her drawn features betrayed the lie. She knew it and smiled, running her hands down her swollen sides with a resigned shrug. "Ill-will and pregnancy grow never less," she quoted lightly. "See—Micail's already asleep."

Deoris would not be distracted. "Where is Arvath?" she asked firmly.

Domaris sighed. "He is not here, he . . ." Her thin face crimsoned, the color flooding into the neck of her shapeless robe. "Deoris, I—I have fulfilled my bargain now! Nor have I complained, nor stinted duty! Nor did I use what Elis . . ." She bit her lip savagely, and went on, "This will be the son he desires! And that should content him!"

Deoris, though she knew nothing of Mother Ysouda's warning, remembered her own; and intuition told her the rest. "He is cruel to you, Domaris?"

"The fault is mine, I think I have killed kindness in the man. Enough! I should not complain. But his love is like a punishment! I cannot endure it any more!" The color had receded from her face, leaving a deathly pallor.

Deoris mercifully turned away, bending to tuck a cover around Micail. "Why don't you let Elara take him nights?" she protested. "You'll get no sleep at all!"

Domaris smiled. "I would sleep still less if he were away from me," she said, and looked tenderly at her son. "Remember when I could not understand why Elis kept Lissa so close to her? Besides, Elara attends even me only in the days, now. Since her marriage I would have freed her entirely, but she says she will not leave me to a strange woman while I am like this." Her laugh was a tiny ghost of its normal self. "*Her* child will be born soon after mine! Even in that she serves me!"

Deoris said sulkily, "I think every woman in this Temple must be bearing a child!" With a guilty start, she silenced herself.

Domaris appeared not to notice. "Childbearing is a disease easily caught," she quoted lightly, then straightened and came close to her sister. "Don't go, Deoris—stay and talk to me a little. I've missed you."

"If you want me," Deoris said ungraciously; then, penitent, she came to Domaris and the two sat on a low divan.

The older woman smiled. "I always want you, little sister."

"I'm not little any more," Deoris said irritably, tossing her head. "Why must you treat me like a baby?"

Domaris suppressed a laugh and lifted her sister's slender, beringed hand. "Perhaps—because you were my baby, before Micail was born." Her glance fell on the narrow, carven girdle which Deoris wore cinctured loosely over her night-dress. "Deoris, what is that?" she asked softly. "I don't believe I've seen you wearing it before."

"Only a girdle."

"How stupid of me," said Domaris dryly. Her slim fingers touched the crimson cord which knotted the links together, strangely twined through the carven wooden symbols. Clumsily, she bent to examine it more closely—and with a sharply indrawn breath, counted the links. The cord, twined into oddly knotted patterns, was treble; thrice sevenfold the flat carved emblems. It was beautiful, and yet, somehow . . .

"*Deoris!*" she breathed, her voice holding sudden sharpness. "Did Riveda give you *this?*"

Scared by her tone, Deoris went sulky and defensive. "Why not?"

"Why not indeed?" Domaris's words were edged with ice; her hand closed hard around Deoris's thin wrist. "And why should he bind you with a—a thing like that? Deoris, answer me!"

"He has the right . . ."

"No lover has that right, Deoris."

"He is *not*—"

Domaris shook her head. "You lie, Deoris," she said wearily. "If your lover were any other man, he would kill Riveda before he let him put that—that *thing* on you!" She made a queer sound that was almost a sob. "Please—don't lie to me any more, Deoris. Do you think you can hide it forever? How long must I pretend not to see that you are carrying a child beneath that—that—" Her voice failed her. How pitifully simple Deoris was, as if by denying a fact she could wish it out of existence!

Deoris twisted her hand free, staring at the floor, her face white and pinched. Guilt, embarrassment and fear seemed to mingle in her dark eyes, and Domaris took the younger girl in her arms.

"Deoris, Deoris, don't look like that! I'm not blaming *you!*"

Deoris was rigid in her sister's kind arms. "Domaris, believe me, I didn't."

Domaris tipped back the little face until her sister's eyes, dark as crushed violets, met her own. "The father is Riveda," she said quietly; and this time, Deoris did not contradict her. "I like this not even a little. Something is very wrong, Deoris, or you would not be acting this way. You are not a child, you are not ignorant, you have had the same teaching as I, and more in this particular matter . . . you *know*—listen to me, Deoris! You know you need not have conceived a child save at your own and Riveda's wish," she finished inexorably, although Deoris sobbed and squirmed to get free of her hands and her condemning eyes. "Deoris—no, look at me, tell me the truth—did he force you, Deoris?"

"*No!*" And now the denial had the strength of truth. "I gave myself to Riveda of my free will, and he is not by law celibate!"

"This is so; but why then does he not take you to wife, or at the very least acknowledge your child?" Domaris demanded, stern-faced. "There is no need of this, Deoris. You bear the child of one of the great Adepts—no matter what I may think of him. You should walk in honor before all, not skulk girdled with a triple cord, forced to lie even to me. Enslaved! Does he know?"

"I—I think. . . ."

"You *think!*" Domaris's voice was as brittle as ice. "Be assured, little sister, if he does *not* know, he very soon shall! Child, child—the man wrongs you!"

"You—you have no right to *interfere!*" With a sudden burst of strength, Deoris twisted free of her sister, glaring angrily though she made no move to go.

"I do have the right to protect you, little sister."

"If I choose to bear Riveda's child . . ."

"Then Riveda must assume his responsibility," said Domaris sharply. Her hands went out to the girdle at her sister's waist again. "As for this foul thing . . ." Her fingers shrank from the emblems even as they plucked at the knotted cords. "I am going to burn it! My sister is no man's slave!"

Deoris sprang up, clutching at the links. "Now you go too far!" she raged, and seized the woman's wrist in strong hands, holding Domaris away from her. "You shall not touch it!"

"Deoris, I *insist!*"

"No, I say!" Though she looked frail, Deoris was a strong girl, and too angry to care what she did. She flung Domaris away from her with a furious blow that made the older woman cry out with pain. "Let me alone!"

Domaris dropped her hands—then gasped as her knees gave way.

Deoris quickly caught her sister in her arms, just in time to save her from falling heavily. "Domaris," she begged, in swift repentance, "Domaris, forgive me. Did I hurt you?"

Domaris, with repressed anger, freed herself from her sister's supporting arm and lowered herself slowly onto the divan.

Deoris began to sob. "I didn't mean to hurt you, you know I'd never. . . ."

"How can I know that!" Domaris flung at her, almost despairingly. "I have never forgotten what you . . ." She stopped, breathing hard. Micon had made her swear never to speak of that, impressing it on her repeatedly that Deoris had not had, would never have, the slightest memory of what she had almost done. At the stricken misery in Deoris's eyes, Domaris said, more gently, "I know you would never harm me willingly. But if you hurt my child I could not forgive you again: Now—*give me that damned thing!*" And she advanced on Deoris purposefully, her face one of disgust as she unfastened the cords, as if she touched something unclean.

The thin nightdress fell away as the girdle was loosened, and Domaris, putting out a hand to draw the folds together, stopped—jerked her hand back involuntarily from the bared breast. The girdle fell unheeded to the floor.

"Deoris!" she cried out in horror. "Let me see—no, I said *let me see!*" Her voice tightened commandingly as Deoris tried to pull the loosened robe over the betrayal of those naked scars. Domaris drew the folds aside; gently touched the raised sigil that gaped raggedly red across both rounded breasts, running swollen and raw like a jagged parody of a lightning-flash down the tender sides. "Oh, Deoris!" Domaris gasped in dismay. "Oh, little sister!"

"No, please, Domaris!" The girl pulled feverishly at her loosened clothing. "It's nothing . . ." But her frantic efforts at concealment only confirmed Domaris's worst suspicions.

"Nothing, indeed!" said Domaris wrathfully. "I suppose you will try to tell me that those are ordinary burns? More of Riveda's work, I suppose!" She loosed her grip on the girl's arm, staring somberly at her. "Riveda's work. Always Riveda," she whispered, looking down at the cowering girl . . . Then, slowly, deliberately, she raised her arms in invocation, and her voice, low and quiveringly clear, rang through the silent room: "*Be he accurst!*"

Deoris started back, raising her hands to her mouth as she stared in horror.

"Be he accurst!" Domaris repeated. "Accurst in the lightning that reveals his work, accurst in thunder that will lay it low! Be he accurst in the waters of the flood that shall sweep his life sterile! Be he cursed by sun and moon and earth, rising and setting, waking and sleeping, living and dying, here and hereafter! Be he accurst beyond life and beyond death and beyond redemption—forever!"

Deoris choked on harsh sobs, staggering away from her sister as if she were herself the target of Domaris's curses. "No!" she whimpered, "no!"

Domaris paid her no heed, but went on, "Accurst be he sevenfold, a hundredfold, until his sin be wiped out, his karma undone! Be he cursed, he and his seed, unto the sons and the son's sons and their sons unto eternity! Be he accurst in his last hour—and my life ransom for his, lest I see this undone!"

With a shriek, Deoris crumpled to the floor and lay as if dead; but

Micail only twisted slightly beneath his blanket as he slept.

II

When Deoris drifted up out of her brief spell of unconsciousness, she found Domaris kneeling beside her, gently examining the *dorje* scars on her breasts. Deoris closed her eyes, her mind still half blank, poised between relief, terror, and nothingness.

"Another experiment which he could not control?" asked Domaris, not unkindly.

Deoris looked up at her older sister and murmured, "It was not all his fault—he himself was hurt far worse. . . ." Her words had pronounced a final indictment, but Deoris did not realize the fact.

Domaris's horror was evident, however. "The man has you bewitched! Will you always defend . . . ?" She broke off, begging almost desperately, "Listen, you must—a stop must and shall be put to this, lest others suffer! If you cannot—then you are incapable of acting like an adult, and others must intervene to protect you! Gods, Deoris, are you insane, that you would have allowed—this?"

"What right have you—" Deoris faltered as her sister drew away.

"My sworn duty," Deoris rebuked sternly, in a very low voice. "Even if you were not my sister—did you not *know? I* am Guardian here."

Deoris, speechless, could only stare at Domaris; and it was like looking at a complete stranger who only resembled her sister. An icy rage showed in Domaris's forced stillness, in her brittle voice and the smoldering sparks behind her eyes—a cold wrath all the more dreadful for its composure.

"Yet I must consider you in this, Deoris," Domaris went on, tight-lipped.

"You—and your child."

"Riveda's," said Deoris dully. "What—what are you going to do?" she whispered.

Domaris looked down somberly, and her hands trembled as she fastened the robes about her little sister once more. She hoped she would not have to use what she knew against the sister she still loved more than anyone or anything, except her own children, Micail and the unborn. . . . But Domaris felt weak. The treble cord, and the awful control it implied; the fearful form of the scars on Deoris's body; she bent, awkwardly, and picked up the girdle from the floor where it lay almost forgotten.

"I will do what I must," Domaris said. "I do not want to take from you something you seem to prize, but . . ." Her face was white and her knuckles white as she gripped the carven links, hating the symbols and what she considered the vile use to which they had been put. "Unless you swear not to wear it again, I will burn the damned thing!"

"No!" Deoris sprang to her feet, a feverish sparkle in her eyes. "I won't let you! Domaris, give it to me!"

"I would rather see you dead than made a tool—and to such use!" Domaris's face might have been chiselled in stone, and her voice, too, had a rocklike quality as the words clanged harshly in the air. The skin of her face had stretched taut over her cheekbones, and even her lips were colorless.

Deoris stretched imploring hands—then shrank from the clear, contemptuous judgment in Domaris's eyes.

"You have been taught as I have," the older woman said. "How could you permit it, Deoris? You that Micon loved—you that he treated almost as a disciple! You, who could have . . ." With a despairing gesture, Domaris broke off and turned away, moving clumsily toward the brazier in the near corner. Deoris, belatedly realizing her intention, sprang after her—but Domaris had already thrust the girdle deep into the live coals. The tinder-dry wood blazed up with a flickering and a roar as the cord writhed like a white-hot snake. In seconds the thing was only ashes.

Domaris turned around again and saw her sister gazing helplessly into the flames, weeping as if she saw Riveda himself burning there— and at the sight, much of her hard, icy anger melted away. "Deoris," she said, "Deoris, tell me—you have been to the Dark Shrine? To the Sleeping God?"

"Yes," Deoris whispered.

Domaris needed to know no more; the pattern of the girdle had told her the rest. *Well for Deoris that I have acted in time! Fire cleanses!*

"Domaris!" It was a pathetic, horrified plea.

"Oh, my little sister, little cat . . ." Domaris was all protective love now, and crooning, she took the trembling girl into her arms again.

Deoris hid her face on her sister's shoulder. With the burning of the girdle, she had begun to dimly see certain implications, as if a fog had lifted from her mind; she could not cease from thinking of the things that had taken place in the Crypt—and now she knew that none of it had been dream.

"I'm afraid, Domaris! I'm so afraid—I wish I were dead! Will they—will they burn me, too?"

Domaris's teeth gritted with sudden, sick fear. For Riveda there could be no hope for clemency; and Deoris, even if innocent—and of that, Domaris had grave doubts—bore the seed of blasphemy, begotten in sacrilege and fostered beneath that hideous treble symbol—*A child I myself have cursed!* And with this realization, an idea came to her; and Domaris did not stop to count the cost, but acted to comfort and protect this child who was her sister—even to protect that other child, whose black beginnings need not, perhaps, end in utter darkness. . . .

"Deoris," she said quietly, taking her sister's hand, "ask me no questions. I can protect you, and I will, but do not ask me to explain what I must do!"

Deoris swallowed hard, and somehow forced herself to murmur her promise.

Domaris, in a last hesitation, glanced at Micail. But the child still sprawled in untidy, baby sleep: Domaris discarded her misgivings and turned her attention once more to Deoris.

A low, half-sung note banished the brilliance from the room, which gave way to a golden twilight; in this soft radiance the sisters faced one another, Deoris slim and young, the fearful scars angry across her breasts, her coming motherhood only a shadow in the fall of her light robes—and Domaris, her beautiful body distorted and big, but still somehow holding something of the ageless calm of what she invoked. Clasping her hands, she lifted them slowly before her; parted and lowered them in an odd, ceremonious manner. Something in the gesture and movement, some instinctive memory, perhaps, or intuition, struck the half-formed question from Deoris's parted lips.

"Be far from us, all profane," Domaris murmured in her clear soprano. "Be far from us, all that lives in evil. Be far from where we stand, for here has Eternity cast its shadow. Depart, ye mists and vapors, ye stars of darkness, begone; stand ye afar from the print of Her footsteps and the shadow of Her veil. Here have we taken shelter, under the curtain of the night and within the circle of Her own white stars."

She let her arms drop to her sides; then they moved together to the shrine to be found in every sleeping-room within the Temple precincts. With difficulty, Domaris knelt—and divining her intention, Deoris knelt quickly at her side and, taking the taper from her sister's hand, lighted the perfumed oil of devotion. Although she meant to honor her promise not to question, Deoris was beginning to guess what Domaris was doing. Years ago she had fled from a suggestion of this rite; now, facing unthinkable fear, her child's imminence a faint presence in her womb, Deoris could still find a moment to be grateful that it was with Domaris that she faced this, and not some woman or priestess whom she must fear. By taking up her own part, by touching the light to the incense which opened the gates to ritual, she accepted it; and the brief, delicate pressure of Domaris's long narrow fingers on hers showed that the older woman was aware of the acceptance, and of what it meant . . . It was only a fleeting touch; then Domaris signalled to her to rise.

Standing, Domaris stretched a hand to her sister yet again, to touch her brow, lips, breasts, and—guided by Domaris—Deoris repeated the sign. Then Domaris took her sister in her arms and held her close for a moment.

"Deoris, repeat my words," she commanded softly—and Deoris, awed, but in some secret part of her being feeling the urge to break away, to laugh, to scream aloud and shatter the gathering mood, only closed her eyes for a moment.

Domaris's low voice intoned quiet words; Deoris's voice was a thin echo, without the assurance that was in her sister's.

> *"Here we two, women and sisters, pledge thee,*
> *Mother of Life—*
> *Woman—and more than woman . . .*
> *Sister—and more than sister . . .*
> *Here where we stand in darkness . . .*
> *And under the shadow of death . . .*
> *We call on thee, O Mother . . .*

By thine own sorrows, O Woman . . .
By the life we bear . . .
Together before thee, O Mother, O Woman
Eternal . . .
And this be our plea. . . ."

Now even the golden light within the room was gone, extinguished without any signal from them. The streaming moonlight itself seemed to vanish, and it seemed to the half-terrified, half-fascinated Deoris that they stood in the center of a vast and empty space, upon nothingness. All the universe had been extinguished, save for a single, flickering flame which glowed like a tiny, pulsating eye. Was it the brazier fire? The reflection of a vaster light which she sensed but could not see? Domaris's arms, still close about her, were the only reality anywhere, the only real and living thing in the great spaces, and the words Domaris intoned softly, like spun fibers of silken sound, mantras which wove a silvery net of magic within the mystical darkness. . . .

The flame, whatever it was, glowed and darkened, glowed and darkened, with the hypnotic intensity of some vast heart's beating, in time to the murmured invocation:

"May the fruit of our lives be bound and sealed
To thee, O Mother, O Woman Eternal,
Who holdest the inmost life of each of thy daughters
Between the hands upon her heart. . . ."

And there was more, which Deoris, frightened and exalted, could scarce believe she heard. This was the most sacred of rituals; they vowed themselves to the Mother-Goddess from incarnation to incarnation, from age to age, throughout eternity, with the lesser vow that bound them and their children inextricably to one another—a karmic knot, life to life, forever.

Carried away by her emotion, Domaris went much further into the ritual than she had realized, far further than she had intended—and at last an invisible Hand signed them both with an ancient seal. Full Initiates of the most ancient and holy of all the rites in the Temple or in the world, they were protected by and sealed to the Mother—

not Caratra, but the Greater Mother, the Dark Mother behind all men and all rites and all created things. The faint flickerings deepened, swelled, became great wings of flame which lapped out to surround them with radiance.

The two women sank to their knees, then lay prostrate, side by side. Deoris felt her sister's child move against her body, and the faint, dreamlike stirring of her own unborn child, and in a flutter of insensate, magical prescience, she guessed some deeper involvement beyond this life and beyond this time, a ripple moving out into the turbulent sea which must involve more than these two . . . and the effulgent glory about them became a voice; not a voice that they could hear, but something more direct, something they felt with every nerve, every atom of their bodies.

"Thou art mine, then, from age to age, while Time endures . . . while Life brings forth Life. Sisters, and more than sisters . . . women, and more than women . . . know this, together, by the Sign I give you. . . ."

III

The fire had burned out, and the room was very dark and still. Deoris, recovering a little, raised herself and looked at Domaris, and saw that a curious radiance still shone from the swollen breasts and burdened body. Awe and reverence dawned in her anew and she bent her head, turning her eyes on herself—and yes, there too, softly glowing, the Sign of the Goddess. . . .

She got to her knees and remained there, silent, absorbed in prayer and wonder. The visible glow soon was gone; indeed, Deoris could not be certain that she had ever seen it. Perhaps, her consciousness exalted and steeped in ritual, she had merely caught a glimpse of some normally invisible reality beyond her newness and her present self.

The night was waning when Domaris stirred at last, coming slowly back to consciousness from the trance of ecstasy, dragging herself upright with a little moan of pain. Labor was close on her, she knew it—knew also that she had brought it closer by what she had done.

Not even Deoris knew so well the effects of ceremonial magic upon the complex nervous currents of a woman's body. Lingering awe and reverence helped her ignore the warning pains as Deoris's arms helped her upright—but for an instant Domaris pressed her forehead against her sister's shoulder, weak and not caring if it showed.

"May my son never hurt anyone else," she whispered, "as he hurts me. . . ."

"He'll never again have the opportunity," Deoris said, but her lightness was false. She was acutely conscious that she had been careless and added to her sister's pain; knew that words of contrition could not help. Her abnormal sensitivity to Domaris was almost physical, and she helped her sister with a comprehending tenderness in her young hands.

There was no reproach in Domaris's weary glance as she closed her hand around her sister's wrist. "Don't cry, kitten." Once seated on the divan, she stared into the dead embers of the brazier for several minutes before saying, quietly, "Deoris, later you shall know what I have done—and why. Are you afraid now?"

"Only—a little—for you." Again, it was not entirely a true statement, for Domaris's words warned Deoris that there was more to come. Domaris was bound to action by some rigid code of her own, and nothing Deoris could say or do would alter that; Domaris was in quiet, deadly earnest.

"I must leave you now, Deoris. Stay here until I return—promise me! You will do that for me, my little sister?" She drew Deoris to her with an almost savage possessiveness, held her and kissed her fiercely. "More than my sister, now! Be at peace," she said, and went from the room, moving swiftly despite her heaviness.

Deoris knelt, immobile, watching the closed door. She knew better than Domaris imagined what was encompassed by the rite into which she had been admitted; she had heard of it, guessed at its power—but had never dared dream that one day she herself might be a part of it!

Can this, she asked herself, *be what gave Maleina entry where none could deny her? What permitted Karahama—a saji, one of the no-people—to serve the Temple of Caratra? A power that redeems the damned?*

Knowing the answer, Deoris was no longer afraid. The radiance was gone, but the comfort remained, and she fell asleep there, kneeling, her head in her arms.

IV

Outside, clutched again with the warning fingers of her imminent travail, Domaris leaned against the wall. The fit passed quickly, and she straightened, to hurry along the corridor, silent and unobserved. Yet again she was forced to halt, bending double to the relentless pain that clawed at her loins; moaning softly, she waited for the spasm to pass. It took her some time to reach the seldom-used passage that gave on a hidden doorway.

She paused, forcing her breath to come evenly. She was about to violate an ancient sanctuary—to risk defilement beyond death. Every tenet of the hereditary priesthood of which she was product and participant screamed at her to turn back.

The legend of the Sleeping God was a thing of horror. Long ago— so ran the story—the Dark One had been chained and prisoned, until the day he should waken and ravage time and space alike with unending darkness and devastation, unto the total destruction of all that was or could ever be. . . .

Domaris knew better. It was power that had been sealed there, though—and she suspected that the power had been invoked and unleashed, and this made her afraid as she had never dreamed of being afraid; frightened for herself and the child she carried, for Deoris and the child conceived in that dark shrine, and for her people and everything that they stood for. . . .

She set her teeth, and sweat ran cold from her armpits. "*I must!*" she whispered aloud; and, giving herself no more time to think, she opened the door and slipped through, shutting it quickly behind her.

She stood at the top of an immense stairwell leading down . . . and down . . . and down, grey steps going down between grey walls in a grey haze beneath her, to which there seemed no end. She set her foot on the first step; holding to the rail, she began the journey . . . down.

It was slow, chill creeping. Her heaviness dragged at her. Pain twisted her at intervals. The thud of her sandalled feet jerked at her burdened belly with wrenching pulls. She moaned aloud at each brief torture—but went on, step down, thud, step down, thud, in senseless, dull repetition. She tried to count the steps, in an effort to prevent her mind from dredging up all the half-forgotten, awful stories she had heard of this place, to keep herself from wondering if she did, indeed, know better than to believe old fairy-tales. She gave it up after the hundred and eighty-first step.

Now she was no longer holding the rail, but reeling and scraping against the wall; again pain seized her, doubled and twisted her, forcing her to her knees. The greyness was shot through with crimson as she straightened, bewildered and enraged, almost forgetting what grim purpose had brought her to this immemorial mausoleum. . . .

She caught at the rail with both hands, fighting for balance as her face twisted terribly and she sobbed aloud, hating the sanity that drove her on and down.

"Oh Gods! No, no, take me instead!" she whispered, and clung there desperately for a moment; then, her face impassive again, holding herself grimly upright, she let the desperate need to do what must be done carry her down, into the pallid greyness.

CHAPTER THREE
✠ DARK DAWN ✠

I

The sudden, brief jar of falling brought Deoris sharply upright, staring into the darkness in sudden fear. Micail still slept in a chubby heap, and in the shadowy room, now lighted with the pale pink of dawn, there was no sound but the little boy's soft breathing; but like a distant echo Deoris seemed to hear a cry and a palpable silence, the silence of the tomb, of the Crypt.

Domaris! Where was Domaris? She had not returned. With sudden and terrible awareness, Deoris *knew* where Domaris was! She did not pause even to throw a garment over her nightclothes; yet she glanced unsurely at Micail. Surely Domaris's slaves would hear if he woke and cried—and there was no time to waste! She ran out of the room and fled downward, through the deserted garden.

Blindly, dizzily, she ran as if sheer motion could ward off her fear. Her heart pounded frantically, and her sides sent piercing ribbons of pain through her whole body—but she did not stop until she stood in the shadow of the great pyramid. Holding her hands hard against the hurt in her sides, she was shocked at last into a wide-awake sanity by the cold winds of dawn.

A lesser priest, only a dim figure in luminous robes, paced slowly toward her. "Woman," he said severely, "it is forbidden to walk here. Go your way in peace."

Deoris raised her face to him, unafraid. "I am Talkannon's

daughter," she said in a clear and ringing voice. "Is the Guardian Rajasta within?"

The priest's tone and expression changed as he recognized her. "He is there, young sister," he said courteously, "but it is forbidden to interrupt the vigil—" He fell silent in amazement; the sun, as they talked, had crept around the pyramid's edge, to fall upon them, revealing Deoris's unbound hair, her disarranged and insufficient clothing.

"It is life or death!" Deoris pleaded, desperately. "*I must see him!*"

"My child—I do not have the authority. . . ."

"Oh, you fool!" Deoris raged, and with a catlike movement, she dodged under his startled arm and fled up the gleaming stone steps. She struggled a moment with the unfamiliar workings of the great brazen door; twitched aside the shielding curtain, and stepped into brilliant light.

At the faint whisper of her bare feet—for the door moved silently despite its weight—Rajasta turned from the altar. Disregarding his warning gesture, Deoris ran to fling herself on her knees before him.

"Rajasta, Rajasta!"

With cold distaste, the Priest of Light bent and raised her, eyeing the wild disarray of her clothing and hair sternly. "Deoris," he said, "what are you doing here, you know the law—and why like this! You're only half dressed, have you gone completely mad?"

Indeed, there was some justification for his question, for Deoris met his gaze with a feverish face, and her voice was practically a babble as her last scraps of composure deserted her. "Domaris! Domaris! She must have gone to the Crypt—to the Dark Shrine."

"You *have* taken leave of your senses!" Unceremoniously, Rajasta half thrust her to a further distance from the altar. "You *know* you may not stand here like this!"

"I know, yes, I know, but listen to me! I feel it, I know it! She burned the girdle and made me tell her . . ." Deoris stopped, her face drawn with conflict and guilt, for she had suddenly realized that she was now of her own volition betraying her sworn oath to Riveda! And yet—she was bound to Domaris by an oath stronger still.

Rajasta gripped her shoulder, demanding, "What sort of gibberish is this!" Then, seeing that the girl was trembling so violently that she could hardly stand upright, he put an arm gingerly about her and helped her to a seat. "Now tell me sensibly, if you can, what you are talking about," he said, in a voice that held almost equal measures of compassion and contempt, "if you are talking about anything at all! I suppose Domaris has discovered that you were Riveda's *saji*."

"*I* wasn't! I never was!" Deoris flared; then said, wearily, "Oh, that doesn't matter, you don't understand, you wouldn't believe me anyhow! What matters is this: Domaris has gone to the Dark Shrine."

Rajasta's face was perceptibly altering as he began to guess what she was trying to say. "What—but why?"

"She saw—a girdle I was wearing, that Riveda gave me—and the scars of the *dorje*."

Almost before she had spoken the word, Rajasta moved like lightning to clamp his hand across her lips. "Say that not here!" he commanded, white-faced. Deoris collapsed, crying, her head in her arms, and Rajasta seized her shoulders and forced her to look at him. "Listen to me, girl! For Domaris's sake—for your own—yes, even for Riveda's! *A girdle?* And the—that word you spoke; what of that? *What is this all about?*"

Deoris dared not keep silent, dared not lie—and under his deep-boring eyes, she stammered, "A treble cord—knotted—wooden links carved with . . ." She gestured.

Rajasta caught her wrist and held it immobile. "Keep your disgusting Grey-robe signs for the Grey Temple! But even there that would not have been allowed! You must deliver it to me!"

"Domaris burned it."

"Thank the Gods for that," said Rajasta bleakly. "Riveda has gone among the Black-robes?" But it was a statement, not a question. "Who else?"

"Reio-ta—I mean, the chela." Deoris was crying and stammering; there was a powerful block in her mind, inhibiting speech—but the concentrated power of Rajasta's will forced her. The Priest of Light was well aware that this use of his powers had only the most dubious ethical justification, and regretted the necessity; but he knew that all of Riveda's spells would be pitted against him, and if he was to safeguard others as his Guardian's vows commanded, he dared not spare the girl. Deoris was almost fainting from the hypnotic pressure Rajasta exerted against the bond of silence Riveda had forced on her will. Slowly, syllable by syllable at times, at best sentence by reluctant sentence, she told Rajasta enough to damn Riveda tenfold.

The Priest of Light was merciless; he had to be. He was hardly more than a pair of bleak eyes and toneless, pitiless voice, commanding. "Go on. What—and how—and who . . ."

"I was sent over the Closed Places—as a channel of power—and when I could no longer serve, then Larmin—Riveda's son—took my place as scryer. . . ."

"Wait!" Rajasta leaped to his feet, pulling the girl upright with him. "By the Central Sun! You are lying, or out of your senses! A boy cannot serve in the Closed Places, only a virgin girl, or a woman prepared by ritual, or—or—a boy cannot, unless he is . . ." Rajasta was pasty-faced now, stammering himself, almost incoherent. "Deoris. *What was done to Larmin?*"

Deoris trembled before Rajasta's awful eyes, cowering before the surge of violent, seemingly uncontrollable wrath and disgust that surged across the Guardian's face. He shook her, roughly.

"Answer me, girl! *Did he castrate the child?*"

She did not have to answer. Rajasta abruptly took his hands from her as if contaminated by her presence, and when she collapsed he let her fall heavily to the floor. He was physically sick with the knowledge.

Weeping, whimpering, Deoris moved a little toward him, and he spat, pushing her away with his sandalled foot. "Gods, Deoris—you of all people! Look at me if you dare—you that Micon called sister!"

The girl cringed at his feet, but there was no mercy in the Guardian's voice: "On your knees! On your knees before the shrine you have defiled—the Light you have darkened—the fathers you have shamed—the Gods you have forgotten!"

Rocking to and fro in anguished dread, Deoris could not see the compassion that suddenly blotted out the awful fury on Rajasta's face. He was not blind to the fact that Deoris had willingly risked all hopes of clemency for herself in order to save Domaris—but it would take much penance to wipe out her crime. With a last, pitying look at the bent head, he turned and left the Temple. He was more shocked than angry; more sickened even than shocked. His maturity and experience foresaw what even Domaris had not seen.

He hastened down the steps of the pyramid, and the priest on guard sprang to attend him—then stopped, his mouth wide.

"Lord Guardian!"

"Go you," said Rajasta curtly, "with ten others, to take the Adept Riveda into custody, in my name. Put him in chains if need be."

"The Healer-priest, Lord? Riveda?" The guard was bug-eyed with disbelief. "The Adept of the Magicians—in *chains?*"

"The damned filthy sorcerer Riveda—Adept and *former* Healer!" With an effort, Rajasta lowered his hoarse voice to a normal volume. "Then go and find a boy, about eleven years old, called Larmin— Karahama's son."

Stiffly, the priest said, "Lord, with your pardon, the woman Karahama has no child."

Rajasta, impatient with this reminder of Temple etiquette which refused the *no-people* even a legal existence, said angrily, "You will find a boy of the Grey Temple who is called Larmin—and don't bother with that nonsense of pretending not to know who he is! Don't harm or frighten the boy, just keep him safely where he can be produced at a moment's notice—and where he can't be conveniently murdered to destroy evidence! Then find . . ." He paused. "Swear you will not reveal the names I speak!"

The priest made the holy sign. "I swear, Lord!"

"Find Ragamon the Elder and Cadamiri, and bid them summon the Guardians to meet here at high noon. Then seek the Arch-priest Talkannon, and say to him quietly that we have at last found evidence. No more—he will understand."

The priest hurried away, leaving, for the first time in easily three centuries—the Temple of Light unattended. Rajasta, his face grim, broke into a run.

II

Just as Domaris had, he hesitated, uncertain, at the entrance to the concealed stairs. Was it wise, he wondered, to go alone? Should he not summon aid?

A rush of cool air stirred up from the long shaft beneath him; borne out of unfathomable spaces came a sound, almost a cry. Incredibly far down, dimmed and distorted by echo, it might have been the shriek of a bat, or the echoes of his own sighing breath—but Rajasta's hesitation was gone.

Down the long stairway he hurried, taking the steps two and three at a time, steadying himself now against one sheer wall, now against the shuddering railing. His steps clattered with desperate haste, waking hurried, clanging echoes—and he knew he warned away anyone below, but the time was past for stealth and silence. His throat was dry and his breath came in choking gasps, for he was not a young man and ever at his back loomed the nightmare need for haste that pushed him down and down the lightless stairs, down that grey and immemorial shaft through reverberating eternities that clutched at him with tattered cobweb fingers, his heels throwing up dust long, long undisturbed, to begrime the luminous white of his robes . . . Down and down and down he went, until distance became a mockery.

He stumbled, nearly falling as the stairs abruptly ended. Staring dizzily about, trying to orient himself, Rajasta again felt the hopeless futility of his plight. He knew this place only from maps and the tales and writings of others. Yet, at last, he located the entrance to the great arched vault, though he was not sure of himself until he saw the monstrous sarcophagus, the eon-blackened altar, the shadowy Form swathed in veils of stone. But he saw no human being within the shrine, and for a moment Rajasta knew fear beyond comprehension, not for Domaris but for himself . . .

A moan rose to his ear, faint and directionless, magnified by the echoing darkness. Rajasta whirled, staring about him wildly, half mad from fear of what he might see. Again the moaning sounded, and this time Rajasta saw, dimly, a woman who lay crumpled, writhing, in the fiery shroud of her long hair, before the sarcophagus. . . .

"Domaris!" On his lips the name was a sob. "Domaris! Child of my soul!" In a single stride he was beside the inert, convulsed body. He shut his eyes a moment as his world reeled: the depth of his love for Domaris had never been truly measured until this moment when she lay apparently dying in his frightened arms.

Grimly he raised his head, glancing about with a steady wrath. *No, she has not failed!* he thought, with some exultation. *The power was unchained, but it has again been sealed, if barely. The sacrilege is undone—but at what cost to Domaris? And I dare not leave her, not even to bring aid. Better, in any case, she die than deliver her child here!*

After a moment of disordered thought, he bent and raised her in his arms. She was no light burden—but Rajasta, in his righteous anger, barely noticed the weight. He spoke to her, soothingly, and although she was long past hearing, the tone of his voice penetrated to her darkened brain and she did not struggle when he lifted her and, with a dogged desperation, started back toward the long stairway. His breath came laboringly, and his strained face had a look no one would ever see as he turned toward that incredibly distant summit. His lips moved; he breathed deeply once—and began climbing.

CHAPTER FOUR
✠ THE LAWS ✠
OF THE TEMPLE

I

Elara, moving around the court and singing serenely at her work, dropped the half-filled vase of flowers and scurried toward the Guardian as he crossed the garden with his lifeless burden. Alarmed anxiety widened her dark eyes as she held the door, then ran around him to clear cushions from a divan and assist Rajasta to lay the inert body of Domaris upon it.

His face grey with exhaustion, the Guardian straightened and stood a moment, catching his breath. Elara, quickly taking in his condition, guided him toward a seat, but he shook her off irritably. "See to your mistress."

"She lives," the slave-woman said quickly, but in anticipation of Rajasta's command, she hurried back to Domaris's side and bent, searching for a pulse-beat. Satisfied, she jumped up and spent a moment seeking in a cabinet; then returned to hold a strong aromatic to her mistress's pinched nostrils. After a long, heart-wrenching moment, Domaris moaned and her eyelids quivered.

"Domaris—" Rajasta breathed out the word. Her wide eyes were staring, the distended pupils seeing neither priest nor anxious attendant. Domaris moaned again, spasmodically gripping nothing with taloning hands, and Elara caught them gently, bending over her mistress, her shocked stare belatedly taking in the torn dress, the bruised arms and cheeks, the great livid mark across her temples.

Suddenly Domaris screamed, "No, no! No—not for myself, but can you—no, no, they will tear me apart—let me go! Loose your hands from me—Arvath! Rajasta! Father, father . . ." Her voice trailed again into moaning sobs.

Holding the woman's head on her arm, Elara whispered gently, "My dear Lady, you are safe here with me, no one will touch you."

"She is delirious, Elara," Rajasta said wearily.

Tenderly, Elara fetched a wet cloth and blotted away the clotted blood at her mistress's hairline. Several slave-women crowded at the door, eyes wide with dread. Only the presence of the Priest stilled their questions. Elara drove them out with a gesture and low utterances, then turned to the Priest, her eyes wide with horror.

"Lord Rajasta, what in the name of all the Gods has come to her?" Without waiting for an answer, perhaps not even expecting one, she bent over Domaris again, drawing aside the folds of the shredded robe. Rajasta saw her shiver with dismay; then she straightened, covering the woman decently and saying in a low voice, "Lord Guardian, you must leave us. And she must be carried at once to the House of Birth. There is no time to lose—and you know there is danger."

Rajasta shook his head sadly. "You are a good girl, Elara, and you love Domaris, I know. You must bear what I have to tell you. Domaris must not—she *cannot*—be taken to the House of Birth, nor—"

"My Lord, she could be carried there easily in a litter, there is not so much need for haste as that."

Rajasta signed her impatiently to silence. "Nor may she be attended by any consecrated priestess. She is ceremonially unclean."

Elara exploded with outrage at this. "A priestess? How!"

Rajasta sighed, miserably. "Daughter, please, hear me out. Cruel sacrilege has been done, and penalties even more terrible may be to come. And Elara—you too are awaiting a child, is that not so?"

Timidly, Elara bowed her head. "The Guardian has seen."

"Then, my daughter, I must bid you leave her, as well; or your child's life too may be forfeit." The Priest looked down at the troubled round face of the little woman and said quietly, "She has been found in the Crypt of the Sleeping God."

Elara's mouth fell open in shock and involuntary dread, and she now started back a pace from Domaris, who continued to lie as if lifeless. Then, resolutely, Elara armed herself with calm and met the

Guardian's eyes levelly, saying, "Lord Guardian, I cannot leave her to these ignorant ones. If no Temple woman may come near her—I was fostered with the Lady Domaris, Lord Guardian, and she has treated me not as a servant but as a friend all my life! Whatever the risk, I will bear it."

Rajasta's eyes lighted with a momentary relief, which faded at once. "You have a generous heart, Elara, but I cannot allow that," he said sternly. "If it were only your own clanger—but you have no right to endanger the life of your child. Enough causes have been set already in motion; each person must bear the penalties which have been invoked. Place not another life on your mistress's head! Let her not be guilty of your child's life, too!"

Elara bowed her head, not understanding. She pleaded, "Lord Guardian, in the Temple of Caratra there are priestesses who might be willing to bear the risk, and who have the right and the power to make it safe! The Healer woman, Karahama—she is skilled in the magical arts. . . ."

"You may ask," conceded Rajasta, without much hope, and straightened his bent shoulders with an effort. "Nor may I remain, Elara; the Law must be observed."

"Her sister—the Priestess Deoris . . ."

Rajasta exploded in blind fury. "Woman! Hold your foolish tongue! Hearken—*least of all* may Deoris come near her!"

"You cruel, heartless, wicked old man!" Elara flared, beginning to sob; then cringed in fright.

Rajasta had hardly heard the outburst. He said, more gently, "Hush, daughter, you do not know what you are saying. You are fortunate in your ignorance of Temple affairs, but do not try to meddle in them! Now heed my words, Elara, lest worse come to pass."

II

In his own rooms, Rajasta cleansed himself ceremonially, and put aside to be burnt the clothing he had worn into the Dark Shrine. He was exhausted from that terrible descent and the more terrible return, but he had learned long ago to control his body. Clothing himself anew in full Guardian's regalia, he finally ascended the pyramid, where Ragamon and Cadamiri awaited him; and a dozen white-clad priests, impassive, ranged in a ghostly procession behind the Guardians.

Deoris still lay prostrate, in a stupor of numbed misery, before the altar. Rajasta went to her, raised the girl up and looked long into her desperate face.

"Domaris?" she said, waveringly.

"She is alive—but she may die soon." He frowned and gave Deoris a shake. "It is too late to cry! You, and you!" He singled out two Priests. "Take Deoris to the house of Talkannon, and bring her women to her there. Let her be clothed and tended and cared for. Then go with her to find Karahama's other brat—a girl of the Grey Temple called Demira. Harm her not, but let her be carefully confined." Turning to the apathetic Deoris once again, Rajasta said, "My daughter, you will speak to no one but these Priests."

Nodding dumbly, Deoris went between her guards.

Rajasta turned to the others. "Has Riveda been apprehended?"

One man replied, "We came on him while he slept. Although he wakened and raved and struggled like a madman, we finally subdued him. He—he has been chained, as you said."

Rajasta nodded wearily. "Let search be made through his house and in the Grey Temple, for the things of magic."

At that moment, the Arch-priest Talkannon entered the chamber, glancing around him with that swift searching look that took in everyone and everything.

Rajasta strode to him and, his lips pressed tight together, confronted him with formal signs of greeting. "We have concrete evidence at last," he said, "and we can arrest the guilty—for we *know!*"

Talkannon paled slightly. "You know—what?"

Rajasta mistook his distressed disquiet. "Aye, we know the guilty, Talkannon. I fear the evil has touched even your house; Domaris still lives, but for how long, no one can tell. Deoris has turned from this evil, and will help us to apprehend these—these demons in human form!"

"Deoris?" Talkannon stared in disbelief and shock at the Priest of Light. "What?" Absently, he wiped at his forehead; then, with a mighty effort, he recovered his composure. When he spoke, his voice was steady again. "My daughters have long been of an age to manage their own affairs," he murmured. "I knew nothing of this, Rajasta. But of course I, and all those under my orders, are at your service in this, Lord Guardian."

"It is well said." Rajasta began to outline what he wanted Talkannon to do . . .

But behind the Arch-priest's back, Ragamon and Cadamiri exchanged troubled glances.

III

"Good Mother Ysouda!"

The old Priestess looked down at Elara with a kindly smile. Seeing the trembling terror in the little dark face, she spoke with gentle condescension. "Have no fear, my daughter, the Mother will guard and be near you. Is it time for you, Elara?"

"No, no, I am all right," said Elara distractedly, "it is my lady, the Priestess Domaris—"

The old lady drew in her breath. "May the gods have pity!" she whispered. "What has befallen her, Elara?"

"I may not tell thee here, Mother," Elara whispered. "Take me, I beg you, to the Priestess Karahama—"

"To the High Priestess?" At Elara's look of misery, however, Mother Ysouda wasted no more time on questions, but drew Elara along the walk until they reached a bench in the shade. "Rest here, daughter, or your own child may suffer; the sun is fierce today. I will myself seek Karahama; she will come more quickly for me than if I sent a servant or novice to summon her."

She did not wait for Elara's grateful thanks, but went quickly toward the building. Elara sat on the indicated bench, but she was too impatient, too fearful to rest as Mother Ysouda had bidden. Clasping and unclasping her hands, she rose restlessly and walked up and down the path.

Elara knew Domaris was in grave danger. She had done a little service in the Temple of Caratra, and had only the most elementary knowledge—but this much she knew perfectly well: Domaris had been in labor for many hours, and if all had been well, her child would have been born without need of assistance.

Rajasta's warning was like a terrible echo in her ears. Elara was a free city woman, whose mother had been milk nurse to Domaris; they had been fostered together and Elara served Domaris freely, as a privilege rather than a duty. She would have risked death without a second thought for the Priestess she loved, almost worshipped—but Rajasta's words, remembered, made a deafening thunder in her mind.

She is contaminated . . . you are generous, but this I cannot allow! You *have no right to endanger the life of your child-to-be . . . place not another crime on Domaris's head! Let her not be guilty of your unborn child's life, too!*

She turned suddenly, hearing steps on the path behind her. A very young priestess stood there; glancing at Elara's plain robe with indifferent contempt, she said, "The Mother Karahama will receive you."

In trembling haste, Elara followed the woman's measured steps, into the presence of Karahama. She knelt.

Not unkindly, Karahama signalled her to rise. "You come on behalf of—Talkannon's daughters?"

"Oh, my Lady," Elara begged, "sacrilege has been done, and Domaris may not be brought to the House of Birth—nor is Deoris permitted to attend her! Rajasta has said—that she is ceremonially unclean. She was found in the Crypt, in the Dark Shrine. . . ." Her voice broke into a sob; she did not hear Mother Ysouda's agonized cry, nor the scandalized gasp of the young novice. "Oh, my Lady, you are Priestess! If you permit—I beg you, I beg you!"

"If I permit," Karahama repeated, remembering the birth of Micon's son.

Four years before, with a few considered words, Domaris had humiliated Karahama before her pupils, sending the "nameless woman"—her unacknowledged half-sister—from her side. "*You have said I must be tended only by my equals,*" Karahama could hear the words as if they had been spoken that very morning. "*Therefore—leave me.*" How clearly Karahama remembered!

Slowly, Karahama smiled, and the smile froze Elara's blood. Karahama said in a her melodious voice, "I am High Priestess of Caratra. These women under my care must be safeguarded. I cannot permit any Priestess to attend her, nor may I myself approach one so contaminated. Bear greetings to my sister, Elara, and say to her—" Karahama's lips curved— "say that I could not so presume; that the Lady Domaris should be tended only by her equals."

"Oh, Lady!" Elara cried in horror. "Be not cruel—"

"Silence!" said Karahama sternly. "You forget yourself. But I forgive you. Go from me, Elara. And mark you—stay not near your mistress, lest your own child suffer!"

"Karahama—" Mother Ysouda quavered. Her face was as white as her faded hair, and she moved her lips, but for a moment no sound came forth. Then she begged, "Let me go to her, Karahama! I am long past my own womanhood, I cannot be harmed. If there is risk, let it fall on me, I will suffer it gladly, gladly, she is my little girl—she is like my own child, Karahama, let me go to my little one—"

"Good Mother, you may not go," said the High Priestess, with sharp sternness. "Our Goddess shall not be so offended! What—shall Her Priestesses tend the unclean? Such a thing would defile our Temple. Elara, leave us! Seek aid for your lady, if there is need, among the Healers—but seek no woman to aid her! And—heed me, Elara— stay you afar from her! If harm comes to your child, I shall know you disobedient, and you will suffer full penalty for the crime of abortion!" Karahama gestured contemptuous dismissal, and as the woman, sobbing aloud, rushed from their presence, Mother Ysouda opened her mouth to make angry protest—and checked it, despairing. Karahama had only invoked the literal laws of the Temple of Caratra.

Again—very slightly—Karahama smiled.

CHAPTER FIVE
✠ THE NAMING ✠ OF THE NAME

I

Toward sunset, Rajasta, gravely troubled, went to Cadamiri's rooms.

"My brother, you are a Healer—priest—the only one I know who is not a Grey-robe." He did not add, *The only one I dare to trust,* but it was understood between them. "Do you fear—contamination?"

Cadamiri grasped this also without explanation. "Domaris? No, I fear it not." He looked into Rajasta's haggard face and asked, "But could no priestess be found to bear the risk?"

"No." Rajasta did not elaborate.

Cadamiri's eyes narrowed, and his austere features, usually formidable, hardened even more. "If Domaris should die for lack of skilled tending, the shame to our Temple will live long past the karma which might be engendered by a fracture of the Law!"

Rajasta regarded his fellow-Guardian thoughtfully for a silent moment, then said, "The slave-woman brought two of Riveda's Healers to her—but . . ." Rajasta let the appeal drop.

Cadamiri nodded, already seeking the small case which contained the appurtenances of his art. "I will go to her," he said with humility; then added, slowly, as if against his will, "Expect not too much of me, Rajasta! Men are not—instructed in these arts, as you know. I have only the barest gleaming of the secrets which the Priestesses guard for such emergencies. However, I will do what I may." His face was

349

sorrowful, for he loved his young kinswoman with that passionate love which a sworn ascetic may sometimes feel for a woman of pure beauty.

Swiftly they passed through the halls of the building, pausing only to pick three strong lesser priests in the event of trouble. They did not speak to one another as they hurried along the paths to Domaris's home, and parted at the door; but although Rajasta was already late for an appointment, he stood a moment watching as Cadamiri disappeared from his view.

In her room, Domaris lay as one lifeless, too weak even to struggle. Garments and bed-linen alike were stained with blood. Two Grey-robes stood, one on either side of the bed; there was no one else in the room, not even the saving presence of a slave-woman. Later, Cadamiri was to learn that Elis had stubbornly remained with her cousin most of the day, defying Karahama's reported threats and doing her ineffectual best—but the air of authority with which the Grey-robes had presented themselves had misled her; she had been persuaded, at last, to leave Domaris to them.

One of the Grey-robes turned as the Guardian entered. "Ah, Cadamiri," he said, "I fear you come too late."

Cadamiri's blood turned to icy water. These men were not Healers and never had been, but Magicians—Nadastor and his disciple Har-Maen. Clenching his teeth on angry words, Cadamiri walked to the bed. After a brief examination he straightened, appalled. "Clumsy butchers!" he shouted. "If this woman dies, I will have you strangled for murder—and if she lives, for torture!"

Nadastor bowed smoothly. "She will not die—yet," he murmured. "And as for your threats . . ."

Cadamiri wrenched open the door and summoned the escort of Priests. "Take these—these filthy *sorcerers!*" he commanded, in a voice hardly recognizable as his own. The two Magicians allowed themselves to be led from the room without protest, and Cadamiri, through half-clenched teeth, called after them, "Do not think you will escape justice! I will have your hands struck off at the wrists and you will be scourged naked from the Temple like the dogs you are! May you rot in leprosy!"

Abruptly Har-Maen swayed and crumpled. Then Nadastor too reeled and fell into the arms of his captor. The white-robed Priests jumped away from them and made the Holy Sign frantically, while

Cadamiri could only stare, wondering if he were going mad.

The two Grey-robed figures rising from the floor, meek and blank-eyed in oddly-shrunken robes, were—not Har-Maen and Nadastor, but two young Healers whom Cadamiri himself had trained. They stared about them, dumb and smitten with terror, and quite obviously oblivious to everything that had happened.

Illusion! Cadamiri clenched his fists against a flood of dread. *Great Gods, help us all!* He gazed helplessly at the quivering, confused young novice-Healers, controlling himself with the greatest effort of his life. At last he said hoarsely, "I have no time to deal with—with this, now. Take them and guard them carefully until I . . ." His voice faltered and failed. "Go! Go!" he managed to say. "Take them out of my sight!"

Almost slamming the door shut, Cadamiri went again to bend over Domaris, baffled and desolate. His sister Guardian had indeed been cruelly treated by—by devils of Illusion! With a further effort, he put rage and sadness both aside, concentrating on the abused woman who lay before him. It was certainly too late to save the baby—and Domaris herself was in the final stage of exhaustion: the convulsive spasms tearing at her were so weak it seemed her body no longer had the strength even to reject the burden of death.

Her eyes fluttered open. "Cadamiri?"

"Hush, my sister," he said in a rough, kindly voice. "Do not try to talk."

"I must—Deoris—the Crypt . . ." Twisting spasmodically, she dragged her hands free of the Guardian's; but so exhausted was she that her eyes dropped shut again on the tears that welled from them, and she slept for a moment. Cadamiri's expression was soft with pity; he could understand, as not even Rajasta would have. This, from infancy, was every Temple woman's ultimate nightmare of obscene humiliation—that a man might approach a woman in labor. When Elis had been bullied into leaving her, her mind—sick and tormented—had receded into some depth of shame and hurt where no one could reach or follow her. Cadamiri's kindness was little better than the obscene brutality of the sorcerers.

When it was clear that there was no more that he could do, Cadamiri went to the inner door and quietly beckoned Arvath to approach. "Speak to her," he suggested gently. It was a desperate measure—if her husband could not reach her, probably no one could.

Arvath's face was pinched and pallid. He had waited, wracked by fear and trembling, most of the day, seeing no one save Mother Ysouda, who hovered about him for a time, weeping. From her he had learned for the first time of the dangers Domaris had deliberately faced; it had made him feel guilty and confused, but he forgot it all as he bent over his wife.

"Domaris—beloved—"

The familiar, loving voice brought Domaris back for a moment— but not to recognition. Agony and shame had loosed her hold on reason. Her eyes opened, the pupils so widely distended that they looked black and blind, and her bitten-bloody lips curved in the old, sweet smile.

"*Micon!*" she breathed. "Micon!" Her eyelids fluttered shut again and she slept, smiling.

Arvath leaped away with a curse. In that instant, the last remnant of his love died, and something cruel and terrible took its place.

Cadamiri, sensing some of this, caught restrainingly at his sleeve. "Peace, my brother," he implored. "The girl is delirious—she is not here at all."

"Observant, aren't you?" Arvath snarled. "Damn you, *let me go!*" Savagely, he shook off Cadamiri's hands and, with another frightful curse, went from the room.

Rajasta, still standing in the courtyard, unable to force himself to go, whirled around with instant alertness as Arvath reeled staggering out of the building.

"Arvath! Is Domaris . . . ?"

"Domaris be damned forever," the young Priest said between his teeth, "and you too!" He tried to thrust his way past Rajasta, too, as he had Cadamiri; but the old man was strong, and determined.

"You are overwrought or drunken, my son!" said Rajasta sorrowfully. "Speak not so bitterly! Domaris has done a brave thing, and paid with her child's life—and her own may be demanded before this is over!".

"And glad she was," said Arvath, very low, "to be free of *my* child!"

"Arvath!" Rajasta's grip loosed on the younger Priest as shock whitened his face. "Arvath! She is your wife!"

With a furious laugh, he pulled free of Rajasta. "My wife? Never! Only harlot to that Atlantean bastard who has been held up all my life as a model for my virtue! Damn them both and you too! I swear—but that you are just a stupid old man . . ." Arvath let his menacing fist fall to his side, turned, and in an uncontrollable spasm of retching, was violently sick on the pavement.

Rajasta sprang to him, murmuring, "My son!"

Arvath, fighting to master himself, thrust the Guardian away. "Always forgiving!" he shouted, "Ever compassionate!" He stumbled to his feet and shook his fist at Rajasta. "I spit on thee—on Domaris—and on the Temple!" he cried out in a breaking falsetto—and, elbowing Rajasta savagely aside, rushed away, into the gathering darkness.

II

Cadamiri turned to see a tall and emaciated form in a grey, shroud-like garment, standing a little distance from him. The door was still quivering in its frame from Arvath's departure; nothing had stirred.

Cadamiri's composure, for the second time that day, deserted him. "What—how did you get in here?" he demanded.

The grey figure raised a narrow hand to push aside the veil, revealing the haggard face and blazing eyes of the woman Adept Maleina. In her deep, vibrant voice she murmured, "I have come to aid you."

"You Grey-robe butchers have done enough already!" Cadamiri shouted. "Now leave this poor girl to die in peace!"

Maleina's eyes looked shrunken and sad then. "I have no right to resent that," she said. "But thou art Guardian, Cadamiri. Judge by what you know of good and of evil. I am no sorceress; I am Magician and Adept!" She stretched her empty, gaunt hand toward him, palm upward—and as Cadamiri stared, the words died in his throat; within her palm shone the sign he could not mistake, and Cadamiri bent in reverence.

Scornfully, Maleina gestured him to rise. "I have not forgotten that Deoris was punished because she aided one no priestess might dare to touch! I am—hardly a woman, now; but I have served Caratra, and my skill is not small. More, I hate Riveda! He, and worse, what he has done! Now stand aside."

Domaris lay as if life had already left her—but as Maleina's gaunt, bony hands moved on her body, a little voiceless cry escaped her exhausted lips. The woman Adept paid no more heed to Cadamiri, but murmured, musingly, "I like not what I must do." Her shoulders straightened, and she raised both hands high; her low, resonant voice shook the room.

"*Isarma!*"

Not for nothing were true names kept sacred and secret; the intonation and vibration of her Temple name penetrated even to Domaris's withdrawn senses, and she heard, though reluctantly.

"Who?" she whispered.

"I am a woman and thy sister," Maleina said, with gentle authority, calming her with a hand on the sensitive centre of the brow chakra. Abruptly she turned to Cadamiri.

"The soul lives in her again," she said. "Believe me, I do no more than I must, but now she will fight me—you must help me, even if it seems fearful to you."

Domaris, all restraint gone, roused up screaming, in the pure animal instinct for survival, as Maleina touched her; Maleina gestured, and Cadamiri flung his full weight to hold the struggling woman motionless. Then there was a convulsive cry from Domaris; Cadamiri felt her go limp and mercifully unconscious under his hands.

With an expression of horror, Maleina caught up a linen cloth and wrapped it around the terribly torn thing she held. Cadamiri shuddered; and Maleina turned to him a sombre gaze.

"Believe me, I did not kill," she said. "I only freed her of . . ."

"Of certain death," Cadamiri said weakly. "I know. I would not have—dared."

"I learned that for a cause less worthy," said Maleina, and the old woman's eyes were wet as she looked down at the unconscious form of Domaris.

Gently she bent and straightened the younger woman's limbs, laid a fresh coverlet over her.

"She will live," said Maleina. "This—" she covered the body of the dead, mutilated child. "Say no word about who has done this."

Cadamiri shivered and said, "So be it."

Without moving, she was gone; and only a shaft of sunlight moved where the Adept had stood a moment before. Cadamiri clutched at the foot of the bed, afraid that for all his training he would fall in a faint. After a moment he steadied himself and made ready to bear the news to Rajasta; that Domaris was alive and that Arvath's child was dead.

CHAPTER SIX
✠ THE PRICE ✠

I

They had allowed Demira to listen to the testimony of Deoris, wrung from her partially under hypnosis, partially under the knowledge that her sworn word could not be violated without karmic effect that would spread over centuries. Riveda, too, had answered all questions truthfully—and with contempt. The others had taken refuge in useless lies.

All this Demira endured calmly enough—but when she heard who had fathered her child, she screamed out between the words, "No! No, no, no . . ."

"Silence!" Ragamon commanded, and his gaze transfixed the shrieking child as he adjured solemnly. "This testimony shall bear no weight. I find no record of this child's parentage, nor any grounds save hearsay for believing that she is daughter to any man. We need no charges of incest!"

Maleina caught Demira in her arms, pressing the golden head to her shoulder, holding the girl close, with an agonized, protective love. The look on the woman's face might have belonged to a sorrowing angel—or an avenging demon.

Her eyes rested on Riveda, seeming to burn out of her dark, gaunt face, and she spoke as if her voice came from a tomb. "Riveda! If the Gods meted justice, you would lie in this child's place!"

But Demira pulled madly away from her restraining hands and ran screaming from the Hall of Judgment.

All that day they sought her. It was Karahama who, toward nightfall, found the girl in the innermost sanctuary of the Temple of the Mother. Demira had hanged herself from one of the crossbeams, a blue bridal girdle knotted about her neck, her slight distorted body swaying horribly as if to reprove the Goddess who had denied her, the mother who had forsworn her, the Temple that had never allowed her to know life. . . .

CHAPTER SEVEN
✠ THE DEATH CUP ✠

I

Silence . . . and the beating of her heart . . . and the dripping of water as it trickled, drop by slow drop, out of the stone onto the damp rock floor. Deoris stole through the black stillness, calling almost in a whisper, "*Riveda!*" The vaulted roof cast the name back, hollow and guttural echoes: "*Riveda . . . veda . . . veda . . . eda . . . da. . . .*"

Deoris shivered, her wide eyes searching the darkness fearfully. Where have they taken him?

As her sight gradually became accustomed to the gloom, she discerned a pale and narrow chink of light—and, almost at her feet, the heavy sprawled form of a man.

Riveda! Deoris fell to her knees.

He lay so desperately still, breathing as if drugged. The heavy chains about his body forced him backward, strained and unnaturally cramped . . . Abruptly the prisoner came awake, his hands groping in the darkness.

"Deoris," he said, almost wonderingly, and stirred with a metallic rasp of chains. She took his seeking hands in hers, pressing her lips to the wrists chafed raw by the cold iron. Riveda fumbled to touch her face. "Have they—they have not imprisoned you too, child?"

"No," she whispered.

Riveda struggled to sit up, then sighed and gave it up. "I cannot," he acknowledged wearily. "These chains are heavy—and cold!"

In horror, Deoris realized that he was literally weighed down with bronze chains that enlaced his body, fettering hands and feet close to the floor so that he could not even sit upright—his giant strength oppressed so easily! *But how they must fear him!*

He smiled, a gaunt, hollow-eyed grimace in the darkness. "They have even bound my hands lest I weave a spell to free myself! The half-witted, superstitious cowards," he muttered, "knowing nothing of magic—they are afraid of what no living man could accomplish!" He chuckled. "I suppose I *could,* possibly, bespeak the fetters off my wrists—if I wanted to bring the dungeon down on top of me!"

Awkwardly, because of the weight of the chains and the clumsiness of her own swelling body, Deoris got her arms half-way around him and held him, as closely as she could, his head softly pillowed on her thighs.

"How long have I been here, Deoris?"

"Seven days," she whispered.

He stirred with irritation at the realization that she was crying softly. "Oh, stop it!" he commanded. "I suppose I am to die—and I can stand that—but I will *not* have you snivelling over me!" Yet his hand, gently resting upon hers, belied the anger in his voice.

"Somehow," he mused, after a little time had passed, "I have always thought my home was—out there in the dark, somewhere." The words dropped, quiet and calm, through the intermittent drip-dripping of the subterranean waters. "Many years ago, when I was young, I saw a fire, and what looked like death—and beyond that, in the dark places, something . . . or some One, who knew me. Shall I at last find my way back to that wonderworld of Night?" He lay quiet in her arms for many minutes, smiling. "Strange," he said at last, "that after all I have done, my one act of mercy condemns me to death—that I made certain Larmin, with his tainted blood, grew not to manhood—complete."

Suddenly Deoris was angry. "Who were you to judge?" she flared at him.

"I judged—because I had the power to decide."

"Is there no right beyond power?" Deoris asked bitterly.

Riveda's smile was wry now. "None, Deoris. None."

Hot rebellion overflowed in Deoris, and the right of her own unborn child stirred in her. "You yourself fathered Larmin, and insured that taint its further right! And what of Demira? What of the child you, of your own free will, begot on me? Would you show that child the same mercy?"

"There were—things I did not know, when I begot Larmin." In the darkness she could not see the full grimness of the smile lurking behind Riveda's words. "To your child, I fear I show only the mercy of leaving it fatherless!" And suddenly he raised up in another fit of raving, heretical blasphemies, straining like a mad beast at his chains; battering Deoris away from him, he shouted violently until his voice failed and, gasping hoarsely, he fell with a metallic clamor of chains.

Deoris pulled the spent man into her arms, and he did not move. Silence stole toward them on dim feet, while the crack of light crept slowly across her face and lent its glow at last to Riveda's rough-hewn, sleeping face. Heavy, abandoned sleep enfolded him, a sleep that seemed to clasp fingers with death. Time had run down; Deoris, kneeling in the darkness, could feel the sluggish beating of its pulse in the water that dripped crisply, drearily, eroding a deep channel through her heart, that flowed with brooding silence . . .

Riveda moved finally, as if with pain. The single ray of light outlined his face, harshly unrelenting, before her longing eyes. "Deoris," he whispered, and the manacled hand groped at her waist . . . then he sighed. "Of course. They have burned it!" He stopped, his voice still hoarse and rasping. "Forgive me," he said. "It was best— you never knew—*our* child!" He made a strange blurred sound like a sob, then turned his face into her hand and with a reverence as great as it was unexpected, pressed his lips into the palm. His manacled hand fell, with a clashing of chains.

For the first time in his long and impersonally concentrated life, Riveda felt a deep and personal despair. He did not fear death for himself; he had cast the lots and they had turned against him. *But what lot have I cast for Deoris? She must live—and after me her child will live—that child!* Suddenly Riveda knew the full effect of his actions, faced responsibility and found it a bitter, self-poisoned brew. In the darkness, he held Deoris as close and as tenderly as he could in the circumstances, as if straining to give the protection he had too long neglected . . . and his thoughts ran a black torrent.

But for Deoris the greyness was gone. In despair and pain she had finally found the man she had always seen and known and loved behind the fearful outer mask he wore to the world. In that hour, she was no longer a frightened child, but a woman, stronger than life or death in the soft violence of her love for this man she could never manage to hate. Her strength would not last—but as she knelt beside him, she forgot everything but her love of Riveda. She held his chained body in her arms, and time stopped for them both.

She was still holding him like that when the Priests came to take them away.

II

The great hall was crowded with the robes of priests: white, blue, flaxen, and grey-robed, the men and women of the Temple precincts mingled before the raised däis of judgment. They parted with hushed murmurings as Domaris walked slowly forward, her burning hair the only fleck of color about her, and her face whiter than the pallid glimmer of her mantle. She was flanked by two white-robed priests who paced with silent gravity one step behind her, alert lest she fall— but she moved steadily, though slowly, and her impassive eyes betrayed nothing of her thoughts.

Inexorably they came to the däis; here the priests halted, but Domaris went on, slow-paced as fate, and mounted the steps. She spared no glance at the gaunt, manacled scarecrow at the foot of the däis, nor for the girl who crouched with her face hidden in Riveda's lap, her long hair scattered in a dark tangle about them both. Domaris forced herself to climb regally upward, and take her place between Rajasta and Ragamon. Behind them, Cadamiri and the other Guardians were shadowy faces hidden within their golden hoods.

Rajasta stepped forward, looking out over the assembled Priests and Priestesses; his eyes seemed to seek out each and every face in the room. Finally he sighed, and spoke with ceremonious formality: "Ye have heard the accusations. Do you believe? Have they been proved?"

A deep, threatening, ragged thunder rolled the answer: "*We believe! It is proved!*"

"Do you accept the guilt of this man?"

"*We accept!*"

"And what is your will?" Rajasta questioned gravely. "Do ye pardon?"

Again the thunder of massed voices, like the long roll of breakers on the seashore: "*We pardon not!*"

Riveda's face was impassive, though Deoris flinched.

"What is your wall?" Rajasta challenged. "Do ye then condemn?"

"*We condemn!*"

"What is your will?" said Rajasta again—but his voice was breaking. He knew what the answer would be.

Cadamiri's voice came, firm and strong, from the left: "Death to him who has misused his power!"

"*Death!*" The word rolled and reverberated around the room, dying into frail, whispering echoes.

Rajasta turned and face the judgment seat. "Do ye concur?"

"We concur!" Cadamiri's strong voice drowned other sounds: Ragamon's was a harsh tremolo, the others mere murmurs in their wake. Domaris spoke so faintly that Rajasta had to bend to hear her, "We—concur."

"It is your will. I concur." Rajasta turned again, to face the chained Riveda. "You have heard your sentence," he charged gravely. "Have you anything to say?"

The blue, frigid eyes met Rajasta's, in a long look, as if the Adept were pondering a number of answers, any one of which would have shaken the ground from under Rajasta's feet—but the rough-cut jaw, covered now by a faint shadow of reddish-gold beard, only turned up a little in something that was neither smile nor grimace. "Nothing, nothing at all," he said, in a low and curiously gentle voice.

Rajasta gestured ritually. "The decree stands! Fire cleanses—and to the fire we send you!" He paused, and added sternly, "Be ye purified!"

"What of the *saji?*" shouted someone at the back of the hall.

"Drive her from the Temple!" another voice cried shrilly.

"Burn her! Stone her! Burn her, too! Sorceress! Harlot!" It was a storm of hissing voices, and not for several minutes did Rajasta's upraised hand command silence. Riveda's hand had tightened on Deoris's shoulder, and his jaw was set, his teeth clenched in his lip. Deoris did not move. She might have been lying dead at his knees already.

"She shall be punished," said Rajasta severely, "but she is woman—and with child!"

"Shall the seed of a sorcerer live?" an anonymous voice demanded; and the storm of voices rose again, drowning Rajasta's admonitions with the clamor and chaos.

Domaris rose and stood, swaying a little, then advanced a step. The riot slowly died away as the Guardian stood motionless, her hair a burning in the shadowy spaces. Her voice was even and low: "My Lords, this cannot be. I pledge my life for her."

Sternly, Ragamon put the question: "By what right?"

"She has been sealed to the Mother," said Domaris; and her great eyes looked haunted as she went on, "She is Initiate, and beyond the vengeance of man. Ask of the Priestesses—she is sacrosanct, under the Law. Mine be her guilt; I have failed as Guardian, and as sister. I am guilty further: with the ancient power of the Guardians, invested in me, I have cursed this man who stands condemned before you." Domaris's eyes rested, gently almost, on Riveda's arrogant head, "I cursed him life to life, on the circles of karma . . . by Ritual and Power, I cursed him. Let my guilt be punished." She dropped her hands and stood staring at Rajasta, self-accused, waiting.

He gazed back at her in consternation. The future had suddenly turned black before his eyes. *Will Domaris never learn caution? She leaves me no choice.* . . . Wearily, Rajasta said, "The Guardian has claimed responsibility! Deoris I leave to her sister, that she may bring forth, and her fate shall be decided later—but I strip her of honor. No more may she be called Priestess or Scribe." He paused, and addressed the assembly again. "The Guardian claims that she has cursed—by ancient Ritual, and the ancient Power. Is that misuse?"

The hall hissed with the sibilance of vague replies; unanimity was gone, the voices few and doubtful, half lost in the vaulted spaces. Riveda's guilt had been proved in open trial, and it was a tangible guilt; this was a priestly secret known but to a few, and when it was forced out like this, the common priesthood was more bewildered than indignant, for they had little idea what was meant.

One voice, bolder than the rest, called through the uneasy looks and vague shiftings and whispers: "Let Rajasta deal with his Acolyte!" A storm of voices took up the cry: "On Rajasta's head! Let Rajasta deal with his Acolyte!"

"Acolyte no longer!" Rajasta's voice was a whiplash, and Domaris winced with pain. "Yet I accept the responsibility. So be it!"

"*So be it!*" the thronged Priests thundered, again with a single voice.

Rajasta bowed ceremoniously. "The decrees stand," he announced, and seated himself, watching Domaris, who was still standing, and none too steadily. In anger and sorrow, Rajasta wondered if she had the faintest idea what might be made of her confession. He was appalled at the chain of events which she—Initiate and Adept—had set in motion. The power vested in her was a very real thing, and in cursing Riveda as she had, she had used it to a base end. He knew she would pay—and the knowledge put his own courage at a low ebb. She had generated endless karma for which she, and who knew how many others, must pay . . . It was a fault in him, also, that Domaris should have let this happen, and Rajasta did not deny the responsibility, even within himself.

And Deoris. . . .

Domaris had spoken of the Mystery of Caratra, which no man might penetrate; in that single phrase, she had effectively cut herself off from him. Her fate was now in the hands of the Goddess; Rajasta could not intervene, even to show mercy. Deoris, too, was beyond the Temple's touch. It could only be decided whether or no this Temple might continue to harbor the sisters. . . .

Domaris slowly descended the steps, moving with a sort of concentrated effort, as if force of will would overcome her body's frailty. She went to Deoris and, bending, tried to draw her away. The younger girl resisted frantically, and finally, in despair, Domaris signaled to one of her attendant Priests to carry her away—but as the Priest laid hands on the girl, Deoris shrieked and clung to Riveda in a frenzy.

"No! Never, never! Let me die, too! I won't go!"

The Adept raised his head once more, and looked into Deoris's eyes. "Go, child," he said softly. "This is the last command I shall ever lay upon you." With his manacled hands, he touched her dark curls. "You swore to obey me to the last," he murmured. "Now the last is come. Go, Deoris."

The girl collapsed in terrible sobbing, but allowed herself to be led away. Riveda's eyes followed her, naked emotion betrayed there, and his lips moved as he whispered, for the first and last time, "Oh, my beloved!"

After a long pause, he looked up again, and his eyes, hard and controlled once more, met those of the woman who stood before him robed in white.

"Your triumph, Domaris," he said bitterly.

On a strange impulse, she exclaimed, "*Our* defeat!"

Riveda's frigid blue eyes glinted oddly, and he laughed aloud. "You are—a worthy antagonist," he said.

Domaris smiled fleetingly; never before had Riveda acknowledged her as an equal.

Rajasta had risen to put the final challenge to the Priests. "Who speaks for mercy?"

Silence.

Riveda turned his head and looked out at his accusers, facing them squarely, without appeal.

And Domaris said quietly, "I speak for mercy, my lords. *He could have let her die!* He saved Deoris, he risked his own life—when he could have let her die! He let her live, to bear the scars that would forever accuse him. It is but a feather against the weight of his sin— but on the scales of the Gods, a feather may balance against a whole human soul. I speak for mercy!"

"It is your privilege," Rajasta conceded, hoarsely.

Domaris drew from her robe the beaten-gold dagger, symbolic of her office. "To your use, this," she said, and thrust it into Riveda's hand. "I too have need of mercy," she added, and was gone, her white and golden robes retreating slowly between the ranks of Priests.

Riveda studied the weapon in bis hands for a long moment. By some strange fatality, Domaris's one gift to him was death, and it was the supreme gift. In a single, fleeting instant, he wondered if Micon had been right; had he, Domaris, Deoris, sowed events that would draw them all together yet again, beyond this parting, life to life . . . ?

He smiled—a weary, scholarly smile. He sincerely hoped not.

Rising to his feet, he surrendered the symbol of mercy to Rajasta— long centuries had passed since the mercy-dagger was put to its original use—and in turn accepted the jewelled cup. The Adept held it, as he had the dagger, in his hands for a long, considering minute, thinking—with an almost sensuous pleasure, the curious sensuality of the ascetic—of darkness beyond; that darkness which he had, all his life, loved and sought. His entire life had led to this moment, and in a swift, half-conscious thought, it occurred to him that it was precisely this he had desired—and that he could have accomplished it far more easily.

Again he smiled. "The wonder-world of Night," he said aloud, and drained the death-cup in a single draught; then, with his last strength, raised it—and with a laugh, hurled it straight and unerring toward the däis. It struck Rajasta on the temple, and the old man fell senseless, struck unconscious at the same instant that Riveda, with a clamor of brazen chains, fell lifeless on the stone floor.

CHAPTER EIGHT
✠ LEGACY ✠

I

The small affairs of everyday went on with such sameness that Deoris was confused. She lived almost in a shell of glass; her mind seemed to have slid back somehow to the old days when she and Domaris had been children together. Deliberately she clung to these daydreams and fancies, encouraging them, and if a thought from the present slipped through, she banished it at once.

Although her body was heavy, quickened with that strange, strong other life, she refused to think of her unborn child. Her mind remained slammed shut on that night in the Crypt—except for the nightmares that woke her screaming. *What monster demon did she bear, what lay in wait for birth . . . ?*

On a deeper level, where her thoughts were not clear, she was fascinated, afraid, outraged. Her body—the invincible citadel of her very being—was no longer her own, but invaded, defiled. *By what night-haunted thing of darkness, working in Riveda, has she been made mother—and to what hell-spawn?*

She had begun to hate her rebel body as a thing violated, an ugliness to be hidden and despised. Of late she had taken to binding herself tightly with a wide girdle, forcing the rebellious contours into some semblance of her old slenderness, although she was careful to arrange her clothing so that this would not be too apparent, and to conceal it from Domaris.

Domaris was not ignorant of Deoris's feelings—she could even understand them to some faint extent: the dread, the reluctance to remember and to face the future, the despairing horror. She gave the younger girl a few days of dreams and silence, hoping Deoris would come out of it by herself . . . but finally she forced the issue, unwillingly, but driven by real necessity. This latest development was no daydream, but painfully real.

"Deoris, your child will almost certainly be born crippled if you bind the life from him that way," she said. She spoke gently, pityingly, as if to a child. "You know better than that!"

Deoris flung rebelliously away from her hand. "I won't go about shamed so that every slut in the Temple can point her finger at me and reckon up when I am to give birth!"

Domaris covered her face with her hands for a moment, sick with pity. Deoris had, indeed, been mocked and tormented in the days following Riveda's death. *But this—this violence to nature! And Deoris, who had been Priestess of Caratra!*

"Listen, Deoris," she said, more severely than she had spoken since the disasters, "if you are so sensitive, then stay within our own courts where no one will see you. But you must not injure yourself and your child this way!" She took the tight binding in her hands, gently loosening the fastenings; on the reddened skin beneath were white lateral marks where the bandages had cut deep. "My child, my poor little girl! What drove you to this? How could you?"

Deoris averted her face in bitter silence, and Domaris sighed. *The girl must stop this—this idiotic refusal to face the plain facts!*

"You must be properly cared for," said Domaris. "If not by me, then by another."

Deoris said a swift, frightened, "No! No, Domaris, you—you won't leave me!"

"I cannot if I would," Domaris answered; then, with one of her rare attempts at humor, she teased, "Your dresses will not fit you now! But are you so fond of these dresses that you come to this?"

Deoris gave the usual listless, apathetic smile.

Domaris, smiling, set about looking through her sister's things. After a few minutes, she straightened in astonishment. "But you have no others that are suitable! You should have provided yourself . . ."

Deoris turned away in a hostile silence; and it was evident to the stunned Domaris that the oversight had been deliberate. Without further speech, but feeling as if she had been attacked by a beast that leaped from a dark place, Domaris went and searched here and there among her own possessions, until she found some lengths of cloth, gossamer-fine, gaily colored, from which the loose conventional robes could be draped. *I wore these before Micail's birth,* she mused, reminiscent. She had been more slender then—they could be made to fit Deoris's smaller slighter body. . . .

"Come then," she said with laughter, putting aside thoughts of the time she had herself worn this cloth, "I will show you one thing, at least, I know better than you!" As if she were dressing a doll, she drew Deoris to her feet, and with a pantomime of assumed gaiety, attempted to show her sister how to arrange the conventional robe.

She was not prepared for her sister's reaction. Deoris almost at once caught the lengths of cloth from her sister's hands, and with a frantic, furious gesture, rent them across and flung them to the floor. Then, shuddering, Deoris threw herself upon the cold tiles too, and began to weep wildly.

"I won't, I won't, I won't!" Deoris sobbed, over and over again. "Let me alone! I don't want to. I didn't want this! Go away, *just go away!* Leave me alone!"

II

It was late evening. The room was filled with drifting shadows, and the watery light deepened the vague flames of Domaris's hair, picked out the single streak of white all along its length. Her face was thin and drawn, her body narrowed, with an odd, gaunt limpness that was new. Deoris's face was a white oval of misery. They waited, together, in a hushed dread.

Domaris wore the blue robe and golden fillet of an Initiate of Caratra, and had bidden Deoris robe herself likewise. It was their only hope.

"Domaris," Deoris said faintly, "what is going to happen?"

"I do not know, dear." The older woman clasped her sister's hand tightly between her own thin blue-veined ones. "But they cannot harm you, Deoris. You are—*we are,* what we are! That they cannot change or gainsay."

But Domaris sighed, for she was not so certain as she wanted to seem. She had taken that course to protect Deoris, and beyond doubt it had served them in that—else Deoris would have shared Riveda's fate! But there was a sacrilege involved that went deep into the heart of the religion, for Deoris's child had been conceived in a hideous rite. Could any child so conceived ever be received into the Priest's Caste?

Although she did not, even now, regret the steps she had taken, Domaris knew she had been rash; and the consequences dismayed her. Her own child was dead, and through the tide of her deep grief, she knew it was only what she should have expected. She accepted her own guilt but she resolved, with a fierce and quiet determination, that Deoris's child should be safe. She had accepted responsibility for Deoris and for the unborn, and would not evade that responsibility by so much as a fraction.

And yet—*to what night-haunted monster, working in Riveda, had Deoris been made mother? What hell-spawn awaited birth?*

She took Deoris by the hand and they rose, standing together as their judges entered the room: the Vested Five, in their regalia of office; Karahama and attendant Priestesses; Rajasta and Cadamiri, their golden mantles and sacred blazonings making a brilliance in the dim room; and behind Karahama, a grey-shrouded, fleshless form stood, motionless, with long narrow hands folded across meager breasts. Beneath the grey folds a dim color burned blue, and across the blazing hair the starred fillet of sapphires proclaimed the Atlantean rites of Caratra in Maleina's corpse-like presence—and even the Vested Five gave deference to the aged Priestess and Adept.

There was sorrow in Rajasta's eyes, and Domaris thought she detected a glint of sympathy in the impassive face of the woman Adept, but the other faces were stern and expressionless; Karahama's even held a faintly perceptible triumph. Domaris had long regretted her moment of pique, those long years ago; she had made a formidable enemy. *This is what Micon would have called karma . . . Micon!* She tried to hold to his name and image like a talisman, and failed. Would he have censured her actions? He had not acted to protect Reio-ta, even under torture!

Cadamiri's gaze was relentless, and Domaris shrank from it; from

Cadamiri, at least, they could expect no mercy, only justice. The ruthless light of the fanatic dwelt in his eyes—something of the same fervor Domaris had sensed and feared in Riveda.

Briefly, Ragamon the Elder rehearsed the situation: Adsartha, once apprentice Priestess of Caratra, *saji* to the condemned and accursed Riveda, bore a child conceived in unspeakable sacrilege. Knowing this, the Guardian Isarma had taken it upon herself to bind the apostate Priestess Adsartha with herself in the ancient and holy Mystery of the Dark Mother, which put them both forever beyond man's justice . . . "Is this true?" he demanded.

"In the main," Domaris said wearily. "There are a few minor distinctions—but you would not recognize them as important."

Rajasta met her eyes. "You may state the case in your own way, daughter, if you wish."

"Thank you." Domaris clasped and unclasped her hands. "Deoris was no *saji*. To that, I believe, Karahama will bear witness. Is it not true, my sister *and more than my sister*. . . ." Her use of the ritual phrase was deliberate, based on a wild guess that was hardly more than a random hope. "Is it not true that no maiden can be made *saji* after her body is mature?"

Karahama's face had gone white, and her eyes were sick with concealed rage that she, Karahama, should be forced into a position where she was bound by solemn oath to aid Domaris in all things! "That is true," Karahama acknowledged tautly. "Deoris was no *saji*, but *SA#kti SidhA#na* and, thus, holy even to the Priest of Light."

Domaris went on quietly, "I bound her to Caratra, not altogether to shield her from punishment nor to protect her from violence, but to guide her again toward the Light." Seeing Rajasta's eyes fixed on her in almost skeptical puzzlement, Domaris added, on impulse, "Deoris too is of the Light-born, as much as I am myself; and I—felt her child also deserved protection."

"You speak truth," Ragamon the Elder murmured, "yet can a child begotten in such foul blasphemy be so received by the Mother?"

Domaris faced him proudly. "The Rites of Caratra," she said with quiet emphasis, "are devoid of all distinctions. Her Priestesses may be of royal blood—of the race of slaves—or even the *no-people*." Her eyes dwelt for an instant upon Karahama. "Is that not so, my sister?"

"My sister, it is so," Karahama acknowledged, stifled, "even had

Deoris been *saji* in truth." Under Maleina's eyes she had not dared keep silence, for Maleina had taken pity on Karahama too, years before; it had not been entirely coincidence which had brought Demira to Maleina's teaching. The three daughters of Talkannon looked at one another, and only Deoris lowered her eyes; Domaris and Karahama stood for almost a full minute, grey eyes meeting amber ones. There was no love in that gaze—but they were bound by a bond only slightly less close than that binding Domaris to Deoris.

Cadamiri broke the tense silence with blunt words: "Enough of this! Isarma is not guiltless, but she is not important now. The fate of Deoris has yet to be decided—but the child of the Dark Shrine must never be born!"

"What mean you?" Maleina asked sternly.

"Riveda begot this child in blasphemy and sacrilege. The child cannot be acknowledged, nor received. It must never be born!" Cadamiri's voice was loud, and as inflexible as his posture.

Deoris caught at her sister's hand convulsively, and Domaris said, faltering, "You cannot mean . . ."

"Let us be realistic, my sister," said Cadamiri. "You know perfectly well what I mean. Karahama . . ."

Mother Ysouda, shocked, burst out, "That is against our strictest law!"

But Karahama's voice followed, in honeyed and melodious, almost caressing tones. "Cadamiri is correct, my sisters. The law against abortion applies only to the Light-born, received and acknowledged under the Law. No letter of the Law prevents snuffing out the spawn of black magic. Deoris herself would be better freed from that burden." She spoke with great sweetness, but beneath her levelled thick brows she sent Deoris such a look of naked hatred that the girl flinched. Karahama had been her friend, her mentor—and now this! In the past weeks, Deoris had grown accustomed to cold glances and averted faces, superstitious avoidance and whispering silence . . . even Elis looked at her with a hesitant embarrassment and found excuses to call Lissa away from her side . . . yet the ferocious hatred in Karahama's eyes was something different, and smote Deoris anew.

And in a way she is right, Domaris thought in despair. *How could any Priestess—or Priest—endure the thought of a child brought so unspeakably to incarnation?*

"It would be better for all," Karahama repeated, "most of all for Deoris, if that child never drew breath."

Maleina stepped forward, motioning Karahama to silence. "Adsartha," said the woman Adept severely—and the use of her priest-name wakened response even in the frightened, apathetic Deoris. "Your child was truly conceived within the Dark Shrine?"

Domaris opened her lips, but Maleina said stiffly, "I beg you, Isarma, allow her to speak for herself. That was on the Night of Nadir, you say?"

Timidly, Deoris whispered assent.

"Records within the Temple of Caratra, to which Mother Ysouda may testify," Maleina said, with chilly deliberateness, "show that each month, at the dark of the moon—observe this, with *perfect* regularity—Deoris was excused her duties, because at this time she was sacramentally impure. I myself noted this in the Grey Temple." Maleina's mouth tightened briefly as if with pain, remembering in whose company Deoris had spent most of her time in the Grey Temple. "The Night of Nadir falls at moon-dark . . ." She paused; but Domaris and the men only looked baffled, though from Karahama's heavy-lidded eyes, something like comprehension glinted. "Look you," Maleina said, a little impatiently. "Riveda was Grey-robe long before he was sorcerer. The habits of the Magicians are strict and unbreakable. He would not have allowed a woman in the days of her impurity even to come into his presence! As for taking her into such a ritual—it would have invalidated his purpose entirely. Must I explain the rudimentary facts of nature to you, my brothers? Riveda may have been evil—but believe me, he was not an utter fool!"

"Well, Deoris?" Rajasta spoke impersonally, but hope began to show upon his face.

"On the Nadir-night?" Maleina pressed.

Deoris felt herself turning white and rigid; she would not let herself think why. "No," she whispered, trembling, "no, I wasn't!"

"Riveda was a madman!" Cadamiri snorted. "So he violated his own ritual—what of it? Was this not just another blasphemy? I do not follow your reasoning."

Maleina faced him, standing very erect. "It means this," she said with a thin, ironic smile. "Deoris was already pregnant and Riveda's rite was a meaningless charade which he, himself, had thwarted!" The woman Adept paused to savor the thought. "What a joke on him!"

But Deoris had crumpled, senseless, to the floor.

CHAPTER NINE
✠ THE JUDGMENT ✠ OF THE GODS

I

After lengthy consideration, sentence had been pronounced upon Domaris: exile forever from the Temple of Light. She would go in honor, as Priestess and Initiate; the merit she had earned could not be taken from her. But she would go alone. Not even Micail could accompany her, for he had been confided by his father to Rajasta's guardianship. But by curious instinct, choice in her place of exile had fallen on the New Temple, in Atlantis, near Ahtarrath.

Deoris had not been sentenced; her penance could not be determined until after her child's birth. And because of the oath which could not be violated, Domaris could claim the right to remain with her younger sister until the child was born. No further concession could be made.

One afternoon a few days later, Rajasta sat alone in the library, a birth-chart spread before him—but his thoughts were of the bitter altercation which had broken out when Deoris had been carried away in a faint.

"They do *not* hide behind mysteries, Cadamiri," Maleina had said quietly, heavily. "I who am Initiate of Ni-Terat—whom you call Caratra here—I have seen the Sign, which cannot be counterfeited."

Cadamiri's wrath had burst all bonds. "So they are to go unpunished, then? One for sorcery—since even if her child is not child to the Dark Shrine, she concurred in the ritual which would have made it so—and the other for a vile misuse of the holy rites? Then let us make all our criminals, apostates, and heretics Initiates of the Holy Orders and have done with it!"

"It was not misuse," Maleina insisted, her face grey with weariness. "Any woman may invoke the protection of the Dark Mother, and if their prayers are answered, no one can gainsay it. And say not they go unpunished, Priest! They have thrown themselves upon the judgment of the Gods, and we dare not add to what they have invoked! Know you not," her old voice shook with ill-hidden dread, "they have bound themselves and the unborn till the end of Time? Through all their lives—*all* their lives, not this life alone but from life to life! Never shall one have home, love, child, but the pain of the other, deprived, shall tear her soul to shreds! Never shall one find love without searing the soul of the other! Never shall they be free, until they have wholly atoned; the life of one shall bear on the hearts of both. We could punish them, yes—in this life. But they have willfully invoked the judgment of the Dark Mother, until such time as the curse of Domaris has worked itself out on the cycles of karma, and Riveda goes free." Maleina's words rolled to silence; fading echoes settled slowly. At last, the woman Adept murmured, "The curses of men are little things compared to that!"

And for this, even Cadamiri could find no answer, but sat with hands clasped before him for some time after all others had left the hall; and none could say whether it was in prayer, or anger, or shock.

II

Rajasta, having read the stars for Deoris's unborn child, finally called Domaris to him, and spread out the scroll before her. "Maleina was right," he said. "Deoris lied. Her child could not possibly have been conceived on the Nadir-night. Not possibly."

"Deoris would not lie under that oath, Rajasta."

Rajasta looked shrewdly at the girl he knew so well. "You trust her still?" He paused, and accepted. "Had Riveda but known that, many lives would have been saved. I can think of nothing more futile than taking a girl already pregnant into a—a rite of that kind." His voice had a cold irony that was quite new to him.

Domaris, unheeding of it, caught her hands to her throat, and whispered weakly, "Then—her child is not—not the horror she fears?"

"No." Rajasta's face softened. "Had Riveda but known!" he repeated. "He went to his death thinking he had begotten the child of a foul sorcery!"

"Such was his intent." Domaris's eyes were cold and unforgiving. "Men suffer for their intentions, not their actions."

"And for them he will pay," Rajasta retorted. "Your curses will not add to his fate!"

"Nor my forgiveness lighten it," Domaris returned inflexibly, but tears began to roll slowly down her cheeks. "Still, if the knowledge had eased his death . . ."

Gently, Rajasta placed the scroll in her hand. "Deoris lives," he reminded her. "Wherever Riveda may be now, Domaris, the crudest of all hells to him—he who worshipped the forces of Life with all that was best in him, so that he even bent in reverence to you—this would be cruellest to him, that Deoris should hate his child; that she, who had been Priestess of Caratra, should torture herself, binding her body until it is like enough that the child will be born crippled, or worse!"

Domaris could only stare at him, speechless.

"Do you think I did not know that?" Rajasta murmured softly. "Now go. Take this to her, Domaris—for there is now no reason for her to hate her child."

III

His white robes whispering, Rajasta paced soberly to the side of the man who lay on a low, hard pallet in a small, cold room as austere as a cell. "Peace, younger brother," he said—then, quickly preventing him: "No, do not try to rise!"

"He is stronger today," said Cadamiri from his seat by the narrow window. "And there is something which he will say only to you, it seems."

Rajasta nodded, and Cadamiri withdrew from the room. Taking

the seat thus vacated, Rajasta sat looking down at the man who had been Riveda's chela. The long illness had wasted the Atlantean to emaciation again, but Rajasta hardly needed Cadamiri's assurances to tell him that Reio-ta of Ahtarrath was as sane as the Guardian himself.

Now that the madness and vacancy were gone from his face, he looked serious and determined; the amber eyes were darkly intelligent. His hair had been shaven from his scalp during his illness, and was now only a soft, smooth dark nap; he had been dressed in the clothing of a Priest of the second grade. Rajasta knew that the man was twenty-four, but he looked many years younger.

Suddenly impelled to kindness, Rajasta said gently, "My younger brother, no man may be called to account for what he does when the soul is left from him."

"You are—kind," said Reio-ta hesitantly. His voice had lost its timbre from being so little used over the years, and he was never to speak again without stammering and faltering in his speech. "But I was—at fault be—before." More shakily still, he added, "A man who loses—loses his soul as if it were a toy!"

Rajasta saw the rising excitement in his eyes and said, with gentle sternness, "Hush, my son, you will make yourself ill again. Cadamiri tells me there is something you insist upon telling me; but unless you promise not to overexcite yourself . . ."

"That fa-face has never left my memory for—for an instant!" Reio-ta said huskily. His voice steadied, dropped. "He was not a big man—rather, gross and florid—heavy of build, with great long hands and a wide nose flat at the bridge over large jaws and great teeth—dark hair going grey at the temples, and such eyes! And his mouth—smiling and cruel, the smile of a big tiger! He—he looked almost too good-natured to be so ruthless—and heavy brows, almost sand-colored, and rough, curt speech. . . ."

Rajasta felt as if he were stifling. It was all he could do to mutter the words, "Go on!"

"Two special marks he had—a gap between his great front teeth—and such eyes! Have you seen the pr-Priestess, Karahama? Cat's eyes, tiger's eyes—the eyes in his face might have been her own. . . ."

Rajasta covered his face with his hand. A hundred memories rushed over him. *I have been blinder than Micon! Fool—fool that I was not to question Micon's tale of kind men who brought him to*

Talkannon's house! Fool to trust . . . Rajasta gritted his teeth, uncovered his eyes, and asked, still in that stifled voice, "Know you whom you have described, my son?"

"Aye." Reio-ta dropped back on the pillow, his eyes closed, his face weary and resigned. He was sure Rajasta had not believed a single word. "Aye, I know. Talkannon."

And Rajasta repeated, in stunned and bitter belief, *"Talkannon!"*

CHAPTER TEN
⁜ BLACK SHADOWS ⁜

I

Domaris laid the scroll in her sister's lap. "Can you read a birth-chart, Deoris?" she asked gently. "I would read this to you, but I have never learned."

Listlessly, Deoris said, "Karahama taught me, years ago. Why?"

"Rajasta gave me this for you. No," she checked her sister's protest, "you have refused to face this thing until the time was past when I could have forced action. Now we must make some arrangement. Your child must be acknowledged. If your own position means nothing to you, think of your child's as one of the *no-people!*"

"Does it matter?" Deoris asked indifferently.

"To you, now, perhaps not," Domaris returned, "but to your child—*who must live*—it is the difference between living humanly or as an outcaste." Her eyes dwelt sternly on the rebellious young face. "Rajasta tells me you will bear a daughter. Would you have her live as Demira?"

"Don't!" cried Deoris convulsively. She slumped, and defeat was in her face. "But who, now, would acknowledge me?"

"One has offered."

Deoris was young, and against her will a gleam of curiosity lightened her apathetic face. "Who?"

"Riveda's chela." Domaris made no attempt to soften it; Deoris had denied too many facts. Let her chew on this one!

383

"Ugh!" Deoris sprang up defiantly. "No! Never! He's mad!"

"He is no longer mad," Domaris said quietly, "and he offers this as partial reparation."

"Reparation!" Deoris cried in rage. "What right has he . . . ?" She broke off as she met Domaris's unwavering stare. "You really think I should allow—"

"I do advise it," said Domaris inflexibly.

"Oh, Domaris! I hate him! Please, don't make me. . . ." Deoris was crying piteously now, but the older woman stood unbending at her side.

"All that is required of you, Deoris, is that you be present at the acknowledgement," she said curtly. "He will ask . . ." She looked straight into her sister's eyes. "He will *allow* no more!"

Deoris straightened, and tottered back into her seat, white and miserable. "You are hard, Domaris . . . Be it as you will, then." She sighed. "I hope I die!"

"Dying is not that easy, Deoris."

"Oh, Domaris, *why?*" Deoris begged, "Why do you make me do this?"

"I cannot tell you that." Relenting somewhat, Domaris knelt and gathered her sister into her arms. "You know I love you, Deoris! Don't you trust me?"

"Well, yes, of course, but . . ."

"Then do this—because you trust me, darling."

Deoris clung to the older woman in exhaustion. "I can't fight you," she murmured, "I will do as you say. There is no one else."

"Child, child—you and Micail are all I love. And I shall love your baby, Deoris!"

"I—cannot!" It was a bewildered cry of torment, of shame.

The older woman's throat tightened and she felt tears gathering in her eyes; but she only patted the listless head and promised, "You will love her, when you see her."

Deoris only whimpered and stirred restlessly in her arms, and Domaris, letting her embrace loosen, bent to retrieve the scroll, wincing a little—for she was not altogether free of pain.

"Read this, Deoris."

Obediently but without interest the girl glanced at the traced figures, then suddenly bent over them and began to read with furious concentration, her lips moving, her small fingers gripping the parchment so tightly that Domaris thought for a moment it would tear across. Then Deoris flung herself forward, her head pillowed on the scroll, in a passion of wild weeping.

Domaris watched with puzzled consternation, for she—even she— did not wholly understand the girl's terrible fear and its sudden release; even less could she know of that single night Deoris had hoarded apart like a treasure in her memory, when Riveda had been not Adept and teacher, but lover . . . Still, intuition prompted her to take Deoris very gently into her arms again, holding her with tender concern, not speaking a word, hardly breathing, while Deoris sobbed and wept until she could weep no more.

Domaris was relieved beyond telling; grief she could understand, but Deoris's childlike, dazed lethargy, the fits of furious rage which alternated with apathy, had frightened the older woman more than she knew. Now, as Deoris lay spent on her shoulder, her eyes closed and her arm around Domaris's neck, it was for a moment almost as if all the years had rolled back and they were again what they had been before Micon's coming . . .

With a flash of inner, intuitive sight, Domaris knew what had been wrought of love; and some touch of her own loss and grief returned, transfigured. *Micon, Riveda—what matter? The love and bereavement are the same.* And to the depths of her being Domaris was glad—glad that after so long, Deoris could at last weep for Riveda.

II

But Deoris was dry-eyed again, sullen and rigidly polite, when she was confronted with Reio-ta outside the hall where they must go before the Vested Five. Her memory of him was still that of a mad chela ghosting cat-footed after the dark Adept—this handsome, self-possessed young Priest startled her. For a moment she actually did not know who he could be. Her voice stumbled as she said, formally, "Prince Reio-ta of Ahtarrath, I am grateful for this kindness."

Reio-ta smiled faintly without raising his eye to her. "There is no d-debt, Deoris, I am y-yours to command in all things."

She kept her eyes fixed upon the blue hem of her loose, ungainly garment, but she did take his offered hand, touching him with scared hesitation. Her face burned with shame and misery as she felt his eyes study her awkward body; she did not raise her own to see the sadness and compassion in his gaze.

The ceremony, though very brief, seemed endless to Deoris. Only Reio-ta's strong hand, tightly clasped over her own, gave her the courage to whisper, faintly, the responses; and she was shaking so violently that when they knelt together for the benediction, Reio-ta had to put his arm around her and hold her upright.

At last Ragamon put the question: "The child's name?"

Deoris sobbed aloud, and looked in appeal at Reio-ta, meeting his eyes for almost the first time.

He smiled at her, and then, seeing the Vested Five, said quietly, "The stars have been read. This daughter of mine I name—Eilantha."

Eilantha! Deoris had climbed high enough in the priesthood to interpret that name. *Eilantha*—the effect of a sown cause, the ripple of a dropped stone, the force of karma.

"Eilantha, thy coming life is acknowledged and welcome," the Priest gave answer—and from that moment Deoris's child was Reio-ta's own, as if truly begotten of him. The sonorous blessing rolled over their bent heads; then Reio-ta assisted the woman to rise, and although she would have drawn away from him, he conducted her ceremoniously to the doorway of the hall, and retained her fingers for a moment.

"Deoris," he said gravely, "I would not b-burden you with cares. I know you are not well. Yet a few things must be said between us. Our child . . ."

Again Deoris sobbed aloud and, violently wrenching her hands away from his, ran precipitately away from the building. Reio-ta called after her sharply in hurt puzzlement, then started to hasten after the fleeing girl, fearful lest she should fell and injure herself.

But when he turned the corner, she was nowhere to be seen.

III

Deoris came to rest finally in a distant corner of the Temple gardens, suddenly realizing that she had run much further than she had intended. She had never come here before, and was not certain which of the out-branching paths led back toward the house of Mother Ysouda. As she turned hesitantly backward and forward, trying to decide precisely where she was and which way to go, a crouching form rose up out of the shrubbery and she found herself face to face with Karahama. Instinctively Deoris drew back, resentful and frightened.

Karahama's eyes were filled with a sullen fire. "You!" the Priestess spat contemptuously at Deoris. "*Daughter of Light!*" Karahama's blue garment was rent from head to foot; her unkempt, uncombed hair hung raggedly about a face no longer calm but congested and swollen, with eyes red and inflamed, and lips drawn back like an animal's over her teeth.

Deoris, in an excess of terror, shrank against the wall—but Karahama leaned so close that she touched the girl. Suddenly, with awful clarity, Deoris knew: Karahama was insane!

"Torturer of children! Sorceress! Bitch!" A rabid wrath snarled in Karahama's voice. "Talkannon's proudest daughter! Better I had been thrown to die upon the city wall than see this day! And you for whom I suffered, daughter of the high lady who could not stoop to see my poor mother—and what of Talkannon now, Daughter of Light? He will wish he had hanged himself like Demira when the priests have done with him! Or has the proud Domaris kept *that* away from you, too? Rend your clothing, Talkannon's daughter!" With a savage gesture, Karahama's clawed hands ripped Deoris's smock from neck to ankle.

Screaming with fright, Deoris caught the torn robe about her and sought to twist free—but Karahama, leaning over her, pressed Deoris back against the crumbling wall with a heavy, careless hand against her shoulder.

"Rend your clothing, Daughter of Light! Tear your hair! Daughter of Talkannon—who dies today! And Domaris, who was cast out like a harlot, cast out by Arvath for the barren stalk she is!" She spat, and shoved Deoris violently back against the wall again. "And you—*my sister, my little sister!*" There was a vague, mocking hint of Domaris's intonation in the phrase, a sing-song eeriness, an echo like a ghost. "And your own womb heavy with a sister to those children you wronged!" Karahama's tawny eyes, lowered between squinting lashes, suddenly widened and she looked at Deoris through dilated pupils, flat and beast-red, as she shouted, "May slaves and the daughters of harlots attend your bed! May you give birth to monsters!"

Deoris's knees went lifeless under her and she collapsed on the sandy path, crouching against the stones of the wall. "Karahama, Karahama, curse me not!" she implored. "The Gods know—*The Gods know I meant no harm!*"

"She meant no harm," Karahama mocked in that mad, eerie sing-song.

"Karahama, the Gods know I have loved you. I loved your daughter, curse me not!"

Suddenly Karahama knelt at her side. Deoris cringed away—but with easy, compassionate hands the woman lifted her to her feet. The mad light had quite suddenly died from her eyes, and the face between the dishevelled braids was sane again and sorrowful.

"So, once, was I, Deoris—not innocent, but much hurt. Neither are you innocent! But I curse you no more."

Deoris sobbed in relief, and Karahama's face, a mask of pain, swam in a ruddy light through her tears. The crumbling stones of the garden wall were a rasping pain against her shoulders, but she could not have stood, unsupported. Suddenly she could hear the low, insistent lapping of the tide, and knew where she was.

"You are not to blame," said Karahama, in a voice hardly louder than the waves. "Nor he—nor I, Deoris! All these things are shadows, but they are very black. I bid you go in peace, little sister . . . your hour is upon you, and it may be that you will do a bit of cursing yourself, one day!"

Deoris covered her face with her hands—and then the world went dark about her, a dizzy gulf opened out beneath her mind, and she heard herself screaming as she fell—fell for eternities, while the sun went out.

CHAPTER ELEVEN
✠ VISIONS ✠

I

When Deoris failed to return, Domaris slowly grew anxious, and finally went in search of her sister—a search that was fruitless. The shadows stretched into long, gaunt corpses, and still she sought; her anxiety mounted to apprehension, and then to terror. The words Deoris had flung at her in anger years ago returned to her, a thundering echo in her mind: *On the day I know myself with child, I will fling myself into the sea . . .*

At last, sick with fright, she went to the one person in all the Temple precincts on whom Deoris now had the slightest claim, and implored his assistance. Reio-ta, far from laughing at her formless fears, took them with an apprehension that matched her own. Aided by his servants, they sought through the night, through the red and sullen firelight of the beaches, along the pathways and in the thickets at the edge of the enclosure. Near morning they found where she had fallen; a section of the wall had given way, and the two women lay half in, half out of the water. Karahama's head had been crushed by fallen stones, but the scarred, half-naked form of Deoris was so crumpled and twisted that for sickening minutes they believed that she, too, was lifeless.

They carried her to a fisherman's hut near the tide-mark, and there, by smoldering candlelight, with no aid save the unskilled hands of Domaris's slave-girl, was born Eilantha, whose name had been written that same day upon the rolls of the Temple. A tiny, delicately-formed girl-child, thrust two months too soon into an unwelcoming world, she was so frail that Domaris dared not hope for her survival. She wrapped the delicate bud of life in her veil and laid it inside her robes against her own breast, in the desperate hope that the warmth would revive it. She sat there weeping, in reborn grief for her own lost child, while the slave-girl tended Deoris and aided Reio-ta to set the broken arm.

After a time the infant stirred and began feebly to wail again, and the thin sound roused Deoris. Domaris moved swiftly as she stirred, and bent over her.

"Do not try to move your arm, Deoris; it is broken at the shoulder."

Deoris's words were less than a whisper. "What has happened? Where?" Then memory flooded back. "Oh! Karahama!"

"She is dead, Deoris," Domaris told her gently—and found herself wondering, in a remote way, whether Deoris had flung herself over the wall and Karahama had been killed in attempting to prevent it—whether they had simply fallen—or whether Karahama had thrust her sister over the wall. No one, not even Deoris, was ever to know.

"How did you find me?" Deoris asked, without interest.

"Reio-ta helped me."

Deoris's eyes slipped wearily shut. "Why could he not . . . attend to his own affairs . . . this one last time?" she asked, and turned her face away. The child at Domaris's breast began its whimpering wail again, and Deoris's eyes flickered briefly open. "What is . . . I don't . . . ."

Cautiously, Domaris lowered the infant toward her sister, but Deoris, after a momentary glimpse at the little creature, shut her eyes again. She felt no emotion except faint relief. The child was not a monster—and in the wrinkled, monkey-like face she could discern no resemblance whatever to Riveda.

"Take it away," she said tiredly, and slept.

Domaris looked down at the young mother, with despair in her face which lightened to a haunted tenderness. "Thy mother is tired and ill, little daughter," she murmured, and cradled the baby against her breasts. "I think she will love thee—when she knows thee."

But her steps and her voice dragged with exhaustion; her own strength was nearly gone. Domaris had never fully recovered from the brutal treatment she had received at the hands of the Black-robes; moreover, she dared not keep this a secret for long. Deoris was not, as far as Domaris could judge, in physical danger; the child had been born easily and so swiftly that there had been no time even to summon help. But she was suffering from exposure and shock.

Domaris did not know if she dared to take any further responsibility. With the baby still snuggled inside her robes, she sat down on a low stool, to watch and think. . . .

II

When Deoris awoke, she was alone. She lay unmoving, not asleep, but heavy with weariness and lassitude. Gradually, as the effect of the drugs began to weaken, the pain stole back, a slow pulsing of hurt through her torn and outraged body. Slowly, and with difficulty, she turned her head, and made out the dim outline or a basket of reeds, and in the basket something that kicked and whimpered fretfully. She thought dully that she would like to hold the child now, but she was too weak and weary to move.

What happened after that, Deoris never really knew. She seemed to lie half asleep through all that followed, her eyes open but unable to move, unable even to speak, gripped by nightmares in which there was no clue to what was real—and afterward there was no one who could or would tell her what really happened on that night after Riveda's child was born, in the little hut by the sea. . . .

It seemed that the sun was setting. The light lay red and pale on her face, and on the basket where the baby squirmed and squalled feebly. There was a heat-like fever in Deoris's hurt body, and it seemed to her that she moaned there for a long time, not loudly but desolately like a hurt child. The light turned into a sea of bloody fire, and the chela came into the room. His dark, wandering glance met hers . . . He wore bizarrely unfamiliar clothing, girt with the symbols of a strange priesthood, and for a moment it seemed to be Micon who stood before her, but a gaunt, younger Micon, with unshaven face. His secret eyes rested on Deoris for a long time; then he went and poured water, bending, holding the cup to her parched lips and supporting her head so gently that there was no hurt. For an instant it seemed Riveda stood there, nimbused in a cloud of the roseate sunset, and he bent down and kissed her lips as he had done so rarely in her life; then the illusion was gone, and it was only the solemn young face of Reio-ta looking at her gravely as he replaced the cup.

He stood over her for a minute, his lips moving; but his voice seemed to fade out over incredible distances, and Deoris, wandering in the vague silences again, could not understand a word. At last he turned abruptly and went to the reed-basket, bending, lifting the baby in his arms. Deoris, still gripped by the static fingers of nightmare, watched as he wandered about the room, the child on his shoulder; then he approached again, and from the pallet where Deoris was lying he lifted a long loose blue shawl, woven and fringed deeply with knots—the garment of a Priestess of Caratra. In this he carefully wrapped the baby, and, carrying her clumsily in his hands, he went away.

The closing of the door jarred Deoris wholly awake, and she gasped; the room was lurid with the dying sunlight, but altogether empty of any living soul except herself. There was no sound or motion anywhere save the pounding of the waves and the crying of the wheeling gulls.

She lay still for a long time, while fever crawled in her veins and throbbed in her scarred breasts like a pulsing fire. The sun set in a bath of flames, and the darkness descended, folding thick wings of silence around her heart. After hours and hours, Elis (or was it Domaris?) came with a light, and Deoris gasped out her dream—but it sounded delirious even to her own ears, all gibberish and wild entreaties. And then there were eternities where Domaris (or Elis) bent over her, repeating endlessly, "Because you trust me . . . you do trust me . . . do this because you trust me . . ." There was the nightmare pain in her broken arm, and fever burning through her veins, and the dream came again and again—and never once, except in her unquiet slumber, did she hear the crying of the small and monkey-like child who was Riveda's daughter.

She came fully to her senses one morning, finding herself in her old rooms in the Temple. The feverish madness was gone, and did not return.

Elis tended her night and day, as gently as Domaris might have; it was Elis who told her that Talkannon was dead, that Karahama was dead, that Domaris had sailed away weeks before for Atlantis, and that the chela had disappeared, no one knew where; and Elis told her, gently, that Riveda's child had died the same night it was born.

Whenever Deoris fell asleep she dreamed—and always the same dream: the dark hut where her child had been born, and she had been dragged unwillingly back from death by the chela, whose face was bloodied by the red sunlight as he carried away her child, wrapped in the bloodstained fragments of Karahama's priestly robes . . . And so she came at last to believe that it had never happened. Everyone was very kind to her, as to a child orphaned, and for many years she did not even speak her sister's name.

BOOK FIVE
✠ TIRIKI ✠

❖ ❖ ❖

"When the Universe was first created out of nothing, it at once fell apart for lack of cohesion. Like thousands of tiny tiles that have no apparent meaning or purpose, all the pieces are identical in shape and size, though they may differ in color and pattern; and we have no picture of the intended mosaic to guide us. No one can know for sure what it will look like, until the last tile is finally fitted into place . . . There are three tools for the task: complete non-interference; active control over each and every movement; and interchange of powers until a satisfactory balance is achieved. None of these methods can succeed, however, without consent of the other two; this we must accept as a fundamental principle—else we have no explanation for what has already transpired.

"The problem is, as yet, unsolved; but we proceed, in waves. An advance in general knowledge is followed by a setback, in which many things are lost—only to be regained and excelled in the next wave of advancement. For the difference between that mosaic and the Universe is that no mosaic can ever become anything more than a picture in which motion has ended—a picture of Death. We do not build toward a time when everything stands still, but toward a time when everything is in a state of motion pleasing to all concerned—rock, plant, fish, bird, animal and man.

"It has never been, and never will be, easy work. But the road that is built in hope is more pleasant to the traveler than the road built in despair, even though they both lead to the same destination."

—from The Teachings of Micon of Ahtarrath,
as taken down by Rajasta the Mage

❖ ❖ ❖

CHAPTER ONE
✠ THE EXILE ✠

I

It was deep dusk, and the breeze in the harbor was stiffening into a western wind that made the furled sails flap softly and the ship rise and fall to the gentle rhythm of the waves. Domaris stared toward the darkening shores, her body motionless, her white robes a spot of luminescence in the heavy shadows.

The captain bowed deeply in reverence before the Initiate. "My Lady—"

Domaris raised her eyes. "Yes?"

"We are about to leave the port. May I conduct you to your cabin? Otherwise, the motion of the ship may make you ill."

"I would rather stay on deck, thank you."

Again the captain bowed, and withdrew, leaving them alone again.

"I too must leave you, Isarma," said Rajasta, and stepped toward the rail. "You have your letters and your credentials. You have been provided for. I wish . . ." He broke off, frowning heavily. At last, he said only, "All will be well, my daughter. Be at peace."

She bent to kiss his hand reverently.

Stooping, Rajasta clasped her in his arms. "The Gods watch over thee, daughter," he said huskily, and kissed her on the brow.

"Oh, Rajasta, I can't!" Domaris sobbed. "I can't bear it! Micail—my baby! And Deoris . . ."

"Hush!" said Rajasta sternly, loosing her pleading, agonized hands;

but he softened almost at once, and said, "I am sorry, daughter. There is nothing to be done. You *must* bear it. And know this: my love and blessings follow you, beloved—now and always." Raising his hand, the Guardian traced an archaic Sign. Before Domaris could react, Rajasta turned on his heel and swiftly walked away, leaving the ship. Domaris stared after him in astonishment, wondering why he had given her—an exile under sentence—the Sign of the Serpent.

A mistake? No—Rajasta does not make such mistakes.

After what seemed a long time, Domaris heard the clanking of anchor-chains and the oar-chant from the galley. Still she stood on the deck, straining her eyes into the gathering dusk for the last sight of her homeland, the Temple where she had been born and from which she had never been more than a league away in her entire life. She remained there motionless, until long after night had folded down between the flying ship and the invisible shore.

II

There was no moon that night, and it was long before the woman became conscious that someone was kneeling at her side.

"What is it?" she asked, tonelessly.

"My Lady—" The flat, hesitant voice of Reio-ta was a murmuring plea, hardly audible over the sounds of the ship. "You must come below."

"I would rather remain here, Reio-ta, I thank you."

"My Lady—there is—something I m-must show thee."

Domaris sighed, suddenly conscious of cold and of cramped muscles and of extreme weariness, although she had not known it until now. She stumbled on her numb legs, and Reio-ta stepped quickly to her side and supported her.

She drew herself erect at once, but the young Priest pleaded, "No, lean on me, my Lady . . ." and she sighed, allowing him to assist her. She thought again, vaguely and with definite relief, that he was nothing at all like Micon.

The small cabin allotted to Domaris was lighted by but a single, dim lamp, yet the slave-women—strangers, for Elara could not be asked to leave her husband and newborn daughter—had made it a place of order and comfort. It looked warm and inviting to the exhausted Domaris: there was a faint smell of food, and a slight pungent smoke from the lamp, but all these things vanished into the perimeter of her consciousness, mere backdrop to the blue-wrapped bundle lying among the cushions on the low bed . . . clumsily wrapped in fragments of a stained blue robe, it squirmed as if alive . . .

"My most revered Lady and elder sister," Reio-ta said humbly, "I would b-beg you to accept the care of my acknowledged daughter."

Domaris caught her hands to her throat, swaying; then with a swift strangled cry of comprehension she snatched up the baby and cradled it against her heart "Why this?" she whispered. "*Why this?*"

Reio-ta bent his head. "I-I-I grieve to take her from her m-mother," he stammered, "but it was—it was—you know as well as I that it would be death to leave her there! And—it is my right, under the law, to take my d-daughter where it shall please me."

Domaris, wet-eyed, held the baby close while Reio-ta explained simply what Domaris had not dared to see . . .

"Neither Grey-robe nor Black—and mistake not, my Lady, there are Black-robes still, there will be Black-robes until the Temple falls into the sea—and maybe after! They would not let this child live—they b-believe her a child of the Dark Shrine!"

"But . . ." Wide-eyed, Domaris hesitated to ask the questions his words evoked in her mind—but Reio-ta, with a wry chuckle, divined her thought easily.

"To the Grey-robes, a sacrilege," he murmured. "And the B-Black-robes would think only of her value as a sacrifice! Or that—that she had b-been ruined by the Light-born—was not the—the incarnation of the—" Reio-ta's voice strangled on the words unspoken.

For another moment, Domaris's tongue would not obey her, either; but at last she managed to say, half in shock, "Surely the Priests of Light . . ."

"Would not interfere. The Priests of Light—" Reio-ta looked at Domaris pleadingly. "They cursed Riveda—*and his seed!* They would not intervene to save her. But—with this child gone, or vanished—Deoris too will be safe."

Domaris buried her face in the torn robe swathed abut the sleeping infant. After a long minute, she raised her head and opened tearless eyes. "Cursed," she muttered. "Yes, this too is karma. . . ." Then, to Reio-ta, she said, "She shall be my tenderest care—I swear it!"

CHAPTER TWO
✠ THE MASTER ✠

I

The soft, starlit night of Ahtarrath was so still that the very steps of their bare feet on the grass could be heard. Reio-ta gave Domaris his hand, and she clutched at his fingers with a grip that betrayed her emotion before this ordeal; but her face was serene in its lovely, schooled calm. The man's eyes, brooding secretly under dark lashes flashed a swift, approving look at her as his other hand swept aside the heavy sacking curtain that screened the inner room. Her hand was cold in his, and a sense of utter desolation seemed to pass from her to him. She was calm—but he was fleetingly reminded of the moment when he had led the trembling Deoris before the Vested Five.

Full realization suddenly welled over Reio-ta, lashing him with almost unbearable self-loathing. His remorse was a living thing that sprang at him and clawed at his vitals; a lifetime, a dozen lifetimes could never wipe out anything he had done! And this sudden insight into the woman beside him, the woman who should have been his sister, was a further scourge. She was so desperately, so utterly alone!

With a gentle, deprecatory tenderness, he drew her into the austere inner chamber, and they faced a tall, thin-faced old man, seated on a plain wooden bench. He rose at once and stood quietly surveying them. It was not until many months later that Domaris learned that the ancient Priest Rathor was blind, and had been so from birth.

Reio-ta dropped to his knees for the ancient's blessing. "Bless me,

Lord Rathor," he said humbly, "I bring n-news of Micon. He died a hero—and to a noble end—and I am not blameless."

There was a long silence. Domaris, at last, stretched imploring hands to the old man; he moved, and the movement broke the static pattern of self-blame in the younger Priest's face. Reio-ta continued, gazing up at the aged Rathor, "I b-bring you the Lady Domaris—who is the mother of Micon's son."

The ancient master raised one hand, and breathed a single sentence; and the softness of his voice stayed with Domaris until the moment of her death. "All this I know, and more," he said. Raising Reio-ta, he drew him close and kissed the young Priest upon the forehead. "It is karma. Set your heart free, my son."

Reio-ta struggled to steady his voice. "M-Master!"

Now Domaris also would have knelt for Rathor's blessing, but the ancient prevented her. Deliberately, the master bent and touched his lips to the hem of her robe. Domaris gasped and quickly raised the old man to his feet. Lifting his hand, Rathor made a strange Sign upon her forehead—the same Sign Domaris had yielded to Micon at their first meeting. The ancient smiled, a smile of infinite benediction . . . then stepped back and re-seated himself upon his bench.

Awkwardly, Reio-ta took her two hands in his own. "My Lady, you must not cry," he pleaded, and led her away.

CHAPTER THREE
✠ LITTLE SINGER ✠

I

With the passing of time, Domaris grew somehow accustomed to Ahtarrath. Micon had lived here, had loved this land, and she comforted herself with such thoughts; yet homesickness burned in her and would not be stilled.

She loved the great grey buildings, massive and imposing, very different from the low, white-gleaming structures in the Ancient Land, but equally impressive in their own fashion; she grew to accept the terraced gardens that sloped down everywhere to the shining lakes, the interlacing canopies of trees taller than she had ever seen—but she missed the fountains and the enclosed courts and pools, and it was many years before she could accustom herself to the many-storied buildings, or climb stairs without the sense that she violated a sacred secret meant for use in temples alone.

Domaris had her dwelling on the top floor of the building which housed the unmarried Priestesses; all the rooms which faced the sea had been set aside for Domaris and her attendants—and for one other from whom she was parted but seldom, and never for long.

She was instantly respected and soon loved by everyone in the New Temple, this tall quiet woman with the white streak in her blazing hair; they accepted her always as one of themselves, but with reserve and honor accorded to one who is a little strange, a little mysterious. Ready always to help or heal, quick of decision and slow of anger, and always with the blond and sharp-featured little girl toddling at her heels—they loved Domaris, but some strangeness and mystery kept them at a little distance; they seemed to know instinctively that here was a woman going through the motions of living without any real interest in what she was doing.

Only once did Dirgat, Arch-priest of the Temple—a tall and saintly patriarch who reminded Domaris slightly of Ragamon the elder—come to remonstrate with her on her apparent lack of interest in her duties.

She bowed her head in admission that the rebuke was just. "Tell me wherein I have failed, my father, and I will seek to correct it."

"You have neglected no iota of your duty, daughter," the Arch-priest told her gently. "Indeed, you are more than usually conscientious. You fail us not—but you fail yourself, my child."

Domaris sighed, but did not protest, and Dirgat, who had daughters of his own, laid his hand over her thin one.

"My child," he said at last, "forgive me that I call you so, but I am of an age to be your grandsire, and I—I like you. Is it beyond your power to find some happiness here? What troubles you, daughter? Open your heart. Have we failed to give you welcome?"

Domaris raised her eyes, and the tearless grief in them made the old Arch-priest cough in embarrassment. "Forgive me, my father." she said. "I sorrow for my homeland—and for my child—my children."

"Have you other children, then? If your little daughter could accompany you, why could not they?"

"Tiriki is not my daughter," Domaris explained quietly, "but my sister's child. She was daughter to a man condemned and executed for sorcery—and they would have slain the innocent child as well. I brought her beyond harm's reach. But my own children . . ." She paused a moment, to be sure that her voice was steady before she spoke. "My oldest son I was forbidden to bring with me, since he must be reared by one—worthy—of his father's trust; and I am exiled." She sighed. Her exile had been voluntary, in part, a penance self-imposed; but the knowledge that she had sentenced herself made it no easier to bear. Her voice trembled involuntarily as she concluded bleakly, "Two other children died at birth."

Dirgat's clasp tightened very gently on her fingers. "No man can tell how the lot of the Gods will fall. It may be that you will see your son again." After a moment he asked, "Would it comfort you to work among children—or would it add to your sorrow?"

Domaris paused, to consider. "I think—it would comfort me," she said, after a little.

The Arch-priest smiled. "Then some of your other duties shall be lightened, for a time at least, and you shall have charge of the House of Children."

Looking at Dirgat, Domaris felt she could weep at the efforts of this good and wise man to make her happy. "You are very kind, father."

"Oh, it is a small thing," he murmured, embarrassed. "Is there any other care I can lighten?"

Domaris lowered her eyes. "No, my father. None." Even to her own attendants, Domaris would not mention what she had known for a long time; that she was ill, and in all probability would never be better. It had begun with the birth of Arvath's child, and the clumsy and cruel treatment she had received—no, cruel it had been, but not clumsy. The brutality had been far from unintentional.

At the time, she had accepted it all, uncaring whether she lived or died. She had only hoped they would not kill her outright, that her child might live . . . But that had not been their idea of punishment. Rather it was Domaris who should live and suffer! And suffer she had—with memories that haunted her waking and sleeping, and pain that had never wholly left her. Now slowly and insidiously, it was enlarging its domain, stealing through her body—and she suspected it was neither a quick nor an easy death that awaited her.

She turned back her face, serene and composed again, to the Arch-priest, as they heard tiny feet—and Tiriki scampered into the room, her silky fair hair all aflutter about the elfin face, her small tunic torn, one pink foot sandalled and the other bare, whose rapid uneven steps bore her swiftly to Domaris. The woman caught the child up and pressed her to her heart; then set Tiriki in her lap, though the little girl at once wriggled away again.

"Tiriki," mused the old Arch-priest. "A pretty name. Of your homeland?"

Domaris nodded . . . On the third day of the voyage, when nothing remained in sight of the Ancient Land but the dimmest blue line of mountains, Domaris had stood at the stern of the ship, the baby folded in her arms as she remembered a night of poignant sweetness, when she had watched all night under summer stars, Micon's head pillowed on her knees. Although, at the time, she had hardly listened, it seemed now that she could hear with some strange inward ear the sound of two voices blended in a sweetness almost beyond the human: her sister's silvery soprano, interlaced and intermingled with Riveda's rich chanting baritone . . . Bitter conflict had been in Domaris then, as she held in her goose-fleshed arms the drowsing child of the sister she loved beyond everything else and the only man she had ever hated—and then that curious trick of memory had brought back Riveda's rich warm voice and the brooding gentleness in his craggy face, that night in the star-field as Deoris slept on his knees.

He truly loved Deoris at least for a time, she had thought. *He was not all guilty, nor we all blameless victims of his evil-doing. Micon, Rajasta, I myself—we are not blameless of Riveda's evil. It was our failure too.*

The baby in her arms had picked that moment to wake, uttering a strange little gurgling croon. Domaris had caught her closer, sobbing aloud, "Ah, little singer!" And Tiriki—*little singer*—she had called the child ever since.

Now Tiriki was bound on a voyage of exploration: she toddled to the Arch-priest, who put out a hand to pat her silky head; but without warning she opened her mouth and her little squirrel teeth closed, hard, on Dirgat's bare leg. He gave a most undignified grunt of astonishment and pain—but before he could chide her or even compose himself, Tiriki released him and scampered away. As if his leg had not been hard enough, she began chewing on a leg of the wooden table.

Dismayed but stifling unholy laughter, Domaris caught the child up, stammering confused apologies.

Dirgat waved them away, laughing as he rubbed his bitten leg. "You said the Priests in your land would have taken her life," he chuckled, "she was only bearing a message from her father!" He gestured her last flustered apologies to silence. "I have grandchildren and great-grandchildren, daughter! The little puppy's teeth are growing, that is all."

Domaris tugged a smooth silver bangle from her wrist and gave it to Tiriki. "Little cannibal!" she admonished. "Chew on this—but spare the furniture, and my guests! I beg you!"

The little girl raised enormous, twinkling eyes, and put the bangle to her mouth. Finding it too large to get into her mouth all at once—although she tried—Tiriki began to nibble tentatively on the rim; tumbled down with a thump on her small bottom, and sat there, intent on chewing up the bracelet.

"A charming child," Dirgat said, with no trace of sarcasm. "I had heard that Reio-ta claimed paternity, and wondered at that. There's no Atlantean blood in this blonde morsel, one can see it at a glance!"

"She is very like her father," said Domaris quietly. "A man of the Northlands, who sinned and was—destroyed. The chief Adept of the Grey-robes—Riveda of Zaiadan."

The Arch-priest's eyes held a shadow of his troubled thoughts as he rose, to take his departure. He had heard of Riveda; what he had heard was not good. If Riveda's blood was predominant in the child, it might prove a sorry heritage. And though Dirgat said nothing of this, Domaris's thoughts echoed the Arch-priest's, as her glance rested on Riveda's daughter.

Once again, fiercely, Domaris resolved that Tiriki's heritage should not contaminate the child. *But how can one fight an unseen, invisible taint in the blood—or in the soul?* She snatched Tiriki up in her arms again, and when she let her go, Domaris's face was wet with tears.

CHAPTER FOUR
✠ THE SPECTRE ✠

I

The pool known as the Mirror of Reflections lay dappled in the lacy light filtering through the trees, repeating the silent merging of light with darkness that was the passing of days, and then of years.

Few came here, for the place was uncanny, and the pool was credited with having the ability to collect and reflect the thoughts of those who had once gazed into its rippling face, wherever they might be. In consequence the place was lonely and forsaken, but there was peace there, and silence, and serenity.

Thither came Deoris, one day, in a mood of driving unrest, the future stretching blank and formless before stormy eyes.

The whole affair had been, after all, something like using a bullwhip to kill a fly. Riveda was dead. Talkannon was dead. Nadastor was dead, his disciples dead or scattered. Domaris was in exile. And Deoris herself—who would bother to sentence her, now that the child of sacrilege was dead? More, Deoris had been made an Initiate of the highest Mystery in the Temple; she could not be simply left to her own devices after that. When she had recovered from her illness and her injuries, she had entered upon a disciplinary period of probation; there had been long ordeals, and a period of study more severe than any she had ever known. Her instructor had been none other than Maleina. Now that time, too, was ended—but what came after? Deoris did not know and could not guess.

Throwing herself down on the grassy margin of the pool, she gazed into the depths that were stained a darker blue than the sky, thinking lonely, bitter thoughts, yearning rebelliously for a little child of whom she had scarcely any conscious recollection. Tears gathered and slowly blurred the bright waters, dripping unheeded from her eyes. Tasting their salt on her lips, Deoris shook her head to clear her vision, without, however, taking her intent, introspective gaze from the pool.

In her mood of abstraction, of almost dreamy sorrow, she saw without surprise the features of Domaris, looking upward at her from the pool: a thinner face, the fine boning distinct, and the expression a look of appeal—of loving entreaty. Even as she looked, the lips widened in the old smile, and the thin arms were held out, in a compelling gesture, to fold her close . . . How well Deoris knew that gesture!

A vagrant wind ruffled the water and the image was gone. Then, for an instant, another face formed, and the pointed, elfin features of Demira glinted delicately in the ripples. Deoris covered her face with her hands, and the sketched-in ghost vanished. When she looked again, the ripples were ruffled only by lifting breezes.

CHAPTER FIVE
✠ THE CHOSEN PATH ✠

I

In these last years, Elis had lost her old prettiness, but had gained dignity and mature charm. In her presence, Deoris felt a curious peace. She took Elis's youngest child, a baby not yet a month old, in her arms and held him hungrily, then handed him back to Elis and with a sudden, despairing move, she flung herself to her knees beside her cousin and hid her face.

Elis said nothing, and after a moment Deoris lifted her eyes and smiled weakly. "I am foolish," she admitted, "but—you are very like Domaris."

Elis touched the bent head in its coif of heavy dark plaits. "You yourself grow more like her each day, Deoris."

Deoris rose swiftly to her feet as Elis's older children, led by Lissa— now a tall, demure girl of thirteen—rushed into the room. Upon seeing the woman in the blue robes of an Initiate of Caratra, they stopped, their impulsive merriment checked and fast-fading.

Only Lissa had self-possession enough to greet her. "*Kiha* Deoris, I have something to tell you!"

Deoris put her arm around her cousin's daughter. Had she ever carried this sophisticated little maiden as a naughty toddler in her arms? "What is this great secret, Lissa?"

Lissa turned up excited dark eyes. "Not really a secret, *kiha* . . . only that I am to serve in the Temple next month!"

A dozen thoughts were racing behind Deoris's calm face—the composed mask of the trained priestess. She had learned to control her expressions, her manner—and almost, but not quite, her thoughts. She, Initiate of Caratra, was forever barred away from certain steps of accomplishment, Lissa—Lissa would surely never feel anything like her own rebellion . . . Deoris was remembering; she had been thirteen or fourteen, about Lissa's age, but she could not remember precisely *why* she had been so helplessly reluctant to enter the Temple of Caratra even for a brief term of service. Then, in the relentless train of thought she could never halt or slow once it had begun in her mind, she thought of Karahama . . . of Demira . . . and then the memory that would not be forced away. If her own daughter had lived, the child she had borne to Riveda, she would have been just a little younger than Lissa—perhaps eight, or nine—already approaching womanhood.

Lissa could not understand the sudden impetuous embrace into which Deoris pulled her, but she returned it cheerfully; then she picked up her baby brother and went out on the lawns, carefully shepherding the others along before her. The woman watched, Elis smiling with pride, Deoris's smile a little sad.

"A young priestess already, Elis."

"She is very mature for her age," Elis replied. "And how proud Chedan is of Lissa now! Do you remember how he resented her, when she was a baby?" She laughed reminiscently. "Now he is like a true father to her! I suppose Arvath would be glad enough to claim her now! Arvath generally decides what he wants to do when it is too late!"

It was no secret any more; a few years ago Arvath had belatedly declared himself Lissa's father and made an attempt to claim her, as Talkannon had done with Karahama in a similar situation. Chedan had had the last word, however, by refusing to relinquish his stepdaughter. Arvath had undergone the strict penances visited on an unacknowledged father, for nothing—except, perhaps, the good of his soul.

A curious little pang of memory stung Deoris at the mention of Arvath; she knew he had been instrumental in pronouncing sentence upon Domaris, and she still resented it. He and Deoris did not meet twice in a year, and then it was as strangers. Arvath himself could advance no further in the priesthood, for as yet he had no child.

Deoris turned to take her departure, but Elis detained her for a moment, clasping her cousin's hand. Her voice was gentle as she spoke, out of the intuition which had never yet failed her. "Deoris—I think the time has come for you to seek of Rajasta's wisdom."

Deoris nodded slowly. "I shall," she promised. "Thank you, Elis."

Once out of her cousin's sight, however, Deoris's countenance was a little less composed. She had evaded this for seven years, fearing the condemnation of Rajasta's uncompromising judgment . . . Yet, as she went along the paths from Elis's home, her step hurried.

What had she been afraid of? He could only make her face herself, know herself.

II

"I cannot say what you must do," Rajasta told her, rigid and unbending. "It is not what I might demand of you, but what you will demand of yourself. You have set causes into motion. Study them. What penalties had been incurred on your behalf? What obligations devolve upon you? Your judgment of yourself will be harsher than mine could ever be—but only thus can you ever be at peace with your own heart."

The woman kneeling before him crossed her arms on her breast, in strict self-searching.

Rajasta added a word of caution. "You will pronounce sentence upon yourself, as an Initiate must; but seek not to meddle again with the life the Gods have given you three times over! Death may not be self-sentenced. It is Their will that you should live; death is demanded only when a human body is so flawed and distorted by error that it cannot atone, until it has been molded into a cleaner vehicle by rebirth."

Momentarily rebellious, Deoris looked up. "Lord Rajasta, I cannot endure that I am set in honor, called Priestess and Initiate—I who have sinned in my body and in my soul."

"Peace!" he said sternly. "This is not the least of your penance, Deoris. Endure it in humility, for this too is atonement, and waste is a crime. Those wiser than we have decided you can serve best in that way! A great work is reserved for you in rebirth, Deoris; fear not, you will suffer in minute, exact penance for your every sin. But sentence of death, for you, would have been the easy way! If you had died—if we had cast you out to die or to fall into new errors—then causes and crimes would have been many times multiplied! No, Deoris, your atonement in this life shall be longer and more severe than that!"

Chastened, Deoris turned her eyes to the floor.

With a hardly audible sigh, Rajasta placed a hand upon her shoulder. "Rise, daughter, and sit here beside me." When she had obeyed, he asked quietly, "How old are you?"

"Seven-and-twenty summers."

Rajasta looked at her appraisingly. Deoris had not married, nor— Rajasta had taken pains to ascertain it—had she taken any lover. Rajasta was not certain that he had been wise in allowing this departure from Temple custom; a woman unmarried at her age was a thing of scorn, and Deoris was neither wife nor widow. . . . He thought, with a creeping sorrow that never left him for long, of Domaris. Her grief for Micon had left her emotions scarred to insensitivity; had Riveda so indelibly marked Deoris?

She raised her head at last and her blue eyes met his steadily. "Let this be my sentence," she said, and told him.

Rajasta looked at her searchingly as she spoke; and when she was finished he said, with a kindness that came nearer to unnerving her than anything in many years, "You are not easy on yourself, my daughter."

She did not flinch before him. "Domaris did not spare herself," Deoris said slowly. "I do not suppose I will ever see my sister again, in this life. But . . ." She bent her head, feeling suddenly almost too shy to continue. "I—would live, so that when we meet again—as our oath binds us to do in a further. We—I need not feel shame before her."

Rajasta was almost too moved to speak. "So be it," he pronounced at last. "The choice is your own—and the sentence is—just."

CHAPTER SIX
✠ WITHOUT ✠ EXPECTATIONS

I

In the eleventh year of her exile, Domaris discovered that she could no longer carry on her duties unaided, as she had done for so long. She accepted this gracefully, with a patient endurance that marked everything she did; she had known for a long time that she was ill, and would in all probability never be better.

She went about those duties which remained with an assured serenity which gave justice to all—but the glowing confidence was gone, and all the old sparkling joy. Now it was a schooled poise that impressed her personality, a certain grave attention that lived in the present moment, refusing equally the past and the future. She gave respect and kindness to all, accepting their honor with a gentle reserve; and if this homage ever struck at her heart with a sorrowful irony, she kept it hidden in her heart.

But that Domaris was more than a mere shell, no one could doubt who saw her in the quiet moments of the Ritual. Then she lived, and lived intensely; indeed she seemed a white flame, the very flesh of her seemed to glow. Domaris had not the slightest idea of her impact on her associates, but she felt then a strange, passive happiness, a receptivity—she never quite defined it, but it was compounded of a lively inner life that touched mystery, and a sense of Micon's nearness,

417

here in his own country. She saw it with his eyes, and though at times the gardens and still pools roused memories of the enclosed courts and fountains of her homeland, still she was at peace.

Her Guardianship was still firm and gentle, but never obtrusive, and she now reserved for herself a period of each day which she devoted to watching the harbor. From her high window she gazed, with a remote and terrible loneliness, and every white sail which left the harbor laid a deeper burden of solitude on her heart. The incoming ships lacked, for her, the same poignant yearning that washed over her as she waited, quiescent, for something—she did not know what. There was a doom upon her, and she felt that this interval of calm was just that—an interval.

She was seated there one day, her listless hands still, when her serving woman entered and informed her, "A woman of nobility requests audience, my Lady."

"You know that I see no one at this hour."

"I informed her of that, Lady—but she insisted."

"Insisted?" Domaris expostulated, with an echo of her old manner.

"She said she had travelled very far, and that the matter was one of grave importance."

Domaris sighed. This happened, now and again—usually some barren woman in search of a charm that would produce sons. Would they never cease to plague her? "I will see her," she said wearily, and walked with slow dignity to the anteroom.

Just at the door she stopped, one hand clutching at the door-frame, and the room dipped around her. *Deoris! Ah, no—some chance resemblance, some trick of light—Deoris is years away, in my homeland, perhaps married, perhaps dead.* Her mouth was suddenly parched, and she tried, unsuccessfully, to speak. Her face was moonlight on white marble, and Domaris was trembling, not much, but in every nerve.

"Domaris!" And it was the loved voice, pleading, "Don't you recognize me, Domaris?"

With a great gasp, Domaris reached for her sister, stretching out her arms hungrily—then her strength failed, and she fell limp at Deoris's feet.

Crying, shaking with fright and joy, Deoris knelt and gathered the older woman in her arms. The change in Domaris was like a blow in the face, and for a moment Deoris wondered if Domaris was dead—if the shock of her coming had killed her. Almost before she had time to think, however, the grey eyes opened, and a quivering hand was laid against her cheek.

"It is you, Deoris, it is!" Domaris lay still in her sister's arms, her face a white joy, and Deoris's tears fell on her, and for a time neither knew it. At last Domaris stirred, unquietly. "You're crying—but there is no need for tears," she whispered, "not now." And with this she rose, drawing Deoris up with her. Then, with her kerchief, she dried the other's tears and, pinching the still-saucy nose, said, elder-sisterly, "Blow!"

II

When they could speak without sobbing, or laughing, or both, Domaris, looking into the face of the beautiful, strange, and yet altogether familiar woman her sister had become, asked shakily, "Deoris, how did you leave—my son? Is he—tell me quickly—is he well? I suppose he would be almost a man now. Is he much like—his father?"

Deoris said very tenderly, "You may judge for yourself, my darling. He is in the outer room. He came with me."

"O merciful Gods!" gasped Domaris, and for a moment it seemed she would faint again. "Deoris, my baby—my little boy . . ."

"Forgive me, Domaris, but I—I had to have this one moment with you."

"It is all right, little sister, but—oh, bring him to me *now!*"

Deoris stood and went to the door. Behind her Domaris, still shaking, crowded to her side, unable to wait even a moment. Slowly and rather shyly, but smiling radiantly, a tallish young boy came forward and took the woman in his arms.

With a little sigh, Deoris straightened herself and looked wistfully at them. There was a little pain in her heart that would not be stilled as she went out of the room . . . and when she returned, Domaris was seated on a divan and Micail, kneeling on the floor at her feet, pressed a cheek already downy against her hand.

Domaris raised happy, questioning eyes at Deoris, startled by seeing. "But what is this, Deoris? Your child? How—who—bring him here, let me see," she said. But her glance returned again and again to her son, even as she watched Deoris unwrapping the swaddling bands from the child she had carried in. It was partly pain to see Micail's features; Micon was so keenly mirrored in the dark, young, proud face, the flickering half-smile never absent long from his lips, the clear storm-blue eyes under the bright hair that was his only heritage from his mother's people . . . Domaris's eyes spilled over as she ran her thin hand over the curling locks at the nape of his neck.

"Why, Micail," she said, "you are a man, we must cut off these curls."

The boy lowered his head, suddenly shy again.

Domaris turned to her sister again. "Give me your baby, Deoris, I want to see—him, her?"

"A boy," said Deoris, and put the yearling pink lump into Domaris's arms.

"Oh, he is sweet, precious," she cooed over him lovingly, "but . . . ?" Domaris looked up, hesitant questions trembling on her lips.

Deoris, her face grave, took her sister's free hand and gave Domaris the only explanation she was ever to receive. "Your child's life was forfeited—partly through my fault. Arvath was debarred from rising in the priesthood because he had no living son. And the obligation, which you had—failed—could be said to pass to me . . . and . . . Arvath was not unwilling."

"Then this is—Arvath's son?"

Deoris seemed not to hear the interruption, but continued, quietly, "He would even have married me, but I would not tread on the hem of your robe. Then—it seemed a miracle! Arvath's parents are here, you know, in Ahtarrath, and they wished to have his son to bring up, since Arvath is not—has not married again. So he begged me to undertake this journey—there was no one else he could send—and Rajasta arranged that I should come to you and bring Micail, since when he comes to manhood he must claim his father's heritage and his place. So—so I took ship with the children, and . . ." She shrugged, and smiled.

"You have others?"

"No. Nari is my only child."

Domaris looked down at the curly-headed child on her knee; he sat there composed and laughing, playing with his own thumbs—and now that she knew, Domaris fancied she could even see the resemblance to Arvath. She looked up and saw the expression on her sister's face, a sort of wistfulness. "Deoris," she began, but the door bounced open and a young girl danced into the room, stopping short and staring shyly at the strangers.

"*Kiha* Domaris, I am sorry," she whispered. "I did not know you had guests."

Deoris turned to the little maiden; a tall child, possibly ten years old, delicate and slender, with long straight fine hair loosely falling about her shoulders, framing a pointed and delicate little face in which glimmered wide, silver-blue eyes in a fringe of dark lashes . . .

"Domaris!" Deoris gasped, "Domaris, *who* is *she*? Who is that child? *Am I mad or dreaming?*"

"Why, my darling, can't you guess?" Domaris asked gently.

"Don't, Domaris, I can't bear it!" Deoris's voice broke on a sob. "You—never saw Demira—"

"Sister, look at me!" Domaris commanded. "Would I jest so cruelly? Deoris, it is your baby! Your own little girl—Tiriki, Tiriki darling, come here, come to your mother—"

The little maiden peered shyly at Deoris, too timid to advance, and Domaris saw dawning in her sister's face a hope almost too wild for belief, a crazy half-scared hope.

"But, Domaris, my baby died!" Deoris gasped, and then the tears came, hurt, miserable sobs, lonely floods she had choked back for ten years; the tears she had not been able to shed then; the nightmarish misery. "*Then it wasn't a dream!* I dreamed Reio-ta came and took her away—but later they told me she died—"

Deoris put the little boy down and went swiftly to her sister, clasping the dark head to her breast. "Darling, forgive me," Domaris said, "I was distracted, I did not know what to say or do. I said that to some of the Temple people to keep them from interfering while I thought what I might do; I never believed it would—oh, my little sister, and all those years you thought . . ." She raised her head and said, "Tiriki, come here."

The little girl still hung back, but as Deoris looked longingly at her, still only half daring to believe the miracle, the child's generous small heart went out to this beautiful woman who was looking at her with heartbreaking hope in her eyes. Tiriki came and flung her arms around Deoris in a tight hug, looking up at the woman timidly.

"Don't cry—oh, don't!" she entreated, in an earnest little voice that thrust knives of memory into Deoris's heart. "*Kiha* Domaris—is this my mother?"

"Yes, darling, yes," she was reassured—and then Tiriki felt herself pulled into the tightest embrace she had ever known. Domaris was laughing—but she was half crying, too; the shock or joy had been almost too great.

Micail saved them all. From the floor, holding Deoris's baby with a clumsy caution, he said in a tone of profound boyish disgust:

"*Girls!*"

CHAPTER SEVEN
⁜ THE UNFADING ⁜ FLOWER

I

Domaris laid aside the lute she had been playing and welcomed Deoris with a smile. "You look rested, dear," she said, drawing the younger woman down beside her. "I am so happy to have you here! And—how can I thank you for bringing Micail to me?"

"You—you—what can I say?" Deoris picked up her sister's thin hand and held it to her own. "You have already done so much. Eilantha—what is it you call her—*Tiriki*—you have had her with you all this time? How did you manage?"

Domaris's eyes were far away, dim with dreamy recollection. "Reio-ta brought her to me. It was his plan, really. I did not know she was in such terrible danger. She would not have been allowed to live."

"Domaris!" Shocked belief was in the voice and the raised eyes. "But why was it kept secret from me?"

Domaris turned her deep-sunken eyes on her sister. "Reio-ta tried to tell you. I think you were—too ill to understand him. I was afraid you might betray the knowledge, or . . ." She averted her eyes. "Or try to destroy her yourself."

"Could you think . . . ?"

"I did not know *what* to think, Deoris! It is a wonder I could think at all! And certainly I was not strong enough to compel you. But, for varying reasons, neither Grey nor Black-robes would have let her live.

And the Priests of Light . . ." Domaris still could not look at her sister. "They cursed Riveda—*and his seed.*" There was a moment of silence; then Domaris dismissed it all with a wave of her hand. "It is all in the past," she said steadily. "I have had Tiriki with me since then. Reio-ta has been a father to her—and his parents love her very much." She smiled. "She has been terribly spoilt, I warn you! Half priestess, half princess . . ."

Deoris kept her sister's white hand in hers, looking at her searchingly. Domaris was thin, thin almost to gauntness, and only lips and eyes had color in her white face; the lips like a red wound, the eyes sometimes feverishly bright. And in Domaris's burning hair were many, many strands of white.

"But Domaris! You are ill!"

"I am well enough; and I shall be better, now that you are here." But Domaris winced under her scrutiny. "What do you think of Tiriki?"

"She is—lovely." Deoris smiled wistfully. "But I feel so strange with her! Will she—love me, do you think?"

Domaris laughed in gentle reassurance. "Of course! But she feels strange, too. Remember, she has known her mother only two days!"

"I know, but—I want her to love me now!" There was more than a hint of the old rebellious passion in Deoris's voice.

"Give her time," Domaris advised, half-smiling. "Do you think Micail really remembered *me?* And he was much older. . . ."

"I tried hard to make him remember, Domaris! Although I saw little of him for the first four or five years. He had almost forgotten me, too, by the time I was allowed to be with him. But I tried."

"You did very well." There was tearful gratitude in her eyes and voice. "I meant that Tiriki should know of you, but—she has had only me all her life. And I had no one else."

"I can bear it, to have her love you best," Deoris whispered bravely, "but only just—bear it."

"Oh, my dear, my dear, surely you know I would never rob you of that."

Deoris was almost crying again, although she did not weep easily now. She managed to still the tears, but in her violet-blue eyes there was an aching *acceptance* which touched Domaris more deeply than rebellion or grief.

A childish treble called, "*Kiha* Domaris?" and the women, turning, saw Tiriki and Micail standing in the doorway.

"Come here, darlings." Domaris invited, but it was at her son she smiled, and the pain in her heart was a throbbing agitation, for she saw Micon looking at her. . . .

The boy and girl advanced into the room valiantly, but with a shyness neither could conquer. They stood before their mothers, clinging to one another's hands, for though Tiriki and Micail were still nearly strangers, they shared the same puzzlement; everything had become new to both. All his life Micail had known only the austere discipline of the priesthood, the company of priests; in truth he had never completely forgotten his mother—but he felt shy and awkward in her presence. Tiriki, though she had known hazily that Domaris had not actually borne her, had all her life been petted and spoiled by Domaris, idolized and given such complete and sheltering affection that she had never missed a mother.

The strangeness welled up again, and Tiriki dropped Micail's hand and ran to Domaris, clinging jealously to her and hiding her silver-gilt hair in Domaris's lap. Domaris stroked the shining head, but her eyes never left Micail. "Tiriki, my dearest," she admonished softly, "don't you know that your mother has longed for you all these years? And you do not even greet her. Where are your manners, child?"

Tiriki did not speak, hiding her eyes in bashfulness and rebellious jealousy. Deoris watched, the knife thrusting into her heart again and again. She had outgrown her old possessiveness of Domaris, but a deeper, more poignant pain had taken its place; and now, overlaid upon the scene it seemed she could almost see another silver-gilt head resting upon her own breast, and hear Demira's mournful voice whispering, *If Domaris spoke kindly to me, I think I would die of joy . . .*

Domaris had never seen Demira, of course; and despite what Deoris had said to comfort the little *saji* girl, Domaris would have treated Demira with arrogant contempt if she had seen her. *But really,* Deoris thought with sadness and wonder, *Tiriki is only what Demira would have been, given such careful, loving fosterage. She has all Demira's heedless beauty, her grace, and a poised charm, too, which Demira lacked—a sweetness, a warmth, a—a confidence!* Deoris found herself smiling through her blurry vision. *That is Domaris's work,* she told herself, *and perhaps it may be all for the best. I could not have done so much for her.*

Deoris put out her hand to Tiriki, stroking the bright, feathery hair. "Do you know, Tiriki, I saw you but once before you were taken from me, but in all these years there has been no day when you were absent from my heart. I thought of you always as a baby, though—I did not expect to find you almost a woman. Maybe that will make it—easier, for us to be friends?" There was a little catch in her voice, and Tiriki's generous heart could not but be moved by it.

Domaris had beckoned Micail to her, and apparently forgotten their existence. Tiriki moved closer to Deoris; she saw the wistful look in the violet-blue eyes, and the tact so carefully instilled by her beloved Domaris did not fail her. Still timidly, but with a self-possession that surprised Deoris, she slipped her hand into the woman's.

"You do not seem old enough to be my mother," she said, with such sweet graciousness that the boldness of the words was not impertinent; then, on impulse, Tiriki put her arms about her mother's waist and looked up confidingly into her face . . . At first, Tiriki's only thoughts had been, *What would Kiha Domaris want me to do? I must not make her ashamed of me!* Now she found herself deeply affected by Deoris's restrained sorrow, her lack of insistence.

"Now I have a mother and a little brother, too," the little girl said, warmly. "Will you let me play with my little brother?"

"To be sure," Deoris promised, still in the same restrained manner. "You are almost a woman yourself, so he will grow up to believe he has two mothers. Come along now, if you like, and you shall watch the nurse bathe and dress him, and afterward you shall show us the gardens—your little brother and me."

This, it soon became clear, had been exactly the right thing to say and do; the right note to strike. The last reserve dropped away quickly. If Tiriki and Deoris were never really to achieve a mother-and-daughter relationship, they did become friends—and they remained friends through the long months and years that slipped away, virtually without event.

Arvath's son grew into a sturdy toddler then a healthy lad: Tiriki shot up to tallness and lost the last baby softness in her face. Micail's voice began to change, and he too grew tall; at fifteen the resemblance to Micon had become even more pronounced; the dark-blue eyes sharp and clear in the same way, the face and slender strong body animated with the same intelligent, fluid restlessness . . .

From time to time Micon's father, the Prince Mikantor, Regent of the Sea Kingdoms, and his second wife, the mother of Reio-ta, claimed Micail for a few days; and often they earnestly besought that their grandchild, as heir to Ahtarrath, might remain at the palace with them.

"It is our right," the aging Mikantor would say somberly, time and again. "He is Micon's son, and must be reared as befits his rank, not among women! Though I do not mean to demean what you have done for him, of course. Reio-ta's daughter, too, has place and rank with us." When saying this, Mikantor's eyes would always fix Domaris with patient, sorrowful affection; he would willingly have accepted her, too, as a beloved daughter—but her reserve toward him had never softened.

On each occasion that the subject arose, Domaris, with quiet dignity, would acknowledge that Mikantor was right, that Micon's son was indeed heir to Ahtarrath—but that the boy was also her son. "He is being reared as his father would wish, that I vow to you, but while I live," Domaris promised, "he will not leave me again. While I live—" Her voice would dwell on the words. "It will not be long. Leave him to me—until then."

This conversation was repeated with but a few variations every few months. At last the old Prince bowed his head before the Initiate, and ceased from importuning her further . . . though he continued his regular visits, which became if anything more frequent than before.

Domaris compromised by allowing her son to spend a great deal of time with Reio-ta. This arrangement pleased all concerned, as the two rapidly became intimate friends. Reio-ta showed a deep deference to the son of the older brother he had adored and betrayed—and Micail enjoyed the friendliness and warmth of the young prince. He was at first a stiff, unfriendly boy, and found it difficult to adjust to this unrestricted life; Rajasta had accustomed him, since his third year, to the austere self-discipline of the highest ranks of the Priest's Caste. However, the abnormal shyness and reserve eventually melted; and Micail began to display the same open-hearted charm and joyfulness that had made Micon so lovable.

Perhaps even more than Reio-ta, Tiriki was instrumental in this.

From the first day they had been close, with a friendliness which soon ripened into love; brotherly and unsentimental love, but sincere and deep, nonetheless. They quarrelled often, to be sure—for they were very unlike: Micail controlled, calm of manner but proud and reserved, inclined to be secretive and derisive; and Tiriki hot-tempered beneath her poise, volatile as quick silver. But such quarrels were momentary, mere ruffles of temper—and Tiriki always regretted her hastiness first; she would fling her arms around Micail and beg him, with kisses, to be friends again. And Micail would pull her long loose hair, which was too fine and straight to stay braided for more than a few minutes, and tease her until she begged for mercy.

Deoris rejoiced at their close friendship, and Reio-ta was altogether delighted; but both suspected that Domaris was not wholly pleased. Of late, when she looked into Tiriki's eyes, an odd look would cross her face and she would purse her lips and frown a little, then call Tiriki to her side and hug her penitently, as if to make up for some unspoken condemnation.

Tiriki was not yet thirteen, but already she seemed altogether womanly, as if something worked like yeast within her, awaiting some catalyst to bring sudden and complete maturity. She was a fey, elfin maiden, altogether bewitching, and Micail all too soon realized that things could not long continue as they were; his little cousin fascinated him too greatly.

Yet Tiriki had a child's innocent impulsiveness, and when it came it was very simple; a lonely walk along the seashore, a touch, a playful kiss—and then they stood for several moments locked tight in one another's arms, afraid to move, afraid to lose this sudden sweetness. Then Micail very gently loosed the girl and put her away for him. "Eilantha," he whispered, very low—and Tiriki, understanding why he had spoken her Temple name, dropped her eyes and stood without attempting to touch him again. Her intuition set a final seal on Micail's sure young knowledge. He smiled, with a new, mature responsibility, as he took her hand—only her hand—in his own.

"Come, we should return to the Temple."

"O, Micail!" the girl whispered in momentary rebellion, "now that we have found each other—must we lose this again so quickly? Will you not even dare to kiss me again?"

His grave smile made her look away, confused. "Often, I hope. But not here or now. You are—too dear to me. And you are very young, Tiriki—as am I. Come." His quiet authority was once again that of an older brother, but as they mounted the long terraced path toward the Temple gateway, he relented and turned to her with a quick smile.

"I will tell you a little story," he said with soft seriousness, and they sat down on the hewn steps together. "Once upon a time there was a man who lived within a forest, very much alone, alone with the stars and the tall trees. One day he found a beautiful gazelle within the forest, and he ran toward her and tried to clasp his arms around her slender neck and comfort his loneliness—but the gazelle was frightened and ran from him, and he never found her again. But after many moons of wandering, he found the bud of a lovely flower. He was a wise man by then, because he had been alone so long; so he did not disturb the bud where it nodded in the sunshine, but sat by it for long hours and watched it open and grow toward the sun. And as it opened it turned to him, for he was very still and very near. And when the bud was open and fragrant, it was a beautiful passion-flower that would never fade."

There was a faint smile in Tiriki's silver-grey eyes. "I have heard that story often," she said, "but only now do I know what it means." She squeezed his hand, then rose and danced up the steps. "Come along," she called merrily. "They will be waiting for us—and I promised my little brother I would pick him berries in the garden!"

CHAPTER EIGHT
✠ DUTY ✠

I

That spring the illness Domaris had been holding at bay finally claimed her. All during the spring rains and through the summer seasons of flowers and fruits, she lay in her high room, unable to rise from her bed. She did not complain, and turned away their solicitude easily; surely she would be well again by autumn.

Deoris watched over her with tender care, but her love for her sister blinded her eyes, and she did not see what was all too plain to others; and, too often, neither Deoris nor any other could help the woman who lay there so patiently, powerless through the long days and nights. Years had passed since anyone could have helped Domaris.

Deoris learned only then—for Domaris was too ill to care any longer about concealment—how cruelly her sister had been treated by the Black-robes. Guilt lay heavy on the younger woman after that discovery—for something else came out that Deoris had not known before: just how seriously Domaris had been injured in that strange, dreamlike interlude which even now lay shrouded, for Deoris, in a dark web of confused dreams—the illusive memory of the Idiots' Village. What Domaris at last told her not only made clear exactly why Domaris had been unable to bring Arvath's first child to term, it made it amazing that she had even been able to bear Micon's.

Prince Mikantor finally got his dearest wish, and Micail was sent to the palace; Domaris missed her son, but would not have him see her suffering. Tiriki, however, would not be so constrained, but defied Deoris and even Domaris, for the first time in her life. Childhood was wholly behind her now; at thirteen, Tiriki was taller than Deoris, although slight and immature, as Demira had been. Also, like Demira, there was a precocious gravity in the greyed silver of her eyes and the disturbed lines of her thin face. Deoris had been so childish at thirteen that neither sister noticed, or realized, that Tiriki at that age was already grown; the swifter maturity of the atavistic Zaiadan type escaped their notice, and neither took Tiriki very seriously.

Everyone did what they could to keep her away on the worst days; but one evening when Deoris, exhausted from several days almost without sleep, napped for a moment in the adjoining room, Tiriki slipped in to see Domaris lying wide-eyed and very still, her face was white as the white lock in her still-shining hair.

Tiriki crept closer and whispered, "*Kiha*—?"

"Yes, darling," Domaris said faintly; but even for Tiriki she could not force a smile. The girl came closer yet, and picked up one of he blue-threaded hands, pressing it passionately to her cheek, kissing the waxen fingers with desperate adoration. Domaris tiredly shifted her free hand to clasp the little warm ones of the child. "Gently, darling," said Domaris. "Don't cry."

"I'm not crying," Tiriki averred, raising a tearless face. "Only—can't I do anything for you, *Kiha* Domaris? I—you—it hurts you a lot, doesn't it?"

Under the child's great-eyed gaze, Domaris only said, quietly, "Yes, child."

"I wish I could have it instead of you!"

The impossible smile came then and flickered on the colorless mouth. "Anything rather than that, Tiriki darling. Now run away, my little one, and play."

"I'm not a baby, *Kiha*! Please, let me stay with you," Tiriki begged, and before the intense entreaty Domaris closed her eyes and lay silent for a space of minutes.

I will not betray pain before this child! Domaris told herself—but a drop of moisture stood out on her lower lip.

Tiriki sat down on the edge of the couch. Domaris, ready to warn her away—for she could not bear the lightest touch, and sometimes, when one of the slave-women accidentally jarred her bed, would cry out in unbearable torture—realized with amazement that Tiriki's movements had been so delicate that there was not the slightest hurt, even when the girl bent and twined her arms around Domaris's neck.

Why, Domaris thought, *she's like a little kitten, she could walk across my body and I would feel no hurt! At least she's inherited something good from Riveda!*

For weeks now, Domaris had borne no touch except her sister's, and even Deoris's trained hands had been unable to avoid inflicting torment at times; but now Tiriki . . . The child's small body fitted snugly and easily into the narrow space at the edge of the couch, and she knelt there with her arms around her foster-mother for so many minutes that Domaris was dumbfounded.

"Tiriki," she rebuked at last—reluctantly, for the child's presence was curiously comforting—"you must not tire yourself." Tiriki only gave her an oddly protective, mature smile, and held Domaris closer still. And suddenly Domaris wondered if she were imagining it—*no, it was true,* the pain was gradually lessening and a sort of strength was surging through her worn body. For a moment the blessedness of relief was all Domaris could understand, and she relaxed, with a long sigh. Then the relief disappeared in sudden amazement and apprehension.

"Are you better now, *Kiha?*"

"Yes," Domaris told her, resolving to say nothing. It was absurd to believe that a child of thirteen could do what only the highest Adepts could do after lengthy discipline and training! It had been but a fancy of her weakness, no more. Some remnant of caution told her that if it were true, then Tiriki, for her own safety, must be kept away . . . But keeping Tiriki away was easier to resolve than to do.

In the days that followed, though Tiriki spent much time with Domaris, taking a part of the burden from the exhausted Deoris, Domaris maintained a severe control over herself. No word or movement should betray her to this small woman-child.

Ridiculous, she thought angrily, *that I must guard myself against a thirteen-year-old!*

One day, Tiriki had curled up like a cat beside her. Domaris permitted this, for the child's closeness was comforting, and Tiriki, who had been a restless child, never fidgeted or stirred. Domaris knew she was learning patience and an uncanny gentleness, but she did not want the girl to overtax herself, so she said, "You're like a little mouse, Tiriki. Aren't you tired of staying with me?"

"No. Please don't send me away, *Kiha* Domaris!"

"I won't dare, but promise me you will not tire yourself!"

Tiriki promised, and Domaris touched the flaxen hair with a white finger and lay still, sighing. Tiriki's great grey cat's eyes brooded dreamily . . . *What can the child be thinking about? What a little witch she is! And that curious—healing instinct. Both Deoris and Riveda had had something like that,* she remembered, *I should have expected as much . . .* But Domaris could not follow the train of thought for long. Pain was too much a part of her now; she could not remember what it was like to be free of it.

Tiriki, her small pointed face showing, faintly, the signs of exhaustion, came out of her reverie and watched, helpless and miserable; then, in a sudden surge of protectiveness she flung her arms lightly around Domaris and pressed gently to her. And this time it was not a fancy: Domaris felt the sudden quick flow of vitality, the rapid surging ebb of the waves of pain. It was done unskillfully, so that Domaris felt dizzy and light-headed with the sudden strength that filled her.

The moment she was able, she sharply pushed Tiriki away. "My dear," she said in wonder, "you mustn't . . ." She broke off, realizing that the girl was not listening. Drawing a long breath, Domaris raised herself painfully up on one elbow. "Eilantha!" she commanded shortly. "I am serious! You must never do that again! I forbid it! If you try—I will send you away from me altogether!"

Tiriki sat up. Her thin face was flushed and a queer little line was tight across her brow. "*Kiha,*" she started, persuasively.

"Listen, precious," Domaris said, more gently, as she lay herself on her pillow again, "believe me, I'm grateful. Someday you will understand why I cannot let you—rob yourself this way. I don't know how you did it—that is a God-given power, my darling . . . but not like this! And not for me!"

"But—but it's *only* for you, *Kiha!* Because I love you!"

"But—little girl—" Domaris, at a loss for words, lay still, looking up into the quiet eyes. After a long moment, the child's dreamy face darkened again.

"*Kiha,*" Tiriki whispered, with strange intentness, "when—where—where and when was it? You said—you told me . . ." She stopped, her eyes concentrated in an aching search of the woman's face, her brows knitted in a terrible intensity. "Oh, *Kiha,* why is it so hard to remember?"

"Remember what, Tiriki?"

The girl closed her eyes. "It was you—you said to me—" The great eyes opened, haunted, and Tiriki whispered, "Sister—and more than sister—here we two, women and sisters—pledge thee, Mother—where we stand in darkness." Her voice thickened, and she sobbed.

Domaris gasped. "You don't remember, you can't! Eilantha, you cannot, you have been spying, listening, you could not . . ."

Tiriki said passionately, "No, no, it was *you,* Kiha! It was! I remember, but it's like—a dream, like dreaming about a dream."

"Tiriki, my baby-girl—you are talking like a mad child, you are talking about something which happened before . . ."

"It did happen, then! It did! Do you want me to tell you the rest?" Tiriki stormed. "Why won't you believe me?"

"But it was before you were born!" Domaris gasped. "*How can this be?*"

White-faced, her eyes burning, Tiriki repeated the words of the ritual without stumbling—but she had spoken only a few lines when Domaris, pale as Death, checked her. "No, no Eilantha! Stop! You mustn't repeat those words! Not ever, ever—until you know what they mean! What they imply . . ." She held out exhausted, wasted arms. "*Promise me!*"

Tiriki subsided in stormy sobs against her foster-mother's breast; but at last muttered her promise.

"Some day—and if I cannot, Deoris will tell you about it. One day—you were made Devotee, dedicated to Caratra before your birth, and one day . . ."

"You had better let me tell her now," said Deoris quietly from the doorway. "Forgive me, Domaris; I could not help but hear."

But Tiriki leaped up, raging. "You! You had to come—to listen, to spy on me! You can never let me have a moment alone with *Kiha* Domaris, you are jealous because I can help her and you cannot! I hate you! I hate you, Deoris!" She was sobbing furiously, and Deoris stood, stricken, for Domaris had beckoned Tiriki to her and her daughter was crying helplessly in her sister's arms, her face hidden on Domaris's shoulder as the woman held her with anxious, oblivious tenderness. Deoris bent her head and turned to go, without a word, when Domaris spoke.

"Tiriki, hush, my child," she commanded. "Deoris, come here to me—no, there, close to me, darling. You too, baby." she added to Tiriki, who had drawn a little away and was looking at Deoris with resentful jealousy. Domaris laid one of her worn, wax-white hands in Tiriki's and stretched out her other hand to Deoris. "Now, both of you," Domaris whispered, "listen to me—for this may be the last time I can ever talk to you like this—the last time."

CHAPTER NINE
✠ THE SEA AND ✠ THE SHIP

I

As summer gave way to autumn, even the children abandoned the hope and pretense that Domaris might recover. Day after day she lay in her high room, watching the sun flicker on the white waves, dreaming. Sometimes when one of the high-bannered *wing-bird* ships slid over the horizon, she wondered if Rajasta had received her message . . . but not even that seemed important any more. Days, then months slipped over her head, and with each day she grew paler, more strengthless, worn with pain brought to the point beyond which even pain cannot go, weary even with the effort of drawing breath to live.

The old master, Rathor, came once and stood for a long time close to her bedside, his hand between her two pale ones and his old blind eyes bent upon her worn face as if they saw not some faraway and distant thing, but the face of the dying woman.

As the year turned again, Deoris, pale with long nights and days of nursing her sister, was commanded unequivocally to take more rest; much of the time, now, Domaris did not know her, and there was little that anyone could do. Reluctantly, Deoris left her sister to the hands of the other Healer-priestesses, and—one morning—took her children to the seashore. Micail joined them there, for since his mother's illness he had seen little of Tiriki. Micail was to remember this day, afterward, as the last day he was a child among children.

Marion Zimmer Bradley

Tiriki, her long pale hair all unbraided, dragged her little brother by the hand as she flew here and there. Micail raced after them, and all three went wild with shouting and splashing and rowdy playing, chasing in and out of the sloshing waves on the sand. Even Deoris flung away her sandals and dashed gaily into the tidewaters with them. When they tired of this, Tiriki began to build in the sand for her little brother, while Micail picked up shells at the high-water mark and dumped them into Tiriki's lap.

Deoris, sitting on a large sun-warmed rock to watch them, thought, *They are only playing at being children, for Nari's sake and mine. They have grown up, those two, while I have been absorbed in Domaris . . .* It did not seem quite right, to Deoris, that a boy of sixteen and a girl of thirteen should be so mature, so serious, so adult—though they were acting, now, like children half their age!

But they quieted at last, and lay on the sand at Deoris's feet, calling on her to admire their sand-sculpture.

"Look," said Micail, "a palace, and a Temple!"

"See my pyramid?" little Nari demanded shrilly.

Tiriki pointed. "From here, the palace is like a jewel set atop a green hill . . . Reio-ta told me, once. . . ." Abruptly she sat up and demanded, "Deoris, did I ever have a real father? I love Reio-ta as if he truly were my father, but—you and *Kiha* Domaris are sisters; and Reio-ta is the brother of Micail's father . . ." Breaking off again, she glanced unquietly at Micail.

He understood what she meant immediately, and reached out to tweak her ear—but his impulse changed, and he only twitched it playfully instead.

Deoris looked soberly at her daughter. "Of course, Tiriki. But your father died—before you could be acknowledged."

"What was he like?" the girl asked, reflectively.

Before Deoris could answer, little Nari looked up with pouting scorn. "If he died before 'nowledging her, how could he *be* her father?" he asked, with devastating small-boy logic. He poked a chubby finger into his half-sister's ribs. "Dig me a hole, Tiriki!"

"Silly baby," Micail rebuked him.

Nari scowled. "Not a baby," he insisted. "My father was a Priest!"

"So was Micail's, Nari; so was Tiriki's," Deoris said gently. "We are all the children of Priests here."

But Nari only returned to the paradox he had seized on with new vigor. "If Tiriki's father died *before* she was born, then she don't have a father because he wasn't live to be her father!"

Micail, tickled by the whimsy of Nari's childish innocence, grinned delightedly. Even Tiriki giggled—then sobered, seeing the look on Deoris's face.

"Don't you want to talk about him?"

Again pain twisted oddly in Deoris's heart. Sometimes for months she did not think of Riveda at all—then a chance word or gesture from Tiriki would bring him back, and stir again that taut, half-sweet aching within her. Riveda was burned on her soul as ineradicably as the *dorje* scars on her breasts, but she had learned calm and control. After a moment she spoke, and her voice was perfectly steady. "He was an Adept of the Magicians, Tiriki."

"A Priest, like Micail's father, you said?"

"No, child, nothing like Micail's father. I said he was a Priest, because—well the Adepts are like Priests, of a sort. But your father was of the Grey-robe sect, though they are not regarded so highly in the Ancient Land. And he was a Northman of Zaiadan; you have your hair and eyes from him. He was a Healer of great skill."

"What was his name?" Tiriki asked intently.

For a moment, Deoris did not answer. It occurred to her then Domaris had never spoken of this, and since she had raised Tiriki as Reio-ta's daughter, it was her right not to . . . At last Deoris said, "Tiriki, in every way that matters, Reio-ta is your father."

"Oh, I know, it isn't that I don't love him!" Tiriki exclaimed, penitently—but as if drawn by an irresistible impetus, she went on, "But tell me, Deoris, because I remember, when I was only a baby— Domaris spoke of him to another Priestess—no, it was a Priest—oh, I can't remember really, but . . ." She made a strange little helpless gesture with her hands.

Deoris sighed. "Have it as you will. His name was Riveda."

Tiriki repeated the name curiously. "Riveda. . . ."

"I did not know that!" Micail broke in, with sudden disquiet. "Deoris, can it be the same Riveda I heard talk in the Priest's Court as a child? Was he—the sorcerer, the heretic?" He stopped short at the dismay in Deoris's eyes, her pained mouth.

Nari raised his head and clamored, "What's a heretic?"

Micail, immediately repenting his rash outburst, unfolded his long legs and hoisted the little boy to his shoulder. "A heretic is one who does wicked things, and I will do a wicked thing and throw you into the sea if you do not stop plaguing Deoris with foolish questions! Look, I think that ship is coming to anchor, come, let's watch it; I'll carry you on my shoulder!"

Nari crowed in shrill delight, and Micail galloped off with him. Soon they were little more than tiny figures far along the beach.

Deoris came out of her daydream to find Tiriki slipping her hand into hers, saying with a low voice, "I did not mean to trouble you, Deoris. I—I only had to be sure that—that Micail and I were not cousins twice over." She blushed, and then said, entreatingly, "Oh, Deoris, you must know why!" For the first time, of her own will, Tiriki put up her face for her mother's kiss.

Deoris caught the slender child in her arms. "Of course I know, my little blossom, and I am very happy," she said. "Come—shall we go and see the ship too?" Hand in hand, close together, they followed the trail of Micail's hurrying feet through the sand until all four stood together again.

Deoris picked up her son (Nari at least was hers alone, for a time at least, she was thinking) and listened smiling as Micail, his arm around Tiriki, talked of the *wing-bird* which was gliding to harbor. The sea was in his blood as it had been in his father's; on the long voyage from the Ancient Land he had been made with joy.

"I wonder if that ship is from the Ancient Land?" Tiriki said curiously.

"I would not be surprised," Micail answered wisely. "Look—they're putting out a boat from the ship, though; that's strange, they don't usually land boats here at the Temple, usually they go on to the City."

"There is a Priest in the first boat," Tiriki said as the small craft beached. Six men, common sailors, turned away along the lower path, but the seventh stood still, glancing up toward where the Temple gleamed like a white star atop the hill. Deori's heart nearly stopped; it was . . .

"Rajasta!" Micail cried out, suddenly and joyously; and, forgetting his new-found dignity, he sped swiftly across the sands toward the white-robed man.

The Priest looked up, and his face glowed as he saw the boy. "My dear, dear son!" he exclaimed, clasping Micail in his arms. Deoris, following slowly with her children, saw that the old Guardian's face was wet with tears.

His arm about Micail, Rajasta turned to greet the others; Deoris would have knelt, but he embraced her with his free arm. "Little daughter, this is a lucky omen for my mission, though it is not a mission of joy," he told her. To her own surprise, Deoris discovered that she was weeping. Rajasta held her close, with a sort of dismayed embarrassment, comforting her awkwardly as she sobbed, and little Nari tugged at his mother's skirt.

"You'd spank *me* for that, D'ris," he rebuked shrilly.

Deoris laughed at this, recovering her composure somewhat. "Forgive me, Lord Rajasta," she said, flushing deeply, and drew Tiriki forward. "A miracle befell me, my father, for when I came here I found—my own small daughter, in Domaris's care."

Rajasta's smile was a benediction. "I knew of that, my daughter, for Reio-ta told me of his plan."

"You knew? And all those years . . . ?" Deoris bent her head. It had, indeed, been wisest that she learn to think of her child as lost to her forever.

Tiriki clung to Deoris, bashfully, and Rajasta laid his hand on her silky head. "Do not be frightened, little one; I knew your mother when she was younger than you, and your father was my kinsman. You may call me Uncle, if you wish."

Nari peeped from behind his sister. "*My* father is a Priest!" he said valiantly. "Are you my Uncle, too, Lord Guardian?"

"If you like," said Rajasta mildly, and patted the tangled curls. "Is Domaris well, my daughter?"

Deoris paled in consternation. "Did you not receive her letter? *You do not know?*"

Rajasta, too, turned pale. "No, I have had no word—all is confusion at the Temple, Deoris, we have had no letters. I have come on Temple business, though indeed I had hoped to see you both. What—what has befallen her?"

"Domaris is dying," Deoris said unsteadily.

The Priest's pale cheeks looked haggard—for the first time in her life, Deoris realized that Rajasta was an old, old man. "I feared—I felt," the Guardian said, hoarsely, "some premonition of evil upon her. . . ." He looked again at Micail's thin, proud face. "You are like your father, my son. You have his eyes . . ." But Rajasta's thoughts went on beyond his words: *He is like Domaris, too.* Domaris, whom he loved as more than a daughter—no one begotten of his own flesh had ever been half so dear to Rajasta; and Deoris said she was dying! *But the essential part of Domaris,* he reminded himself sternly and sadly, *has long been dead. . . .*

They dismissed the children as they neared the dormitory of the Priestesses. Alone together, Rajasta and Deoris climbed the stairs. "You will find her very changed," Deoris warned.

"I know," said Rajasta, and his voice held a deep sorrow; he leaned heavily on the young woman's offered arm. Deoris tapped gently on the door.

"Deoris?" a faint voice asked from within, and Deoris stepped aside for the Guardian to precede her. She heard her own name again, raised questioningly, then a glad cry: "Rajasta! Rajasta—my father!"

Domaris's voice broke in a sob, and Rajasta hastened to her side. Domaris tried to raise herself, but her face twisted with pain and she had to fall back. Rajasta bent and elapsed her gently in his arms, saying, "Domaris, my child, my lovely child!"

Deoris very quietly withdrew and left them alone.

CHAPTER TEN
✠ KARMA ✠

I

Standing on the terrace, listening for the shouts of the Temple children in the lower gardens, Deoris heard a quiet step behind her, and looked up into Reio-ta's smiling eyes.

"The Lord Rajasta is with Domaris?" he asked.

Deoris nodded; her eyes grew sad. "She has been living only for this. It will not be long now."

Reio-ta took her hand and said, "You must not grieve, Deoris. She has been—less than living—for many years."

"Not for her," Deoris whispered, "but only for myself. I am selfish—I have always been selfish—but when she is gone I shall be alone."

"No," said Reio-ta, "you will not be alone." And, without surprise, Deoris found herself in his arms, his mouth pressed to hers. "Deoris," he whispered at last, "I loved you from the first! From the moment I came up out of a—a maelstrom that had drowned me, and saw you lying on the floor of a Temple I did not recognize, at the feet of—a Grey-robe, whose name I did not even know. And the terrible burns on you! I loved you then, Deoris! Only that gave me the strength to—to defy . . ."

Matter-of-factly, Deoris supplied the name that, after so many years, his tongue still stumbled on. "To defy Riveda. . . ."

"Can you care for me?" he asked passionately. "Or does the past hold you still too close?"

Mutely Deoris laid her hand in his, warmed by a sudden confidence and hope, and knew, without analyzing it, that it was of this that she had waited all her life. She would never feel for Reio-ta the mad adoration she had known for Riveda; she had loved—no, worshipped Riveda—as a suppliant to a God. Arvath had taken her as a woman, and there had been friendship between them and the bond of the child she had given him in her sister's place—but Arvath had never touched her emotions. Now, in full maturity, Deoris found herself able and willing to take the next step into the world of experience. Smiling, she freed herself from his arms.

He accepted it, returning her smile. "We are not young," he said. "We can wait."

"All time belongs to us," she answered gently. She took his hand again, and together they walked down into the gardens.

II

The sun was low on the horizon when Rajasta called them all together on a terrace near Deoris's apartments. "I did not speak of this to Domaris," he told them soberly, "but I wished to say to you tonight what I mean to tell the Priests of this Temple tomorrow. The Temple in our homeland—the Great Temple—is to be destroyed."

"Ah, no!" Deoris cried out.

"Aye," said Rajasta, with solemn face. "Six months ago it was discovered that the great pyramid was sinking lower and lower into the Earth; and the shoreline has been breached in many places. There have been earthquakes. The sea had begun to seep beneath the land, and some of the underground chambers are collapsing. Ere long—ere long the Great Temple will be drowned by the waves of the sea."

There was a flurry of dismayed, confused questions, which he checked with a gesture. "You know that the pyramid stands above the Crypt of the Unrevealed God?"

"Would we did not!" Reio-ta whispered, very low.

"That Crypt is the nadir of the Earth's magnetic forces—the reason the Grey-robes sought to guard it so carefully from desecration. But ten years and more ago . . ." Involuntarily Rajasta glanced at Tiriki, who sat wide-eyed and trembling. "Great sacrilege was done there, and Words of Power spoken. Reio-ta, it seems, was all too correct in his estimation, for we still had not rooted out the worms at our base!" For a moment Rajasta's eyes were stark and haunted, as if seeing again some horror the others could not even guess at. "Later, spells even more powerful than theirs were pronounced, and the worst evils contained, but—the Unrevealed God has had his death-wound. His dying agonies will submerge more than the Temple!"

Deoris covered her face with her hands.

Rajasta went on, in a low, toneless voice, "The Words of Power have vibrated rock asunder, disrupted matter to the very elements of its making; and once begun at so basic a level the vibrations cannot be stilled until they die out of their own. Daily about the Crypt, the Earth trembles—and the tremors are spreading! Within seven years, at the most, the entire Temple—perhaps the whole shoreline, the city and the lands about for many and many a mile—will sink beneath the sea—"

Deoris made a muffled, choking sound of horror.

Reio-ta bowed his head in terrible self-abasement. "Gods!" he whispered, "I—I am not guiltless in this."

"If we must speak of guilt," Rajasta said, more gently than was his habit, "I am no less guilty than any other, that my Guardianship allowed Riveda to entangle himself in black sorceries. Micon shirked the begetting of a son in his youth, and so dared not die under torture. Nor can we omit the Priest who taught him, the parents and servants who raised him, the great-great-grandsire of the ship's captain who brought Riveda's grandmother and mine from Zaiadan . . . no man can justly apportion cause and effect, least of all upon a scale such as this! It is karma. Set your heart free, my son."

There was a long pause. Tiriki and Micail were wide-eyed, their hands clasped in the stillness, listening without full understanding. Reio-ta's head remained bowed upon his clasped hands, while Deoris stood as rigid as a statue, her throat clasped shut by invisible hands.

Finally, dry-eyed, pale as chalk, she ran her tongue over dry lips and croaked, "That—is not all, is it?"

Rajasta sadly nodded agreement. "It is not," he said. "Perhaps, ten years from now, the edges of the catastrophe will touch Atlantis as well. These earthquakes will expand outwards, perhaps to gird the world; this very spot where we now stand may be broken and lie beneath the waters some day—and it may be, also, there is nowhere that will be left untouched. But I cannot believe it will come to that! Men's lives are a small enough thing—those whose destiny decrees that they should live, will live, if they must grow gills like fishes and spend their days swimming unimaginable deeps, or grow wings and soar as birds till the waters recede. And those who have sown the seeds of their own death will die, be they ever so clever and determined . . . but lest worse karma be engendered, the secrets of Truth within the Temple must not die."

"But—if what you say is so, how can they be preserved?" Reio-ta muttered.

Rajasta looked at him and then at Micail. "Some parts of the earth will be safe, I think," he replied at last, "and new Temples will rise there, where the knowledge may be taken and kept. The wisdom of our world may be scattered to the four winds and vanish for many an age—but it will not die forever. One such Temple, Micail, shall lie beneath your hand."

Micail started. "Mine? But I am only a boy!"

"Son of Ahtarrath," Rajasta said sternly, "usually it is forbidden that any should know his own destiny, lest he lean upon the Gods and, knowing, forbear to use all his own powers . . . yet it is necessary that you know, and prepare yourself! Reio-ta will aid you in this; though he is denied high achievement in his own person, the sons of his flesh will inherit Ahtarrath's powers."

Micail looked down at his now slight, strong hands—and Deoris suddenly remembered a pair of tanned, gaunt, twisted hands lying upon a tabletop. Then Micail flung back his head and met Rajasta's eyes. "Then, my father," he said, and put out his hand to Tiriki, "we would marry as soon as might be!"

Rajasta gazed gravely at Riveda's daughter, reflecting. "So be it," he said at last. "There was a prophecy, long ago when I was still young—*A child will be born, of a line first risen, then fallen; a child who will sire a new line, to break the father's evils forever.* You are young . . ." He glanced again into Tiriki's child-face; but what he saw there made him incline his head and add, "But the new world will be mostly young! It is well; this, too, is karma."

Shivering, Tiriki asked, "Will only the Priests be saved?"

"Of course not," Rajasta chided gently. "Not even the Priests can judge who is to die and who is to live. Those outside the Priesthood shall be warned of danger and told where to seek shelter, and assisted in every way—but we cannot lay compulsion on them as on the Priesthood. Many will disbelieve, and mock us; even those who do not may refuse to leave their homes and possessions. There will be those who will trust to caves, high mountains, or boats—and who can say, they may do well, or better than we. Those who will suffer and die are those who have sown the seeds of their own end."

"I think I understand," said Deoris quietly, "why did you not tell Domaris of this?"

"But I think she knows," Rajasta replied. "She stands very close to an open door which views beyond the framework of one life and one time." He stretched out his hands to them. "In other Times," he said, in the low voice of prophecy, "I see us scattered, but coming together again. Bonds have been forged in this life which can never separate us—any of us. Micon, Domaris—Talkannon, Riveda—even you, Tiriki, and that sister you never knew, Demira—they have only withdrawn from a single scene of an ending drama. They will change—and remain the same. But there is a web—a web of darkness bound around us all; and while time endures, it can never be loosed or freed. It is karma."

III

Since Rajasta had left her, Domaris had drifted in dreamless reverie, her vague thoughts bearing no relation to the pain and weakness of her spent body. Micon's face and voice were near, and she felt the touch of his hand upon her arm—not the frail and careful clasp of his maimed hands, but a strong and vital grip upon her wrist. Domaris did not believe that there was immediate reunion beyond death, but she knew, with serene confidence, that she and Micon had forged bonds of love which could not fail to draw them together again, a single bright strand running through the web of darkness that bound them one to another. Sundered they might be, through many lives, while other bonds were fulfilled and obligations discharged; but they would meet again. Nor could she be parted from Deoris; the strength of their oath bound them one to the other, and to the children they had dedicated from life to life forever. Her only regret was that in this life she would not see Micail grow to manhood, never know the girl he would one day take to wife, never hold his sons. . . .

Then, with the clarity of the dying, she knew she need not wait to see the mother of Micail's children. She had reared her in her lonely exile, sealed her unborn to the Goddess they would all serve through all of Time. Domaris smiled, her old joyous smile, and opened her eyes upon Micon's face . . . *Micon?* No—for the dark smile was crowned with hair as flaming bright as her own had once been, and the smile that answered hers was young and unsteady as the clasp of his still-bony young hand upon hers. Beyond him, for an instant, she saw Deoris; not the staid Priestess but the child of dancing, wind-tangled ringlets, merry and sullen by turns, who had been her delight and her one sorrow in her carefree girlhood. There, too, was Rajasta, smiling, now benevolent, now stern; and the troubled, hesitant smile of Reio-ta.

All my dear ones, she thought, and almost said it aloud as she saw the pale hair of the little *saji* maiden, the child of the *no-people,* who had slipped away from Karahama's side to lead Domaris to Deoris that day in the Grey Temple—but no; time had slid over them. It was the face of Tiriki, flushed with sobbing, that swam out of the light. Domaris smiled, the old glorious smile that seemed to radiate into every heart.

Micon whispered, "Heart of Flame!" Or was it Rajasta who had spoken the old endearment in his shaking voice? Domaris did not see anything in particular now, but she sensed Deoris bending over her in the dim light. "Little sister," Domaris whispered; then, smiling, "No, you are not little any more . . ."

"You look—so very happy, Domaris," said Deoris wonderingly.

"I *am* very happy," Domaris whispered, and her luminous eyes were wide twin stars reflecting their faces. For a moment a wave of bewilderment, half pain, blurred the shining joy; she stirred, and whispered rackingly, "*Micon!*"

Micail gripped her hand tight in his own. "Domaris!"

Again the joyous eyes opened. "Son of the Sun," she said, very clearly. "Now—it is beginning again." She turned her face to the pillow and slept; and in her dreams she sat once more on the grass beneath the ancient, sheltering tree in the Temple gardens of her homeland, while Micon caressed her and held her close, murmuring softly into her ear . . .

IV

Domaris died, just before dawn, without waking again. As the earliest birds chirped outside her window, she stirred a little, breathed in her sleep, "How still the pool is today—" and her hands, lax-fingered, dropped over the edge of the couch.

Deoris left Micail and Tiriki sobbing helplessly in each other's arms and went out upon the balcony, where she stood for a long time motionless, looking out on greyish sky and sea. She was not consciously thinking of anything, even of loss and grief. The fact of death had been impressed on her so long ago, that this was only confirmation. *Domaris dead? Never!* The wasted, wan thing, so full of pain, was gone; and Domaris lived again, young and quick and beautiful . . .

She did not hear Reio-ta's step until he spoke her name. Deoris turned. His eyes were a question—hers, answer. The words were superfluous.

"She is gone?" Reio-ta said.

"She is free," Deoris answered.

"The children—?"

"They are young; they must weep. Let them mourn her as they will."

For a time they were alone, in silence; then Tiriki and Micail came, Tiriki's face swollen with crying, and Micail's eyes bloodshot above smeared cheeks—but his voice was steady as he held, "Deoris?" and went to her. Tiriki put her arms around her foster-father and Reio-ta held her close, looking over her shining hair at Deoris. She in turn looked silently from the boy in her arms to the girl who clung to the Priest, and thought, *It is well. These are our children. We will stay with them.*

And then she remembered two men, standing face to face,

opposed in everything yet bound by a single law throughout Time—as she and Domaris had been bound. Domaris was gone, Micon was gone, Riveda, Demira, Karahama—gone to their places in Time. But they would return. Death was the least final thing in the world.

Rajasta, his old face composed and serene, came out upon the balcony and began to intone the morning hymn:

> *"O beautiful upon the horizon of the East,*
> *Lift up thy light unto day, O eastern Star,*
> *Day-star, awaken, arise!*
> *Lord and giver of Life, awake!*
> *Joy and giver of Light, arise!"*

A shaft of golden light stole over the sea, lighting the Guardian's white hair, his shining eyes, and the white robes of his priesthood.

"Look!" Tiriki breathed. "The Night is over."

Deoris smiled, and the prism of her tears scattered the morning sun into a rainbow of colors. "The day is beginning," she whispered, "the new day!" And her beautiful voice took up the hymn, that rang to the edges of the world:

> *"O beautiful upon the horizon of the East,*
> *Day-Star, awaken, arise!"*

✠ AFTERWORD ✠

One of the questions writers are asked ad nauseam is this:

"Where do you get your ideas?"

When answering this I tend to be rude and dismissive, because it makes it sound as if "ideas" were some sort of gross infestation, alien to the asker's kind, implying that being able to get "ideas" was unusual; whereas I cannot even imagine a life without having, every hour or so, more "ideas" than I could ever use in a lifetime.

More rationally I know that the asker is only seeking, without being sufficiently articulate to say so, some insight into a creative process unknown to him or her; and when I am asked whence arose the idea for such a book as *Web of Darkness,* I really can answer that I have no idea. Where *do* dreams come from?

One of my earliest memories, when I was the merest tot, was of building great imposing structures with the many building-blocks of wood-ends which my father, a carpenter, gave us to supplement the small and unimaginative supply of toy blocks in the playroom; when asked what I was building, I invariably replied "temples." The word was alien even to me; I suspected that they were "something like churches" (which I *did* know) "only much *more.*" I remember seeing a picture of Stonehenge, and *recognizing* it; I did not see that actual construct till in my forties; yet when I did, the "shock of recognition" was still there. I was not taken to enough movies (and those mostly of the slapstick or cowboy variety, not very interesting to such a child as I was), and in my infancy there was no television; so where did I find the wish to recapture the imposing structures of Indian or Egyptian temples, great rows of columns occupied always in my imagination by masses of priests and priestesses clad in long sweeping cloaks, whose colors defined what they did?

The only actual physical images of my childhood (I am speaking of four years old, before I could read anything much but *Alice in Wonderland)* were from a book of Tanglewood Tales with the wonderful landscapes and images of an ancient world which surely never existed except perhaps in Wordsworth's "Ode on Intimations of Immortality" (a poem which well might have been read to me before I was able to understand it—my mother was a romantic). But I knew that this world of images existed; I recognized them in the Maxfield Parrish landscapes; and when my mind (fed on Rider Haggard and Sax Rohmer), long before I discovered fantasy or science fiction via the pulps, began to teem with these characters and incidents, I can only imagine that I fitted them mentally into the temples and scenes I had constructed with my blocks, as a playwright fits his characters onto the stage of a certain toy theatre he may have owned in childhood.

Where do dreams come from anyway? From that mysterious source and that alone can I seek for the "idea" of *Web of Light* and *Web of Darkness.* And into that mysterious fountain I dipped again years later for the visions which brought me MISTS OF AVALON.

Where do dreams come from?

—**Marion Zimmer Bradley**